Mary Agnes Tincker

By the Tiber

Mary Agnes Tincker

By the Tiber

ISBN/EAN: 9783337280567

Printed in Europe, USA, Canada, Australia, Japan

Cover: Foto ©Andreas Hilbeck / pixelio.de

More available books at **www.hansebooks.com**

BY THE TIBER.

BY THE AUTHOR OF

"SIGNOR MONALDINI'S NIECE."

"CAINA ATTENDE."

BOSTON:
ROBERTS BROTHERS.
1881.

TO

MR. J. C. HOOKER

This Book

IS GRATEFULLY DEDICATED BY THE AUTHOR.

Rome, January, 1881.

CONTENTS.

BY THE TIBER.

CHAPTER I.

A FAIRY STORY.

ONCE upon a time, as a royal exile who was visiting Rome rode out with his friends to the chase, they passed a certain rude stone house set in a vineyard. This house had been a sepulchre in ancient times; but the dust of the dead was blown away, and the vase which had held it was set in a museum, and the marbles that had adorned it were torn off to ornament the palaces of the living, and over its crumbling foundations had been built a new house wherein dwelt Gigi, the vine-dresser, with his daughter Felicità and her step-mother, Nanna.

It was a rough place; but the poppies grew brilliantly all about its foundations, and wall-flowers nodded out of reach above, and an ivy-vine crept up, stone by stone, and draped itself around a small square window set close beside the only remaining skeleton window of the ruin. This window opened on a narrow road of the Agro Romano; and when the chase went by in the early morning, there was a face framed in its cornice of leaves. Felicità looked out at the horsemen, and laughed and blushed when they all looked up at her. When the prince took off his hat to her she only laughed and blushed the more, and no more thought of saluting him than she would have thought of saluting the sun when it burned her face.

After they had passed, one looked back and drank that face of hers with thirsty eyes; and Felicità looked after him across the dark green vines. When he was hidden from her eyes by a turn of the road, a miracle of nature was wrought in the girl; for her heart, knocking strongly at some hitherto unopened door of her soul, wakened her dormant imagination, that sprang like a butterfly from the chrysalis; so that, leaning from her window, she still saw the gallant cavalier on his roan steed, and knew that his flashing eyes were as black as carbon, and that his swarthy cheek kept the vivid color that had kindled at her glance.

The girl's face was worth looking back to see, though its outlines were not perfect. A wealth of shining black hair was braided into a coronet about her beautiful head, and her eyes were large, brown, and sparkling. For the color of her soft, full face and neck, it would have looked pink if you had held an orange-blossom to it, but, cheek to cheek with a red rose, it showed pure white. Then her blushes were always coming and going, — soft, light blushes that were not a flame, but only the light of a flame.

So Felicità looked after the unknown cavalier, and thought of him till she forgot to laugh and jest as usual when Marco Bandini came to see her that evening. Marco was her promised husband, and they were to be married the next Easter. Gigi and Nanna had arranged the marriage, and she was content with it; for Marco was gardener in a neighboring villa, and had put a pile of golden scudi in the great bank at Rome.

But now new fancies began to flutter through the girl's life, — fancies simple and innocent at first, like the little white butterflies that go fauning about in early spring. But summer hastens after spring, and the butterflies of July have painted wings.

One day Felicità disappeared and left no trace.

CHAPTER II.

FELICITÀ INFELICE.

THE father and Marco searched, of course; but they might as well have searched for the dust of the dead whose home they had invaded. They raved, of course; but they might as well have raved against the wind that bore that dust away. The mocking smile, the cold surprise, the helpless shrug of the shoulders, which met their questions, were utterly baffling Nanna, threatened by both, and beaten by her husband, called on all the saints to witness that she knew nothing of the girl's abduction or flight.

Gigi raved himself to death. He was very nearly a beast, this vine-dresser,— dull and easy-humored when all went well, and lashing himself into a blind fury when he was crossed; and his fury, having nothing else to spend itself upon, turned its poison backward, and gave him a paralytic stroke. He might have recovered had he chosen to keep quiet; but with returning health came returning passion, and a second stroke followed the first one. Only when death was at hand did the beast in him lie down, and something of higher calm look out of his eyes.

And then, at last, Felicità, the ghost of herself, came stealing in one evening, and sank sobbing on her knees by his bedside, and dropped a purse of gold into his chilling hand. He asked no questions, and she told no tales. His hand let slip the gold,

motioned to touch her bowed head, and fell short of
it. And then death blindfolded him, and took him
away to other scenes.

When all was over, Nanna whispered a sharp question into the girl's ear, and received a sobbing answer.
"He is sick, and his mother and sisters came and sent
me away. He is sorry that he took me. He will
die."

Nanna went herself to see if the story were true,
and was driven away with contumely. She had to
be content with the gold that Felicità had brought;
she took it, and they lived on together.

Marco kept away from them. Had her father been
living, her lover would have wished to kill Felicità;
but Gigi's death had fallen like a frost upon his wrath,
and he let her alone. He kept a constant watch upon
her, though. There was a certain point in the wall
of the villa whence he could see the green door with
rough gray steps leading up to it, and the window
with the ivy, and a slope of grass with a solitary
cypress standing above it. Day after day he watched,
but caught no glimpse of her, till, when weeks had
passed, he began to long for the sight of her with
other feelings than those of jealous anger; and when
weeks had multiplied, he came to think that, if but
she would ask him, he would forgive her anything.

At last, as he gazed at her window one morning in
the spring, Felicità appeared there with an infant in
her arms, and stood framed in the ivy. His heart
leaped to her so gladly that it took in even the child.
Standing there with the little one nestled into her
neck, she seemed to say to him, We are inseparable.
If you take one, you must take both.

It was an apparition. She stayed only long enough
to say so much.

Marco returned to his work; but sunset found him
again on guard, and again rewarded.

This time Felicità stood in the open door, and looked out on the road to right and left, as if to see if any one were within sight. It was a still, bright evening, burnished with a sunset that made the very turf look like cloth of gold. The climbing ivy above her head pushed a few leaf-tips out of the shade and lighted them like lamps. The cypress, impervious to the sunshine, glowed sullenly on its westward side, and stretched a long pointed shadow, shaped like a dagger, down the shining green.

"If she comes out, I will take her!" said Marco, breathlessly.

Felicità hesitated, clasped her babe closer, then came out slowly, step by step, walked across the green, and seated herself in the shadow of the cypress. Sitting there motionless, she looked like the figure of a woman damaskeened on a sword-blade.

A month later she and Marco were married. She gave herself to him willingly enough, threw herself away on him, indeed, as a thing no longer of any value. He gave up his place, bade the step-mother never come near them, and took Felicità and her child to a new home. This was a deserted villa away among the Sabine mountains, in a hidden spot above which Palestrina climbs the height where once stood the temple of Fortune, *Fortunæ Sanctæ,* and of the infant Jove, where the broken olive-tree ran with honey and oil, and the ever-burning lamp under its lofty arch warned the distant mariners off the Tironian shore to worship the goddess of the sea.

Felicità went unresistingly; but as she went, the weight of every milestone they passed was added to her heart. She performed her duties faithfully in that green solitude to which her husband had brought her, but she seldom smiled, or seemed interested in anything but her child. She would bend over the babe for hours, gazing down into his face as one

may gaze into a deep lake down which some price-
less, irrecoverable treasure has sunk, and now and
then her eyes would light up suddenly for a moment
as if she had caught a glimpse of a lost delight.

One might have believed that her husband would
be jealous; but he showed no sign of displeasure. He,
too, had his dreams, not of a fleeting sweetness sunk
forever in the past, but of a glorious future when the
earth should no longer be the possession of a few, but
for mankind, and when every man should dare to
speak his boldest thought without fear of imprison-
ment or exile.

To this man, whose passionate intelligence had
burst the crust of the *contadino* without taking on
the still harder shell of conventionality, a king or
ruler was but a man raised on the will of the people,
and sustained on that will, like a ball tossing on the
top of a fountain-jet, which may at any moment withdraw and let it roll into obscurity, or be crushed underfoot.

Let Felicità caress and pamper her child, then, and
teach him to scorn a common life, and whisper to
him that his dead father had been the companion
of kings. Later, when the young mind should begin
to awaken, he, too, would help to train the boy,
would use his daintinesses and his disdains for a
purpose worthy of them. The two streams of blood
in his veins should never unite; they should forever
foam and fret against each other till they filled him
with a hatred more intense than any mere *contadino*
could feel.

Meantime he meant to make a gardener of him,
not a mere workman but an artist; and he employed
a young teacher from the seminary in the town to
come down for an hour every day and instruct the
little Vittorio, since the mother was not willing to
send him to school.

"A boy who has been taught reading, writing, and Latin ought to be able to learn the rest himself," said Marco. "I will teach him botany; and he will have a chance to see gardens when he is older."

When Vittorio was five years old his mother died in giving birth to a daughter.

Marco found a trusty nurse for the two little ones, and went steadily on with his work, his imagination meantime digging under the *débris* of ruined governments to find the golden foundations of a lost paradise.

"It is long in coming," he said to Garibaldi, who came to his house more than once.

"Patience!" replied the soldier. "Patience and faith! When you see the aurora, you may be sure that the day is coming. The spirit of freedom does not rest, nor turn back, any more than the sun does, when once it has set its face toward a people."

"If only I could talk as you do!" said Marco, gazing admiringly at his hero. "If only I had the gift of stirring people up! But I can only speak in such a fury that people shut their hearts against my words, as they shut their windows against a tempest."

"Be silent then," said Garibaldi, smiling. "Acts are better than words. You may not know the famous old law of the joust and tournament: 'The lance does not liberate the sword, but the sword liberates the lance.' All the words we can utter do not free us from the duty of acting when the time comes; and one good blow for the right will cover the silence of a life."

"I am going to be a soldier," said a clear, sweet voice beside the two. "Marco has given me a sword."

"Bravo, little Duke!" said Garibaldi, turning to

the child. "And whom are you going to fight against?"

"Traitors," replied Vittorio, unsheathing his toy sword and looking up into the questioner's face with brilliant, serious eyes.

"He's a good bit of steel," said the soldier; and, giving him a light blow on the cheek, added, "That is your confirmation."

CHAPTER III.

VITTORIO.

YEARS passed, and Vittorio more than answered his step-father's expectations. He was beautiful in person and refined in tastes, and the hate that had been nourished in his soul was to the hate of Marco what the spirit of a high-mettled horse is to that of a mule. He was becoming too restive, indeed, and the quiet and solitude of his villa life were irritating him so much that he welcomed the prospect of other employment than that of merely helping Marco.

A friend of Marco's, the gardener in Villa Cesarini, in Genzano, sent for Vittorio to come to him on a certain day of the summer which completed his twenty-fourth year. A Neapolitan prince, who had just bought a large villa within the walls of Rome, was coming to see the Cesarini gardens. He wanted a gardener; and if the young man would be on the spot when he made his visit, the situation might be procured for him.

"I would rather meet him there in the open air than go to see him in Rome," Vittorio said. "I will not wait in any man's anteroom, nor stand, cap

in hand, while he sits talking to me. I should be
sure to do something that would make him refuse
me."

There was little likelihood of Vittorio's being
refused for any other reason than a want of humility, for he had studied his art with the passion with which such a nature turns to the one
pleasure and distraction possible to it. He could
not be intimate with gentlemen, he would not asso-
ciate with *contadini*, and he therefore made himself
intimate with nature. He studied the ways and
habits of plants, their virtues and vices, their laws
and their histories. All his soul, poetic, fiery, ambi-
tious, and outraged, having no human consolation,
turned to the flowers, and found in them a fair new
world wherein he was not without honor. The
flowers tried to please Vittorio, Marco said. And,
indeed, he was notable for his success with them.

He set out early one summer morning for Genzano,
making the last part of the journey, from Albano, on
foot, glad of a walk which might a little quiet his
nervous agitation. He had resolved to accept the
situation if it were offered him; but the necessity
was bitter. It seemed a tacit acknowledgment of a
social position which he had always tacitly protested
against.

Arriving at Villa Cesarini, he exchanged a few
words with the gardener, and went into the garden to
wait, strolling about, and examining everything.

That long row of hydrangeas that leaned so heavily
on the rail with their weight of pink and violet-
colored balls would look well set beside still waters;
so he thought. All the water should be colored with
flowers. "I wish there were a pond. A fountain-
basin is nothing. I will have somewhere a wide thin
sheet of a cascade with a crowd of scarlet flowers
behind it, and some scarlet flowers where it falls to

send a red light along the ripples. That should be
in a place that has strong lights and shades; perhaps,
an ivy wall behind, a tree hanging over, and the
south sun pouring in, with something dense to splinter
the beams up into a sharp rain."

He paused in a little open terrace, and looked down
upon Lake Nemi's misty mirror, all liquid green and
purple, with a dream of a white cloud sailing over.
The emerald banks pushed into the water, which
seemed to have colored itself from them, in many a
graceful curve and point. Far away on its bosom
was a tiny boat. Across the water, Nemi hung upon
the hillside, its whitely dropping waterfall a motionless line in the distance. "After all," said Vittorio,
"what can be done with a few acres of almost level
land! One needs distance, a lake and a mountain."

His mind was always breaking bounds in this way.
When one has only imaginary possessions, one may
as well wish grandly.

Vittorio had nothing, and worse than nothing.
When he lifted his head, aware of the shadowy
coronet in his hair, the blouse clung to and scorched
him like the shirt of Nessus; and when he would
have contented himself with the blouse, the proud
blood in his veins foamed up, and assailed him, heart
and brain, in a blind rage of protest. The canopy
which he could almost feel waving its crested fringe
over his head flouted the mire in which his feet
were entangled. All the joints of his life were
torn and dislocated by these strong horses of fate,
tied to his vitals and pulling in opposite ways.

Turning away from the terrace, he went down the
winding path, and paused again in a shaded opening
below. It was an exquisite spot, so perfectly imi-
tating one of Nature's graceful, careless moods that
Nature herself might have believed it her own work.
There was no view into the distance: the place was

only an opening of the path into a grassy, irregular space closely shut in by trees. From under the terrace above dropped a scattered rain, like water from the eaves, — dropped and stole into little rills among the grass, and united into a pool on a bed of yellow pebbles, and ran away in a little brook that scarcely dared to murmur above its breath. Over the pool leaned a weeping willow. Vittorio stood beneath the willow, and gazed into this pool, which reflected his face.

Nothing could be more beautiful than both his face and form. His beauty was of that character of mingled Arabic and Italian which can be compared only with itself. Golden bronze and sunset crimson do not describe its rich shadow and bloom. The long tapering lines of the limbs, the features which art could only copy, not improve, the liquid dark eyes, the unsmiling lips, the shining black hair in a mass of loose waves, the small brown hands, — there was not a flaw in them. His dress, though in some sort a workman's, was graceful. An antique intaglio in red carnelian buttoned the blue collar of his belted blouse, and a broad-brimmed hat of very dark blue crushed the hair half over his forehead, and curled up at the sides showing his profile. In the wide black band of the hat was set a small gray feather with a scarlet tip.

While he stood thus, three persons came into the terrace above, a lady and gentleman accompanied by the gardener. The gentleman passed on after a moment, to examine the place, which he had never visited before ; the lady remained on the terrace, her feet on a mat of ivy and myrtle, one knee slightly bent to an ancient capital of a column placed there as a seat. She looked off a moment toward Nemi, then downward to the dim bower from whence a musical tinkle of water-drops came faintly to her ear.

At first she could see nothing.   Vittorio, looking into the pool, saw her face reflected clearly.   It looked down upon him as from the sky, only the leaf-flecked blue behind and around it, a face with the proud, white, and almost sullen oval of a young Juno.   A dress of dark blue showed through the rustic parapet, and a shawl of fine white wool bound her head, and dropped on her shoulders.   A red rose had just been pushed into the locks behind her left ear, and a bunch of red roses were half falling out of her belt.   She wore Vittorio's colors.

His stern and bitter expression softened as he gazed at the reflected image ; and, after a moment, his heart began to tremble faintly, like the water in which that image lay.   He would have passed the lady indifferently if they had met in the common way ; he had more than once opposed a curling lip to the admiring smiles of fine ladies ; but alone with her in this ideal world, shot through by a glance from the woman above, and her shadow below, he could not be indifferent.

The Donna Adelaïde, gazing steadily downward, saw indistinctly the shape beneath the willow, saw the dark-blue hat with its red-tipped feather, the beautiful profile and the graceful figure.   But she did not see the pool with her own face in it.

Neither moved, and nature stood motionless around them.   The sunshine seemed to have crystallized about the scene.   The faintly heard bells ringing the noon Angelus from the towers of Nemi was all the sound they heard, except the water-drops and their own hearts.

"What beautiful creature is this ?" whispered the lady to herself.   "Why does he not look up ?   He is perhaps one of the *Alpinisti*.   They are about here somewhere ; and the hat looks like.   I have half a mind to drop him a rose."

She glanced around, and, seeing that her father was
at a distance, talking over with the gardener some ar-
rangement of azaleas and camellias which he wished to
reproduce in his own villa, she drew one of the roses
from her belt, and held it in her hand hanging over
the parapet. Her backward glance and her gesture
were all mirrored below.

Vittorio looked suddenly up as the rose rustled
down to his feet; but the lady was gazing off toward Nemi, and did not seem aware of his vicinity.
He stooped for the rose, and hid it in his bosom.
The next instant he heard voices above, the face disappeared from the terrace, and presently steps came
down the path.

The gardener appeared, followed by an elderly gentleman. After them came the Donna Adelaïde. Her
figure was tall and straight, proud rather than graceful, and her slight arched foot seemed scarcely to
touch the path. One hand held lightly the long, dark-
blue folds of her dress; the other hung lightly by her
side. Her head was as proudly erect as if the *fascia
alba* that bound it had been the ancient diadem of
the Orient. She glanced coldly at the man under
the willow, and bit her lip with a quick, involuntary
pressure when she saw his blouse.

"This is the young man whom I have recommended
to your Excellency," said the gardener. "Would you
like to speak to him?"

Vittorio touched his hat, but did not remove it,
and waited to be spoken to. His heart ached with a
sudden spasm. Here was his master!

The prince glanced at him as from an immeasura-
ble distance. "You might come to Rome to-morrow,
and see the place," he said, and passed on.

Vittorio muttered a word of assent, then quite removed his hat to the lady, and looked at her earnestly
as she passed him. She glanced him over compre-

hensively, but without the slightest sign of salutation. What sort of gardener was this who wore a hat that a gentleman might wear for a caprice, and clean shoes that fitted him perfectly, and who buttoned his cotton blouse at neck and wrist with antique *intagli*, and fastened his leather belt with an antique bronze buckle which she might herself have worn? To be sure, any gardener or *contadino* might dig such things out of the ground; but, then, they always sold them for their superiors to wear.

She passed him with just as much notice as she might have given to a tree; but she had dropped her rose to him, he knew. And that rose, like a live coal dropped upon an altar prepared for it, burned on his heart with a fire never to be extinguished. It burned not only his heart; it consumed every interest of his past life, every hope that he had cherished for the future. Politics, rank, kingdoms and republics, — what did they matter to him? He knew them no more. Before the Donna Adelaïde had traversed the long loop of the descending path, and come back to that part directly beneath where Vittorio stood, a dazzlingly sweet passion had taken entire possession of him.

Passing beneath, the Neapolitan turned her head, and looked deliberately and steadily up into his face as he looked down, and though her own was immovably cold, quick sparks were flickering in her dark eyeballs.

"Heavens! how beautiful he is!" she whispered to herself as she went on.

"Is that man a Swiss gardener?" she demanded of their guide, who was himself Swiss.

"He is Italian, Eccellenza," replied the man, thinking that she could not have looked at Vittorio, whose face was the soul of Italy.

"Is he of your town?" the prince inquired carelessly, not interested in the least, but intending to be amiable.

" Oh, no ! he is not *roba di Genzano*," the gardener answered. " His mother was a Roman *contadina*, and his father, they say, was the Duke of Monteforte."

Adelaïde turned quickly to loosen her floating scarf from an oleander branch that had caught it, and hid the smile that sprang to her lips. Even in the dark she had not mistaken the son of a clod for the son of a gentleman !

For Vittorio, he stood there rapt before a transfigured life. It was as when, standing upon a mountain-top, when the rain has ceased, with the blue above, and the level sunbeams underfoot, one sees close at hand in the plain the dusky wall of cloud and slanting rain extending from the earth to the heavens, and almost within arm's reach upon its front, the sudden glory of the rainbow set its foundations of red and blue and yellow on the dazzled stones and grass of the valley.

Vittorio felt as if a rainbow had dropped its airy splendor about him.

So comes love in the lands of the sun, as swift as an arrow from a bow.

———◆———

CHAPTER IV.

UNDER THE ROSE.

THE purchaser of Villa Mitella, a man of immense wealth, had also purchased his title of prince. His family was of the lower nobility of the South of Italy, and had counts and cavaliers in Naples and Sicily. The villa grounds were large, and the gardens highly cultivated; but there was a newly added portion of land which had not yet been laid out. The new part included a small but

commodious house. This house, with the *casino*,
or palace, as it was usually called, and the gardener's house, were not set within the gardens, but
made a part of the walls. The palace faced the west,
the gardener's house was at the eastern extremity of
the grounds, and the newly acquired house, called by
common consent the *casuccia*, faced the south. The
north wall was not interrupted by any building.

Vittorio's house, though small, was a charming
little nest. The ground floor opened only into the
garden, and was reserved for tools. An outside stair
led up to a picturesque vaulted room with a wide
lattice. A bedroom beside this, and two rooms
above, comprised the apartment. One of the upper
rooms served as a kitchen, and an outside stair
descended from it to a narrow street which ran
beneath the eastern walls of the villa.

Here Vittorio lived quite alone. In the morning
he made his own coffee, and once a day came an old
woman to bring his dinner and put the apartment in
order. He remained in the house while she was
there, showed her out into the back street when she
had finished, and locked and barred the door behind
her. A very assuming young man for a gardener,
she considered him, and remarkably *curioso* in all his
ways; but she took care not to transgress the bounds
he set her. The "Signor Vittorio," she had called
him at first; but he corrected her incisively. "My
name is Vittorio." "As if to call him Signore were
an insult," she said to her cronies.

Save for this old woman, the street door of the
house was very seldom opened. Vittorio never went
out in the evening, and seldom even by day, except
when business required; and the men he employed
entered by a small gate in the wall close to the corner of the *casuccia*.

Marco came to Rome to see his step-son after a few

weeks. Ringing the bell of the south gate, as he had been told to do, he was admitted by one of the assistant gardeners, and after a few minutes' search found Vittorio among the orange-trees. He was examining them carefully, and cutting the finest buds into a little basket, and so absorbed in his occupation that he started on hearing a step near him, and colored deeply with surprise and anger as he turned to see who it was.

" Oh ! I thought it was one of the men," he said ; " and I don't allow them to come here."

The two saluted each other rather dryly. Their affection had never been demonstrative. Their sympathy consisted in a common hate of their social superiors, and a common love of their own profession ; but their personal tastes and habits were quite diverse.

" You don't allow the men to come here ? " Marco repeated interrogatively, as he followed Vittorio to a fountain set against a wall near by.

" No ; they have nothing to do here, and they have no right to go so near to the palace. The gate is opened only by permission, and when it is necessary, and there is no other entrance except through the palace and through my house." ·

As he replied, Vittorio went up the steps at the side of the fountain, and, pushing away the veiling ivy, set the basket of orange-buds on a little spray-wet shelf of the rock-work. Two white pigeons, that had been drinking there in the cool shade on the brim of the marble basin, fluttered away for a moment, then returned to their spray-catching and their billing and cooing.

Marco stood back in a thicket of red and white camellias, and looked about him. " I would like to see what you are doing," he said. " And I have but a little time to stay, for I must take the evening train to Valmontone. That *benedetta* diligence takes six

hours on the road. I started at seven o'clock this
morning, and have only just arrived. How do you
get along ?"

" Very well. I couldn't be better off."

Marco's clouded eyes flashed out a sharp glance
into his companion's face. He had found Vittorio
paler and thinner than when they parted.

" You were cutting orange-buds," he said, glancing
up at the mossy shelf where they were set. " They
say that the Donna Adelaïde is to be married to-
morrow."

" Yes," Vittorio answered briefly, moving away.

They walked about the garden, looking at the flowers and at the work begun in the new land. Coming to the gardener's house, they went in and drank a
glass of wine together, and Vittorio gave his step-
father a present for Rosa. It was a beautiful Gre-
cian scarabeo of lapis-lazuli, with a Minerva engraven
on it.

" I found two of them when I made the new drain,"
he said, " and I thought this would please Rosa. The
other is a Victory, and I have kept it for my name.
They belong to me as much as to any one. They were
under the wall ; and the land under the wall belongs
to nobody."

" *Sicuro!*" replied Marco with tranquil acquiescence, examining the gem, and mentally calculating
its value.

Presently they went out again, and, after strolling
about for a while, paused behind a half-moon laurel
hedge, through which was visible a company of ladies
and gentlemen breakfasting in the open air.

Palazzo Mitella was a solid pile, with a wing at
either side extending farther back into the garden,
and thus enclosing three sides of a paved square, into
which opened the long windows of the surrounding
rooms. The table was set in this open court, and

five or six persons were seated there. The city without was swimming in heat, and just sinking into a languid mid-day sleep; but in this secluded spot, as silent as the heart of a forest, a faint and fitful breath of air from the east passed over the garden, and cooled and scented its wings before reaching the company.

Marco gazed at the scene with that gloomy, taciturn face of his, marked the glittering china and silver, the rose-red and golden-yellow of the wines, the fruits and flowers, the obsequious servants. He noted the company, their easy attitudes, almost lounging in the large leather-covered arm-chairs, and listened to their low-voiced talk and light laughter. "Outside," he thought, "the hungry beggar drops his head upon the curbstone to sleep, and the poor mother hushes her child's cries that they may not be turned away from the doorway in which they have taken refuge, and the ragged children cluster on the church steps, thankful for a crust of bread. While these — who laid the first stone around which have petrified all the insolent privileges and crushing power under which we groan? Some man no better than I am, who did a deed for which I should be hanged if I did it to-day. It is time for us to move. This play of the great is respectable only because the actors put on such serious airs. If once we, the spectators, should laugh aloud, all the world would see how ridiculous it is. Ah, may they hear a laugh that will chill the marrow in their bones!"

The glance and breath of this man's face might well have scorched what it touched; but the laurel screen through which he gazed held bright and unscathed its glossy, scented leaves, proud with the memories of many a triumph. Its unfading green had never wreathed such brows as his.

Marco turned his eyes, without turning his head,

to speak to his companion; but the words were arrested on his lips by the look in Vittorio's face. It could hardly be called an expression: it was an absorption. Vittorio gazed into the face of the Donna Adelaïde, his whole being drowned in the contemplation of her, and utterly calm in the intensity of that trance.

Marco's own face changed as he watched him, and grew calm with something of the same intensity. He recollected, read, and understood. There was no mistaking the utter passion of Vittorio's gazing eyes.

Then he looked back at the lady. She was no longer to him merely a member of the class which he hated; she was an individual, and her slender white arms, stronger than Samson's, were wreathed about the pillars of a temple into which were built the hopes of his life.

She sat there in careless ease, a long white robe falling about her, half hiding the dim gilding and the lions' claws of her chair, a red silk turban folded about the thick tresses of her dark hair. She scarcely replied to the young man who sat beside her, and gave only an absent word to the others; yet Marco's piercing eyes detected in her something of purpose, some alertness of attention under her apparent languor and abstraction. That play of the hand and arm, those movements of the head that made its fringed drapery wave as if a breeze had passed over it, that pushing out of the small foot from beneath its flowing drapery, — it was not all unconscious. She was playing off these graces on some one. It was not the man at her side. Who was it?

While he looked she raised a cluster of red roses from her lap, touched them to her lips, as if breathing their perfume, then veiling her face from the others with them, gave a quick, searching glance around the garden, probed with her flashing eyes the laurel screen, and let them melt there for an instant. Then she dropped the roses, and resumed her languid coolness.

The blood that rushed to Marco's face sang so loudly in his ears that he did not hear the breath at his side sharply drawn as if it had been held long suspended.

Both turned away involuntarily; but in turning, Vittorio snatched a laurel leaf, and threw the hand holding it up over his head, and held it there a moment, the gesture full of a fiery exultation. He seemed to have crowned himself.

It was several minutes before Marco could control himself to ask calmly, "What part of the palace will they live in when they come back? They say that an apartment is prepared for them here."

Vittorio pointed to the north wing. He did not seem to have found his voice. Marco walked in that direction, and he was obliged to follow, slipping from one hedge and grove to another, to remain unseen by the company at the table, till they stood close to the palace. This north wing had but two stories above the ground floor, and ended in a *loggia* along the whole *primo piano*. Two long windows opened into this *loggia*, and a narrow stair, half hidden near the outer wall, descended from it into the garden. The *loggia* and stair, and the corner of the garden that surrounded them, were all wreathed and smothered in roses. There were roses for every month in the year, overlapping each other in constantly increasing richness, — roses piled on roses, till the ground was a pink and white carpet with their falling petals, and the bridal apartment was like a casket in which the Persian attar has been spilt.

If Vittorio had looked into Marco's face he would scarcely have known him; for never had he seen in it that glittering, ferocious joy. It was such a light as shines in the eyes of the tiger when he quivers with repressed force and eagerness, the instant before launching himself upon the prey of which he is sure.

Felicità was avenged !

------◆------

CHAPTER V.

ORANGE-BUDS.

THE north wing of the palace had been newly fitted up as a bridal apartment, and the Donna Adelaïde had already taken possession of it. She was to be married early in the morning in church, and leave Rome immediately to spend two months in the country.

On the evening before her wedding she dismissed her maid early, everything being prepared for her toilet in the morning. The bridal dress and veil glimmered whitely from sofas and chairs in the *sala* adjoining her bedroom, the cases containing her bridal jewels lay on the dressing-table, with the delicate gloves and shoes, and her trunks stood already packed in the anteroom.

"You can go now, Lucia," she said. " I will finish undressing myself. But first set all the doors open, so that I can walk a little. I feel nervous and wide-awake. A sleeping-potion ? No; it would make my eyes look heavy in the morning."

Following the maid into the *sala*, she listened to her steps as she passed through the anteroom, then locked both doors after her. She had no mind to be watched that night; and now, when the freedom of married life was so near, she was all the more impatient of the restrictions and oversight of girlhood.

Haughty, passionate, and unscrupulous, she had yet a sort of vicious nobleness, and scorned the pettinesses of her life as heartily as she scorned its duties. She was marrying for freedom. Her family had selected her husband, and she had accepted him willingly. He was rather a weak youth, and only a count; but he was rich, and he opened a new life for her. She gave very little thought to him, indeed, except the contemptuous one that his authority was not likely to give her much annoyance. Her mind was occupied with a future in which he played a subordinate part. And yet this future, now that it was near enough to be read, did not satisfy her. Of uncultivated intellect, neither literature nor art offered itself to fill the great space outside her girlish life. Feminine occupations she cared little for. Nature delighted her only to the extent of an unintelligent pleasure in beautiful scenes. The most beautiful landscape had but one word to say to her. Of the infinite volumes it contained she knew nothing and cared nothing. She required a magnificent landscape about her palace or villa, as she required fine furniture in her rooms, and thought no more of one than of the other. Excitement, stirring scenes, pageants, and power, — these were her aspirations. She felt in herself the struggle of energies impatient to be employed, without possessing the natural piety which might have directed them to noble work. She was supremely egotistic, and wished to enjoy life fully, and to be not only a law to herself, but a law to others. Yet now, looking at that near future which had promised so much when it was vague and distant, she could define nothing but a continuation of pettinesses indefinitely multiplied, — the same conversations, made up of gossip and scandal; the same vapid receptions, in which the sole ambition possible was to have the most beautiful toilet and receive

the most compliments; the same monotonous drives
through familiar scenes; and a church function now
and then to dawdle through with the usual carelessly
performed affectation of devotion.

The palace was quite still. All had retired early,
in preparation for the morning. Every door and
shutter was closed and bolted. Adelaïde walked
restlessly to and fro from the anteroom to the
boudoir opening into the *loggia,* her tall figure in its
flowing white dress looking spirit-like in the dim
rooms, lighted only by two candles from the bedroom.
After a little while she extinguished these, and softly
opened one of the western windows overlooking the
city. The moon was in the south, and its beams
shot by without entering the room. All the city was
flooded with a melancholy splendor, and the mountains on the horizon lay like a sleeping caravan of
gigantic camels with huge shapes sunk into outlines
that seemed to stir with the soft breathing of deep
repose. Beside her, as she leaned from the window,
were heads of carven stone that caught the light
along their cold, unconscious brows.

Adelaïde leaned farther out, and the quiet moon-
beams suddenly felt an unquiet soul thrust among
them, and trembled on that hair and forehead, fever-
ish and palpitating with life. She gazed over the
city with gleaming eyes. It was the first time that
she had ever seen it in silence and solitude like this,
the first time in all her life that she had ever opened
her window at night, and the situation had for her
something of the zest of an adventure.

Presently a company of *contadini* came up the
street on their way out of the city. One of them
played a mandolin, and they all walked silently to
the music.

Adelaïde drew quickly back, and closed the window
and the shutters. An open window with a lady in it

would have been a strange sight at that hour of night. Irritated still more then at being so cramped, she crossed the room, opened one of the garden windows, and looked out on a scene of enchantment. The fountains fell with a foamy plash, the paths were paved with mother-of-pearl, the illuminated trees and shrubs rained a silvery light onto the turf, and the deep shadows were as soft as clouds. Now and then a faint breeze came in from the mountains, spent with its long journey, put the heavy odors aside like a curtain, and swooned away among the roses. Up against the sky on every side was reared the garden wall, with its vases full of long, pointed aloe-leaves, like swords guarding this paradise.

Leaning from the window, Adelaïde met that soft rush of sound which is the silence of nature : the touch of leaf to leaf, the stirring of a bird in its nest, the fluttering down, all at once, of a cloud of flower-petals, the fanning of a moth's wing, the gathering of cool mists into dew, and the falling of the dewdrop, the rustling of the petals of a ripe rosebud which in the morning will be a rose, the murmur of multitudinous growth; and, above all, that indefinite consciousness of harmonies too grand for the ear to gather which is felt when the soul strains upward and outward from the tethers of the body, and knows that the stars are singing. For they sing ! No ship that sails but makes its song upon the water; no wave comes up the shore without its silken murmur; no bird nor bee that flies but the air hums or rustles against its wings. And shall the swift worlds be mute ? They sing, they sing !

The Donna Adelaïde did not think of the music of the spheres; but she felt some influence which made walls and a roof intolerable. Wrapping herself hastily in a black mantle, and drawing the hood over her head, she opened one of the long windows of the

loggia, and slipped silently down the stair and into
the garden. She wandered through the flowery alleys,
now bathed in a white light that ran glistening over
her silken domino, now hidden in the shades, a
blacker shadow. There was no danger here of observation. The palace was barred like a prison, the
casuccia was not inhabited, and the gardener's house
— she walked in that direction to make sure that its
windows were blind. Yet, after all, she would not
have cared if Vittorio had seen her, she thought.
He was not like any one else. He was the only person she knew who never annoyed her. Besides, he
adored her, and his adoration pleased her. The
Count Belvedere, her husband of to-morrow, was
fiacco even in his devotion to her; and she liked the
strong taste of life.

She sauntered on, thinking idly of Vittorio, since
she must think of something. He was the only thing
new in her life. Everything else was stale. She
liked his disdainful ways, his daintinesses, his severe
silence, and the rare smile that came only when a
flower pleased him. "It is a pity the Monteforte
would not own him, instead of the imbecile they
took," she thought. "One can see that he belongs to
them; and the proofs they did not find, they could
have made. I could then have married him, and
been a duchess."

She reached the eastern extremity of the garden,
and, pausing in a thicket of oleanders, saw through
the flowers Vittorio's windows wide open. The moonlight lay whitely on the ledge of the wide casement,
and a faint golden light stole out to meet it from a
little lamp burning before a Madonna. There was
no other light, and no sign of life. On the outer wall
hung a mantle of jasmine full of little white stars
that shone shyly back to the moon.

"He is imprudent to sleep with his windows
open," the lady thought, walking on.

Close beside the rose-thickets of her apartment was a group of pines standing in a circle, like a round temple, of which the trunks were the pillars, and the crowded green umbrellas they held aloft, the roof. In the midst of these trees was a round marble pedestal, from which a slender column of water shot far up into the pine-scented. dusk of the green roof, and fell in spray on the daisied turf. This was the fountain and grove of Undine. Seen from without, it might have been a water-nymph dancing there. The pedestal and the falling spray sparkled in the light; but all above was in a deep shadow, through which a dim and tremulous whiteness outlined the drapery of an invisible form.

As Adelaïde paused beside one of the trees, she heard a long, deep sigh, — the sigh of one who sleeps, and mourns in sleeping.

Startled, she drew her mantle closer, and stepped farther into the shade. There lay Vittorio asleep, one arm bent under his head, the other thrown out into the light, which it seemed to grasp with an upturned palm. So Endymion might have slept, and in his dream have grasped the shining vesture of Diana.

"Was ever any other human creature so beautiful?" murmured Adelaïde, bending to look at him. "He is like a fairy prince!"

As she bent there, smiling into his sleeping face, a nightingale burst into sudden song among the roses.

Vittorio stirred, raised himself on to his elbow, and listened, his face turned toward the palace. The song wavered and ceased, and as it fell into silence, a single word broke from his lips. "Adelaïde!" he exclaimed, and stretched his arms out toward her windows. Then, moved by some seeing instinct, he turned and saw standing there beside the fountain a slender form all in black.

He rose to his feet, silent and breathless; and at the same moment, with a silken rustling like that of the falling waters, the sharp blackness parted and slipped to the ground, revealing a white shape with swan's-down bordered folds sweeping the daisies: Undine stepped from her pedestal!

"Vittorio!" said Undine.

He breathed again, and in that breath cast himself at her feet.

"Why are you here, Vittorio?" asked the Donna Adelaïde gently.

"Forgive me!" he exclaimed. "I could not stay in the house. I have not slept for a week. To-morrow you will be a bride!"

"Yes," she replied quietly. "And I want to see my wreath. You would not show it to Lucia. Show it to me now."

His passion recalled her wavering fancy, and her quiet confounded him. He dropped his face forward into the dewy grass at her feet. "I am but your servant!" he groaned out. "Even here and now, outside the cruel world you live in, I am but your servant!"

"You are Vittorio!" she replied, with involuntary emphasis and significance; then added hastily, "bring me the wreath."

He looked up into her face, then rose to do her bidding.

The wreath lay above the fountain where he had placed it that evening, safe and fresh. Nothing could reach it there, unless a bird should dash through the spray to peck its sweet waxen buds.

Adelaïde stepped quite out into the moonlight as Vittorio came back. "How beautiful!" she exclaimed. "But is it long enough? Try it on my head."

She bent before him, and he, as in a dream, laid the wreath on her head.

"It fits me perfectly," she said, and stood erect and crowned, looking at him with her steady eyes. "Yet I did not give you a measure."

"I measured the Diana," he said, and glanced at a statue that shone out from the laurels.

"You tried my wreath on her head!"

"No; I would not allow the wreath to touch any head but yours. But I measured that, and allowed for the soul."

She smiled, still looking at him steadily. "You think that a soul would expand the brain, then?"

"Naturally," he replied.

"And if you measured the Diana for my girdle, you would allow for a heart?" she asked.

"No; I should make the girdle shorter."

"Why?" she asked wonderingly.

"The goddesses of this world have no hearts," said Vittorio. "But Diana's heart was strong. It beat her side out full with love. She did not marry a count for his money and his name; she loved a shepherd."

Vittorio's bitterness prevented the Donna Adelaïde being overwhelmed by her imagination, though it could not prevent her being fascinated. It was at variance with the soft enchantment of the scene, and kept her obligations in her memory. After a moment's silence she bent her head again, and bade him take off her wreath.

He removed it with trembling care, and had turned away to replace it, when she spoke again.

"*Felicissima notte*, Vittorio. Go home, and shut your windows, as I am going to do. To-morrow I leave Rome for the country, and I wish to find you alive and well when I return, as I shall not if you breathe the night air in this reckless way. We shall meet again. *Addio!*"

She went swiftly away, and a moment later he heard her window close.

"We shall meet again." The words fell like balm on his bruised spirit. He did not ask what they might mean. He only welcomed them.

The next morning, when Lucia brought the bridal wreath, her mistress saw that it was made of flowers, not of buds. She smiled, but said nothing.

With the wedding and the summer visits of the Contessa Belvedere we have nothing to do. Early in October they returned to the palace again. They arrived in time for breakfast, after which they had coffee in the garden. Then, one by one, the company dropped away to rest before the afternoon drive.

The Countess seemed to have gone in; but in fact she only pretended to go, returning swiftly among the screening shrubs to a little nook hedged in by orange-trees, where a passion-vine hung along the wall. Here Vittorio bent with one knee on the ground, while he pretended to disentangle a broken branch. He had been watching the newly married couple through the trees, and his brows were black with anger. He scarcely glanced up as the lady swept toward him, her silken skirts rustling on the grass in long purple folds.

"You here, Vittorio?" she said, with a light affectation of surprise. "I have come for some passion-flowers."

"It is a pity to break them," he said gloomily; "and roses would suit you better. You might as well wear a crucifix at a ball as put a passion-flower in your bosom when you are gay."

"They suit me, and I want them," she replied.

He began reluctantly to break the flowers. "Within an hour you will throw them away, or worse," he said.

"Perhaps not," she returned, without a sign of displeasure. "But what could be worse than throwing them away?"

"Giving them to Count Belvedere," he answered.

She laughed softly, and put the flowers he gave her into her bosom. "Why should you object to that?"

"Because I hate him!" said Vittorio, and, turning away, knelt down to his work again.

The Count's voice was heard calling his wife. He never allowed her to be long out of his sight.

Adelaïde bent quickly toward Vittorio, and laid her hand on his shoulder. "I hate him more than you can do," she whispered. "And now stay where you are a little while, that he may not know you were here."

Before he could catch her hand, it was withdrawn, and she ran away, checking her pace when she came in sight of the palace windows, and arranging the flowers in the white laces on her bosom as she went.

"I went to get some passion-flowers," she said, smiling at her husband as he came to meet her. And, putting her hand in his arm, she drew him indoors.

Poor Vittorio! that his goddess was but a light woman, he might suspect; but he was far from imagining that he was but one of her many caprices, and that all the baffled energies of her nature were flowing toward the one open channel of intrigue. If she sank from the starry heights on which his fancy had placed her, the skies, for him, sank with her, and she was still the highest and best he knew.

He stood there in a tumult of emotion that destroyed all thought, till a slight sound near aroused him. A mandarin orange had dropped from one of the branches against the wall, where they grew beside the large, sorrowful stars of the passion-flower.

Vittorio absently stooped for the fruit, and put it

to his lips; but instead of a delicate fresh sweetness, his mouth was scorched by an intense strength of rind and pulp where all perfumes of fruit and flower seemed to have been concentrated.

He cast it away, washed his mouth in a fountain near by, and, stealing along by the wall, went into his own house.

CHAPTER VI.

APPLE-BLOSSOMS.

WHILE the golden *mandarini* were dropping through Italian odors to burn the lips of the rejected scion of a coroneted race, far away across the ocean, a daughter of the North stood dreaming in a sunlight as rich, if more tempered, with ducal strawberry-leaves crushed beneath her republican feet, and heard a crimson apple fall from a laden tree to the bright turf below. Primeval forests swept over the hills, luxuriantly dark, and full of mystery; purple mountains propped a purple sky, in which were other mountains of more than snowy whiteness, — whole alpine ranges, with avalanches of mist-entangled sunshine, and dazzling angles of airy glaciers. Between forest and mountain a broad river wound dreamily to and fro, and ever onward. Wherever a leaf was seen, there October had laid its rainbow coloring; and, swathing the mountains, filming the nearer hills, and filtered through the forests, lay the slumbrous richness of the autumn haze.

The only sign of human life visible was in the tall and slender figure of Valeria Ellsworth moving slowly down the fruit-scented orchard to a vine-hung cottage near the highway. Her last October dream in her native land was ended. It was time to go. The carriage was at the door, and the trunks were on the steps. Through the sounding forest, like an arrow through the heart of solitude, the coming train was rushing to its station in the near valley; and beyond the mountains lay the seaside town from which on the morrow a steamer would bear her across the ocean to the scene of ideal lives.

Valeria was alone in the world and without a home, and her fortunes were all bound inside her closely crushed curls of brown hair. She had chosen her life to be single and artistic, — chosen not with laborious reasoning, but with a swift instinct of what was best fitted for her. The pros and cons had all been weighed, not consciously, perhaps, but in the long, slow balance of experience. For her early youth was passed. She was now thirty-five years old. Her first need was a home quite her own, as much her own as the shell is the home of the nut. Some people have a certain outward insensibility or positiveness which makes promiscuous social intercourse tolerable and even pleasant, and dulls the contact with alien substances; but she was so sensitively strung that the outer personality of a protecting and harmonious privacy was an absolute necessity. Without it, all that she was was worse than lost. This home was not possible to her in her native land, but might be possible in another.

The last good-byes were said, and she turned away from the door. The vine-draped cottage went all into crooked lines as she looked back; the fences fell, the trees were blurred, the whole place was ruined in her tears.

How beautiful was her native land, with its winters, which she was leaving! How fine were those storms, thick with snow-flakes and snow-birds, where the drifts reveal the ways of the wind as it tears a tall

3

tree up by the roots as with one hand, and with the
other fashions a frail snow-anemone that a human
breath would break, but that the blasts of air swerve
out of their courses to spare, as it hangs trembling
in fairy beauty, the pet and nursling of the whirl-
winds!

How nobly stirring was that fearless outcry of indignation over wrong, that fearless searching out of
iniquity, that confident breasting of any height that
the world can raise, that bold curiosity which is the
base of all knowledge! Atalanta, thou swift runner
among nations, stumbling a little over the golden
apples, but overtaken only by love! "A soul feminine saluteth thee" across the seas!

"Will the Olympians give me anything in exchange?" the traveller asked; and answered herself,
"Yes, if they give me four walls of my own to shield
me from the world, and my own roof for a *balda-
chino.*"

After a few hours came the final parting, and then
the awful hour when, for the first time to her, all the
world went down behind the sea.

But Nature is as unwearied in her wiles as she is
inexhaustible in her treasures. The transparent highway down which the light sank in green and blue,
the foam that ran under the water to show its milky
beryl, the waves that beckoned like sirens from many
an unstable mimic island, all that life in which, while
most reposing, they were yet as unresting as their
own beating hearts, — it was first a distraction, and
then a delight. Then London, which she found and
left in a November fog; then Paris, the *bonbonnière* of
the world; and still onward, till there rose a certain
height with a cross set upon it; and, "I think I
climbed there and set that cross," Valeria said to
her travelling companion. "And I must have played
here in some sunny, forgotten childhood."

Then, one after another, the towns which so disappoint and so satisfy at once, — the satisfaction deep, the disappointment superficial. "I know now," said Valeria, "why everybody loves Italy, and feels at home in it: it is because it is like ourselves, — a mingling of splendors and miseries. Mrs. Browning calls it the 'land of souls.' It is the land of souls in bodies."

———◆———

CHAPTER VII.

CASA PASSARINA.

VALERIA accompanied Mrs. Grey, her travelling companion, to a large boarding-house where that lady always stopped when in Rome. Casa Passarina occupied the second floors, or, more properly, the *secondi piani*, of three houses all thrown into one apartment, which had its ups and downs of high rooms for high prices and low rooms for moderate ones. The centre of the house, comprising dining-room, drawing-room, and boudoir, was common property. The eastern end of the long apartment had a number of comfortable low bedrooms, which were called sunny, because on clear mornings the sun looked into them for half an hour out of the corner of his eye; and the western end contained some rather showy chambers, and two small suites occupied by two of the ladies.

The American boarders divided the house into up and down town; the English, into West End and City; and all were pleased with their lodgings wherever they might be situated. For the house was thoroughly well kept, and the landlady, the Widow Passarina, a treasure of her kind. She was a large, pleasant-faced woman between fifty and sixty years of age, gracefully cordial in manners, and full of life and tact. She assumed that all the members of her family, as she called it, were devotedly fond of each other, and wished infinite good to herself; she knew how to sympathize with the present plaintiff without saying anything against the absent defendant, and had such a pleading manner of admonishing a quarrelsome or insolent person that she seemed to be imploring the grace of a benignant sovereign.

The family gave her something to do, indeed, in the way of peace-making; for it comprised members from the four quarters of the earth. There were Americans and English, pretending to like each other immensely, but missing no opportunity to give each other a little wholesome correction; there were Germans, hated up by French and down by Danes and diagonally by various other nations; and there was an Irishman who loved everybody so much, himself first of all, that everybody in turn was angry with him.

But these enmities were, after all, chiefly geographical, and did not prevent a good deal of pleasant talk and some kind feeling between the belligerents; the more so that there were other differences, more near and bitter than national ones, which formed new angles of opinion and new alliances. National foes could forget their cicatrized wounds for the moment, and meet half-way to resent the bleeding wounds of a newer warfare.

> "Saxon and Norman and Dane, though we be,
>   We are each all Dane"

in the papal or anti-papal cause.

It must be owned that this combat was not conducted on either side with a very admirable dignity.

It consisted chiefly of what we may figuratively call kicks and pinches and twits, and small triumphs celebrated after the manner of the "cock that crows in the morn," rather than of the swift sabre-thrust that leaves a saddle empty, or the fine artillery-thunder that opens a new red river-bed through the solid ranks of the foe. It was, however, a copy in small of the social state of Rome at that time, which suggested the idea of two armies drawn up face to face, each one trembling in its shoes, and whispering in its ranks the most injurious things of the other.

How the great actors in the drama liked their chorus, or if they gave it a thought, would be hard to guess. It is doubtful if either Prometheus or Jove would have felt himself greatly helped or honored on seeing a lady partisan, with a fly-away bonnet miraculously sustained on a chignon which projected it quite beyond the outline of the skull, and a nose very much in the air at the other extremity of the head, refuse haughtily to partake of refreshment at a reception where her rival Titaness or Olympianess was admitted. It might have been considered wiser by some had she smilingly accepted a seat at the table, and with it the opportunity to poison her opponent in a cup of tea.

At the earnest prayer of the Signora Passarina, the subject of the Pope and the Italian kingdom was partially avoided in open discussion ; but the *bianchi* and the *neri* showed their colors, notwithstanding. The *nere* liked to wear yellow ribbons upon occasion, and to come rustling in to breakfast in the papal court toilet, to show that they were just from the Vatican, and they had a way of leaving the *Voce della Verità* newspapers about, of reckoning time by *festa* days instead of days of the month, and the hours of the day from *Ave Maria*, which left no doubt as to their opinions. The position of a new-comer might

always be guessed by observing how she would reply
to a question as to the time of day.   On their side,
the *bianchi* opposed the tricolor to the yellow, the
Libertà to the *Voce*, the *Venti Settembre* to the
dicciotto Giugno, and the smile of the conqueror to
the bile of the conquered.

In short, human nature on one side did precisely
what human nature on the other side would have
done, had their positions been reversed; and that
one of these parties did not leave the house, or chase
the other away, was due to the fact that there was an
element of justice and common-sense in each which
knew how to soften the asperities of that partisanship which was only a conviction of the passions.
Mr. O'Hara, a *cameriere segreto* of the Pope, took
pains to be very polite to Captain Marini of the
king's guards when the latter came to see Miss Lilian
Marshall; and the Signora Passarina, whose liberal-
ism was whispered to be without bounds, almost
went on her knees to every Monsignore who crossed
her threshold.   Others helped; and, thanks to the
multiplicity of these conflicting influences, the modi-
cum of harmony necessary to preserve the community
was saved from destruction.

When our two travellers arrived at Casa Passarina,
early on a bright November morning, Mrs. Grey asked
to be shown the rooms already engaged for them.

"Your old rooms were taken," the Passarina said.
"But there are still better."

Valeria, who had listened to Mrs. Grey's glowing
descriptions on the way, looked with astonishment at
these chambers, and asked herself if she was to live
in an old curiosity shop.   In the hurry and excitement of travel she had scarcely glanced at any of the
rooms she had occupied since leaving her own beautiful American chamber, with its plate-glass windows
that went up or down at a touch, and stopped where

they were bid, its hot and cold water, ever ready at the bright faucets, and, above all, its obvious and unmistakable cleanliness.

"I dare say you may feel disappointed at first, since you have been brought up on fresh paint," Mrs. Grey said; "but you will be delighted by and by. Passarina bought this furniture at sales and in out-of-the-way places before people had fairly waked up to the value of old things; and now you could scarcely get such stuff for money."

"I should hope not!" said Valeria, and pointed to a little skeleton-iron stand on which rested an object which she had not beheld since her childish days, — a white delf basin and pitcher, both a little chipped and slightly leaning to one side, the pitcher capable of holding two quarts.

Mrs. Grey calmly poured water into the basin. "I presume," she remarked, "that you did not expect to live in an old Roman house, and have the Mississippi or the Connecticut — or was it the Penobscot? — flow through your dressing-room."

"O foam-bells of Arethusa!" ejaculated Valeria, *sotto voce*, gazing at the chipped pitcher. "O spirits of the vasty deep! O shades of Diocletian and Caracalla! — But I want you to understand," she said, with a sudden turn, "that American rivers are not to be sneered at even in Rome."

From the depths of a large fringed towel in which Mrs. Grey's face was being dried, issued a few half-stifled bars of "Hail Columbia."

Valeria looked about her. "I will own," she said presently, "that those spindle-legged, intarsio bureaus have an air of prim gentility, like proper ancient maidens who wear the most heavenly old laces over their flat, narrow gowns; and the chairs that stand on hoofs or claws bring certain quaint mythological stories to mind. There is a large red-leather three-

legged chair on hoofs that I. am going to take into
my own room at once.   How many charming people
must have sat in this chair!   I will add one to their
number," seating herself.   "The bedsteads are brass.
They could n't be better unless they were silver or
gold.   And will you look at that altogether too lovely
lamp!   Italy is the land of beautiful lamps.   We
shall find Aladdin's here some day.   And, Mrs.
Grey, will you see what she has given you for a
paper-weight, and what I am going to take away
from you instantly?   It is a fragment of *cipollino*
from some ancient pilaster, fluted on one side, the
fresh fractures all glittering green and silver.   It is
probably a petrified bit of one of the four rivers of
Paradise."

"Would n't you like to exchange rooms with me?"
Mrs. Grey asked, viewing these depredations with a
wondering smile; for Valeria had carried the chair to
the door of her own room, and laid the paper-weight
on the cushion of it, preparatory to walking them
both quite away.

"Oh, no, thank you!   I prefer my own.   Besides, it
will be so pleasant to see the sweetness with which
you are going to allow me to take all the loveliest
things out of your chamber, and give you in exchange
all the ugliest things in mine.   And you know perfectly well that you would rather have a neat, respectable little bronze lizard than this broken bit of *cipollino*, which you would have called rubbish if I had
not told you that it is beautiful.   It would be still
more beautiful with a fresh, fragrant pink laid on
it.   How I love pinks!   Did you see the little St.
John's bouquet that Lombardi painted for me last
year when he was here, — a bunch of pinks set round
with lavender, the long, long stems bound around
with a bright golden straw gathered from a newly
cut wheat-field?   It was a sonnet in color.   You

shall have my lizard. Here he is. See what a society air he has! Does n't he look like a nice, slim young man in a tail-coat? If you could turn him over, you would find a little starched white cravat all properly tied. You shall have my pretty blue chintz arm-chair, too. It will just suit you. You were made for chintz. And you can sit contentedly in a blue chair. I cannot. It is like sitting on the sky. Even the gods and goddesses had the grace to put a cloud under them when they sat down. There should be sumptuary laws for the use of blue."

"Are you insane, my dear?" exclaimed Mrs. Grey mildly, looking at her back hair in a hand-glass.

"Perfectly!" responded Valeria. "But don't be alarmed. My insanity is not catching."

"I never heard you rattle on so before," the lady said plaintively.

"Because you never before saw me on a *festa* day that calls out all my population. There are *gamins* in my city. It is n't half a dull town when the people are wide awake."

Mrs. Grey resignedly gave herself little soft dabs of pearl-powder. Valeria carried away her spoil, came back, stood looking out into the street for a moment, then went and kissed her companion on both cheeks.

"It is the first time you have ever kissed me," Mrs. Grey said beamingly. She liked all her lady friends to kiss her.

"It is not at all a personal kiss, you know," Valeria explained. "It means that I am so overflowing with contentment just at this moment that I must kiss some one. I am glad that your soft, sweet, though somewhat powdery cheeks happen to be in the way. Half the kisses we give, you know, and the best half, are not meant for the persons who receive them. A great part are meant for the persons who give them."

"I assure you that I am not so hypocritical," Mrs. Grey said disapprovingly.

"It is not hypocrisy," was the quick reply.

"And why not, pray?"

"I've forgotten why. When you have your conclusion, the premises go to the rag-bag. It is annoying to keep a great rubbish of whys and wherefores about one's mind. But the conclusion is correct. Oh! you need not look so incredulous and superior. I know my conclusions from my impressions by the feel of them, as quickly as I know the touch of a crystal from the touch of a flower. If you had piled up a mountain in order to get a mouse out of it, would n't you recognize that mouse instantly as an elaborated animal every time it caught your eyes, even though you might have mislaid the mountain?"

Mrs. Grey looked at her companion, stretched her mind to its utmost, and grasped her.

"You will forgive me if I say that you are the least in the world like a carpet-bagger," she said. "I never saw any one who had such a hatred of what she considers unnecessary possessions, or who travels through life, both physically and mentally, in such light marching order."

Valeria reciprocated the look. What an odd way some people have of making those personal remarks! she thought. They are constantly calling one's attention to one's self. Yet I seldom criticise them, though it would be easy to do so. They must be taught better. But how? Probably by destroying their self-complacency. "I wonder," she said aloud, "that you could not have found a finer comparison than a carpet-bagger. Out of civility, I could think of a thousand fine things to say to you which you do not in the least merit."

"No; the only fine thing I could have thought of would have been the troubadour with his pack and his lute," Mrs. Grey said.

There was a moment of silence, thoughtful and secretly pained on one side, watchful and complacent on the other. Then Valeria went toward her own room, singing softly as she went, —

> "Senza terra, e senza tetto,
> Di valsente sprovveduto,
> Va ramingo il poveretto
> Col fardello e col liuto.
> Il liuto ed il fardello
> Non toccar del menestrello."

Having passed the door, still singing, she closed it behind her. Then, sinking into her red-leather, three-legged, antelope-hoofed chair, and dismissing two large tears with her benediction, she set herself to studying out what wind and weather of life, and chymistry of human nature had formed that thought, that the apparent object of almost every human affection is but the feather to an arrow which has elsewhere its mark.

She had scarcely begun that most delightful of wild Diana hunts, the chase of an idea, with the fluttering garments of a hundred fanciful nymphs on the wind, and the silvery glad baying of the hounds of the seven senses, now one catching the scent, now another, and the whizzing of arrowy thoughts, all sweeping along in that speed and life of upper air which makes one smile unconsciously, when the door of her room opened and Mrs. Grey appeared.

"Pray don't stay here moping all alone," she said. "Come out and be introduced to some of the ladies." Then seeing the only half-comprehending face that Valeria turned upon her, she added, "What are you laughing at?"

"Nothing," replied Valeria.

There were several ladies in the house who had known Mrs. Grey on her former visits to Rome, and they came to welcome her back. She was one of those persons, *tanto buono che non val niente*, who never have enemies. People forgot all about her when she disappeared; and when she came back, saw her with something of that pleased surprise we feel on perceiving an unappropriated cushion at the other end of the long, hard bench on which we have been sitting.

The first visitor was Miss Chaplin, a maiden lady of fifty-five. Catholic maiden ladies of a certâin age go to Rome as the sparks fly upward. Miss Chaplin was tall, pale, gentle, and slow of speech, and had an air of grace and but half-faded beauty hanging about her like a veil.

"Miss Ellsworth is a convert, and quite as devoted as you are," Mrs. Grey said in introducing the two to each other.

Miss Chaplin looked at Valeria with her sweet, pale smile, then bent and kissed her, holding her hand a moment while sitting beside her.

Mrs. Carini was another visitor, — a dreadful little woman, puffing with spirit and enthusiasm, and a desire to know everything and tell everything, never letting any one complete a sentence unless he had strength of lungs to shout her down. After half an hour's verbal combat with this lady, one could not help wishing that the engineer who ran that machine *would* come. She told and asked the news, directed everybody what to do, pronounced upon everything, and made herself so annoying even where she wished to please, that it was a pity.

"Miss Cromo hasn't come back yet," she said. "She is later than usual this year. She went to Switzerland and from there to Paris, where she is buying her winter things. She expects to come back in a week or two, and I am quite impatient; for I want to see how her dresses are made."

Others came in, and Miss Chaplin and Valeria retired to a window to talk over a subject most interesting to them both. This was but two or three years after that 20th of September which gave Rome to Italy, and party feeling still ran high. The one side watched jealously to preserve its as yet unsteady foothold, and menaced whatever endangered it; the other listened for the tramp of allied armies that never came, and believed that the echoes dying away about the world were the multitudinous voices of rising nations. They could not believe that the old thunderous music of the centuries was a song that is sung, and that there should survive of it only the sigh that trembles along the heart-strings of the penitent, and the canticle of the soul which has triumphed only over itself.

Valeria was surprised to learn that she would be able to practise her religion without the slightest hinderance, and that even priests could go about the streets without insult.

"I have heard that it was different," she said; "and I came here almost believing that martyrdom was again possible. Ever since I first thought of coming to Italy, I have been haunted by a presentiment that I was to suffer something peculiar in Rome from no fault of my own, something relating to my religion, a suffering which should be almost, or quite, to death."

"Yet you came," Miss Chaplin said.

"Oh! that would not have prevented my coming," Valeria replied seriously. "It is always 'sweet and becoming' to die for a noble cause. However," she added with a smile, "as there seems to be no present hope of our being thrown to the lions, we must try to reconcile ourselves to being let alone — is it severely?"

The other visitors withdrew, leaving but one with Mrs. Grey. This was a lady about forty years of age, small, very quietly dressed, and very quiet of manner, though she talked in her way nearly as much as Mrs. Carini did. Every time she addressed Mrs. Grey, she said "dear Mrs. Grey." She held by the hand a little girl of six years, and from time to time she caressed the child, and smiled into her sweet and serious face. Her smiles were all an effort of the will, and though well meant, were rather mechanical.

"You must know Miss Pendleton," Miss Chaplin said to Valeria. "She is very good. She wished to be a nun; but her family made so much opposition that she yielded to them. But she lives the life of a nun. She lodges in a convent, and devotes her life to charitable works. She is very kind to that child, who is an orphan niece of Mrs. Gordon, one of the boarders here. Mrs. Gordon is too much occupied with society and with finding a husband for her daughter to trouble herself much about the child."

Valeria had some knowledge of human nature, and the rare habit of using her knowledge. She did not study faces, she read them intuitively; and never had she neglected a warning given her by some face in despite of itself, without repenting afterward of that negligence. Most persons are as easily deceived by those whom they know to be deceitful, and as blindly influenced by those whom they know to be intriguing, as though the alphabet of human nature were unknown to them.

Miss Pendleton's face had that unpleasant contradiction of a remarkably suave manner over unmistakable indications of a strong and persistent will. The will might be rightly directed; but if wrongly directed, this outward sweetness and prudence would make the woman strong for evil. A frank nature resents such a combination.

Coldness has the right to be reserved; but one does not like to be caressed through a veil.

Miss Pendleton rose, and, still holding little Marie by the hand, came to the window, smiling as usual, to make Valeria's acquaintance.

"I wish she had not that habit of drawing her mouth up tightly, as if she did not mean to let a word pass without being questioned," Valeria thought. "It reminds one of a prison. Perhaps she is excellent. I think she is. But she is too guarded to be pleasant. And I wish that she would not love me so much all at once."

Little Marie performed her blushing salutations with careful, but timid grace. "She is going with me to a Benediction in Sant' Andrea," Miss Pendleton said.

"But you have already been with me this morning to a Benediction in San Carlino, little dear," Miss Chaplin said to the child. "You can receive only one Benediction in a day. The Lord has no more for you now. It is useless for you to go."

The fair face clouded for an instant, then brightened with an angelic smile. "I like to see Him bless other people," said Marie.

CHAPTER VIII.

A FAMILY MEETING.

OUR travellers did not join the family till dinner-time of the day after their arrival. Mrs. Grey was employed in getting rid of a freckle, and Valeria in refreshing herself after the fatigues, mental and physical, of their journey, with an immense sleep. After nearly twenty-four hours' immersion in that sweet and all-restoring Lethe, rousing herself from time to time to say, "Not yet! not yet!" and dreaming deliciously away into unconsciousness again, Nature gave the signal of assent to returning life. "All hail to my sisters Eve and Aphrodite!" she said. "The one fresh out of nothingness, as the other out of the sea, and I out of sleep. Mrs. Grey, I am just half an hour old."

"Your inexperienced age will, I hope, excuse our being a little late to dinner," Mrs. Grey remarked.

The people at the dinner-table were very pleasant. Each had a smile for the new-comers. The news of the day were told; the inevitable quarrels were decked with smiles and roses, and seemed to be rather amusing little imps. The dinner was well served, and several of the ladies who were going out afterward wore gay toilets.

Valeria sat between Lilian Marshall, a tall American girl with brilliant dark eyes and a wild-rose color, and Mr. Clive Willis, a novelist.

The pretty coquette, who rejoiced in her beauty as a butterfly in its wings, and flirted as naturally as she breathed, complimented the novelist over the shoulders of Valeria, who could not believe that the few magazine stories she had written had made her famous, and was not quite pleased at being made ridiculous by over-praise.

From the other side came responsive compliments, of which also she was the vicarious recipient.

"Do you know what I am going to write next?" she asked at length, confidentially.

"Do tell me!" exclaimed Lilian Marshall, not caring a fig, but looking up with a glowing interest which displayed her fine eyes to the greatest advantage.

"A new version of Pyramus and Thisbe," said Valeria. "The wall is to be a simple New England woman, and Thisbe will have such eyes! Pyramus is to be an author, and he will have?"— she glanced at Mr. Clive Willis's head — "yes, he will have curly black hair."

"How charming!" said Miss Marshall coolly, helping herself to a bunch of golden-green, rose-clouded muscatels, while the gentleman hid his blushes in a wine-glass. "And do tell me who is to be the lion, and if he will tear poor Thisbe into inch pieces."

"Do not imagine that he will be a soft-hearted Snug, the joiner," was the stern reply. "The lion will be a pretty woman!"

Lilian gave a little cry. "Thisbe is lost!"

"I will eat up the vile, pretty woman myself!" cried Mr. Willis, recovering from his momentary abasement.

Valeria leaned backward slightly, that Lilian's glance of beaming gratitude might have its full effect, unimpeded by her neck-ribbon. "I had forgotten that you are a lion," she said.

Refreshed and made better acquainted by this short dialogue, the three pursued their dinner for a moment in silence.

Mrs. Gordon, an elderly, showy woman, sat opposite with her daughter Fanny, who was twenty years old, and had a nice little head to put a bonnet on.

"I am positive that we shall every one of us appear in print this year," the young lady said. "It is quite too dreadful. Mr. Willis is writing a novel of Italian society, or society in Italy, and now we have another writer."

Both writers looked at the girl.

"I will put you in print if you want me to, my dear," Valeria said kindly. "It would n't take me two minutes."

The girl's face shone with delight. "I will run away if you do!" she protested.

"I should not like my daughter to be made pub-

lic," Mrs. Gordon said, studying doubtfully over the
last part of Valeria's speech, and comparing it with
the countenance of the speaker.

"It would be such a pity for the world to lose
those ears!" Mr. Willis said, glancing at the lovely
pink shells with which nature had adorned the young
lady's head. "I promise not to paint your whole
portrait, Miss Fanny. I never do that for any one,
though I am accused of it. My portraits are compo-
sitions. For example, I see a woman with wonderful hair. I take her scalp, so to speak, and throw
away the woman. Some stupid man, myself probably, misses an opportunity to say a bright thing. I
take the opportunity, and — may I be allowed to
hope? — say the bright thing. It seems to me harmless."

"Your characters are frequently charming, Mr.
Willis," Mrs. Gordon said. "But you must excuse
my saying that, according to my view, you lay too
much stress upon good impulses, and too little on
good principles."

"I own," the author replied humbly, "that I prefer good impulses acted upon, to good principles only
talked about."

"But," she began —

"Precisely!" he struck in, foreseeing a sermon,
"But allow me to make a comparison. A human
being, we may say, is a spirit leading a beast. The
principles, good or bad, are with the spirit; the impulses, good or bad, with the beast. Now a good
spirit may have a bad beast, but a bad spirit seldom,
if ever, has a good beast. An angel leading a lamb is
very fine, but unusual; an angel conquering a tiger
is sublime, but also unusual. Given, then, the aver-
age human soul, a fallen and fettered angel, don't
you think that the sort of animal he has to manage
is a matter of importance? Don't you think that he

might get an occasional fall if he were mounted on a wildcat or a donkey?"

"I bet my money on the donkey!" called out Master Thomas Clouden, a dreadful American boy, from the opposite end of the table.

"*A propos* of donkeys," began a very delicate voice —

"In my opinion," said Professor Wagner, in a very loud tone. He had for some time been trying to obtain a hearing.

Everybody looked at him.

"In my opinion," he repeated in a subdued key, "there is no greater outrage than to show up a person in print."

The Professor, who had lost his hair at thirty, yet who wore the most beautiful blond curls at sixty, had figured in a recent story as Professor Wignor.

"Dante showed up people," Mr. Willis said.

The German, being an enthusiastic Dantean scholar, paused to recover from this shock. He could see the evident retort, could see his way, indeed, to retort on the probable rejoinder; but he was too good a chessplayer to be satisfied with foreseeing only two moves.

"And some of the great painters showed their enemies up on canvas, which amounts to the same thing," added Lilian, and gave the Professor a smile which had on him something of the effect of a sunstroke.

"I do not say that you are quite wrong," Mr. Willis resumed. "It is unjustifiable and indelicate to betray confidences, or to punish publicly a private offence. But a single malicious and dishonest person may originate a gossip so wide-spread as to amount to publicity. Thistles have winged seeds. A person of that character should be exposed. Poison ought always to be labelled. They told a little story in the United States during the last war which is *à propos.*

I suppose I may tell it now without offending any
one.   Some of the Northerners were dissatisfied that
their government had allowed so many Southerners
to go free after having taken the oath of allegiance,
and insisted that the Southerners acted upon the rule
that 'All is fair in love and war.'   One day a rattle-
snake was found in the Northern camp.   'Swear it,
and let it go!' cried one of the soldiers.   There are
individuals who privately do public mischief behind
the screen of the delicacies and scruples of honest
people."

"*A propos* of donkeys," resumed the delicate voice,
finding an opening; and went on to relate the sorrows
and sufferings of the donkey on whose back she had
that very morning made the ascent of Monte Cavo,
and the fiendish cruelty of the driver, whom she was
resolved to call before the proper authorities when
she should have discovered where the proper authorities might be found.   It is a common illusion with
strict and law-abiding new-comers in Italy, that they
are going to correct a great many inconveniences
which are different from the inconveniences they
made up their minds to bear at home.   This was Mrs.
Ellis, a very nice lady from Boston, in the United
States, where she had lived a life of the most exquisite
gentility for fifty years, and this was her first visit to
Europe.

Seeing the company attentive, she set forth the case
eloquently, even trying to include the Signora Passarina by occasional explanations in Italian, of which
language she was not a perfect mistress.   "The poor
animal became so impatient that he not only refused
to go forward, he turned quite round, and faced the
other way," she said; "and that horrible man gave him
the most dreadful blows, — *tanti bastimenti*," she explained to the Passarina, and was shocked that the
company could be so cruel as to smile.

Tommy Clouden smiled vacantly, then went for a dictionary. Ten minutes after he was heard exploding with laughter, to the surprise of everybody.

The family had a pleasant way of taking their after-dinner coffee in the drawing-room, where those who did not go out usually spent the evening together. A piano-forte, a card-table, and a chess-table afforded amusement to those who believed that there is nothing more to say in the world; while those who looked upon silence as a demon, or a very stupid fellow, or who secretly knew that it is a sublime presence which they had not the moral composure to face, kept up a babel-of tongues to drive it away.

Mr. Willis came to Valeria with Jean Ingelow's last novel in his hand. "Do you like the bobolink after it has become a rice-bird?" he asked.

Valeria gave the book back to him. "I am not yet prepared to read it," she said. "I resent too much the ceasing of the song."

"You prefer poetry, then?" he asked.

"I prefer everything," she replied. He smiled.

"There are many and various beauties in the world," remarked Miss Vardon, who was trailing her silken flounces up and down the room, and glancing at herself in the mirrors while waiting for a friend's carriage to come and take her to a reception.

"I see only too many," Mr. Willis replied mournfully. "Sometimes, I confess, I cannot help wishing that 't' other dear creature' were away."

"It is perfectly useless to say anything serious to you," the lady remarked scornfully. "Is that my carriage, James?" And exit, with a very grand air.

Enter Lilian Marshall, the white folds of an opera-cloak dropping from her shoulders, a white rose shining like a star in her dark hair, a feathery white fan in her hand, and her face brilliant with color. She smiled brightly, too happy and triumphant not to be

amiable, said a sweet good-night to all, and went off
to the theatre, followed by her aunt, Mrs. Clouden,
and by Mr. Clive Willis.

Professor Wagner, with a look which said that
then was the moment, if Mephistopheles wished to
make a contract with him, accepted absently Miss
Chaplin's compassionate invitation to a game of chess
in the boudoir. Mrs. Gordon retired to her apartment in the West End to receive some mysterious
important visitor. Miss Fanny Gordon, who had
been hovering about the piano-forte, asked Mrs. Grey
if she was fond of music. Mrs. Carini smiled toward
Valeria, and made a motion to approach her. Valeria
fled from the room.

Pausing in the anteroom to give a servant some
orders, she saw Mrs. Gordon come out, escorting with
great politeness a departing visitor. This was a tall,
slight lady, most singularly, but gracefully, swathed
in black from head to foot. It was wonderful how
anything but a statue could stand in such drapery,
that did not fall in folds, but swept and clung about
her form from the veiled head to the feet. It was a
pallid face, with dark hair dropping low on the forehead, and dark eyes that seemed to plunge into the
object they glanced at. The shape of the face was a
sullen oval. The smile was brilliant, and full of life.

A footman rose as this lady appeared, and opened
the door, accompanying her out.

"It is the Countess Belvedere," Mrs. Gordon said
beamingly to Valeria, smiling at the door through
which her visitor had passed. "She is the daughter
of Prince Mitella. Isn't she beautiful?"

Valeria did not reply except by a bow. She felt
silent, as if something important had happened to her.
Her heart trembled for a moment under the passing
glance of that woman, like a quiet pool into which a
wild bird has dashed an instant on the wing.

CHAPTER IX.

AMONG THE NERI.

A FEW days after her arrival in Rome Valeria had her first audience of the Pope.

She had looked forward to this event with a profound interest. From childhood the name of Pius IX. had been familiar to her, at first as a strange name of strange dread, later as a name suggesting as strange a reverence.

The unquestioned ruler of the largest body of subjects in the world, the discrowned heir of the longest line of kings that the world has known, and singular, in his own office, for length of days, and for the events which had marked his reign, — it did not need the Catholic faith to make him an object of vivid interest. But she had that faith, and held it with enthusiasm.

Her enthusiasm was not, however, that pernicious partisanship which believes that the Church can ever need the prop of a lie; and she had none of that vicious prudence which would conceal the crime of a Catholic lest Catholicism might suffer thereby.

The Spouse of the King of the Cæsars of the earth must not be suspected.

Animated, then, by a faith which was above the reach of circumstances, and a tender reverence for that priesthood among whom she had found her wisest counsellors and kindest friends, she prepared to meet the teacher of them all.

The carriage came to the door for her and Mrs. Grey toward noon, and they were driven through bright, crowded *piazze* and dark and narrow streets, over the Ponte Sant' Angelo, past the two "musi-

cal water-trees" of St. Peter's, under the great arch
by the bell-tower, through the echoing street that
circles those gigantic yellow walls, and into the court
of St. Damasus. The thought that this was the
famous Vatican Palace, which had for so many years
stood on a cloud among her castles in Spain, the real
rattling stones of its court under her carriage wheels,
the real yellow stones of its walls all about her, was
scarcely dwelt upon ; and it was impossible to think
with any interest that those long rows of casements
enclosed the *loggie* of Raphael, and that all the gods
and goddesses of Olympus and the Nile and the
Indus stood within these walls, mute and cold, discrowned of all save beauty, in the presence of the
God of gods. To Valeria the palace had but one
occupant, Pius IX.

"My dear," Mrs. Grey said, "you must take off
your gloves."

Mrs. Grey acted as ballast whenever her companion got off the solid ground of the commonplace.
The shock was not so great as it might have been,
however; for it brought to mind another command:
*Take the shoes from off thy feet, for the place whereon
thou standest is holy ground.*

Valeria removed her gloves, pushed her rustling
train behind her, rearranged Mrs. Grey's veil drapery,
and looked at the picturesque Swiss guard, as she
was bid.

Monsignor Fenelon, who was to present them, made
his appearance, and conducted them into one of the
Raphael *loggie,* where twenty ladies and gentlemen
were waiting. They took their places near the door.

"He will enter by this door," Monsignor explained ;
"then you must kneel. He will pass down the line,
giving each one his hand to kiss ; and he may make
a little address when that is over."

"I want to kiss his foot," Mrs. Grey whispered.

Monsignor nodded, and glanced inquiringly at Valeria.

"No," she replied to the glance, "I want to see his face."

At the opposite side of the long, narrow room, at the end of the line, stood a very tall gray-haired prelate in a purple silk robe talking with some ladies, who seemed to be under his care. He walked about very much at his ease, speaking with different persons. Presently he crossed the room, and shook hands with Monsignor Fenelon, addressing him in English.

"This lady has a letter of introduction for you," Monsignor Fenelon said, and. presented Valeria to Monsignor Nestore.

Valeria rose from her chair, but he motioned her to sit again. "Come and bring me your letter at a quarter past two this afternoon," he said in the manner of one used to command. "I shall then have time to see you a few minutes before others come. I dine at two, and receive at half past two."

The curtain was withdrawn from the door, and Monsignor Nestore returned to his place. The Swiss guards entered, and took their places at the lower end of the room, and a moment later the doorway was filled with a crowd of prelates picturesque in scarlet, purple, and black. The company knelt. Valeria, with her hands tightly and unconsciously clasped, glanced over those figures to discover the supreme one. They entered, and, separating, disclosed a form all in white, the robe, the face, the hair. But the beaming eyes were brown, and the smiling lips were human with sweet and kindly life. "A delicious old man," one of the least reverent of the company pronounced him afterward.

The Pope gave his hand to Monsignor Fenelon to kiss, then laid it on his shoulder while listening to the few words that were spoken to him in a low

voice. Valeria could not unclasp her hands, could
not remove her eyes from his face, even after Mrs.
Grey had kissed his foot, and her own turn had
come.

The Pope looked at her, smiled, laid his hand upon
her head, murmured a few words, and passed on. " It
is the hand that holds the keys!" she thought, as she
felt its light pressure on her hair.

It was all over in a few minutes, and they drove
home to find the family at breakfast.

All the *neri* asked for the Holy Father, and had
heard that he was in excellent health. All the
bianchi asked for the Pope, and had heard that he
was failing rapidly. All the *neri* prayed that he
might be spared, since after him would come the
deluge. All the *bianchi* responded with an emphatic
" Poh !"

After breakfast Valeria drove to Monsignor Nestore's. She found him dining with his chaplain, the
table drawn up before the sofa on which Monsignor
sat. He motioned her to a seat beside him while he
read her letter. Then, after a few kind inquiries and
offers of service, he led her to a large, bright drawing-
room, where a dozen or more ladies and gentlemen
were waiting.

Monsignor Nestore received informally two or three
hours of every afternoon, and if any inferior persons
came, they never displayed their inferiority while in
his house. Uncompromisingly dignified, cultivated,
yet brusque, this prelate liked no trifling in his presence, and allowed none in his house. The person who
could not say something sensible might remain silent,
and he did not hesitate to administer a sharp rebuke
if he thought that it was deserved. Full of courage
and common-sense, travelled, familiar with courts,
intimate with the leading spirits of that party which
in the West is called ultramontane, of which he was

a conspicuous member, it was a privilege to know him, even if one did not always agree with him.

There was always some one worth seeing at these receptions. Here was Louis Veuillot, then on a visit to Rome; and the lovely Countess Steinberg, whose windows the mob had broken two years before, when she illuminated for the Pope's coronation *festa ;* and a distinguished missionary Monsignore just returned from China; and an English lady just from Lourdes, full of a miraculous cure which she had witnessed there; and the fine, old-school Vicomtesse de Valois, who, in spite of ill-health, had made a pilgrimage from Belgium to throw herself *au pieds du Saint Père.* And here was our Valeria, with the wild pine-scents of her native State yet lingering in her nostrils, and her eyes full of pleased wonder over this wonderful Roman life.

Monsignor presented her rather sweepingly to the company, giving them that slight biographical sketch of her which he sometimes did give of persons so presented, and at which his friends were wont to smile. They often smiled at his little characteristic peculiarities. Valeria somewhat blushingly made her courtesy, then settled contentedly into the sofa before the fire, accepted the screen given her by her host, and prepared to listen. It is so delightful to hear people talk when they have something worth saying.

It was a pleasant room. How many, in all parts of the world, will remember it, now that its life has dropped to ashes ! The bright sun pouring in at the southern windows; the bright wood-fire on the hearth; the portrait of Francis Joseph of Austria, given to Monsignor by the Emperor himself; the large gilded arm-chairs ranged about the walls; the case of tropical birds opposite the southern windows; the table piled with choice books near the western windows; the

little boudoir sofa before the fire, with always one
or two ladies nestled into its cushions ; Don Giovanni,
the little chaplain, coming and going, now with a
letter, now with a private message from some one
who must see Monsignore immediately and alone;
and, above all, the tall figure of Monsignor Nestore
himself, leaning on the mantelpiece, or going about
among his guests, speaking fluently in five languages,
seeing that no one was neglected, listening to what
some isolated knot of gentlemen were talking about,
having a word for all, — a little dogmatical sometimes, but never mean, never unkind, never trivial.

Peace to his gray hairs, that were laid in the grave
just as the scarlet *berretta* of a cardinal was settling
upon them ! He was well hated ; not only with the
manly bitterness of political and religious opposition,
but with the hate of Rome.

For Rome means hate. It is love spelt backward ;
and the witches know that there is no curse so bitter
as a backward-spoken blessing, no blasphemy so bold
as a backward-muttered prayer. All history laughs
at the sentimental legend of " Roma, Amor."

Before Valeria left his house that day Monsignor
Nestore invited her to assist at his Mass the next
morning in the crypt of St. Peter's.

It was a golden opportunity, for in the long list of
clergymen from all parts of the world who seek the
privilege of saying a Mass at the tomb of St. Peter,
each one has to await his turn, and only six persons
are admitted at a time to the crypt.

Valeria was up, therefore, by daylight, and driving
through the golden freshness of the December sunrise,
which found the streets nearly empty. A warmer air
met her as she raised the heavy curtain of the church,
the perpetual spring of St. Peter's.

The nave was dim, the side aisles dark ; but the
dome had caught the rising sunlight, and all beneath

it was glorious. Seated on the steps of the great altar were Madame de Valois and her companion. Valeria joined them, and waited, watching the sunlight creeping down to the stone Apostles visible through the windows of the façade.

Presently a group of Liliputian figures issued from the sacristy, and crossed the church toward the pilaster of St. Veronica, growing more human in size as they came nearer, and standing revealed Monsignor Nestore and his attendants. The ladies followed him, a little door inside the railing under the balcony was opened, and they all went down the stairway inside the foundations of the pilaster.

To one accustomed to the thin walls of brick or wood of the New World, there is a peculiar and romantic charm in these hidden stairways, in these immense piles of apparently solid masonry threaded with narrow, vaulted passages, and pierced with hidden loopholes through which, far up behind a statue, or a vase, or an acanthus leaf of some beautiful capital, a human head may be thrust out, as small and as unnoted as a fly on the ceiling.

The little chapel of the crypt was glowing with lamps and with candles when they stepped into it out of the shadows. It is the jewel-case of St. Peter's; for, set in the midst of its mosaics and its gold, is the "lordly male sapphire" of the keystone of the arch of the Christian faith, the venerated remains of St. Peter.

Monsignor put on his vestments before the altar, and said Mass. Outside, in the confession, Canova's kneeling Pope seemed to pray with them, looking in through the iron screen.

When it was over Valeria went to take her coffee with Madame de Valois, spent a pleasant hour with her, then returned to Casa Passarina to find two or three ladies waiting to see her.

They had come on business concerning which they were very urgent and enthusiastic. The government, under pretence of making excavations, was going to remove the Stations of the Cross from the Colosseum, where that devotion had been made every Friday in the time of the Popes, — the Colosseum having been consecrated to the martyrs; and these ladies proposed to go the next day, with as large a company as they could collect, and make the devotion for the last time.

It was, in fact, more a protest against the action of the government than a devotion, though some of the ladies engaged in the enterprise were sincerely religious, and felt both grieved and scandalized at what they considered the desecration of a holy shrine. The really prudent motive of the government was not known till afterward, when it was said that either the Colosseum must have been put in a state which would make it impossible to occupy it for any meeting whatever, or the use of it must have been conceded for a great political demonstration, which would have been red republican in nature, if not in name.

"It is time for you to show your colors," one of the ladies urged, seeing Valeria hesitate. "We must let them see what we think of this. No Catholic has a right to hide his opinions now."

"I have already shown my colors in a way that no one could mistake," Valeria replied; "and I am willing to do anything that I ought. But don't you think that these flashes of gunpowder are rather undignified? Besides, I don't like to pray out of spite."

"Do you think that we wish to pray out of spite?" asked the Countess Steinberg, reproachfully.

"Dear madam, it is the last thing that I would think of you!" exclaimed Valeria, who admired the lady sincerely,—admired not only her pathetic, graceful beauty, but her fine, enthusiastic nature. "But neither must you believe," she added, "that I would hesitate to join you from coldness or cowardice. I cannot decide now, but will send you word in the evening."

They went, a little discontented, and she set herself to thinking over the matter. But the conclusion seemed to be forever flying at her approach, and the arguments accumulating on either side,—on the four-and-twenty sides, or the eight-and-forty sides, on the sides that never ceased to present themselves, and complicate themselves in an inextricable tangle.

"Order!" she cried at last, bringing down an imaginary hammer. "Ideality has the floor."

There was a momentary lull in her mind; then the discussion proceeded something in the following manner.

Faith (in whose breast Ideality had hidden her face). Shall the Lord listen in vain to-morrow over the spot where once he leaned to receive in his arms the ascending souls of martyrs, and still leaned, patient and loving, when only a feeble prayer came up? Shall all be mute to-morrow?

A quiet Voice (supposed to be Reason). "Non vox sed votum, non clamor sed amor, non cordula sed cor psallit in aure Dei." Let each one sacrifice in his own soul to-morrow.

Another Voice. But example? Besides, it looks as if one were afraid.

Fourth Voice. You are afraid. You fear the frown of a friend. You fear ridicule. You are afraid that some one will say that you are afraid.

Courage. Hear, hear!

Prudence (in a sarcastic voice). I have been invited here to-day to speak,—an unusual compliment from this parliament, which has ordinarily only words of scorn for me. I will not deign to retaliate; though I might remind the honorable members of certain occasions on which, looking on from my place of banishment, I have seen this assembly present the pitiable Icarian spectacle of —

Chair. Order!

Prudence (taking out a note-book and reading). Infallible rules: 1st. When you are in doubt what to do, do nothing; 2d. A word once spoken, or an act once performed, not all the king's horses can bring it back again; 3d. Take ten years to think over any proposition coming from women. (*Hisses.*)

A shrill Voice. The chair, being a woman, ought —

Chair. I am not a woman; I am a soul.

Another Voice. If Prudence came here only to read a set of musty old proverbs —

Third Voice. Prudence never does say anything original.

Common-Sense (roughly). Question!

Prudence (who has been whispering with Reason). In the first place, you are bound to obey and respect the government under which you live, when it does not command you to commit a wrong or omit a plain duty. In the second place, as subordinate members of a party, you are neither called upon nor permitted to take part in a demonstration where your superiors do not lead you.

Several Voices. Our leaders are in church triumphant! (*Interruptions, hubbub, riot, chaos.*)

Valeria put on her bonnet, as one puts a cloth over a bee-hive, drove to Monsignor Nestore, and told him the whole story.

"Don't go," he said. "It's a piece of nonsense. Those ladies will be called before the Questore."

"Two heads are better than one," she said to herself, with a sigh of relief, as she left him; "especially when one of them is my head."

The next afternoon, in common with half Rome, Valeria had an errand which took her to the Roman Forum, and she arrived just in time to see half a dozen lady ringleaders marched out of the Colosseum under the escort of a policeman, and conducted to parts unknown. The Countess Steinberg had been arrested for organizing a political demonstration. The other ladies voluntarily accompanied her to the office of the Questore, where she was informed that, if she repeated the offence, she would be sent over the frontier, and forbidden to return to Italy.

"Banished from Rome!" It had quite an heroic sound.

The next day the Countess Steinberg's tables were laden with the visiting-cards of the *neri*, foremost among them the enamelled pasteboard of Monsignor Nestore.

"The day after my windows were broken, two years ago, a thousand cards were left on me," she told Valeria. "To-day there must be fifteen hundred."

"It would be well to send a list of your cards to the Questore," Valeria suggested. "Do you think that your visitors would object?"

———◆———

CHAPTER X.

KATE CROMO.

ONE day, when Valeria came in from a walk, she was told that Miss Cromo had returned. The people in the house said a good deal about Miss Cromo, her goings and comings, her sayings and doings. She seemed to be a person of consequence among them.

"What sort of person is she?" Valeria had asked of Miss Chaplin. "Shall I like her?"

"She is very clever," Miss Chaplin replied, "and very amusing. She can caricature a person perfectly. She could make you laugh at your best friend."

"Oh, no, she could not!" Valeria replied decisively. "I would not allow her to try. But you have not answered me."

Miss Chaplin became circumspect. "If she should take a fancy to you, she would be very useful; she has been in Rome so long, and knows so many people."

"And if she should take a fancy against me, what then?"

"I think that she will like you," was the reply, spoken with a reserve which prevented further questioning.

"Do tell me something of Miss Cromo," Valeria said afterward to Mr. O'Hara, the Irish boarder. "I hear so much of her, yet can understand nothing."

He laughed. "She is very clever," he said. "Very clever!" he repeated, nodding his head.

Valeria looked attentively at the speaker. She liked Mr. O'Hara, yet was constantly being vexed with him. "I hope you do not flatter yourself that you are charitable now," she said with great frankness. "Because you might just as well have called her a rascal."

He became serious. "I have no wish nor intention to say anything of the kind. She is a very interesting lady."

Valeria's next effort was with Mr. Clive Willis. "I have been trying to form some idea of Miss Cromo; but no one will give me a definite answer. I shall not ask you."

"If she had been a man, she would have been a lawyer," he said concisely. "And if she were a man and a lawyer, and I needed some one to prove that I never .existed, and that all who imagined to have seen me were suffering from an optical illusion, and that my own notion that I existed was an hallucination, and, since a person who never existed cannot have an hallucination, that I never even fancied that I existed; and then, this having been all satisfactorily proved to the world, if I needed that my counsel should turn about the next day, and prove to all the world that he never said any such thing, — I would instantly retain Mr. Kate Cromo for any fee which he should choose to name."

Valeria mused a little while. "I suppose you would n't like to call them fibs," she remarked.

" No, we do not call them fibs," Mr. Willis replied. " They are grafted truths. Pardon me, I don't want to be funny, but suppose that we should call them Cromatics ? "

"Well," Valeria said, putting an end to the subject, " with all your chromatics I have not found the key-note. I will find it myself."

"The key-note is a capital I," he said.

It was not pleasant. Nothing that she had heard of this woman was pleasant. The result of it all was a feeling that no good would come to her from such an acquaintance.

Valeria had a will like the wind's will, which goes inevitably on its general course, yet swerves around impediments, seeming momentarily to turn back at times, but still going ever forward where its face was first set. She liked to softly breathe her wishes, and preferred to give up unimportant ones rather than contend; but she had at need the power of the storm. In the affairs of others she had no will, and she was incurious to a fault. All her life had been passed in retirement, with little society beside books and nature; and, standing, as in a magic circle, surrounded

by these companions, she was only too prone to look
upon the persons and personal interests about her as
mere pictures, or, at most, as scenes in which she was
never to take a part, and actors with whom she had
little or nothing to do. A dreamy veil of unreality
covered it all.

This sort of life had had the natural result of render-
ing her less prompt in social fencing, and, together
with an exceeding sensitiveness, and a habit of seldom
speaking except from the surface, had given many
persons the impression that she was easily influenced,
and not hard to coerce. Her courage and decision
were all for great things; in trifles she was timid.
Yet many littles make a mickle; and it had sometimes happened that her patience had broken under
an accumulation of petty aggressions silently borne,
and that the aggressor had been astonished by a sudden indignant self-assertion, which had left him puzzled ever after to know how to understand her, but
very little disposed to provoke a temper which had
for a moment seemed to him the most proud and
arrogant that he had ever known. To sincere affection her heart was as the heart of a child, pleased,
trusting, and uncritical; to sympathy she gave love;
for sympathy enters where affection waits at the door.
But, then, sympathy is rare.

Conscious of her own disposition, and that self-
defence was to her difficult and troublesome, Valeria
shrank from associating with a person who seemed,
from all that she had heard of her, to be of a positive
and aggressive character. She took the opportunity
to speak to Miss Chaplin on the subject on the day
of Cromo's return, when they went out for a walk
together.

A certain intimacy had sprung up between the
two. They saw each other frequently, and always
with pleasure. Valeria liked those long walks when

they sauntered slowly through the purely Roman streets of the city, stopping now and then to look at some beautifully carved *portone*, or a balcony of flowers high up on a house-front, or the overhanging green of a roof-garden running along the sky, — at any of those beauties which catch the eyes at every turn. Sometimes the open door of a quiet church would invite them, and Miss Chaplin would say, " Let us go in and speak to the Lord a moment; " and, kneeling there before the altar, aware of the bowed head and praying heart beside her, Valeria had a foretaste of the sweetness of heavenly intercourse.

" I want to tell you," she said; " I have been thinking that I would rather not become acquainted with Miss Cromo. There is no need that I should; for I am going to change entirely my mode of life. I did not come here for society, you know; I have no leisure for it, and I have already spent too much time in visiting. I must resume immediately my American habits; rise early, go out to Mass, then write all the forenoon. When the others breakfast, I shall dine. I may walk out, or talk an hour or two before dinner-time; but I shall not go to the table. The Passarina will send me something to my room for supper. I am sorry to miss the bright dinner-table chat, and the occasional evening in the drawing-room. But I must; for they set my eyes too wide open, and I must sleep early. As Miss Cromo does not, you say, come to breakfast, and joins the family only at dinner, we need never meet, or but very rarely."

" It is as well that you should not know her," Miss Chaplin said. " But she will wish to see you."

" I do not see why she should."

" She likes to know every one. Then you are in the house, and she will hear you spoken of."

" Please do not mention me to her. If she should

ask for me, tell her that I am very busy, and avoid introductions."

The next day Miss Chaplin told Valeria that Miss Cromo had asked for her, and expected a visit.

"Say nothing of me," she replied.

A few days later the subject was mentioned again. "She has spoken of you repeatedly, and is greatly surprised that you do not go to see her."

"Say nothing of me," Valeria repeated. "And, by and by, she will understand."

Again, after a day or two, Miss Chaplin returned to the subject. "Really, you must excuse me for boring you, but if you do not go, she will be angry with both of us. I believe that she suspects me of trying to keep you away. She has told me to come and bring you at four o'clock this afternoon."

"Indeed!" said Valeria, opening her eyes widely. "I am going for a drive this afternoon. I hope that you do not make any promises for me."

Another day was set by Miss Cromo, and yet another; and the third time, seeing that Miss Chaplin was nervous and annoyed about the matter, Valeria went.

"But I was never — why, it is being bullied ! — in my life before," she said. "And it seems to me that this woman has very little of either pride or delicacy."

Miss Chaplin was herself vexed enough to speak plainly. "Miss Cromo never allows pride, or delicacy, or the rights of others to stand in the way of her wishes," she said.

Entering a large and rather excessively *bric-à-brac'd* chamber, they were met by a vivacious lady, who kissed 'dear Frances' fondly on both cheeks, and welcomed Valeria as cordially as though she had not dragged her there. Not a word was said of the visit having been delayed. She chatted gayly and amusingly, displayed her treasures, delivered, *à propos*, learned little lectures without appearing to suspect that her hearers might possibly themselves know something of the subjects of which she treated; then, through a series of gossipy transitions, slid into the subject of genealogy, and gave a shining account of her own, in which a celebrated historical personage would have been surprised to find himself included.

Miss Chaplin, having an engagement, was obliged to go away after a few minutes; but Miss Cromo urged Valeria so to stay a little longer, that, charmed and fascinated, she accepted the invitation.

How bright she was! How gay and comical! How comfortable she made her visitor, and how delightfully home-like it was when, unexpectedly, tea was brought in! How pretty she was, too! — with a face that looked fresh in that soft light, and her uncovered brown hair, in which one did not detect a thread of white; with the little birdlike ways, at once so dainty and so decided, and the graceful dress, which, however, was not well suited to her short figure. Miss Cromo always dressed tall. Her self-esteem would not allow her to admit that she could not wear or do anything which the tallest woman in the world could wear or do.

She flattered coarsely, and asked indelicate questions; but she did both with a lover-like air which left one astonished and amused, rather than offended.

"I am almost sixty years old; how old are you?" she asked with a bright, bold smile, and a glance as bright. She never failed to tell her age, and, while taking remarkable care of her person, proclaimed in season and out that she was an old woman.

"I am thirty-five," replied Valeria, and thought that she would like to present the lady with a behavior-book with certain passages strongly marked.

"You are a beauty!" Miss Cromo declared with

the greatest coolness. "I am going to fall in love with you directly, and I want you to come to see me every day. Receive your friends here in my *sala* whenever you like. And bring me in the evening what you have written during the day, and read it to me."

"I never show my manuscript, nor tell what it is," Valeria replied. "I don't like to. I never did in my own family, when father and mother were alive. I could not, though I wrote only insignificant little stories. They had to wait for the print. I have not the habit of telling any one what I am doing. It is, perhaps, odd; but I shrink from it. And now I am more — is it odd? — than ever; for I am dreaming of writing a book. See! I tell you so much."

"What is the name of the book?" Miss Cromo asked promptly.

"I have not yet found one. It is so hard to suit a story with a name. I wouldn't like to Nicodemus the poor thing into nothing. Besides — I — I don't know whether it will be a boy or a girl."

"You darling creature! Tell me what the story is, and we will find a name together."

Valeria laughed. "You are a terrible woman! I am not going to tell you a word more about it!"

"Miss Chaplin says that you are going to write for the *Fair Play*," the lady went on, in no wise disconcerted by this failure, intending, probably, to return to the charge another time. "What are you going to write?"

"Oh, it will be nothing!" Valeria was quite willing to tell all about this. "They want only an occasional short article on some given subject."

"What subject have they given you now?"

"They wish me to answer this question: ' What is the root of the Catholic difficulty in Rome?'"

"When are you going to write it?" pursued the inquisitor in a very business-like manner.

"Not for a week or ten days. I shall have to ask information. That sort of thing is, indeed, outside my province."

"I have promised to write an article now and then for the *Aurora*," Miss Cromo said. "We must tell each other what our subjects are, so as not to write about the same thing. They wanted me to write for *Fair Play;* but I refused."

She did not, however, tell what her subject was, nor did Valeria ask her; and her assertion that she had been asked to write for the *Fair Play* was an invention of the moment.

The conversation then became less personal, and Valeria presently took leave.

"Remember, you are to let me see you every day," was the parting charge of her entertainer. "You are just the friend that I have always wanted. I have never seen any one who suits me so perfectly." And the sentence ended with a rather too warm kiss on her visitor's mouth.

"You handsome creature!" she exclaimed, looking after her. "You step like a young empress!"

"That 'young' is a master-stroke," thought Valeria. "It really is pleasant to hear, though I know just how old I am."

She went thoughtfully to her room, interested, yet unsatisfied. She had never had an intimate friend, and she would have liked to have one, and one as clever and amusing as Miss Cromo. But could she trust her? It was far from sure. The one thing necessary was that her friend should be sincere and loyal, and ready to forgive sometimes, as she surely would be forgiven anything but insincerity and betrayal. Valeria knew that she was herself no saint, and she did not expect to find saints among her

friends. She had not found them anywhere, least of
all among those who appeared to consider themselves
irreproachable. And affection likes to have something to forgive, something to explain and excuse.
That was its peculiar province, she thought. Therefore all that she had heard against Miss Cromo was
as nothing to her. She could quite well think for
herself; and her inclination had ever been to look
with interest on a person who was much criticised.
Popular judgments are frequently so worthless, — a
witless acclamation, like the running of a silly flock of
sheep who crowd pell-mell after one whose nose has
happened to lead him in some new direction. For
the rest, it seemed to her that their characters were
complementary, — she standing apart as a spectator of
social life, the other an active combatant; she un-
ready in defence, the other ever prepared, and scent-
ing the battle afar off; she religiously inclined, her
merest weeds of fancy growing with roots toward the
centre of things, and her butterflies all Psyches;
the other intellectually sceptical and material. She
did not fear the differences, nor entertain any phari-
saical exclusiveness. Each had wit enough to appreciate the other, and they could quarrel amicably.

"If only I could trust her!" she thought.

And still she mused over the interview with a
trouble which she could not define. She would not
admit that she had felt for the first time in her life
how strong is an unscrupulous 'and smiling persistence, and how convincing is mere bold assertion; or
that, at the bottom of her heart, she was sorry for
having yielded, and made the visit she had at first
refused to make. She sought by reason to combat an
instinct which had never deceived her, and succeeded
only in imposing on herself an apparent acquiescence,
which did not silence the doubt. For reason is always
imperfect in judging of character, since the logic of

the Creator overpasses the logic of the schools, and our thought may not grasp the premises of a human soul.

———◆———

CHAPTER XI.

BLACK SPIRITS AND WHITE, BLUE SPIRITS AND GRAY.

ONCE a week during the winter the Signora Passarina opened her house to all the friends of all her boarders, giving them tea at her own expense. On the same day Mrs. Gordon and Miss Cromo received in their own apartments, — the former with closed doors, the latter in a semi-privacy from which she could overlook the crowd outside, and see who her friends' friends were, and also if any of her own subjects allowed themselves to be entangled in profane wiles while on their way to pay their respects to herself. Between these two ladies there was an irreconcilable feud; that is, Mrs. Gordon loftily and severely disapproved of Miss Cromo in every possible way, and Miss Cromo hated Mrs. Gordon from the bottom of her heart, the more bitterly because she had vainly made every effort to establish an intimacy with her. Mrs. Gordon was a favorite in *papalina* society, and was a very honest, if rather a bigoted Catholic. Miss Cromo, who called herself Catholic without having the least reason to do so, was deeply mortified that *papalina* society would not notice her, and believed that Mrs. Gordon was the cause of the Countess Belvedere having given her the cut direct, the Countess Belvedere being conspicuously *papalina*. Silently and coldly all this society passed the little woman by. In vain she begged the few whom she knew to bring their friends to her. They did not refuse;

but the tantalizing prize seemed ever within reach
of her eagerly grasping fingers, while ever it slipped
through them. But still she persisted, having perfect
confidence, and with reason, in her power to hold
what once she had grasped. It mattered little to her
that she "ate humble pie," as she confessed, to make
a friend or conciliate a foe, since she fully intended
that both should afterward be made to feel her
strength. The chief and perhaps only value that
Valeria had in her eyes was in her being a member
of *papalina* society.

These Saturday receptions at Casa Passarina were
considered important by needy artists and professional
people of all sorts. They came to make desirable
acquaintances, and to snap up ingenuous tourists, especially the golden geese of América. There came
now and then certain American ladies, resident in
Rome, who held themselves apart with severe coun-
tenances, which signified that they were on no account
to be approached by the vulgar, and proclaimed to
uninstructed Italians that there were Americans *and*
Americans; and there were also a number of Italian
ladies of the middle class, who could not see the
difference, and were charmed alike with everybody,
since, after all, these foreigners were all so *curiosi* that
it was n't worth while mentioning, unless one of them
should be guilty of some unusually brilliant stupidity.
And there were the tourists, refreshing to see, with
their enthusiasm and their intelligence, with history
and the guide-book at their finger-ends, talking with
expanded hearts of great things under the supercil-
ious eyes of people who dryly talked of little things,
and looked upon great subjects as they would have
looked upon caged bears, thankful that they could
not get near enough to bite them. Those dear tourists in their travelling dresses, or the plain black silks
which they had put into the bottoms of their trunks

in the palpitating hour of packing, and who believed that they were in the very pink of Roman society, and were touching the outer flounce of the millennium! What a wonderful account they would give, when they went home, of these same receptions!

There was little Dr. Kraus, who was but just launched on his profession, and naturally and properly anxious to make his way. Miss Cromo had taken him under her protection, and recommended him to everybody, putting certain high lights into her picture of his capabilities; and he, in return, attended her assiduously for next to nothing, studied over all her little ailments with the solemn anxiety of a court physician, artistically painted her rheumatic knees with iodine, bore her snubs patiently, and was altogether as humble a servant as could be desired. There was Mr. Clive Willis, looking most serious when most amused, and a number of pleasant lady novel-writers. Occasionally some distinguished person came, partly not to slight an invitation, or rudely break a clever little net that some fair hand had cast over him before he was aware, partly to see how queer it all was.

Mr. Clive Willis had, rather impudently, proposed and copied out a motto to be written on the cards for the Passarina Saturdays:—

"Ricchi, e al verde di cotanti,
  Qua venite tutti quanti."

But then, he was always jeering. Miss Cromo said that he mocked himself in the looking-glass.

The first of these receptions took place two or three days after Miss Cromo's return; and that lady invited Valeria to come to her apartment to "help her receive," she said.

"And receive your friends here, my darling,"-she said. "It is so much quieter than out in the Passa-

rina *sala*. You can always use my reception-room
just as if it were your own."

Valeria was surprised at such generosity. "You
are too kind," she said. "But I do not intend to
invite any one, and I shall have very few visitors.
I will come with pleasure and see you receive.
Nothing will make me believe that you need any
help."

Miss Chaplin came to Valeria's room to take her
to Mrs. Gordon's, where she promised to go later.
Miss Chaplin was looking very fair and pretty, with
a good deal of white lace about her silver-gray dress,
and a pink rose in a little mist of mignonette in her
bosom.

"How nice of you to wear flowers!" Valeria said.
"You keep me in countenance. See what a red rose
I found this morning. I'm making believe that it is
a ruby. I have been sighing all my life for a ruby."

"I hope never to be too old to wear flowers," Miss
Chaplin said. "I used to know a beautiful white-
haired lady in America, who often put a rose in her
hair to fasten a lappet or a veil. Once I saw
her with a pale yellow rose like a star, and it was
lovely."

"White hairs," said Valeria, "are the dawn of
heaven, — it is better in Italian, the *alba del para-
diso*, — and it is fitting that there should be a morning star above them."

Miss Cromo had been very much occupied all the
morning, and was but just dressed when Valeria
went into her room, and offered to help her.

"If you would be so very kind," she replied. "I
have not a moment, and there are two or three little
things to do. Clara Vine is in Rome, and is coming
here this afternoon. Will you please find her book
— it is there on the upper shelf — and cut the leaves,
and put it in some conspicuous place? I have never

looked at it. And you might read out some little thing while I am dusting this Dresden set."

"What other notables do you expect?" Valeria asked, searching over the books.

"There is the painter, Mr. Hubert."

Valeria was pleased. "Oh! I have wished to see him. Is he nice?"

"Such a dear old Turveydrop!" Miss Cromo said affectionately, while she wiped with great care a pretty Dresden cup. "And I suppose that his wife will be with him,—a die-away creature who pretends to be sick, and is well as you or I."

Valeria found the book, cut the leaves, opened at random, and read:—

> "We caught a prize in our nets to-day,
>   As we drew the shining mackerel home;
> In the midst of the quivering rainbow lay
>   A face as white as the cold sea-foam."

"If it had been anything but mackerel!" Miss Cromo remarked. "They are as bad as onions."

Valeria turned the leaves: "Here is one called 'Fulgura Frango.' It begins with a description of a tempest, and a note explains that the Liberian basilica is referred to, that there are five bells, and that the *campanone* is named Maria Assunta. Here is the ringing:—

> "When, like an angel voice, there fell,
>   Sudden and sweet and bright,
> Three great golden strokes of a bell
>   Into the stormy night.
> And four great golden strokes of a bell,
>   As they ring at dawn of day,
> Out through the tempest's deafening swell,
>   Cleft their musical way.
> There were wind and thunder echoing far,
>   And the wild rain's headlong fall;
> But the bells of my queen of basilicas
>   Were ringing over them all!

" ' Glory to God ! ' (sang the major bell),
'He has made all things that be.
He is Three in One ; and from heaven to hell
There is no God but He.'
And the four bells sang out, clear and bright,
' Glory to God ! Amen.
Forever and ever ' (through the raging night),
'And ever, and ever, Amen.'
The faithful heart rejoiced aloud
At the chorus clear and sweet:
' Maria Assunta is walking the cloud
With her beautiful shining feet ! '

" ' I am blest ' (she sang down out of the skies),
' With chrism and water and prayer ;
And I break the thunderbolt as it flies,
And scatter the clouds of air.
I call the people, I call the priest,
I mourn the faithful dead ;
And I ring a pæan of joy for the feast.'
' Amen !' the chorus said.
And while she sang so glad and strong,
Over and over again,
And in and out of her steady song,
They braided their bright ' Amen.' "

"They do ring so," Valeria said, interrupting herself. "Maria Assunta, sonorous and slow, and the others dancing about her."

"Very likely," replied Miss Cromo, reaching a feather duster up to a very ugly majolica plate on the wall. "And I dare say Clara Vine believes devoutly that the lightning snaps in pieces under their feet like macaroni. She is very superstitious."

"'Comme toutes les âmes poétiques,'" quoted Valeria, and closed the book, and laid it in solitary state on a little table beside the finest arm-chair in the room.

"Oh, how provoking !" Miss Cromo exclaimed suddenly. "There goes Mrs. Gordon's coal-gas ! They never kindle their fire till the last minute, and for half an hour their gas comes down my chimney. I believe she does it on purpose."

Valeria hastened to open a window. Miss Cromo

gave a little scream. "Don't! I never open my windows in the winter. I will burn a pastile."

"But the gas will be in the room all the same," Valeria said.

"No one will perceive it when I have lighted a pastile," suiting the action to the word.

The company began to come, and Miss Cromo's nostrils breathed the odorous smoke with perfect contentment; while Valeria, who would fain have opened every window, and shaken all shakable articles out in the fresh west-wind, hated the perfume for the poison hidden in it, and fancied that her whole being was full of carbonic-acid gas.

But she watched with pleasure the graceful ease and cordiality with which Miss Cromo received her guests. Whatever she might say about them behind their backs, she certainly was charming to their faces. The arrival of Mr. Hubert, her "dear old Turveydrop," was hailed with murmured rejoicings, intended for his ear alone. She wanted him to talk with a very distinguished lady who was not accustomed to the slip-shod manners of people in general; "and you are so courtly!"

As for Mrs. Hubert, "if you had not come to-day, I should have sent this very evening to inquire if you were ill. I have been so anxious!" and "Mr. Whitney! I did not hope that you would remember me when so many shining people are seeking your society. I wrote begging you to come; but I was afraid you would not."

"Mr. Whitney, my dear?" she had said to Valeria the day before; "certainly I know him. The dear old snob! I could twist him around my fingers."

Dr. Kraus came in, and bowed profoundly before her. He was, apparently, invisible to her eyes. He had been only too visible for the last fifteen minutes, talking in the outer drawing-room with Lilian

6

Marshall. He watched his opportunity, caught her glance, and made another solemn and reverential inclination. The spot where he stood was a void to Miss Cromo. The poor little man looked distressed, but firmly resolved to do his penance, if it should keep him there bowing alternately to the profile, full face, or back of his hostess all the afternoon.

"If you do not instantly speak to that man, I will pinch you when they are all gone away!" Valeria whispered to her.

"Ah! good morning," Miss Cromo said to him. Then, more sharply, "Why don't you pick up Mrs. Smith's glove? Don't you see that she has dropped it? A gentleman should learn to do those things."

He bowed again profoundly,—this time to Miss Cromo's back,—with an expression not devoid of anger, and obediently picked up the glove.

"I wonder he does n't pick it up in his mouth, like a little dog," Valeria thought, looking at him with contempt. "If he had had manliness enough to turn his back and walk out of the room the first time she overlooked him, she would have written him a sweet little note to-morrow, asking why he did n't come here to-day."

A nice-looking couple came in, youthful, with very pleasant manners. The gentleman's face, though noticeably unsmiling, was very agreeable. Miss Cromo introduced him to Valeria,—Dr. Lacelles.

She had heard Mr. O'Hara and Miss Cromo talk of Dr. Lacelles that day at table. "He is an ass!" the Irishman had said; and Miss Cromo had responded with a laugh, "Yes, a solemn ass!"

"If," Valeria reflected, "everybody here should be suddenly bewitched so as to be forced to say to each other's faces what they have said behind their backs, what a scattering there would be!"

A pretty young woman appeared in the door,—a

drooping creature, hesitating there with a light poise, as if a breeze had blown her so far, and would presently float her in.

"Oh, Miss Vine!" Miss Cromo exclaimed, going to meet her with eager affection.

"Our American Sappho!" she said, presenting her to some one. "If you have not read her poems, do so at once. I know them by heart. While you read you will imagine yourself in Athens in the golden age. She sounds every chord. There is one poem on the fishermen which would make your flesh creep. Then the 'Fulgura Frango' is superb. Such a description of a storm! Miss Ellsworth was perfectly entranced by it, and you know Miss Ellsworth is a judge, and herself of the craft. Have you read her last story in the *Aurora*, 'My Dog Tray'?"

"Yes; and I wondered if it were a true story," Miss Vine said, smiling across at Valeria.

Poor Valeria, who was crimson with annoyance at this display, tried to reply with calmness, "I made the story, but God made the dog." And, watching her first opportunity, she slipped from the room.

Three ladies, all of them novel-writers, had met in a corner by the door just as she came out. "What a meeting!" exclaimed one of them gayly. "We must be Macbeth's witches. What shall we talk about? It ought to be something professional. Let's abuse the critics."

"No; let's abuse the publishers," said the second.

"We will abuse them both," the first speaker said, with an air of the greatest satisfaction. "Mrs. Waters shall begin," nodding at the lady who had not spoken.

"I cannot," she replied softly. "They have been too good to me, they have been my best friends."

"Behold a woman writer who loves critics and

publishers!" cried the first speaker. "It only remains that she should love the printer and the proofreader! And yet, she has two eyes, a nose, and a mouth. Did they never, my dear phenomenon, cut you up the least bit, or ignore you crushingly? Did they never spoil your most studied passage, or change the sense of it to something that made you want to murder them?"

"They have found fault sometimes," Mrs. Waters replied pleasantly. "But the faults were there; and if I was not aware of them, it was better for me to know. One improves so. I have learned a good deal from the notices of my books; and sometimes I have been touched by the kindness with which a fault has been pointed out or excused. Of course, now and then, but very rarely, there is one who —" She paused to find an expression which should be gentle enough.

"Who has ears too long for a horse," supplied the first speaker.

"Oh, I would n't say that!" exclaimed Mrs. Waters.

"Of course you would n't, you lamb! and that is the reason why I have said it for you."

Valeria passed this Olympian circle, and was instantly seized upon by Mrs. Carini, and introduced to a gentleman whom that lady was evidently anxious to get away from, and who apparently was not sorry to lose her.

"Mr. Allen would like to make your acquaintance. Sit right down here and talk with him."

"They tell me that you write," began the gentleman, who seemed to be a clergyman.

"It is n't worth mentioning," she said. "So many people write!"

"May I ask what your object is?" he pursued, with the deliberateness of one who meditates a regular siege.

"I beg your pardon. I'm afraid I do not quite understand."

"What do you aim at in what you write?"

"I aim at writing a story."

He remained silent . and grave, looking down. Valeria considered. Should she let the matter rest at that? Or should she frankly say that she had never thought about the matter, and was not prepared to give a reason? Or should she be amiable, and try to find some of those troublesome whys and wherefores which were always being forgotten?

The gentleman turned to her suddenly with a smile on his sober face which was very sweet. "You think me impertinent!" he said; and his voice, losing its somewhat hard and formal quality, had a faint vibration and softness in it, as when, opening a piano, after the first sharp click of the lock, and dull thud of the lid, a fold of sleeve or slipping cover brushes the wires, and stirs a little the tunefulness in them. There was music under the calm exterior of this man.

Valeria's denial was not spoken in words. He surely was not impertinent. He was a kindly, earnest man, who could not and would not learn the art of small talk.

"There is nature to praise, for one thing," she said; "and anything is good which has a tendency to draw people out of the city, and make them remember how far more beautiful is the country."

She paused. He bowed slightly and waited, looking down as though he had entered upon a long silence.

"Then one might give a little harmless amusement, a little timely consolation or courage, or even a warning."

She waited so long that he was forced to speak, but with the air of one who merely speaks an affirmation in order that another may proceed. "I have often found one or all of these in books that I have chanced upon."

"And there is one's own little song to sing over everything that is beautiful and sublime, and one's own little shot to fire at what is evil. And the song and the shot, if they are good for nothing else, are a *sfogo.*"

Another pause. He would have more. It was stimulating, even irritating..

"What can one do," she said, "if a voice that will not be silenced says, 'Write!' and, presumptuous or not, one feels that it is the same voice which spoke to St. John? Inspiration has its handmaidens as well as its apostles. The lighthouse on the headland guides the ship safely over the wide ocean; but the lamp set in the cottage window shows the returned sailor the way up the grassy lane by night. It was worth while setting the lamp there to have him smile in the dark at the sight of it."

The gentleman did not care to push too far one whose voice he had heard tremble, and whose eyes, he suspected, had a reason of their own for being cast down. If Valeria had touched music in him, he perceived that he had stirred deep waters in her. Yet he was interested. He liked to know what people mean and are about in their lives, and he was troubled at finding so many who mean nothing more than a bird or a beast might mean, — a thicker tree for the nest, or a drier cave for the lair; a riper cherry to peck, or a finer lamb to rend and devour.

"Songs to sing; yes," he said. "But should women fire shots? Is not charity, rather, their province?"

She smiled a challenge in his face. "Does Charity, then, stand by sweetly smiling or only helplessly weeping when wrong is done, neither denouncing the oppressor, nor crying out for help for the oppressed?

Such a charity would be a rather insignificant member of the abiding 'these three' of St. Paul. Faith removes mountains; Hope recounts her visions of what lies behind these mountains, without which Faith would not care to remove them. Does Charity only speak soft words, — she the 'greatest of these'? And when Justice drops the sword, who shall take it?"

The minister's cheeks had begun to redden. He forgot the object with which he had begun the conversation.

"She is more than justice!" he said. "She is justice transfigured. Why, when a condemned criminal is recommended to the mercy of the executive, what does it mean but that there are certain circumstances which the letter of the law does not take cognizance of, but which would render his condemnation contrary to the true spirit of justice? What is the charity of the soul that adores God but a burning sense of what is His due? Charity animates both Faith and Hope, and strikes down whatever would weaken the arm of the one or dim the vision of the other. When Justice will not strike, the sword belongs to Charity."

"You have convinced me," Valeria said slyly.

He dropped his head a little. It was not she, he recollected, who had made objections.

"Our neighbors think that we are too much in earnest for a reception," she added, seeing that two or three persons were looking at them. "And here is Mrs. Carini swooping down to carry you off."

Some one was seeking him, and he rose to go. "We have been talking of three ladies, and disputing as to their relative merits," he said, with a faint sparkle of malice in his expression; "and if we have said no evil of them, it may be because we were not allowed time. It seems to me that our conversation may be suitable to the occasion."

Valeria resumed her tour of the room, catching a sentence here and there. "Never make an enemy in Rome!" Mr. O'Hara was saying to some one. "They will do anything here. Last week an Englishman was followed to his apartment in Via Rasella, and murdered on the stair close to his door. He was not robbed. There will never be anything done about it."

Farther on, half out a glass door opening into a garden balcony, Mr. Willis stood talking with Clara Vine. He had broken for her the last scarlet leaf of a woodbine that reached up to the railing, and she, laying it against the back of her delicate glove, was smiling faintly at some thought that it called up. He glanced at her, then over her head at the more brilliant figure of Miss Marshall, who was tranquilly flirting at the other side of the room, then back at her again. It seemed to be a case of " t' other dear creature."

Miss Marshall's present victim was a painter.

"You will never come back to America to live?" she asked reproachfully.

"No; I am better off here. America makes a fine perspective for a view of the world, its features are so grandiose; but I prefer Italy for the foreground. You surely do not mean to return."

"I most certainly shall. I greatly prefer my own country, and I think it my duty to do what I can to improve and beautify it."

"I'm not sure but that your going will turn the balance," he murmured, gazing at her.

Two beautifully dressed women were watching a third, who had just entered, wearing a brown satin dress.

"She has had it dyed, my dear! She has had it dyed, just as I knew she would; and I've won my gloves. I bet with Anne Grey about it. Anne insisted that she would have it dyed black, because she got an ink-spot on the side breadth the last time she wore it last winter. She has put a bow of ribbon over the spot. Why! don't you remember the yellow satin that Miss Murray has been wearing everywhere for three years? Sometimes it was veiled in tulle, sometimes it had black lace flounces, and again she wore it with a brown velvet corsage and bands. When I saw that brown velvet — it was new last winter — I said at once, she will dye it brown. It's always safest to dye yellow goods brown. And here it is launched on a new existence, and we shall see it all winter, wherever a brown satin can appear. Next winter it will have another change into black. Fortunately, one never notices black, unless it is something magnificent. But the yellow was an eyesore. Well, I've won my gloves."

"Perhaps she may have bought a new yellow one just to confound you," whispered the second. "You couldn't very well ask her if it is the same."

"Oh, yes, you could! You can ask anything if you only do it in the right way. If you are very sweet and cool, you can ask a woman where she stole her pocket-handkerchief."

"Hush!" whispered the other, seeing Mr. Willis standing near.

"'A chiel's amang ye takin' notes.'"

Next came a fair American tourist, glowing from sight-seeing, who talked with a scion of young Italy, — a tall, slight young man with bright eyes, looking out of a serious Roman face.

"I am so glad that there is no new thing under the sun!" she said. "If there were, I should give up. There is so much to see! But I wish you wouldn't change anything here. These improvements spoil the picturesque. I would like the old times back."

"You, madam," the Roman said·gravely, but with a deep tremor underneath his voice, "you would be very picturesque in a short red petticoat, no matter if a little soiled and stained, and a white *camicia*, with a copper vase of water on your head, and your feet bare. An artist would want to paint you so, coming down between gray walls, or standing before an ivy-clad ruin. How would *you* like it?"

"Oh! of course it's like the boys and the frogs. But nations, like people, must be content to take their turn; and now it is America's turn. It is like the rousing of the clans in old Scotland,—this race of the nations to waken the world. You have had your time, and we hold the torch now."

The Roman's eyes flashed through the sudden tears that filled them. "Italy shall yet be the torch-bearer a third time," he said. "We slept. We were not dead!"

His companion looked at him, then silently dropped her eyes. She felt as though she had unwittingly insulted his mother.

How touching is that patriotism of theirs, so wounded and so fiery! How jealous they were of every glance that fell upon their own Italia in those first days when she stood with dishevelled locks, and wide dazzled eyes half incredulous of freedom, and breast still panting from under the hoofs that had trampled her! As her stained and tattered robes slipped down, they caught about her the glories of her past, and pinned them with a sword. And, "She shall be the torch-bearer yet a third time!" they said.

"Long live Italia!" Valeria said to herself, and passed by, going to Miss Cromo's apartment again.

That lady was speaking to Miss Chaplin, who had just come in, and was looking at a small crayon portrait that she had not seen before.

"How do you like it? Burton brought it to me

last night as a surprise. I had not known that he
was doing it."

"Is it meant for you?" exclaimed Miss Chaplin.
"Why, it looks like a girl of twenty."

Miss Cromo turned with an angry laugh to a gentleman beside her. "You see how we old women
hate each other!" she cried.

Miss Chaplin blushed slightly. "No," she said.
"Burton has one in his studio that is just like you."

"It looks a hundred years old!" cried Miss Cromo.
"You see, Mr. Smith, how we old women hate each
other."

The sunset faded in the western windows, stars and
candles were lighted, and people began to go away.
With the last echoes of *Ave Maria* the last guests
disappeared, and the belated dinner-table was prepared in Casa Passarina.

Miss Cromo called Valeria to her after dinner.
"Come and talk with me a little while," she said.
"Since you have been guilty of the wonderful dissi-
pation of dining, you cannot think of going to bed
now."

Valeria followed her with pleasure into the deserted room, where a wood fire, fallen into coals, filled
all the place with a red glow, and glistened on the
many ornaments. Another log was thrown on, and
they drew their arm-chairs up before the blaze, and
talked, screen in hand.

"How I like to have you with me!" Miss Cromo
said. "We must go away together next summer.
Where do you think of going?"

"It is hard to tell. I wish to go very early in the
season, and to some quiet country place. I have no
experience here, you know. I have heard that the
small towns are not very practicable, all the best sites
in them being occupied by villas, or convents, so that
strangers have to live in the midst of dingy narrow

streets where the view, and even the air, is lost. Mr.
Willis says he feels angry every time he visits one
of those *paesi*, and sees what a waste of beauty there is
all about, the only idea of the class of people one
could live with being to huddle as closely as possible
together. The convents, he says, have all beautiful
positions, with gardens and bits of forest, and the best
views possible."

"The convents, yes!" Miss Cromo said sharply.
"Here in Italy one promise of the Scriptures, at least,
is fulfilled, 'The meek possess the earth.' It pays to
resign the world here, or, for the matter of that, almost anywhere. The vow of poverty is worth at
least a thousand dollars a year. I wonder some
benevolent person does n't propose that the starving
poor should all take the vow of poverty."

"Our Lord promised that whoever would be willing to lose his life for His sake should find it,"
Valeria said gravely; "and that to those who devoted
themselves to Him, without thinking of food or rai-
ment, their Heavenly Father should provide those
things. I know what your opinions are; but please
do not express them to me. A discussion between
us would not produce any good result. I am devoted
to my religion, and do not wish to hear anything
against it. I attack no one else."

"I could be good if I had you always with me,"
Miss Cromo exclaimed, with a sudden change of voice.
"You do not make hypocritical pretences of piety,
like the rest. It is they who have disgusted me with
religion. Stay by me, my darling! You can do me
immense good. And you may scold me whenever
you will. If I had always had you, I should have
been a good Catholic."

Nothing is more tempting to some women, to most
women, indeed, than the offer of a missionary station
at their own door; and the greater the sinner, or the

more benighted the heathen, the better pleased are they. That a remarkably intelligent, hard-headed, worldly, and mocking little woman, nearly twenty years older than herself, was all ready and eager to be converted by her, did not strike Valeria at the moment as unlikely. That she was being entertained as she had that afternoon seen the "Sappho of America" entertained, did not occur to her. It is one thing to tell lies at a reception, and another thing to tell lies *tête-à-tête.* A sudden enthusiasm sprang up in her heart. She would do all that she could for Miss Cromo. She would bring her Catholic friends to see her. She would ask Monsignor Fenelon to call, and she would persuade Miss Cromo to attend to her religious duties better. And how fond she would be of her! It all flashed through her mind in an instant, and her answer was ready almost before the other had done speaking.

"The less you say about my goodness, the better. I am not a hypocrite, however. I will find some one who is better fitted than I am to correct you of your naughtinesses. I would do anything for you." And, rising, she bent over her companion, and kissed her.

The firelight shone brightly over them. Miss Cromo held both Valeria's hands, and kissed them, then looked up into her face. "I really do want to be good, dear!" she said. The expression of childlike ingenuousness was admirable, but it did not quite suit the elderly face, which had settled into quite other lines. It reminded Valeria of the mature Mrs. Frances Kemble Butler reading the part of Juliet.

She went back to her seat.

"And now tell me what you saw at Mrs. Gordon's," Miss Cromo said, changing the scenes.

"Several persons I knew were there. Among them was Monsignor Nestore."

"You must ask him to come to see me," Miss Cromo said.

"Certainly! And the Countess Belvedere was leaving just as I went in. I was sorry; for she interests me strangely, I cannot say why. It may be an air of mystery which I fancy hangs about her. She has such an odd way of looking at people. Her eyes plunge into them, then slide off like a shadow. I have never heard her speak. Perhaps that would destroy the illusion."

"It certainly would," Miss Cromo replied with bitterness. "She knows how to use her eyes; but as for her tongue, she can talk only gossip. She is perfectly ignorant. And there is no mystery whatever about her. She is simply an infamous woman. She had not been married more than three months before people were talking of her."

Valeria sat and listened in displeased silence to a recital given in language as scandalous as the facts related, more disgusted with Miss Cromo than with the Countess Belvedere. Brought up in a New England town where scandals were almost unknown, in a pure home where modesty of conduct was always observed, and where no unclean word was ever uttered, and intimate with a choice literature from which every disagreeable element was banished, she had always taken for granted that decent language was an indispensable component of decent morals, and that such expressions as she was now listening to with a shiver of disgust could be used only by such persons as the speaker was describing.

"And this woman," Miss Cromo concluded, "is the idol of such pious saints as Mrs. Gordon, Miss Chaplin, and Miss Pendleton. They either pretend that they do not believe, or they suddenly recollect that they must be charitable. Hypocrites!"

"Don't excite yourself," Valeria said lightly. "Tell

me why you gave such a terrible slap to Miss Chaplin this afternoon. It was too bad. You know she is very delicate and frail. I saw her hand tremble. Besides, the picture does look younger than you, though you look wonderfully young and pretty."

Miss Cromo began to laugh, half amused, and still half angry. "Oh, I have the whip hand of Frances," she said. "Sometimes she tries to make little disagreeable speeches. She would like to be disagreeable if she dared. But I have the whip hand of her."

"You shall never have the whip hand of me, little woman," Valeria said in a caressing tone.

"As if I could want to, you darling!" was the fond reply. "It is rather you who command me. You make me do as you like, and you say the most horrible things to me."

"Oh, but you do not know what a number of horrible things I don't say, my dear," Valeria returned. She had caught the tone of Miss Cromo's honeyed audacities, and found it convenient. "There is a Spanish proverb that is à propos: 'You see what I drink, but not the thirst I suffer.' Sometimes I have longed to shake you. For instance, when you kept Dr. Kraus bowing like a Chinese mandarin this afternoon. I wonder you dare do such things; and I wonder still more that people will let you."

Miss Cromo was laughing again. "Of course they will let me! The motto of success is, 'De l'audace, et de l'audace, et toujours de l'audace.' Just assume that you are something, and stand your ground firmly that you are, and people will believe you."

Valeria looked at the speaker a moment in silence, at the small head thrown back, the resolute face with its steely smile, and the lady-like attitude, reposing without lounging. "I do not wonder that you have a contempt for most people," she said presently. "It

is quite true that very few of them have any mind
of their own. It is, perhaps, the secret of many persons' power: contempt of those they lead. They
know the weaknesses of their friends, and of human
nature in general, and while pretending not to see
them, they play upon them. What a number of
puppets you must have!"

She spoke gently, even languidly; but was conscious of a very decided feeling of mingled admiration
and dislike, — admiration for the strength of will, the
wit, and the energy of character of this woman, and
dislike of the use to which she put them.

Miss Cromo bit her lip. She scarcely liked to see
her principles so barely presented. "I have the
greatest respect and regard for my friends," she declared. "I do all I can to please them; and it is but
natural that I should expect a return of complacency."

"Of course I put the subject crudely," Valeria replied. "I had, you may say, made a visit to the kitchen
to see what was the foundation of the wonderful
dish the cook had sent up. Of course it is combined
and sugared and garnished by an artist. *S'intende.*
And you do try to please, and succeed too. I find
you charming when you behave well. I am not sure
but you could drive me a little if you used the whip
softly. And now, good night, dear. I shall ask some
of my friends to come to see you. I want my friends
to be yours."

She bent over Miss Cromo and kissed her, and
stood there a moment smoothing her soft hair. She
felt a desire, almost a need, to love her. It is easier
to love one who is strong. And surely there must be
some real honesty under all the worldliness, some
honor and generosity which affection could reach. It
was not strange that she, being a woman, and alone,
had learned the necessity of wearing armor; and who
knew how many blows she had herself received before

she learned to strike so well? "I think that if I were hard pushed, I also could strike a hard blow," Valeria thought, still touching the silent head that leaned against her arm.

Then there were other things that had been told her, which had aroused her compassion. Miss Cromo had once been poor, and had had to earn her own bread till an opportune inheritance made her independent. And, worse than all, she had had to struggle against the menace of hereditary insanity, to watch and fear, lest, yielding weakly, she should be overcome by worse than death. Who could say that this poison taint in her blood was not the cause of some of her faults?

The head was lifted from her arm. "Love me!" came in a soft murmur. "Only love me!"

"I will love you if you will let me," Valeria replied.

------◆------

CHAPTER XII.

TRYING TO BE "GOOD."

FULL of this new affection, Valeria went the next morning to Monsignor Fenelon and told him all her story. She had quite reckoned on him, knowing how beautifully his stern ideas of duty were tempered by the sweetest charity and by an almost poetical enthusiasm.

He heard her quite through, and hesitated a little before speaking. "I should be sorry to destroy a pleasant illusion for you, or to discourage you in thinking the best you can of any one," he said; "but I am afraid that you are deceived. I have been so several times, and I have no more confidence in her. That she should, or should not, be a Catholic is not

7

the point. I have many Protestant friends whom I value very highly. The trouble is that you cannot depend upon her in any way. Her sole aim and ambition is social success, and to that she would sacrifice anything or anybody. She seems to me like a person who would die grasping her worldly possessions, and crying out, 'Oh, my furniture! Oh, my *roba!*'"

"You will not go, then?" Valeria asked, chilled and disappointed.

"Why should I contribute to her social ambition, for it is nothing but that? Yet I will go soon and call upon her."

"I shall stand by her," Valeria said a little defiantly, rising to go.

"I wish you to," he replied quickly. "And I am sorry that I cannot take the part you ask me to take. I will do so gladly whenever I can feel that she is sincere, and I will gladly own that I have been wrong. I hope that you do not think me too severe."

"I think you strict, Monsignore," Valeria replied. "But I also think that you have earned the right to be so."

The first failure was rather disheartening; but she could not give up without one effort more. Her next appeal was to a lady.

"But what are you laughing at?" she asked, stopping with her story half finished.

"Pray excuse me!" the lady said. "I am laughing at your simplicity. Did she kneel before you, put her hands together, and ask you to hear her say the 'Now I lay me down to sleep'?"

"She said nothing but what was reasonable," Valeria replied, much offended. "I fail to see what there is to laugh at in the subject."

"Wait till you see it develop," the lady said, "and then you will not be vexed with me. Why, my dear, if she were in Constantinople, she would fight for

Mohammedanism like a Turk, and she would never rest till she had become head sultana."

Tired and vexed, Valeria went home, liking Miss Cromo better than ever, since no one else seemed to have any real regard for her. " I will stand by her!" she resolved. "And I will go and tell her now that Monsignor Fenelon is coming to see her."

Professor Wagner and Mr. Willis were with Miss Cromo, and she was laughing. "I saw Mr. Adams this morning," she said, "and he is raving about Lilian Marshall. He says she has the liquid eyes of Domenichino's Cumæan Sibyl. Of course I agreed with him. I always agree with all the raptures of a lover. And Lilian has fine eyes, and that very way of rolling them up that you see in the Borghese palace. But that is nothing to the way she has of showing her eyelashes and her ear. Did you ever see her do that, Mr. Willis ?"

Mr. Willis, with rather a bad grace, protested that he never had.

" It is one of the loveliest effects!" the lady went on with enthusiasm. "She sits with her head turned a little aside, and slightly drooping, and her eyes fixed on the hem of her last flounce. Then she smiles faintly, as if at some sweet thought. I 've seen five men sitting round in a semicircle and staring at that effect with their mouths open. Men are such dear trusting creatures ! It is always the left ear she shows. The right, unfortunately, was injured by being badly pierced. She retains that position about two minutes; then she moves a little, and gives her audience time to shut their mouths before she looks up. In that way she remains unconscious of their admiration. She is such a pretty, clever creature !"

This was to pay her two visitors for having been remiss in their attentions to herself since Miss Marshall's arrival.

"And now," she added, "I must beg you to excuse me, for I have promised to go to Santa Maria Maggiore with Miss Ellsworth, and it must be time for the first vespers."

"You are a wretch to speak so of Miss Marshall," Valeria said, as they drove away from the door. "I have half a mind not to go to church with you."

"Oh, you can fling some holy water in my face as we enter, and I shall probably disappear with an odor of brimstone," was the laughing answer.

They went up to the church door, where a good many people were entering, among them two distinguished-looking Monsignori. Great simplicity of manners is observed in Roman churches. With that exquisite good taste which they have derived from the saints, it is not considered by Italians to be fitting that worldly distinctions should be made prominent in the house of God. Valeria, therefore, was about to do as others do, and pass by, when Miss Cromo touched her arm.

"I am not pious, but I know my manners," she said; and, drawing back for the clergymen, made them a reverential and rather old-fashioned courtesy.

The two *porporati*, not accustomed to such demonstrations, passed by without appearing to be aware of the salutation.

"Pigs!" remarked Miss Cromo, recovering her equilibrium.

They went in. "I shall look at you, and do everything that I see you do," she added. "I intend to behave with the most abject propriety. Where shall we post ourselves? Or shall we walk about?"

"We must first go to the altar of the Blessed Sacrament. As you know your manners so well, I suppose you see the propriety of first paying your respects to the Master of the house."

They crossed the church through the crowd that

was constantly moving to and fro with the subdued greeting of friends, and low-voiced talking in groups, which make of a great Roman function merely a magnificent reception in honor of the saint or the event commemorated. Here and there, along the walls or in nooks of chapels, were a few silent lookers-on or figures bowed in devotion.

The two ladies found places on the steps of a confessional, and seated themselves there.

"I was afraid I would have to go about with you to make my courtesy to all the saints," Miss Cromo remarked, settling herself comfortably against the confessional; "and I am really too old."

"I do not give so much thought to the saints as I ought perhaps," Valeria replied. "When I look upward I see only Christ. I reverence the saints, of course; but I often forget them. It is a defect."

"And God?" asked Miss Cromo, looking at her companion.

Valeria returned her look. "Why, Christ is God!" she said.

An expression of derision, sharp and bitter, passed over Miss Cromo's face, and her lips parted to speak. But, seeing Valeria color, she became serious for a moment. "I wish I had your faith, dear," she said. "You see I was a Unitarian before I became a Catholic, and I 'm afraid I was only plated over, and that the base metal is coming out through." And she began to laugh again.

"I presume that you were the same kind of Unitarian that you are Catholic," Valeria remarked. "My father was Unitarian, and he had a reverent soul."

Miss Cromo's eyes emitted a little sparkle of anger, while her lips were still smiling. "It depends entirely on the shape of head with which one is born," she declared. "Now, my head is deficient in the bump of reverence. I don't know whose fault it is, and I don't mean to accuse any one."

"I think it depends on the sort of heart one has," Valeria replied coldly. "Hush! Here comes the chapter."

The clergy were coming out of the sacristy, and passing across the church toward the Borghese chapel, where the *Immaculata* was celebrated. Miss Cromo watched them with enthusiasm. "What beautiful purple silk stockings! and what lovely yellow clouds along their ermine! And as for the lace I should like to get behind one or two of them with a pair of scissors."

The two got up and began to walk about; saluted some of their acquaintances; went into the chapel of the Blessed Sacrament to look at the veiled Tamar between her twin boys, and the wolf's head that nature had taken a fancy to paint in a block of Egyptian marble; came out again and listened to a hymn sung with a full choir and orchestra,. the music of which rolled in long waves of complex harmony that, from time to time, cast up the refrain, like a pearl on the shore, *Ave Maris Stella;* then, with a rush of advancing sound, caught it away, sweeping it to and fro, hiding it, and again tossing it up, *Ave Maris Stella*, with a breaking froth of *Aves* all about.

Then Miss Cromo said that she must go home. "I want to finish my article for the *Aurora*, and send it by to-night's mail," she said. "And I shall come in and read it to you before posting it."

They went home, and after dinner Miss Cromo came to Valeria's room with her bonnet on, and the manuscript in her hand. "I shall have barely time to hurry through it," she said, "for it is later than I thought. I have already read it to Miss Chaplin."

Valeria wondered a little what extraordinary sort of article this could be which was so displayed, and prepared to hear it with interest.

It began with the meeting of the authoress with a friend from another country, who, after the first salutation, suddenly turned to her and asked, " Will you tell me, pray, what is the root of the Catholic difficulty in Rome ? "

" You see, it is the same question which was asked of you," the reader said, glancing up with her hard, bright smile, then resuming her reading.   The article was an answer to this question.

Valeria sat stupefied, not hearing a word.   This, then, was Miss Cromo's motive in asking her what and when she was going to write, — for a pitiful theft like this !   And what had she hoped to gain ? Had she hoped to intercept her thus every month, and drive her out of the path ?   " I could give her a thousand ideas and never miss them ! " thought Valeria, with a swell of contemptuous pride.

The reading ended, and the reader folded up her manuscript.   " How do you like it ? " she asked, without looking up.   Her nostrils had a slight tension, her lips were slightly compressed, as if she half expected a combat, and were prepared for it.

" Oh, of course it is quite charming ! " Valeria replied, drawling her words a little.   " I am so much obliged ! "

Miss Cromo looked up.   " Have you sent your article yet, my dear ? "

" I told you that I should not send it for a week or ten days, and it is now not more than four."

" What subject are you going to write on ? " was the next question, put with a resolute smile.

" I told you the subject, too."

Miss Cromo's countenance changed.   She had meant to oust Valeria from her connection with the *Fair Play*, if possible ; and she believed that her article had exhausted the subject, as it would have done, indeed, if the study of encyclopædias and dictionaries would have done so.

"Well, I must go now," she said, and hurried away, only half satisfied.

Valeria opened her windows wide. "Come in, pure tramontana, and blow all that is left of her out of the room!" She took up a book. "Come, sweet thoughts, and drive all that is left of her out of my mind!"

In two minutes she was among the gods.

The God of gods be thanked for pure air and poetry!

CHAPTER XIII.

FLITTING.

THE weeks slipped away. The history of one would have answered for that of the week following, by changing the date. In January Mrs. Grey was called to France by the illness of a relative, and Valeria found herself with no acquaintances except those which she had made in Rome. It was unpleasant.

Many persons were very kind and civil; but their kindness was such as people show to those whom they meet frequently, find agreeable, and forget when they are out of sight. All had their own affairs to attend to. She was on their visiting-list; but there was no one upon whose heart her name was written. People are never very much pleased with one who withdraws from that round of receptions and card-leaving which is called society, even though such a retirement might be reasonably explained. In this busy world few have leisure to examine ; they have only time to judge. Therefore some concluded that their attentions were not properly esteemed, and decided not to press them. They were not to blame. They exerted themselves to fulfil their social duties, and expected others to do the same. They could not weigh nicely to find when the exertion might be too great.

One disillusion caused Valeria great disappointment. She had fancied that, in foreign countries, Americans stood by each other, and that they would have a certain union, which did not mean intimacy, indeed, but which would give to each a sense of protection, and at need, the strength of the whole. It was not so. The greater number of those of whom she knew much, either personally or from report, were divided by petty jealousies and dissensions, and seemed to rejoice in each other's misfortunes. They struggled and intrigued for fine acquaintances, and, when they were successful in obtaining them, assumed a state that was pitifully ridiculous. The English had more dignity. They were proud of being English. Americans were ashamed of being American, and longed to be European, and to efface their nationality as much as possible.

Of course this was not true of all; but it was true of all whom she saw much of. There were finer souls, who honored their country and themselves ; but she looked at them from a distance. Circumstances did not bring them together ; and Valeria never sought any one.

It was therefore with a regret not unmingled with anxiety that she saw Mrs. Grey leave Rome. Monsignor Fenelon, too, was going ; and she had depended greatly on him. A diplomatic mission had been offered to him, and he would go away in the spring. She would be left to fight the little battles of pinches and pin-pricks quite alone. "It will be like living in a swarm of mosquitoes without a net," she thought, and then added, with a sort of fear, "I hope that they may not prove worse than mosquitoes!"

"People will forget you if you withdraw so," said a Mrs. Barry, whom the world remembered to call a bore.

"I must bear it then," Valeria replied. "I am not rich enough to find pleasure in society; it is a labor to me, and I am very busy. There are some whom I should be sorry to lose."

She had gone to visit Mrs. Waters, a pleasant lady writer, and had met several ladies in her *sala*.

"I am not very rich, but I like to see my friends," said another lady. "I accept the invitations they are so kind as to give me, and am happy to entertain them when I can." And she held her head very much back, pressed her lips together, and looked down. Reproof was in every crease of her gown, and her very bonnet-strings bristled with a sense of what was due to "society."

This was Miss Murray, whom her kind friends had called "Yellow Satin" the year before, and had already renamed "Dyed Brown," and it was the identical historical gown which now frowned at Valeria. These friends smiled at her; they laughed at her reception days, which seldom brought forth more than two carriages and half a dozen visitors. But they perceived that she was in the right way, and was likely to achieve a modest success, especially as she knew how to smile sweetly when she was snubbed.

"You have nothing else to do," Valeria said to her. "And you have an independent income. It would be a mistake if any one should think that I am pretending to despise society. I am simply expressing my inability to avail myself of the civilities offered me. When I have a house, a maid, a carriage, and even only five thousand a year, I will go to visit somebody every day, or invite some one to visit me. But now I cannot consent to worry my life out, to pinch, and plan, and count *centessimi*, to get a toilet, which will, after all, be outshone by that of everybody about me. Why, my dear Miss Murray, I have such a respect for my friends, that I should not think myself worthy to visit them unless I had diamonds as big as peas."

This speech giving the lady addressed something to think of, she remained silent.

"So do *I* like my friends," Mrs. Barry said, giving Valeria a cold glance. "And I am glad to see them without diamonds."

A beautiful young lady who had been a social star in nearly every great city on the continent, and whose heart, made for better things, was illy satisfied with such conquests, paused beside Valeria in leaving the room. "I understand you perfectly," she said in a low voice, and held out a slender hand. "If I were going to remain in Rome, I should beg permission to come and see you quietly now and then; and I hope to visit you later, if it will not be an intrusion."

"I should know how to prize a visit from you," Valeria replied. "I confess, I do not care much for the pedestal; but I admire the statue."

The ladies went away, one by one. Mrs. Barry came to take a civil, half-friendly leave of Valeria, being after all a good soul, though a stupid one.

"Take my advice and don't let people forget you," she said.

"You are so kind!" said Valeria sweetly. "But I shall be content to be forgotten if you are remembered."

Mrs. Barry went away, considering herself to have been highly complimented.

Mrs. Waters had signed Valeria to stay after the others.

"I know so well the trials of a peripatetic writer," she said. "I have tried all the different miseries of it; but the greatest is, I think, to write in a boarding-house. I have a proposal to make to you. A friend of mine has two rooms which she had engaged till the middle of April; and she has had an invitation to go to Sicily which she is very desirous to accept. But she is responsible for these rooms, having obtained them at much less than their real value. I think they would suit you admirably, and you could take them till the 15th of April at her price, which, I am sure, can be no more than you are paying now. They are in the Albergo dell' Oriente."

"But how could I live alone in a hotel?" Valeria asked.

"It is only a lodging hotel. You have every attendance, and your coffee, from the family. The dinners are sent in. It is not in the least like a public house. It is perfectly quiet and well-ordered, and the people who go there are chiefly tourists, who are out all day, and who are the best class of strangers in Rome. People who come here to study the glories of antiquity for a few weeks will never annoy you. Besides, recommended by me, you will be under the protection of the family. They are respectable, unpretending people, and will be very friendly. Come and see for yourself."

They went down the street of the Triton, entered a quiet vestibule, which attracted but little notice in that crowded thoroughfare, and up the clean white marble stairs to the third story. The look of everything was plain and orderly; but Valeria observed a point of richness here and there in a bronze or statue, or table bearing a slab of verd-antique or some precious marble.

The back rooms were reached by galleries, which surrounded three sides of a dim court, the third side running off behind a church that pushed its little belfry of a single arch close above the last gallery. In the arch two bells were hung. When they stepped into this third gallery the noises from the street were but a faint murmur; when they had reached the end of the last wing, there was a perfect silence. The gallery continued around the corner of the last room, and led to a terrace; and back of the terrace was a garden full of vines, shrubs, and fruit-trees, with yellowing mandarin oranges, and roses, even now in January.

By one of those charming surprises of which the irregular streets of Rome are full, this last chamber, which was three stories from the street, was level with the garden.

Mrs. Waters opened the door, and Valeria uttered an exclamation of pleasure. It was such a pretty room! The colored tiles of the floor, the bright autumn leaves of the wall-paper, the birds and flowers of the ceiling, the gayly striped green hangings, gave the room a warm and cheerful look, while a superb piece of rich, dark carving, a great mirror and table of *cinque-cento* work that had belonged to the Prince of Monaco, added to it a certain dignity. Then there were paintings, and small terra-cotta copies of celebrated statues, and some fine bronzes, and a white column supporting a large vase holding a white lily, and a wood fire in the little fireplace, and a great square of sunshine with the shadow of a bell in it on the floor.

"It is not common, you see," Mrs. Waters said. "In fact, the people are not common. The landlord is a collector of pictures and antiquities, and has been a sort of artist, I believe. His eldest son is a noted artist in Paris. You have a door and window on the gallery,

you see, and a door on the terrace. This little door
in the terrace leads to a private stair by which you
can go out into another street, or into the picture-
gallery below there, where the landlord has a large
and valuable collection. You can go down any time
to see it. It is not now open to the public. This
man is a Syrian, the son of a silk-merchant of Mount
Lebanon, and has lived in Cairo, in Smyrna, in Trieste,
in Vienna, in Venice. He will tell you about the
cedars of Lebanon, and the Syrian summer nights, and
how they sleep on the house-tops, and wake in the
morning with their heads wet with a dew that hurts
them no more than it hurts the flowers. I am glad
you are pleased; and if you say the word, the place
can be yours on the first of February. That will give
you two months and a half, you see."

It seemed too good to be true; but it came true,
nevertheless, and on the first day of February Valeria
found herself the mistress of this charming retreat.

Her flitting from Casa Passarina was not a very
pleasant one; for the mistress of the house was suffi-
ciently displeased at losing two boarders in the middle
of the season to be a little disagreeable; the ladies,
who had constantly interrupted her, were unable to
see how she could wish for greater tranquillity; and
Miss Cromo, who alternated sharp questions and
fond regrets, was disappointed at losing sight of one
whom she was beginning to hate bitterly. She was
one of those who wish to keep a strict watch over
those they hate. She was irritated by that will which
yielded momentarily, then resisted, by the confidence
that evaded alike her most insolent inquisition and
her most honeyed flatteries; and the suspicion that
Valeria understood and despised her made her furious.

She came to visit her after a day or two, and admired everything. "You will have a reception-day,
of course," she said.

"Certainly not! That would be absurd. But I shall be happy to see any one who comes any day after three o'clock."

"What is this?"

Miss Cromo had espied an enormous envelope, with two or three documents and pamphlets half drawn out of it.

"Look and see! I am a shepherdess."

It was Valeria's diploma as a member of the Arcadian Academy, with her new Greek name, that flowed like a brook, and several other documents, all ornamented with the olive-wreath, the crossed shepherd's crooks, the drooping lamb, and the pipes of Pan.

The names of two distinguished Monsignori were inscribed as having proposed and seconded her election.

"It was a surprise to me," Valeria said. "I had not asked it of any one, nor, indeed, thought of it."

Miss Cromo's face was flaming with anger. She was so angry that she forgot her rule never to own to having been slighted.

"They would not have done it for me," she said. "I am a member, but I was proposed by my Italian teacher."

"You are a member?" Valeria said, ignoring her companion's anger. "How glad I am! We can go there together."

"I never go!" Miss Cromo exclaimed with scorn. "It is an anachronism. The organization ought to have dissolved fifty years ago. Nothing can be more ridiculous. I went once or twice at first, and I never was more bored in my life. We sat there two hours listening to a recitation of what they called original poems that hadn't an idea in them, mere rhymed words such as any dunce can string in the Italian language. There was a bishop seated at each side of

me. One had dirty hands, and the other smelt of
tobacco. It was both disgusting and ridiculous."

That day she left Valeria without kissing her, or
calling her darling. The omission did not cause any
grief.

Monsignor Fenelon had understood and approved
of Valeria's flitting ; but Monsignor Nestore had been
harder to reconcile. A lady of any age without a
companion was to him a very doubtful object ; but a
lady in a hotel without a companion was simply not
to be thought of.

She let his first vehement protest effervesce without
speaking. What would people say of her ? A young
lady alone in a hotel in the midst of a crowd of men !
She should pay some respect to the customs of the
people among whom she lived. He was astonished
that Monsignor Fenelon should have consented. It
was not to be thought of. It was highly improper.
He disapproved of the project *in toto.* Why did she
not have a companion, some old woman or some old
man, to go about with her ? Why did she not speak ?
Why did she not say something ? She did speak
when he gave her the opportunity.

" Dear Monsignore, it is so good of you to care ! "
she began ; but got no further.

" Of course I care. I am devoted to you. I do not
wish you to commit an imprudence."

" But listen a moment. In the first place, I am
not a young lady. In the next place, the house is
not in the least like a hotel, and I shall not see so
many gentlemen, nor see them so freely as where I
am. There is a great deal of flirting in Casa Passarina, and Miss Cromo has kindly offered me the use
of her apartment to receive a friend any time I may
want it, and promised that I should not be interrupted.
I do not know why she did. I have no use for it.
In the Hôtel d'Orient I shall live as in a glass case.

No one can approach my room without being seen.
But at the same time I shall scarcely ever meet a
soul in the house. Only the family will be about
me. As to what people will say, they will say just
what they wish to. If they are bad, they will be
malicious; if good, they will find no fault. And,
Monsignore, how in the name of common sense am I
to have a companion when I have scarcely money
enough for myself? Besides, I am not a Becky Sharp,
to need a sheep-dog. Don't be vexed! I really wish
to be prudent as far as I can without being slavish.
Consider, Monsignore, I must live the life of a student,
and I cannot do so in a boarding-house, and I am determined to do so in Rome. There is an immense
deal of good in Rome with all the evil, and I intend
to stay here in spite of everything, and I intend to
conquer every difficulty here; for there is n't one
which I respect enough to be worried about. I always
conquer in the end. Don't oppose me hastily. Monsignor Fenelon has seen the place. Come and see it
yourself, and you will change your mind. I promise
you that if you still oppose, I will give up the project.
Go to-day, if you can, please, and talk with the landlord. To-morrow, I will come to ask your decision."

"Women are stubborn creatures!" Monsignor declared with a half-resigned discontent. "They will
have their own way, though it should ruin them.
I have to make a visit to the Princess N——, the
sister of the Emperor of Austria, to-day. She is in
Rome, and has sent to let me know. If I have time
afterward, I will go and see this place. I do not know
anything about it. And here," he added, "is just a
case in point. I was at the Austrian Court when
Maximilian was made Emperor of Mexico, and I
opposed it with all my strength. It was the work of
the Empress Augusta. She was determined that he
should go; and but for her he would not have gone.

When the troubles began there, I begged that they
would call him back. At last the Empress got angry with me. They were outside Vienna, and I had
gone to pay a visit to them. 'Monsignor Nestore,'
she said, 'we like you as a friend, and we are happy
to see you when you say nothing to displease us.
But if you come here to urge the recall of Maximilian
from his empire, we do not wish to see you any more.'
I rose and bowed. 'Madame,' I said, 'when it comes
to that, I have no more to say. I shall never mention the subject to you again. Of course a woman
must have her way.' And I took my leave. As I
drove into Vienna again, I met the French messen-
gers going out to inform her of Maximilian's ex-
ecution."

"The moral of your story is terrible," Valeria said.
"But if I should come to grief in my obstinacy, I
hope, Monsignore, that you, at least, will not lose your
head."

He lifted his forehead austerely, not pleased that
his warning should be jested with.

The next day she went to him again, feeling
rather anxious. There were visitors, as usual.

"I have been to see the very pleasant rooms that
you are going to occupy in the Hôtel d'Orient,"
Monsignor announced to her in the hearing of all,
"and I am much pleased with them. The landlord
and his wife are excellent, respectable people, and
will take you under their closest protection."   .

"You must go to see her there," he added, turning
to the Countess Steinberg. "And you, Mrs. Gordon.
It is a most unexceptionable place. I am pleased
with it."

"How finely he did that!" Valeria thought, while
thanking him, and answering the ladies' compliments
and questions. "He has set a shield up before me.
No one can find any fault now."

"I should like so much to see this place," said Lady. Merton, one of the visitors. "My carriage is at the door. Can I take you there after I have seen Monsignor a moment?"

The other visitors went, and only Lady Merton and Valeria remained. The English lady, a pretty young widow, had some favors to ask, — admittance to the Vatican Museum and gardens, and audiences of the Pope for friends.

She lingered most unnecessarily, always chatting very much at her ease, and jesting, to the prelate's evident displeasure.

"I cannot make you out!" he said abruptly, standing before the sofa on which the two were sitting. "I have known you a good while; and it is like trying to read a book of which I cannot get beyond the preface."

The lady blushed a little. She was, perhaps, aware that he might have found her coquettish. "I hope you may like the book when you shall have read the whole," she said.

"I am sure he will!" Valeria made haste to say.

"Now, this one," Monsignor resumed, turning to her, "I understand perfectly. Her character is like a clear brook, where I can see every pebble, every single pebble!"

"He is calling you shallow," the lady said, coloring with vexation.

"Not at all!" he replied, with a cutting emphasis. "Some brooks are shallow, yet muddy, and you can see nothing. Others are deep, but transparent. Valeria is not shallow."

Lady Merton rose and took leave with the best grace she could, but deeply mortified.

Monsignor Nestore called Valeria back a moment. "I am pleased with the place," he said, "and I wish to ask your forgiveness for the rude way in which

I spoke to you yesterday. You did not deserve it; and I had no right to speak so."

He held out his hand, and she bent her head over it His was such a sure-footed dignity. He was not afraid to bend lest he should fall.

Those were pleasant days which followed. Shut in a sunny quiet, it was possible to think and to work, — that sweetest of all work which is an exercise of the mind, — that trying of the wings which may fly only as far as the hands can reach perhaps, but is flying nevertheless, and so preferable to creeping. Better fall with many bruises, trying to fly, than creep forever unhurt.

Occasionally, when the sun began to decline, some acquaintance dropped in for half an hour. There were a few kind enough to come thrice for one visit of hers in return. Sometimes several happened to be there at once; and it might be that they were not common people, and then she liked to listen almost in silence. It seemed to her that it would be very pleasant to have a house where the people she liked could come to meet each other, leaving her to listen or to speak, as she should choose.

The weeks flew only too fast.

Sometimes the Syrian landlord would come round by the gallery and terrace to the garden, and would bring her a rose or a cluster of *mandarini* cut with the leaves around them. Now and then he would stop and talk awhile. He told her the Arabic names of things, spoke Arabic that she might hear the beautiful clear language, which in some way is like black coffee, rich and not too sweet, having an aromatic bitter, rather. It is a language which suits a thin-faced, bright-eyed, turbaned, and haughty people. It goes well with their swift horses and gleaming blades, and their tents under the stars.

Then what pleasure for a Northerner to walk in

that little garden of Hesperides, where all the trees
hung full of golden fruit at midwinter, and to see
the lemon-trees that lined the walls pruned of long
branches that could be burned on the fire when the
sun had dried them a few days!

Then there was the picture-gallery, room after room,
crowded with paintings. It was only to cross the
terrace, go down a private stair, and shut herself
in with endless delights. This Sant' Antonio, with
the upward face, and those hands that all the artists
copied, —'hands that Overbeck had stood and praised,
saying, "Raphael never painted. such!" — was designed by Michael Angelo. The Emperor of Russia
would have had it long before, but that the Crimean
War intervened and gave him other things than pictures to think of, and the subject had never been
resumed.

And this other, a Domenichino, full of harmonious form and color, would probably have gone to
Washington; but here, again, a war had broken into
the negotiations; and the seven virtues had been
called out in living colors from the national soul, instead of being hung in glowing canvas in the national
council-chamber. Vigilant Justice, with the jewelled
eye suspended at her throat, and her smooth cheek
reflected in the mirror of Prudence; Force, with the
lion on her shield, listening to Temperance; Faith,
Hope, and Charity softly rounding up the pyramid of
symbolic beauty, — they were but hints of what had
been, beautiful as they were.

Then there was the Spanish picture of a monk
casting devils out of a possessed man, — a picture of
which many stories were told. Men used to stop in
the street when they saw it in a window, and laugh,
and try to imitate the grimace of the man who sup-
ports the demoniac. Pio Nono had sent a letter written by a prince of the Church, and a carriage to take

this picture to the Vatican, and had laughed till he
cried, while the dignified prelates around him tried
to imitate this man's nauseated grimace, which Cer-
vantes might have described. It was irresistible.
One looked at the monk holding up a crucifix, at
the lovely, curious, peeping boy, at the tormented face
of the demoniac, from whose mouth reptiles were
dropping; but ever the eyes went back to that other
figure, and one felt an impulse to make up a face.

Apparently, one little demon of mischief had lingered in the canvas.

They were pleasant days, — such days as one goes
to Rome to see the suns go down upon, and the stars
crown.

But they fled, and March was waning, and she
would not ask to stay beyond her time, since her staying so long had been a favor.

CHAPTER XIV.

WITH MOTHER NATURE.

IT was the last day of March, and a day worthy of
Eden. There had been nothing of the traditional
lion in this month. It had come in like a lamb, and
was going out like an angel.

Valeria took a little travelling-bag, told the people
of the house that she should be away all night, and
drove down to the Piazza San Marco, whence a diligence started every morning for Palestrina. There
was still an hour to wait, and she spent it in the
garden of the Piazza, which was all fresh from a
morning shower, — spent it very childishly, being
childishly pleased that morning.

A bright-faced little boy, with a gold band on his

cap, came by, stood a moment watching the lady who walked about searching the clover borders of the flower-beds, and when he caught a smile from her, came in and asked what she was trying to find.

"A four-leaved clover," she replied. "If you find a four-leaved clover, you can have whatever you wish for."

Then he began searching diligently with her, his round, rosy face bent close to the green turf; and they had a wonderful discourse. For Valeria's childhood had not flown away when its season was past, but had hidden itself in the folds and windings of the years, like a little golden-winged butterfly in a garment, and she knew the thoughts of children, — those wondering, wide-eyed, serious thoughts, that are so proud and shy, and will not utter a word for any force on earth.

The hour was nearly past, and the clover-leaf was not found. Perhaps it does not grow in Rome.

"What would you have wished for if you had found it?" asked the lady.

"Oh, I was searching for it for you!" the boy answered. "I don't want anything."

"Come to think of it, I do not want anything," she replied. "And that is the magical thing we have found, you see, — contentment! They are putting the horses to the carriage over there. I must go. Good-by, little boy! I hope that you will never want anything."

He raised his cap with a modest manliness, stood looking after her till she had taken her seat in the diligence, exchanged another smile with her, and went his way.

The diligence, a remarkably shabby, but perfectly comfortable vehicle, rattled away through the Trajan Forum. It was the first time Valeria had travelled in such a carriage since those days when she had gone

in a great yellow coach with four horses through hundreds of miles of pleasant country roads in the Pine-
tree State, far away across the ocean. Did they travel
in coaches now up hill and down dale through the
lovely woods of Maine ? And were the passengers
ever sea-sick with the rolling of their splendid coach ?

The scent of those Northern pines and cedars seemed
to float across the ocean and the years, swathing in
mists of the past the great umbrella pines of the
South; and where the snow-laden birches had bent like
Eastern courtiers before their Emperor, ivy and grape-
vines swept like a tapestry ; and instead of the little
red school-house was a storied immemorial ruin, and
instead of white cottages looking down from slop-
ing hills, dark castles and convents grasped the beet-
ling cliffs with their claws of stone and iron.

The sky softly clouded over, and a light shower
came down, making the fresh landscape still lovelier.
They stopped a few minutes at the antique Osteria di
Finocchio, and went into the black old kitchen, where
a woman was cooking at a vast, cavernous fireplace,
and men were drinking at the tables. Then on again
under the soft sprinkling of the skies.

The country grew lovelier as they advanced. It
seemed to have rained flowers. The rich valleys and
slopes, where the mountains press closer and crowd
the campagna, were miracles of delicate coloring.
Peach, almond, and cherry trees were swathed in white
and pink mists of bloom, the wide-spreading vineyards
were cobwebbed over with the clouded amber of
newly set canes, rivers of golden-green verdure ran
between the hills, and carpets of the same lay fringed
out under the trees. A soft tumult of lights and
shades chased each other over plain and mountain.
It was an infantine beauty and life, — spring newly
born, and smiling and playing to itself.

As they began the long, gentle ascent that leads to

Palestrina, a light breeze from the west drew the clouds away as softly as a mother might draw the curtain from a sleeping babe she wishes to display, yet fears to waken, and a sudden rainbow, faint, yet perfect, started out and hung trembling above the earth, without disturbing that trance of dewy, silvery air ; and the duplicate bow answered the first as in a whisper. The wide sunbeams that came across the world put off their glory as they caressed the scene, as Hector his plumes for the frightened babe.

Down the steep banks by the roadside hung a thin veil of ivy, pierced with countless blue flowers ; here and there was thrust out a slender branch with a light sprinkle of blossoms like snow-flakes.

Then the gray old city came in sight, slipping down the lap of the hill, with the gray barren rocks above, and the hamlet of San Pietro with its ruined fortress at the summit, and a ruined wall zigzagging from top to bottom.

"Ave, Fortuna Prenestina !" whispered Valeria, leaning out the window. "Hail to the sacred city from which even Rome could not tear the fugitive ! Hail to the ruined fortress of Stefano Colonna, whose brave heart never surrendered ! Hail to the foundations of the wall over which poor Marius was drawn, and which Pompey the Great and cruel Sylla besieged ! Hail to the thrice-destroyed Preneste, the ploughed and sown with salt, which laughs out in wine and roses after the triple destruction !"

"I don't doubt that it's an awfully filthy place," she thought, leaning resignedly back, after having fired off her salute.

The event justified her fears. It was a filthy town. They stopped in the Piazza, before the seminary, set all along its front with fragments of the temple of Fortune ; a boy took her travelling-bag, and conducted her up a long street-stair, then a long house-stair, to an apartment where a large, rosy-faced woman came to meet her, smiling, and breathing quickly with eagerness to make her the most utterly comfortable and contented person on earth. No small reserves nor laundried dignities nor microscopic proprieties could live in the presence of this large, glowing creature. She melted them down with her genial kindness, or laughed them away with her good-natured scorn. She took possession of Valeria, fed and rested her effectually, asked and learned all her affairs, and the reasons of them; insisted that she should marry, and recommended an excellent husband to her; then told her own history in a clear, sketchy style which left nothing to be desired.

Valeria laughed, submitted, and was contented with everything.

"I think that you are the goddess of Fortune," she said. "And if you are, you can procure me a carriage. I wish to drive about a little, before dark."

A carriage? Yes, as many carriages as she wanted. "Felicetta, go and tell Pietro to have his carriage ready at once for Madama Valeria."

"You can be perfectly comfortable here," she pursued. "It may seem rough at first; but you will soon like it. I don't starve my family. There is the best of meat, fowl, and birds; there are fresh eggs, good wine of our own making, fruit; there is every sort of cheese — *c'è tutto!* I have a Danish artist, who has been here eight months, the Signor Eduardo. His studio is up in the old palace, but he eats and sleeps here. His room is down in that other house, where yours will be. I took an apartment below, because I have no rooms to spare here, my family is so large. You can choose the room you like best. Your coffee will be sent down to you; but dinner and supper will be here, unless you want that sent down too. But it is better to come up. It will do you good to see people and talk a little. My husband was a famous painter, and he always said that after working for hours it did him good to talk awhile. He went to Russia to fresco the Emperor's palaces, and was killed on his way back. They made a great deal of him there, and the Grand Duchess Maria sent me a lovely watch and chain. I will show them to you." And the Signora Maria displayed the exquisite royal gift, — a tiny enamelled watch with a chain of fairy delicacy.

The carriage was ready promptly, and Valeria drove to the old palace, where she had another errand besides seeing the famous mosaic. Perhaps she too could have a writing studio there, as the Dane had one for painting.

Troops of filthy, impudent children ran to the carriage, clamoring for *un baiocco*, and followed her up the steps to the grand half-moon concave of the old palace front. An old woman, the *custode*, came out and drove them away, and showed her the mosaic. There was nothing else to see in this deserted and ruined place, unless Madama would like to see the Tempietto at the very top.

Of course she would like to see it. So they went up farther, passing through a grassy enclosed garden, where statues lay fallen from their niches and half hidden in verdure. In the Tempietto, which was an open *loggia* in front of a painted chamber enclosed on three sides, the Signor Eduardo of the Signora Maria was painting with a model. He was a slender young man, scarce over thirty years of age, with exquisitely pure and regular features, blond hair and beard, and blue eyes. He looked calm and modest, even cold. He was a flower of the North.

All round him was unrolled the magnificent panorama of mountain and plain, with Rome crouching at the west under its everlasting mists, and far-stretching

mountains fading toward the east from black to purple,
from purple to violet, from violet to gray, from gray to
silver, and from silver to a dream. And where they
ceased, the eye knew not. Southward, beyond the
Volscian hills, lay the sea in the misty clasp of the
far-off promontory of the Siren.

Down, and into the carriage again went Valeria,
fully content ; for she had already engaged her studio.
It was a bare, grim chamber ; but it had a window
that showed all that beautiful world. They drove
outside the walls, only glancing along, without stopping, since the sun was low. Presently they came
to a road that had an ancient narrow paved road
running beside it, the ancient Via Prenestina. The
town was hidden from them. They stopped at a large
gate in the wall. " It is Villa Frattina," the *vetturino*
said.

In the gate stood a serious, dark-faced man of over
sixty years of age, whom you would have hesitated to
classify. He had too much dignity to be called a *contadino*, or a common laborer ; yet he was dressed like
a laboring man. He carried himself well, was not
too ready with his salutation, and did not smile nor
come forward on being addressed.

" Madama would like to see the villa, with your
permission," the *vetturino* said to this man. " Padro-
nissima ! " was the reply. And Marco Bandini opened
the gate wider, and lifted his straw hat and looked at
her gravely as the lady passed him, but made no further compliments. When she had entered, he went
slowly out and began to talk with the *vetturino*.

A Janus of crumbling gray stone stood at either
hand inside the gate, a path led along the wall under
the trees, and the path that led straight to the house
was bordered with a hedge of box that spread out into
a semicircle set with ancient statues and busts found
on the place. The grounds rose in gardens and ter-

races from the road, all the details of them smothered in foliage, over which, from the summit of the gradual elevation, looked a few fine cypresses.

Valeria walked along the wall in the eastern direction, turned and entered a dark laurel avenue closely overarched with glossy, shining boughs, and pursued that fragrant twilight to the upper terrace, where stood the finest trees, and where rose-bushes were tangled in the hedges and clung to the trunks of cypresses.

The hedges enclosed in the centre a green chamber with statues, and reaches of dark laurel walks stretching to right and left, and below, a great square wrought in a pattern with fine, low box hedge, that was beginning now to sprout with brighter green along its squares and angles and wheels. From this upper terrace, looking through the parted boughs, could be seen a line of purple mountains, showing in bold, yet harmonious undulations against the southern sky. All else was green. There was no other view..

The paths were a glittering yellow with fallen laurel leaves. The place was a wilderness of laurels. Valeria walked hastily through one that led down to the house. An old woman sat on the step twirling her distaff. She smiled, but did not speak. On the ground behind the house was a confused heap of fragmentary sculpture. There were Egyptian heads, filleted heads, and heads ringed all over with short curls, one of them face down. A pretty marble face leaned against the cheek of a gigantic mask, another was hidden on a draped breast where the folds were held by a brooch. There were carven coats of arms, and broken hands and feet. One of the steps leading to the house was formed of milk-white folds of Carrara over a colossal shoulder. The house was not large. The owner had finished the grounds, but the malaria had discouraged him from building a *casino;* and

for many a year the place had been abandoned to
Marco Bandini and his family. Here Vittorio had
dreamed, and here Felicità had died.

When Valeria reached the upper terrace a second
time, the sun was at the horizon, and its last beams
came through the trees, and fell in large splashes of
unradiant orange gold on to the darkening ground.
She had to stoop and touch the leaves it fell on to
make sure that they were not painted.

As she stood there silent in that charmed solitude,
thinking that the place and the hour were fitting for
some shadowy form of the past that should appear, a
slight sound made her turn, and — spirits of immortal
loveliness ! — it was no antique shade, no togaed senator, no fiery Marius, no Horace leaning against a
cypress with an open, twice-read Homer in his hand,
but such a creature as would perhaps have subjected
them all. A girl of eighteen, slim and graceful, with
a heavy, dishevelled crown of black hair, brilliant
dark eyes, red lips smiling over small, milk-white
teeth, and a fresh face and round throat of rosy white,
with a delicate richness in the cheeks where a dimple
nestled.

This vision stood under the darkness of a cypress-
tree, glowing like the evening star, and waited to be
spoken to.

"Come to me if you are human !" Valeria exclaimed. "Whether you are human or not, come to
me !"

The girl advanced with a half-bashful, half-confi-
dent air, laughing, and alternately raising and dropping her brilliant eyes. It was as wonderful as if
one of those splashes of sunlight had taken human
form. It could not have taken a brighter shape, nor
a prettier simple dress, either, than the white *camicia*,
green skirt and corsets, and yellow handkerchief.

"Speak ! What are you ?" Valeria repeated, looking with delight into that face as delicate as a flower and as rich as a fruit.

The girl only hung her head and laughed. She was as simple as a wildwood creature, yet not silly. She laughed from the sweet joy of living, as a brook laughs that runs headlong down from the mountain, no matter where, so that it flows and dances.

"What is your name?" was the next question.

"Rosa," said the girl, finding voice; and, in speaking, a sweet, faintly smiling seriousness settled upon her. In work and thought she could be earnest, you saw, when the time for work and thought should come.

"Of course! I might have known you could have no other name," Valeria said. "What is your mother's name?"

"It was Felicità. But she is dead." She did not lose her smile in saying it. What did she know of death? Her mother's last sigh had swelled the tiny sails of her newly launched life. There must have been a smile in that sigh.

"Is the man at the gate your father?"

"Si, signora."

"Have you brothers and sisters?"

"I have one brother, Vittorio." She spoke with an air of pride. "He is the gardener at Villa Mitella, in Rome."

"Do you live here always?"

"I live here all winter with papa and Betta. But in the summer I go up to the old palace and stay with Chiara. I once had a fever here, and now papa will not let me stay."

She spoke with quiet self-possession, was frank, clear-headed, and prompt.

"What do you do here?" Valeria asked, unable to remove her eyes from that face, which took her observation innocently, and was not disconcerted by it.

"I don't ask what your father and Betta do, but what you do."

"I live here," the girl replied slowly, not seeming quite clear as to this reply.

Yes, she lived there as a peach lives on the bough, ripening in the sun; as a rose hangs on its stem, breathing out odors, and feels the breeze and the dew and the sun, and asks no questions.

Valeria recollected having read that Pliny had mentioned the roses of Preneste as having been famous among the ancients for their fragrance. It was the city of beautiful roses, he said. "Your name is Rosa Prenestina," she exclaimed.

"My name is Rosa Bandini," the girl replied with a slight surprise.

Valeria prepared to go away. "When do you go up to the old palace?" she asked, leading her prize down the steps with her.

"In May."

The two walked down to the gate together; and when Valeria looked back from the carriage in driving away, she saw Rosa hanging on her father's arm, and chattering to him like a magpie.

It was all charming. The filthy little town was set in an atmosphere of beauty, and its past was a record of beauty. Cicero and Juvenal and Cato and Pliny and Plutarch and Aristotle, and who knows how many others, had praised the town as they might have praised a fair woman. Then the old myth of its origin was so pretty! Telemachus, searching for his father, was told by the gods to build a town where he should see men dancing crowned with leaves; and, meeting here *contadini* decorated with branches, he had accepted it as a sign, and founded the city. So out of the dark past the history of this town had sprung, men dancing crowned with leaves; and the fountain of their laughter had never run dry. She had heard it to-day in the rose-white throat of the Rosa Prenestina.

"Well?" asked the Signora Maria when her visitor returned.

"I am delighted. I shall come back in a fortnight. You must give me that room looking toward the east. And I have a room in the old palace where I shall go every day."

"*Brava!* I knew you would like it!"

CHAPTER XV.

ROSA PRENESTINA.

ROSA BANDINI had grown up in solitude, with no playmates but her father, Vittorio, and old Betta, except that, since she had been sent up to the palace in the summer, she had made the acquaintance of Chiara. Her father had never allowed her to know children, and did not now allow her to know girls and boys of her own age.

"Children, especially such as she would see here, corrupt each other," he said.

He and Vittorio had taught her what she knew of books, to read, write, and make accounts, and Chiara had taught her housekeeping, knitting, weaving, and lace-making. Lace-making was her chief employment. Everything in the house on which lace could be put was decorated by her busy fingers, and many a yard was put away for her bridal outfit when she should marry. The most solemn hours of her life were spent in puzzling out a new pattern with her cushion and bobbins.

It will be seen that this was a very old-fashioned little Rose.

She had, however, read something by herself; for
the owner of the villa had been there for a part of one
distant autumn, and had left a case of books, chiefly
history and poetry; and these she found, and pored
over, especially the history of Palestrina. She had
told her father and Vittorio all about the siege of
Casalinga, that was so bravely defended by soldiers
from Preneste, of the nuts that were floated down on
the river to the starving inhabitants, of the rape-
seed they sowed over the walls, showing that they
meant to hold out till it should grow.

They let her talk, and said many a *Brava!* to en-
courage her. They knew that she had not many
pleasures or interests. But she never knew it. Her
joyfulness and sweetness sprang up and fell about her
like a fountain, and all the world looked joyful through
it. Neither did she know that her father and Vittorio
were bitter with the world. They smiled now and
then for her; and if they were never merry, why, that
was their way. She never heard them complain of
anything. Then old Betta was as gay as a cricket, and
cheerful and contented about everything.

Rosa had been to the old palace the year before,
and though she had very little company there, and
never went anywhere, nor saw any one, except in the
presence of Chiara, the *custode,* who was a friend of
her father, she liked the wide view, and to wander
through the deserted rooms and garden, and down
into the beautiful church of Santa Rosalia, that alone,
of all the place, had been preserved in its first beauty.
And she liked to go about with the tourists who came
to see the mosaic. Several times Chiara had let her
open the door of the room for them, and stand while
they looked, and listen to their strange, harsh languages as they talked to each other. She had learned
all the history of the mosaic, and told it off very
proudly to these curious *forastieri.* This was her

festa. And they all praised her, and gazed at her, and
spoke of her to each other; and sometimes they told
her that she was beautiful. She knew that she was
beautiful, she had heard it all her life, and it was one
of the sources of her happiness. It was pleasant to
see that the most serious face smiled when it looked
at her.

The previous year the Danish painter had come
there, and he, too, had glanced at her as he went in
and out; and he was so unmistakably good, so nearly
an angel, as both Chiara and the Signora Maria said,
that she was allowed to speak to him now and then.
He usually painted in the Tempietto when the weather
was fine; but when it was bad, he came down to a
room next that of Chiara, and she could see him at
work; for the door was almost always open.

Rosa would always be seated at such times at
Chiara's window, with her lace-cushion on her lap;
and the painter would glance from time to time across
his easel at that bright face in the gray old room,
and Rosa would glance over her bobbins at the fair-
haired Northerner who made such wonderful pictures.
And if by chance their glances encountered, Rosa
would hang her head and laugh, and by and by begin
to peep up again, like the simple, delicious little fool
that she was.

She wondered much over this artist with his magic
pencil, who painted all the rainbow colors of the campagna, the mountains and the skies. He could make
a fine picture of a donkey with a man and a basket
of greens on his back, of old Peppina with her bundle
of sticks, of Catarina with two hens hanging heads
downward from her hand, of ragged little Tito with
his round face and saucy smile, of the women washing
at the fountain with their skirts turned up, and a wall
of ivy for a background. She had never thought these
things worth a second glance, yet he studied, and

spent days over them. When they were painted she
could see that they were beautiful, but without knowing why, unless it was because he had touched them.

Many of the things that she had admired and
wondered over, the Signor Eduardo cared nothing
for. The fine dresses of some of the ladies, all ribbons and little crimped-up flounces, he had laughed
at, and called ugly; and he hardly glanced at Seconda
Dorelli's coral and gold chain, and large gold rings,
though they were so splendid.

" To be sure," thought Rosa, "he seems to admire
my ear-rings." But when she had motioned to remove one that he might examine it, he had said that
it was not necessary, and had told her to sit still while
he sketched it hanging in her ear. And he did sketch
it very perfectly, and the profile and whole head with
it. It was rather provoking that he had not let her
know what he was going to do, so that she could have
smoothed back those heavy locks of hers that were
always dropping over her eyes. For he had actually
taken them all as they were in disorder.

" No matter," he had said, " the ear-ring is all right."
And he had laughed.

She used to think it all over as she sat in Chiara's
great chamber making lace, think over all that he
said and did; and she found herself very pleasantly
employed.

All this had happened the summer before. The
Dane had stayed till October, and had then gone to
Rome. Rosa cried a little quietly when he went
away, but had not let him see her tears. She was
rather ashamed of crying for anything. It seemed
childish. So she tried to be brave, and had smiled
when he said "Addio" to her. "I shall come back
next summer. Will you be glad to see me, Rosa?"
he had said, looking at her in a way that had made
her drop her eyes, she knew not why.

And now he was back again, and she at the palace,
and he came and went just as he had the year before.
It was just the same, — with a very little difference ;
and the difference was the *signora americana,* Madama Valeria.

Rosa was very fond of the new signora, who was
most kind to her ; but she was *curiosa* for all that.
Most *forastieri* were *curiosi.* She would sometimes
sit and look off toward Rome, or to the eastern mountains, or to the sea, for hours, and never seem to tire.
And she looked into flowers, and examined leaves, and
stopped to look at sun-rays and moon-rays and common pebbles ; and she wanted to know the names of
them all. She looked at the stars, too, and sometimes
told Rosa the names of them, and watched at the
window to see the new moon, and cried out when the
sunlight had gone down like a high tide and left that
little crescent stranded, just as if there never were a
new moon before.

To Rosa these were all very common things, pleasant enough, certainly, to look at once in a while ; but
to look at them every day was very queer.

Sometimes Madama and the Signor Eduardo had
long conversations together which they seemed to
like ; and though they spoke Italian, Rosa did not
understand one half they said, they were so very
learned. Now and then, while they talked, the Signor
Eduardo would turn and see Rosa's serious, puzzled
face, and would smile and say something to her ; and
all the reply she made was a laugh. She was so
simple and unthinking that she laughed at nothing,
as the birds sing, as the fountain runs over.

"Sangue dolce !" the Dane said once, looking at
her with a tender smile. And, indeed, she had sweet
blood as well as a sweet face.

Perhaps, as the days of that summer went by,
her laugh grew less light and empty and frequent.

Sometimes she only smiled. But she was herself no more aware of the change than the swinging rose is, when a heavy dew-drop falls into its heart and steadies it somewhat. She still went about her little duties, and the small routine of her life. If she was sometimes rather absent, that was nothing. She had things to think about. Madama Valeria and the Signor Eduardo seemed to be very good friends, and Chiara had said that perhaps they would one day be married. She was thinking of that. It was very interesting; and, thinking of it, she sometimes forgot to laugh.

It was not strange that they should be much together, talking, and taking long walks in the campagna or up the mountain. They liked the same things, and it was quite natural, quite proper.

"They are going out now to walk," she thought, one day, looking after them with a sweet, light shadow on her face. They were of the same height, for Madama was tall, and she had a red rose in her bonnet, and a little red ruffle at the bottom of her dress, and a great fan covered with painted Chinese women, and black gloves painted with little red and gold flowers. The Signor Eduardo had painted them. Rosa did not know that she sighed, looking after them. She was thinking that it must be a grand thing to be a fine lady, though she had never dreamed of being one, or wished for anything so silly. She was content to be as she was, with her blue-and-white cotton skirt, and deep blue corset, laced over a white *camicia*, and a green handkerchief folded down in pleats from the back of her neck, and tucked into the high bust in front. The Signor Eduardo had once said that her face above that green and blue looked like a pink Arethusa growing out of a reedy brook.

The two whom she watched went upward a little to the long green road that leads from the westward mountain-side down to the campagna.

"I half wish that I had asked Rosa to come with us," Valeria said. "It seems unkind to never offer her any change. But, to tell the truth, when her pretty face is by, your talk is not very interesting. I don't blame you. I merely state the fact, and explain why I do not furnish you with more opportunities to gaze at her. I doubt if so much silent homage be good for a girl who will presently be left quite alone. One must think a little of her as well as of pleasing one's self."

She had been thinking rather impatiently of late: "This man, who is as good as he can be, and has not a particle of vanity, is behaving as badly as if he were a rascal. When he goes away that child will break her heart."

The painter hung his head a little, and was silent. He was a quiet, reserved man, slightly bashful, and as delicate as a woman ought to be. He did not believe that Rosa dreamed of loving him or any one. He had been studying her face unconsciously while studying the problem if indeed a soul would ever float on that *sangue dolce,* if ever she would be anything but a flower.

It was a lovely road, the hedges and walls about it overmantled with vines of large white convolvuli, half hidden at times by clumps of elder-trees, sweet with immense clusters of flaky white blossoms. The flowers were so profuse that at turnings of the road they seemed to have smothered it quite.

At a turn they came upon two gentlemen,—a small, slight Greek priest in his black robe and four-cornered *berretta,* and a tall professor from the seminary. The Professor held a book in his hand, and read aloud as they walked, reading slowly, like a boy at school. He was learning Greek of the other; and every Greek root, as he drew it out, was perfumed with Italian flowers.

Hearing the steps that followed, the two turned their heads.

"It is a peripatetic school," the Greek said, with a singularly sweet smile in his face, that was as pale as a pearl.

"With Aristotle strained through Saint Thomas Aquinas," added the Professor.

"Accept my compliments on the architecture of your Lyceum," Valeria said; and added, "Will the Professor Sardegna be at liberty to-morrow?"

The Professor declared himself to be entirely at her disposition.

Would he give her a reading of Tasso in the Barberini garden the next afternoon?

The Professor would call to escort her to the garden at any hour she might name.

"At four, then." And they separated.

The painter and Valeria gathered flowers, — little white violets, purple bachelor's-buttons, a hundred wild things of all colors. Now and then one of them made a hasty sketch of something that caught their eyes and fancy. They visited the fountain that the Dane had painted, Acqua di Pepe, and drank of its limpid water, noted in all the country round. Then they turned homeward, and went up to the old palace again, where the Dane had left some letters that must be mailed that evening.

Chiara, seeing them return, knew what was wanted, and sent Rosa down with the letters, to spare them the stairs.

Rosa gave the letters with a smile; but there was a certain modest dignity in her manner which did not escape either of them. Her face was perhaps not quite so rosy as usual; but she looked at them calmly, and answered as gently as ever. With all her simplicity, there was something unapproachable about her.

"How sober you are, Rosa *mia!*" Valeria said, "What has happened?"

"Nothing has happened," the girl replied with quiet reserve; and her faint, proud smile would have become a queen.

"*Felicissima sera*, Rosa!" said the Dane, looking at her earnestly.

She replied with sweet composure, and let them go.

But when they were gone, she fled up-stairs, and out into the green, high-walled garden behind the palace. The grass grew tall, there was no one in sight. She ran across the garden, and flung herself down beside a headless statue that lay there, and, hiding her face against the cold marble breast, sobbed out all her passion.

"I don't know what is the matter with me!" she sobbed, beating down a thought that tried to rise. "It must be an *urta dei nervi*. I don't know what else." And she buried her face in the dewy grass, and strove to cool her throbbing temples against the cold marble. And again, when she rose, and stole into the house at twilight, she protested to her own heart, "I don't know what I was crying so for!"

CHAPTER XVI.

COUNTRY LIFE.

IT was a various company that met at the Signora Maria's supper-table that evening, for several new visitors had arrived in the afternoon. At the end of the table sat the Dane, with Valeria below the corner at his right, and a young Swede opposite her. Next the Swede sat two English ladies, who were

making the journey from Rome to Genazzano on
foot ; " shod like horses," said the Signora Maria, who
marvelled greatly over these long walks. Next to
Valeria sat three German ladies.

The German ladies were silent and modest, and
seemed timid ; the English ladies were silent and
reserved, and seemed severe ; the Swede kept up an
almost whispered conversation in Danish with the
Signor Eduardo.   There was an air of constraint over
all.   One of the German ladies, having swallowed
something the wrong way, partly because of embarrassment, and choking a little, nearly cried with
mortification.   .

Clelia, the pretty girl who waited on them, kept
glancing about with bright eyes full of laughter
at these queer *forastieri*, who ate together without
speaking a word.   The Signora Maria, who usually
waited, was employed on some momentous dish in
the kitchen.

" What a pity we have not a Frenchman or a
Russian here to make up the seven nations !" Valeria
said to the Dane.   " We are now but six."

" Yes," he assented smilingly, but could get no further, as she had spoken in English, which he did not
understand well.

The silence deadened.   The Dane exchanged an
amused glance with the waitress, and nodded toward
the kitchen door, with a murmured, " Per carità ! "

Clelia disappeared, and a moment later entered
the Signora Maria, smiling and rubicund, bearing a
great open dish, which had evidently been taken off
her mind as well as off the fire.

. " Now here is something *chic !* " she called out in a
loud, cheery voice, and set the dish down beside the
Dane.   " Help yourself, Eduardo *mio, senza compli-
menti*.   It is too heavy to stand holding.   Or help first
Madama Valeria, if you wish."   And she patted him

on the shoulder, repeating with great good-will her
" Eduardo *mio !* "

" He is so good ! " she added, addressing the company.

The painter, who was accustomed to these compliments, took no notice of them except by a slight
blush and smile.

" It is really *chic*, Signora Maria," one of the ladies
said, having tasted of the dish.

It was home-made macaroni steeped in a rich
giblet sauce, and garnished with little gold-colored
balls, which proved to be the yolks of the number of
eggs which the late hen would have laid that week if
her life had been spared.

" Of course it is ! " responded the landlady, who
was not inclined to hide her light under a bushel;
and she immediately described the manner in which
It was prepared.

She laughed and talked; sang a few lines of a
soldier's song; filled everybody's tumbler with great
splashes of red wine; piled their plates with the most
embarrassing mountains of food; asked how they
liked their food, and told them what other *cic-
cheria* was then being prepared for them in the
kitchen.

" Madama Valeria says that my *agro dolce* is better
than they make in Rome, and Madama Valeria is a
judge of everything, from an *agro dolce* to Dante's
Inferno. She is a very distinguished lady, and has
written a library full of books. She is immensely
rich. Her father was a Senator of the American
States. And when she came here she brought letters
of introduction to the Mayor and the Bishop and the
Princess — "

" Good gracious ! " cried Valeria, astounded at the
gigantic proportions which the very modest story
that had been drawn from her on her arrival had

assumed in the fervid imagination of the Signora
Maria. "Where did you get all this wonderful romance?"

"Everybody says it," the landlady replied with
great dexterity.

The company were all laughing. The ice was
broken. They regarded with a smiling wonder this
great creature, who was as simple as a child, yet had,
at need, no small amount of subtlety; this woman so
generous and enthusiastic, who lost her head with a
facility only equalled by the facility with which she
regained it.

"She is a type!" murmured one of the ladies. "I
could listen to her all day."

The supper ended, they all gathered about a table
in an inner chamber. The Signora Maria was going to show them some antiquities. The other
tables in the room were already piled with antique
vases, lamps, and fragments; but the more precious
articles were locked away in a cabinet. They
consisted chiefly in scarabei, intagli, and ancient
rings, all found in the plain about Palestrina, where
the territory is probably as rich as any in Italy.
For not only did the beautiful natural position of
ancient Preneste invite the rich to build their villas there, but the supreme reputation and magnifi-
cence of the Temple of Fortune, which covered all the
site of the present town, drew worshippers and tribute.
Cicero bears testimony to the splendors of this temple, and the few remains left of it confirm his word.
Pliny praises the roses of Preneste; Cato, its walnuts;
Martial, its wines and the fertility of its soil; Livy
says that it had a territory of twenty miles by twenty-
five, and owned eight cities; and it was so sacred that
those who fled to the shelter of its temple were safe
from Roman justice and vengeance.

All this gave an enchanting value to these precious

little fragments that had so long been hidden in the earth, and had now come to light with all their memories about them. Some had been found by *contadini*, and sold to the Signora Maria's brother, who understood these things, and others had been taken from the soil in their own vineyards.

When the company went away, Clelia and the old servant, Felicetta, came in and played *Morra* with the Signora Maria for a tumbler of wine, and some cherries that were left. The three hands were thrust vigorously out, and each seized her gains eagerly, that the others might not rob her, the *padrona* cheating frankly now and then.

Tired and contented, Valeria went down-stairs, accompanied by Clelia, bearing a long brass lamp, crossed the *piazzetta*, shut herself into her room, and, extinguishing the candle, seated herself by the open window.

The mountain rose steeply at her left, lifting the horizon half-way to the zenith. On its side the Cappuccini church and convent nestled into a grove. Close to her window was the convent of the Sepolte Vite, as silent as the grave, not only now by night, but when the sun shone on its mysterious walls, wherein every face is veiled forever from human sight.

The velvety dusk was sweet with the perfume of elder-blossoms; a fountain dropped with a watery whisper down by the street-side; and through the immensity of silence stretching off eastward toward the mountains, came the liquid notes of a lone bird that sang as though it spoke. Every night that plaintive nightingale sang in the silence between the Cappuccini and the Sepolte Vite.

" I am glad to be in Italy!" Valeria thought, closing her window against the night air.

And again the next day she said, " I am glad to be

in Italy!" when she sat in the pleasant garden of the
Barberini palace, in the lower part of the town, with
the landscape spread out in sunshine from under the
dark roof of ilex-trees over her head, and listened to
Professor Sardegna reading Tasso. As she listened,
the view changed to the garden of Armida, the marble shapes about breathed, and the misty sea-line in
that great mountain hollow at the south drew nearer,
and rippled into sight.

> " D' incontro è il mare ; e di canuto flutto
>   Vedi spumati i suoi cerulei campi."

"Will you take a walk?" the Professor asked,
closing the book.

They wandered down into the campagna, meeting
the *contadini* coming up from their work to sleep in
the city. There were whole families, from grand-
fathers to babies, with laden donkeys, and black pigs
that skipped like goats.

"Nothing would induce them to sleep in the campagna," the Professor said. " They fear the malaria,
and perhaps they fear each other; for those cabins in
the plain do not close like a city house."

These *contadini* have a character which their class
in no other country possess. It cannot be despised,
and disgust is not the feeling that it inspires. If you
do not look at them with compassion, and sometimes
with admiration, you pay them the compliment of
your hatred, which they do not deserve. Perhaps,
though, they are more likely to inspire each and all
of these feelings in turn. The only sentiment which
they can never awaken is respect.

Those souls are like the soil underneath their vineyards and olive-orchards, which is sown through with
ruined glories. The roots of a plant or tree may clasp
a delicate marble hand down in the dark, or slip over
the long, chiselled folds of a Carrara toga, or grow

across a smooth cheek that the sun has not seen for
centuries, or entangle and bear downward a scarabeo
or intaglio that a princess might wear and prize.
Fragments of Christianity and Paganism lie jumbled
together, the balls of Jove Serapis rolled against the
thornless roses of Saint Francis. So in these minds,
where you surprise exquisite bits of knowledge in the
midst of ignorance, delicate traits of culture in roughness, and of beauty in ugliness. You see a rich pink
rose, all dewy with freshness, in a battered hat; you
receive an elegant salutation from a tattered clown;
your servant pays you compliments which you would
like to translate into your own language for the drawing-room; a rough-shod, leather-legginged fellow walks
backward half the length of a church in which is exposed the Sacrament. Who told him that he must
not turn his back upon the king?

You cannot teach them. Their ignorance is so
systematized as to have become a science, and your
new facts have no place there. They would be like
new wine in old bottles; and they know that their
bottles would burst. They are civil to your face,
maybe, but they laugh when you have turned away.
Their easy, amused scorn is as lofty as the scorn of a
philosopher for a fool. The wisest and most philan-
thropic stranger who would instruct them would seem
to them ridiculous. They know things which you do
not know, therefore they consider themselves better
informed. Their habits, as well as their faith, are
founded upon a rock. They live in the midst of petrified customs, and your customs which differ from
them are as laughable in their eyes as you would be
if you walked on your hands instead of your feet.

They do not want your tools, your machines, nor
your books. Their princes do not offer them these
things, therefore they are worthless. What do you
foreigners know of Italy or of them? The only

respectable thing about your interference is your money. They are content to turn over the earth as their fathers did before them; and all the mathematics they want is in their ten fingers.

They gather bunches of little green apples no larger than cherries, and almonds that have only a soft milky kernel, and peaches like green rocks; and their market is filled with this trash, because they will not sacrifice the certain *soldo* of to-day for the hope of three *soldi* to-morrow. It is useless for you to urge them to cultivate their fruit, and make it at least as fine as that of Northern countries. The princes cultivate fruit in their gardens because they are princes; for them, they take what the trees give; and what they cannot sell, the pigs will eat.

You can do nothing with them. Only when the rich and the powerful shall interest themselves in agriculture, will Italian produce equal that of Northern lands; and only when the prince tries to instruct the *contadino* will he consent to learn.

The superstition with which these poor people are so often reproached is scarcely a misfortune. That love of the marvellous has done in them something of the work which knowledge does for the learned. It has kept their souls above the earth on which their feet tread, and it has kept a certain freshness in their hearts. If great thoughts do not expand the mind, it is better that it should be inflated by illusions than to collapse. Moreover, superstition, the Scylla of ignorance, is better than scepticism, the Charybdis of learning. To superstition sublime action is possible; but who would expect heroism from incredulity?

"Madama is silent," the Professor remarked, as Valeria walked along, buried in thought.

"Pardon me! I was thinking how much Father Gioacchino Ventura might have done for the glory of God and of Italy, if he had been permitted; and how much those two noble books of his, the *Donna Catto-lica* and the *Donna Cristiana*, might yet do, if they were only read."

"He died in France," the Professor said.

"Yes; in exile!" was the reply. "When I had read his books, I went in search of him, as on a pilgrimage; and when they told me that he was dead, I had such a sense of loss as few deaths could cause me."

"Have you seen his monument in Sant' Andrea della Valle?" the Professor asked.

"Yes. His dust was brought back and laid with all honor under the pavement, when the troublesome immortal spark was out of it; and his marble likeness was set up, as if preaching, when his voice was silenced forever. It is not Jerusalem alone which has stoned the prophets, and killed them that were sent unto her."

There was silence again, neither wishing to pursue an unpleasant subject.

Then the Professor pointed out a spot where, a few years before, a *contadino* had come upon an ancient sarcophagus in digging a trench on his land. Hoping to find a treasure in it, he carefully removed all the earth, and, without calling help, managed to lift the cover. Within lay the form of a woman, distinct in shape, though quite dark in color. On seeing this awful shadow out of the past, the man fainted. When he regained consciousness, and had called assistance, the figure had quite fallen to dust.

They came to a little wayside chapel where some boys were sweeping the floor, and putting up flowers before a picture of the Madonna, in preparation for some *festa*.

Farther on, where the falling bank at the roadside had disclosed a piece of ancient wall, the Professor picked up a pointed bone arrow-head, and Valeria an ancient silver coin of Greece.

They stopped on a little bridge over a ravine to

look down at the tree-tops, and to see the low sunshine move on the parapet. It moved backward with
a slow strength as the sun went down, but trembled
in moving. The sunshine always trembles as it moves.
Is it because the heart of the earth beats hard, or is
it the heart of the sun ?

The golden air of sunset had grown silver, then
taken a delicate shade of violet; and a star was visible
when they reached the city gate again. It was very
lovely.

"'How good is our life, the mere living,'" thought
Valeria, "especially when one is in Italy and in the
country !"

But, pleasant as such hours were, they did not equal
the long days when she was shut into that great gray
room of the old palace, where the only furniture was a
chair and a table drawn up before the window. There
her fancies had elbow-room ; and though, when she
seated herself, pen in hand, and waited for the procession of her story to march out through that gate
of expression that is so small, so small ! there was
ever a confusion like that of any public procession,
— now a poor little fancy gets its wings crushed by
some hobnailed common-place that will come out,
now "a thought stops the way !" and has to be set
down on its own slip of paper outside, and a general
bustle of many-colored ideas, — it was high *festa* for
all that, and a most pleasant trouble. A few persons
who had put their heads into this studio found it very
bare ; but Valeria was to herself like the old woman
who lived in a shoe.

"I like large, bare rooms," the Dane said, " if only
they are lofty and well-proportioned, and have a good
view from the windows. It has always seemed to me
that small spaces make small talk. When I go into
a room so crowded with furniture that you come out
with your knees and elbows black and blue with
bruises, I never expect to hear anything but scandal."

In company with two or three other visitors in
Palestrina, they went on little excursions to the neighboring towns, to Cave and Genazzano, to Rocca di
Cave and Zagarolo. It was all a dream of delight.
Multitudinous flowers, gray rocks and precipices, picturesque old palaces, mountains as blue as lapis-lazuli,
golden wheat-fields and dark-green vineyards, all nature's cornucopia poured out on the landscape, made
of life something ideal. And delight was business
and beauty was food.

In all these excursions Rosa Bandini accompanied
her new friend; but the Dane was too busy to go.
He had to finish a large picture, and many sketches,
and he was going to Venice, where he would remain
several months, then return to Rome in the spring.
After another year and a half he would go back to
Denmark, and he was laying up Southern sunshine to
last him through many a Northern winter, perhaps
through all the winters of his life.

He was so busy as almost to have given up his
walks with Valeria; but they talked together at the
table and after supper. Sometimes she wondered if
he had any loverlike inclination toward Rosa, and if,
supposing he had, he would be willing to yield to it,
and marry a little blossom of a rustic, who went in
petticoat and corsets, and with a handkerchief, if she
wore anything, on her head.

She tried him one day with a different costume,
when she was just setting out on some excursion with
Rosa. She had snatched off the girl's clean white
apron and thrown it aside, draped a white zephyr
shawl around her shoulders and fastened it with a
pink rose, and caught a black lace veil to her thick hair
with a gilt spear. The dark-blue skirt and little high-
heeled boots were all that could be desired; and no
lady could have been more prettily dressed. Few
ladies could have so well become their dress as Rosa

did, standing there under the gray doorway leading
out into the Tempietto, only the halo of a smile about
her lips, and her dark eyes looking earnestly out from
under her drooping brows at the painter. She did not
laugh. She looked out at him from the shadowed
depths of her heart to see if he, a gentleman, thought
that she could be a lady.

His eyes were caught by that vision, as in a net.
He drew one quick.little breath, and smiled, but said
nothing.

"Did you ever see a person who bore being stared
at so nobly?" Valeria said to him in English. "A
marble statue could not take admiration more tranquilly. See how well the pink rose becomes her!
And pink is a trying color. Is it not a pity that such
a creature should marry a common fellow, who will
perhaps beat her?"

He murmured some unintelligible word, and dropped
his eyes. He had a wonderful faculty for holding his
tongue.

Rosa looked at him steadily with her fathomless,
melancholy eyes, her bearing full of a proud simplicity, then turned away without a word, and went
down-stairs.

It was like trying to bring the equator and the tropic
of Cancer together!

CHAPTER XVII.

"SWEET HOME."

ONE day, late in the summer, Valeria received a
letter from Miss Chaplin, who was yet in Rome,
but about to set out for Paris, on her way to America
with Mrs. Gray.

She wrote that Miss Cromo had taken an apartment, and having moved her effects into it, without arranging them, had gone away for a short *villeggiatura*. In October she would return and put the house in order.

"There is a vacant apartment over hers," Miss Chaplin wrote, "and I thought of you at once when I saw it, though I thought best not to say anything then. I only glanced at it when I went with Miss Cromo, who looked at the whole house. But I procured the keys, and went alone the next day, in order to tell you all about it. I spoke to the man having charge of it, and he will let the apartment for a reasonable price, and keep it till he hears from you."

Then followed a description.

We have already described Villa Mitella, and have mentioned the *casuccia* which was included in its southern wall. It was this house to which Miss Chaplin referred; and it seemed, indeed, to be enclosed in a world of walls. For not only the villa wall, in which more than half its depth was set, stretched at either end of it along the Via Nero, but the opposite side of the street was also walled-in gardens for some distance up and down. Downward there was nothing but walls, Via Nero making a sudden turn around the corner of the villa, and passing by the entrance to the gardener's house at the back of the grounds. Up the street houses were visible at a short distance.

The house was long and narrow, the side on the street; and opposite the middle of it, a second street, Via Claudia, came down a slight rise into Via Nero. Quite near one end of the *casuccia*, almost as though it were a continuation of Via Claudia, an arched opening had been cut, and finished with a gate into the garden. This gate was always kept jealously closed, and had a deep recess both inside and on the street.

As is common with these city gardens in Italy, the
land inside the wall was much higher than the street;
so that the gateway had a long stair inside, and the
earth was almost half-way up the rooms of Miss Cromo's apartment. The wall, that looked like a fortress
on the outside, was on the inside scarcely over the
tops of the rose-bushes.

The *casuccia* had a double roof, and only two stories
above the ground-floor. The lower was reached by a
door at the end looking up the street, and an inside
stair; the upper had an outside stair at the opposite
end. Both apartments had windows on the street
and one window at the end opposite the door. The
upper one alone looked into the garden. This was
by an arched window that had once lighted a stairway
now closed, and it looked out over the inner steps of
the gate, through the shrubs to Vittorio's house, and
over a paradise of flowers and fountains to the opposite wall of the garden, which hid all the world
beyond, except a blue mountain-top.

"Shall I have that window looking into the garden closed up?" the Prince's major-domo asked him.
"I don't think that the Countess will like it."

"What harm will it do?" the Prince replied, rather
impatiently. He was none too well pleased with his
daughter, and very willing to oppose her wishes, when
he did not understand perfectly the reasons for them.
"To close it would be to darken a room. If the lady
likes to look into the garden, she is welcome to. And
if she would like to have some flowers, tell Vittorio
to give her as many as she wants."

Valeria had already been to Rome, and had taken
the apartment on a long lease. While talking with
the major-domo about it in the porter's room of the
villa, a quiet-looking gentleman whom she had found
there, after listening awhile, had asked her if there
were any repairs that she would like to have made in

the house. She divined at once that he was the owner,
but chose not to know visibly.

"I do not doubt that there may be something wanting, sir," she said ; "but the apartment pleases me so
much that I have not, as yet, seen any defects."

"Whenever you do," the Prince said, smiling slightly, "tell my major-domo, and he will do whatever may
be necessary."

Valeria courtesied, and became aware to whom she
was speaking. The Prince made a very magnificent
bow, and retired.

"I was afraid you might object to being in the
house with Miss Cromo," Miss Chaplin said. "Otherwise I thought the place would suit you. It seems
so retired, yet is really central."

"Oh! I do not mind Miss Cromo," Valeria replied.
"We need not disturb each other."

So the bargain was made, and she went back to
stay another week in Palestrina, and finish the last
chapter of her book.

Oh that first book! written with what pleasure,
as if one were singing, and with what pain that we
can so little express what we would write! How
confident we are while writing, how sure to please!
Then, when it is out of our hands, past recall and past
mending, how all our pleasure and confidence seem
to have been an illusion! The faults we saw grow
like evening shadows ; the merits we fancied were
there diminish and disappear. We had imagined
that we had something to say to the world, and, having spoken, we shrink at our own presumption, and
would fain hide ourselves. How can we hope that
an echo will come back to us !

The book was finished and sent, however. She
tore it out of her own hands, that would fain have
written it all over again, and tried to put it out of her
mind as well.

There were a few days left to revisit some of the
pleasant summer haunts : one more long walk through
a ripe wheat-field that stirred in golden waves far
overhead; one more loitering under a deep-shad-
owed fig-tree to see which fig had the golden honey-
drop oozing from its tip that sagged heavy with
sweetness; one more climb to the wild little mountain-top hamlet, with its quiet church lighted up
more by Pietro da Cortona's picture than even by
the airy upper light of the sun, and a last long breath
of that mountain-air, which inebriates like the wine
of the gods, sending the vigor of early youth along
the limbs, and a gladness as of immortal childhood
through the heart, almost lifting the flesh off the soul ;
one more hour with Tasso in the dense warm air
under the ilex boughs of the Barberini garden, with
the landscape swimming in mists, and the honeyed
breath of flowers and fragrant laurel creeping around
the gray old masks and statues, and through the sun-
streaked gloom.   And at last there was but one evening left.

They went over, a half dozen of them, to spend it
at the Generale, a villa just outside the eastern gate
of the city.   It was a modern house of almost palatial
size, built upon solid ancient foundations, and surrounded by gardens and vineyards.   The house was
untenanted, its owners, two young brothers scarcely
over twenty, living in the Piazza of the town ; but
dances and dinners were often given in its large halls,
and there were little garden-parties every afternoon
toward sunset.   The usual place of reception was the
cellar, which opened out by two great doors even with
the garden.   Inside, two large rooms were divided
and supported by fine stone arches, which had the
beauty of strength and proportion, if not of finish.
Hogsheads of wine lay around the dark walls, and
extended into the black grottos that reached far be-

yond the house, under a street and into the mountain. In the circle of light about the open door was a table with chairs. One of the young men filled a decanter of sunny white wine from a hogshead near by, the other went farther back into the grotto and drew a decanter of red wine. No one was allowed to leave their grounds without tasting of their wine.

Outside the sun was setting, making the grape-leaves ruddy, and blushing along the thickly set bunches of white grapes, not yet ripe, till here and there one shone like a carbuncle. There were roses about, and lavender. There was a group of *contadine* outside picking the leaves from mulberry boughs to feed the silkworms. The deep blue mountain chain flushed to a red-purple, and the distant silvery ones became rose-colored. The sky was as clear as a crystal, and there was a moon three days old in it, and soon there would be a star.

The little company sat inside the cellar-door, but looking out, themselves a picture without their knowing it. They talked, laughed, and sipped the cool wine that was the essence of just such days as that in a vanished year. There was the Signor Eduardo, the Professor, two or three young ladies, Rosa, and Valeria.

When the twilight fell, they went out into the garden, and one of their hosts brought a mandolin, and sang to it. He was a laughing young Romeo with a sweet voice, and years of romantic adventure before him. As he sang, the Dane turned his eyes upon Rosa, who sat with hers drooping. It suddenly occurred to him to wonder where all her laughter had flown. He could not recollect when he had heard her laugh. And was it possible that she was proud! If it had been any one else sitting with those folded hands and lowered lids, he would have said that she was proud-looking. But when some one touched and spoke to her, the childlike smile and simple air returned.

Then her eyes wandered, looking at the air, seeming half to seek and half to avoid some object, till they settled and dwelt on the handsome singer.

Young Cesare sat on the corner of a beautiful ancient marble sarcophagus that was filled with earth and bright with pink and white petunias. His moist dark hair escaped in waves from under a soft gray hat with a green and gray feather in it, his dark eyes sparkled, his slight form was thrown into a graceful attitude as he played the mandolin and sang of love.

"Confound him! how handsome he is!" the painter thought, and felt himself old, felt himself ugly, too, with his blond hair and blue eyes, that lacked that Southern fire. "But his family would not let him marry her. They want more money than she will have."

For one minute painting seemed to him a very poor business, and it seemed a very fine thing to be a handsome black-eyed Italian, playing the mandolin among the vines at evening, and singing in a voice more passionate even than the love-song he uttered.

Valeria praised the song and the place and the evening, and rose to go, delighted. For she had caught a little green ray in the blue eyes of Rosa's laggard lover, and she joyfully hoped that he was suffering unutterable torments of jealousy.

They all accompanied her home, and took a cordial leave at the door, for she was to go away early the next morning. Old Chiara stood in the *piazzetta,* waiting to take Rosa up to the palace; and they all went their ways, and the summer dissolved like a dream that leaves one smiling.

The next morning, accompanied by a servant whom

she had engaged in Palestrina, she set out for Rome, " not knowing whither she went."

The apartment was a convenient one, and had been very well put in order for her. Her own part, which occupied all the centre and the western end, consisted of three rooms, the centre being divided, and giving a study looking into the garden, and a bedroom looking into the street, with a little corridor between leading to a large *sala* that occupied all the end of the building. The rest was given up to the servant.

This servant, Marta, proved very good-natured, as Italian servants usually do when well paid and well treated, and allowed their little thefts. But she was immeasurably astonished at her mistress's manner of setting up housekeeping, and at the little need she had of *artisti.*

" But, Madama Valeria, a lady cannot do such things!" she ventured.

Valeria, who had rather imperative ideas as to a servant's place, interrupted her.

" A lady is one who knows how to do everything ; and I am a lady, and I can do everything. I could build a house if I would take the trouble. I do not wish to have any workmen here. You are strong, and must exert yourself, and I shall tell you what to do. I also know how to cook, and how ironing should be done, and how long a pound of coffee ought to last, and how much broth a pound of meat will make. In short, you cannot mention a thing that any woman can know which I do not know perfectly. And you need never tell me what a lady should or should not do, because I, being a lady, know all about it, and you, being a servant, cannot possibly know anything of it."

So Marta was sent up on a ladder to hang curtains, and down on her knees to scrub floors ; and she hammered her fingers black and blue, nailing covers on to chairs; and, when all was completed, she had to own that the result exceeded her expectations.

In a week the house was in order, and, though but scantily furnished, had everything that was necessary for comfort. The rest must wait for better times. And in the mean time it was happiness enough to have a house of her own, all her own to command in, to invite to, or to exclude from, to hide in, to work in, to live in. It had not been life before. It had been only journeying; now it was rest. No more listening ears or peeping eyes at the keyhole, no more alien habits to disjoint her own, no more sulky faces to dampen her sunny mood, no more uncertainty. Seating herself in an arm-chair, she knew that she could sit there ten years, if she chose. It was now worth while to plant a flower, to frame a picture, to embroider a table-cover; for this was home! It was worth while to put lavender and rose-leaves all about in drawers, on shelves, in books and in beds, and to coax even the walls to catch a faint perfume. It was "sweet home!"

Before the week was well over, a great noise began to be made in the apartment underneath. Miss Cromo had returned, and was setting her house in order with much bustle and parade. There was a running about, a thumping of furniture, a driving of nails, a rattling of hand-carts, a sound of voices, with occasional little feminine screams.

Valeria laughed as she heard these demonstrations. "I wonder what she will say when she knows who is overhead! I hope she may not find out till I am ready."

Her servant and the Prince's major-domo were the only persons in town who knew her whereabout, and they had been strictly forbidden to tell any one, on the plea that she was not yet prepared to receive.

She had taken possession of her studio, a charming

little room, and, with a writing-table before the garden-window, was waiting, pen in hand, for a subject. There were such countless little stories waiting to be told, hovering in the very air, as thick as motes in a sunbeam.

It was September now, with still a summer heat. The garden outside was a blaze of color, blooming for itself alone; for the family were all away. Looking out, one saw nothing but reds, and golds, and milk-white shining out of dark green, and the brown wall, with a purple mountain-top over it.

" We must build a city and a few villas around the foot of that mountain. How would a pearl villa look half-way up, with a great many roses and myrtles about it ! A stream of bright water shall come down from the top in all sorts of brook-gambols, divide before it reaches the villa, one half running under ground, and springing up in a fountain inside the wall. The other half, heart-broken at this desertion, shall throw itself downward, and fall on a peak of lapis-lazuli with such force as to be dashed all into spray over the flowers and grass close by the fountain ; and the fountain shall laugh. Cupid and Psyche can spend their honeymoon there." And a great deal more of the like nonsense.

When one has to amuse one's self, one must sometimes be foolish.

Dropping her eyes to a little grove of camellias directly before her window, Valeria saw a man standing there. He must have been there for some time without her being aware of him. He seemed scarcely aware of himself, indeed. His face was partially turned toward her, and his arms hung by his side. He seemed to have paused there unconsciously in deep and not pleasant thought, though his face was calm. One might guess that under the fixed and statuesque beauty of that exterior there was a clash of thought and of passion, a desperate search, as of one in a great strait, and seeking if there should be some means of escape as yet unknown.

After a moment, he started slightly, lifted his eyes enough to show how lustrous they were, and walked slowly on, looking about him. Half absently he lifted here and there a plant too heavy with blossoms, and supported it, or broke off a withered leaf, touching them softly and gravely, as if he reverenced them. Reaching a fountain presently, he sat down on the marble brink, wet both hands in the basin, clasped them over his forehead, and leaned his elbows on his knees, sitting there with his face hidden.

"Something is the matter with that beautiful Vittorio," Valeria thought. "I will not look at him. He believes himself to be unobserved. I hope that his lady love has not played him false, if he has one. How could she!"

She drew back from the window just as Marta came to give her a letter that the postman had brought. "It is from Nell!" she said smilingly, and broke it open. "I wonder where the gay young sailor-girl is now!"

It was in a place which could never suffer from drouth, and could only be defined by certain numbers of latitude and longitude.

"Dear Valeria, don't you like to be on board of a ship that rolls her rail nearly under on both sides? That is what the Azorean is trying to do now, and we are all perfectly satisfied. We are becalmed in a fog, or befogged in a calm, as you please. I have just dropped my blue veil overboard, and a porpoise has carried it off. I have no doubt that he has tied it around his tail in a bow-knot, and is now switching it about, to all intents and porpoises the greatest dandy in the briny deep." And so on.

Valeria took her pen, and wrote at the top of a

sheet, " Nelly's Letter;" then began rapidly to write out a story of an imaginary letter, but a real Nelly.

The sketch was half finished when the door-bell rang, there was a sound of voices in the anteroom, a step in the corridor, and some one entered the *sala*, of which the door at her elbow was open. She was too much occupied to think anything except that it must be Marta.

" Well!" said a voice behind her.

She started up, and confronted Miss Cromo, who stood with wide-open eyes in the studio door.

" I can't believe my eyes! What does it mean?" the lady gasped.

" Why don't you ask me how I dare?" said Valeria, rising to meet her visitor, and really pleased to see her.

" How had you the face to come here and stay, and never tell me?" cried Miss Cromo.

" How had you the face to come in when I am not at home?" was the retort.

" You have spoilt my programme," she added, while Miss Cromo stood looking curiously about her. " I meant to have let my card down by a string from the window over your door, and waited for you to take it in. How did you find out? I forbade everybody to tell."

" I know you did; I suspected some mystery. The major-domo protested that he had forgotten your name, and your very pert servant did n't seem to know anything about you."

" My servant obeys my orders," Valeria said tranquilly. " When she ceases to do so, I shall send her away."

Miss Cromo paused a moment, seemed to check a sharp word, then went on. " I told Burton to ask the postman, and he saw a letter that was brought you this morning."

"What a good detective you would make!" was the response. "But you ought not to teach Burton to spy."

"Show me your house!" Miss Cromo said abruptly; then added, "You have behaved very strangely, very strangely, indeed!"

"It is you who are behaving strangely," Valeria replied with decision. "There is not the slightest reason why you should know anything about my affairs. You have your apartment, and I have mine, and we have both an equal right. I do not interfere with you, and you must not interfere with me. I am not a Dr. Kraus, nor a Burton, nor any of those persons whom you can bully. It's a vulgar word, but it suits the circumstances, and describes a vulgar thing."

Miss Cromo reddened violently, and there seemed to be a tightness in her throat. She put her hand up to her bonnet-strings, coughed a little, and made an effort to control herself. Her voice was almost gentle when she spoke after a minute; but she had not controlled the fury of her eyes.

"If you want to throw me away, you can," she said. "You are the most capricious creature I ever saw."

"I am not capricious, and I do not wish to throw you away," Valeria replied calmly. "I want you to stay within your limits as I stay within mine. You are charming when you behave. Now be amiable, and praise my beginning of housekeeping. Of course the rooms are only half furnished to your eyes, though to mine they do very well. I imagine the rest. You know I can afford so little now. Are n't there some lovely spaces to fill up?"

Miss Cromo was still choking with suppressed anger. She did not wish to quarrel with Valeria, and she was eating her humble pie; but it went hard with her. She never liked to lose an acquaintance. You never know when people may be useful to you, was her motto. They were good for *claquers*, if for nothing else.

Valeria went on, giving her time to recover.

" Of course I shall never have the rooms full, and I do not care to. A plain, bare drawing-room with a lady in it is *bien distingué*, as somebody said of the Frenchman who went to a reception without his decorations. I think it will be the next fashion; just as fashionable ladies are going to wrap themselves in sheets, by and by, with nothing but a great single jewel here and there to hold them on."

" I have n't the least peep into the garden," Miss Cromo said, pausing in the study after her tour of the house. " I had half a mind to take this apartment on that account. How did you know about it ? "

Valeria thought best not to divulge Miss Chaplin's part in the affair ; for though her person was out of reach of the "whip-hand," her reputation was not.

" The Prince came out to Palestrina and offered the house to me on his bended knee," she said. " And the Pope advised me to accept."

" Nonsense ! What secret can it be ? "

" It is one of my caprices not to tell. I dote on mysteries."

Miss Cromo was silent.

" Now don't let us quarrel !" Valeria went on impulsively. " Why need we clash ? I wish well to you. Our aims are so different that we might well get along peacefully together, and it would be unpleasant for both if we were not at peace."

" I have the greatest possible willingness to be at peace with you, my dear," Miss Cromo replied sharply. " The difficulty is entirely on your side."

"Valeria laughed lightly. "Oh, you artful little woman, I know what sort of peace you want! It is the lion and the lamb lying down together, the lamb inside the lion."

"You are such a lamb!" the other remarked significantly.

"You are quite right. I am not a lamb, nor even a sheep. Lambs and sheep were made to be fleeced and eaten. Sit down, please."

"You will, of course, receive," Miss Cromo said, seating herself.

"That depends on whether any one comes to see me. I should be glad to have a few visitors. I might, one of these days, give a little breakfast, now and then; but never a dinner nor a reception, though I were worth millions. I would like a small select circle of friends."

Miss Cromo's face showed a momentary poignant mortification. She was aware that her own society was anything but select.

"Mrs. Caruthers told Miss Chaplin that she would come to see me as soon as I should return to town," Valeria went on hastily, perceiving that she had made a mistake. "She is such a person as I would like to know I am told that she is a very high-minded lady." And then she perceived that she had made another mistake; for her companion looked at her with a sudden, sharp interest which was, to her mind, out of proportion with the importance of the announcement. She did not know what thought was behind those sparkling eyes, but it made her uneasy nevertheless.

The thought was simply that Mrs. Caruthers should not make the proposed visit, and that no lady should go near Valeria whom she could keep away, and no friend be faithful to her whom she could alienate. For such a work her many acquaintances, even the humblest, were of use. It meant that her instinctive hatred was growing with every word that Valeria uttered, and that it had caught in that insane drop of blood in her veins which lent fury to her passions. Yet after the first intent, momentary look, she smiled.

"I am so glad, dear," she said. "You will like her very much. You need more society. It is not wholesome for a person to be so much alone, and always in the clouds; though yours is quite an ideal life. You ought to have visitors in the evening, at least."

"I shall have my club in the evenings."

"What club?" demanded Miss Cromo.

"Oh! have n't I told you that I am going to found a club? I have already two members. At first there will be but seven; and then it will be very difficult for any one to gain admittance."

"What is it about? What is it called?"

"You must ask more prettily than that if you expect to be told."

"Now, you darling, don't tease! You know that you mean to tell me all about it."

"It is called the Millennial Club."

"How very odd! Of course I am one of the two members. Or am I to be the third?"

"Neither. We are not going to admit you. It would cease to be millennial if you were a member. Yours is a reign of terror."

"I will terrify you into admitting me. You know I am as sweet as a kitten when I am pleased. You can make me secretary. I write a good clear hand."

"You can't come in."

"I shall be here the very first one. Why do you call it the Millennial Club? What are you going to do?"

"I will never tell you. I will perish first!"

"Tell me instantly what the club is for!"

"We are going to correct the abuses of the world."

"Just what I should like! How do you correct them? I can be vice-president."

"We shall vote a sufficient income to all the poor people, and let the rest be as rich as they please. We shall reward the good, and punish the bad. But we won't have you."

"It is just what is needed. I will be treasurer."

"One of our first acts will be to burn you in effigy. You will not enter the club in any other form."

"Nothing could be nicer. I will be president. And I will bring a little metal monk I have to put the candles out with to exhort my effigy in her last moments. Perhaps I will have him miraculously extinguish the flames. It will be a scene to paint. And now I must go," she added, rising. "I have some things to do; and then I have promised to take Mr. Green to the Arcadia this afternoon."

"So you are reconciled to the Arcadia," Valeria said.

"I was never out with it," Miss Cromo replied, growing sharp again.

"But you did not like it, you know. You told me it was a bore, and you never went."

"I never said so!" declared Miss Cromo, but without looking at Valeria.

"Don't you recollect telling me about the poems that were nothing but words, and the two bishops, one smelling of tobacco, and the other with dirty hands?"

"Oh! I never said it! I never said it!" cried Miss Cromo, and, looking upward, seemed to call heaven to witness to her sincerity.

Valeria regarded her attentively, and recollected what a lady had once said to her of Miss Cromo: "She will lie you right down to your face."

"I am glad you have changed your mind," she said dryly.

Miss Cromo said no more. There had been no resentment in her denial. She merely wished it to be understood that she was going to deny.

"How is Burton?" Valeria asked, as they went toward the door. "I suppose he is helping you to set your house in order. I should be glad to see him if he has ever a minute to spare me."

Burton was a young painter, and Miss Cromo's factotum. She had sometimes been useful to him, and he was far more useful to her. He was her escort, her errand-boy, her agent, her slave, and she led him a dog's life from which he could not escape. Perhaps he did not wish to escape, and had become so accustomed to his bondage that he would have been lost without it; but he had had his moments of rebellion when the rein had been too tightly drawn. On such occasions her complaints had been loud and long to all her friends. Valeria had herself been wearied by them, for she liked Burton, and considered him to be far more a gentleman than Miss Cromo was a lady. He was a good fellow when not influenced by her.

"A perfect boor, my dear," she would say. "I really shall have to turn him off, for I cannot bear any longer his 'grand, gloomy, and peculiar' ways. Mrs. Polo asked me the other day how I could permit him to speak to me so impudently, and said that I ought to exact more respect. But he is a boor, and that is all that you can say of him." Then, if a service were wanted from the young man, who so good as he? Nor was this a mere selfish and ungrateful caprice, which, being understood, could harm no one. For Burton's reputation for manliness had suffered with his well-wishers, who looked on him as rather a poor-spirited fellow, while those who were indifferent to him believed the evil that Miss Cromo said, and paid no attention to her sweeter moods.

The last that Valeria had heard from him in the spring had excited her compassion. "Burton cannot show any more of his airs," Miss Cromo had said to her gleefully. "He is poor now, completely out of money, and I have got him under my thumb."

She had made no comment on the coarseness of feeling which had dictated this speech, and had checked an impulse to remind the speaker of a bitter time when she had herself been poor, and in need of friendly help.

CHAPTER XVIII.

A GOOD-NATURED FELLOW.

TO say that Vittorio was unhappy would be to give no idea of his state of mind. He was simply in torment.

He had loved the Donna Adelaïde with an impassioned worship which she had herself degraded. But, though degraded, it was not dead. He clung to her broken and dishonored image with a passion that was sometimes half hate; for he had nothing else. Such as she was, she was his. Intense, morbid, ideal, he had never held himself to be bound by the code of a social order which his birth had placed him outside of; and he acknowledged no allegiance save that which he paid to nature. In his way he was singularly honorable, more so than many a pretender to moral excellence. He had no little vices nor meannesses, and he had noble virtues. But his one crime he placed on a pedestal, and defended. It was not a crime for him, he thought; since everything that he could desire on earth was so hedged in that he could obtain nothing without stealing it. This might have been an ideal love if she had willed it so. He would have worshipped her as an angel if she had chosen. But she had come down to him, and now she was his, he said. She could never go up to that ideal height again.

She had never tried to, indeed. She had never, even at the first, attempted to play the rôle of an angel, or made any disguise of her own baseness. She took baseness as a matter of course, not being able to imagine anything different. Nothing would have seemed to her more ridiculous than that a man should give her an ideal worship. She would have thought him an idiot.

She had, then, made no pretence of penitence, but had merely become prudent. Her family suspected her, she said. They had put a young man in the garden on purpose to watch her. She dropped all that wild adventurous spirit which had at first made her prepare for and baffle every suspicion. She was afraid. She explained, and sought to conciliate Vittorio. Sometimes she had moments of haughty impatience with him; and then afterward she humbled herself. She was a hypocrite, and he knew it. He knew that she was tired of him, but also that she was afraid of him. What he did not know, what he was wild to know, was if some one else had taken his place. He felt that it must be so, yet could find out nothing. Sometimes he had seemed to be on the point of discovery; then all had dissolved before him like a mist. The same means which she had used to baffle others, she was now using to baffle him. He felt sure of it.

And this young man whom she pretended to believe was set to spy upon her, — Vittorio believed that he was hired by her to guard her against him.

He had known the fellow by sight all his life. Bruno was from the little mountain-town of San Pietro, above Palestrina, and knew no more of gardening than a cat knows.

"Pretend that you are glad to have him here, and want his help, and that will deceive them," she had said to Vittorio.

"Vittorio wants him, though I don't see the need," she said to her family. "Still, as he has a certain sum allowed him to hire what assistance he wants, I suppose he may spend it as he likes. Since you will keep such a strange, assuming fellow, of course you must yield to his caprices."

The truth was, Vittorio did not pay the young man a penny. The mystery was, who did pay him. He certainly did not lack money; and he never did anything of work except when some one of the family was in sight.

"Why should he pretend to work before them if they put him here as a spy?" Vittorio asked.

"Because they want him to deceive you, and he makes them think that he works like that all the time."

It was a tangle; and perhaps if they had all spoken the truth to each other's faces, the matter would have been no clearer; for not one would have believed what any other said. The truth was a fish which they never took from any other person's hook in that *acqua torbida* which composed their social element. They believed what they saw, and nothing more.

The Prince had refused to dismiss Vittorio. "His sulkiness does not trouble me, and he is a good gardener," he said. "He never brings people about, nor asks favors. I believe that he is an honest fellow. Let him keep Bruno, if he likes."

This Bruno was a vulgarly handsome fellow of twenty-two, or thereabouts. He was lazy, pleasure-loving, and unprincipled. He was not vindictive, he was even called good-natured; but it was that good-nature which is not incompatible with any cruelty or crime. In the childish days when he had gone down into the fields to work, he had been a cleverer little thief than the other boys of his age, and had lied with greater dexterity. He had never had any scruples of conscience about it. He did not know what conscience meant. His father and mother, who were good, pious people in their way, lied with an absolute tranquillity, quite as a matter of course, and reckoned how much they could steal from the rich without being guilty of a mortal sin, and never intimated, probably never suspected, that honesty had any positive boundaries. His companions had had a great admiration for him in those days; for he had known how to invent stories and circumstances, and to prepare whole chapters for any *dénouement* which he had fixed upon with a dexterity and forethought which could not have been excelled. He had a great talent for this sort of enterprise.

But he had no talent for labor, nor for study, nor for denying himself anything that he wanted; and his early life had been hateful to him.

A rather unpleasant circumstance had taken him away from that life when he was scarcely fourteen.

We have said that Bruno was good-natured; and the proof of the rule was that once in a great while he got into a terrible fury. It was seldom; but these exceptions were strong enough to make themselves remembered. It was not his fault, he said. People should let him alone. If Gian had n't held his arms, nothing would have happened.

As it was, the unfortunate Gian, who had got Bruno down in a fight, and held him pinioned with one hand while he beat him with the other, had been nearly killed. For Bruno's fingers at least were free, and they had got his knife out, and pricked Gian in the side; and when Gian, feeling that sharp point, had loosened his hold, he had received two furious stabs, and had fallen bathed in blood.

Bruno had had to fly, of course, and had run half-way to Rome, believing that Gian was dead. And he did well to run; for that the boy was not dead would not have saved his life. Those people have quick feelings, and Gian's brothers would not have waited for the slow life to return to that pale face of his before plunging their daggers in little Bruno's palpitating heart.

He reached Rome, and he stayed there, half starving for a while, but after a few weeks finding a place as errand-boy in a house where there appeared to be a great many errands to do. Little by little, he had shown that he could perform sly commissions with uncommon success, and he learned that such talents always found employment. His life suited him admirably now. To follow some person about the city all day, and report everything that he had done, without his knowing that he was watched; or to keep guard over a certain house, and tell who entered it; or to give a *lira* or a cigar to some house-porter, and draw from him all that he knew about the tenants; or to make friends with the servants and find out still more private affairs, — that was to feel himself a person of consequence.

There was a variety of adventure and of unexpected incidents and combinations in this life which kept him continually merry. He did not always know for whom he was working, and he never showed any curiosity. When he did know, he pretended ignorance; and never by word or look hinted at the secret intelligence that really existed, except with his most intimate associates in the same business. The servant-girls were invaluable to him. He knew Marta, who

lived with the American lady in the *casuccia*, and just
how Madama Valeria sat always by the garden window
looking out, and just what she had in her house, and
who visited her, and whom she visited. Yet he never
glanced up at her window, nor seemed aware of her
existence. If he wished to know if she were there,
he went behind the trees and peeped.

"What have they let that apartment for?" the
Countess Belvedere had asked angrily, on seeing a
curtain at the window. "Find out who is there."

This had been said to her maid. The Countess
affected not to know Bruno, and he affected not to
know that he was in her service. He could not have
proved it. If he had made such an assertion, she
would have stared at him with her bold eyes, and
scorned to answer. A gentleman's gentleman had
placed him in the garden, and given him his orders;
and he knew better than to ask any questions. His
own safety depended on his discretion. At a hint of
betrayal, who knew how many would have been against
him?

So when, on giving the maid a detailed account of
Valeria's affairs, Lucia had cast an angry glance at the
window, and said, "I wish that she would go out of
that house!" he understood perfectly well that he was
to make the American lady wish to move away. But
he knew equally well that he must use great caution,
though the lady did not seem to be a person of much
consequence. She went out but little, had few visitors,
and was not rich, certainly. Still, their way was to
act cautiously and circuitously.

She sat all day watching what went on in the garden. Of course she was watching. What else was
she there for? Of course she suspected something;
for there was something to suspect. Of course her
mind was occupied with such things. All the people
he knew occupied their minds with the affairs of

others ; it was his own profession ; what else should she think of ?

And he knew perfectly well what to do. No violence, — oh, no ! Only a bungler would be rude. He knew a man who would hang about and smile impudently in her face whenever she came down her steps. There was another who would follow her home when she went out. There were certain things that he could say or cause to be said to the grocer's men up the street which would make them stare at her whenever she went by, and come out and look after her, and do everything but speak to her. These people could go to her door with strange inquiries and stranger messages.

It was not necessary to do anything great. All that was needed was a series of petty annoyances which would sound like nothings, when told, but which would make her wish to go away. Besides, some means must be used to injure her credit with her friends, so that, if she should tell any tales, they might not be believed. But this belonged to higher circles than his, to people who knew her friends. Still even there he could help. He could tell his employers, or have told to them, any story which they might wish to repeat. But they must give him a hint.   •

It was not the first affair of the kind in which he had. been employed. Why, only the winter before they had smiled and looked and whispered a French lady out of town. Somebody wanted her to go, and go she did. ' Yet if she had described her grievances, no one would have believed that she actually had to go in consequence of them. She was alone, and though she had friends, they were not relatives, and she had no real protection. She could not complain of any one in particular ; for the moment she fixed her eyes threateningly on one whom she had met too often, he disappeared. The next time it was another. In all, it had taken about twenty of them; and they had grinned and whispered and stared her out of Rome. Nobody would believe her. They thought that her imagination deceived her. It was a great help to Bruno and his friends that outside of their happy circle most people were as stupid as idiots about such affairs, and did not wish to inform themselves. They would know that a man was a liar, yet believe all that he said; they would know that he was subtle and intriguing, yet refuse to believe that he would seek to attain his ends by any but the most bungling means. This stupidity was a great help to them.

Then there was that other, a gentleman this time. They had driven him crazy. Bruno almost died of laughter when he thought of it. They began by watching and following him with pretended secrecy, till they had attracted his attention. Then they sent a brigand two or three times to hang about his door, and on the stair. Then they made friends with a waiter in the hotel where he boarded, and had the man drop salt or sugar out of a tiny paper into his soup or wine, so that he had not dared to taste either. They had stared at him fixedly and strangely. At first the man had been astonished, then nervous, then terrified; and after a month or two he had begun to act very strangely; and at last, he had actually become insane. It was great fun.

That the French lady had been truly a lady, and a delicate and refined woman, and that the gentleman had been honorable and cultivated, though not too strong of mind, only made the fun the greater. If they had been dishonest persons, they would have been let alone.

This smiling, good-natured human reptile would have known perfectly well how to apply the torture of the drop by drop of water. He was, indeed, invaluable to his employers, who did not like to descend to

small details. It was enough for them to give their
money, and a hint; and they preferred to give only
such a hint as could be made nothing of in a court of
justice. Not that courts of justice would ever dream
of having anything to do with them, however. They
were too respectable. But it was best to be always
on the safe side. They even gave their money in
a prudent way. "Here are five *lire* for that good
fellow who picked up the cane I dropped this morning.
It is a valuable cane, and I should have been very
sorry to lose it." And perhaps the so-called five *lire*
were five times five, or ten times five, and a sign had
indicated what cane was to be picked up next.

It is always best to be prudent. Prudence is a
great virtue. Does she not hold the mirror to Justice?

Bruno was at Villa Mitella to keep watch on Vittorio, that he did not find out certain affairs which
were none of his business, and to try to persuade him
to go away, to emigrate, to jump into the Tiber, if he
had a fancy to do so, and to make himself generally
useful.

He did not dislike Vittorio. He merely thought
him a fool. He had always thought him a fool.
A fellow who stood apart from everybody, neglecting
advantages which would have given him place and
money, and glowering at fortune, — what was such a
fellow but a fool? If he, Bruno, had had Vittorio's
chance with the Countess Belvedere, he would have
made his fortune by it, and climbed, who knows where?
But the fellow was a fool, and bent on destruction.
Still he wished him no harm, though Vittorio treated
him scornfully. Bruno was good-natured.

Bruno's good-nature was a certain physical quality
combined with indifference. He was self-centred, and
had no outward clinging fibres to tear. Wherever
he was, there was the thing which he loved best, —
himself. Such natures roll as easily as balls. Their

particles all press toward the centre, and wherever they may roll or stop, they are always right side up. Only they do not like to get into a corner.

Bruno always carried a knife. All his fellows did. All the boys in Palestrina had carried them when he was young, and those who were rich enough carried revolvers. The law does not allow men or boys to carry weapons, you say? What of that? What was the law? It had never touched him. Bruno looked upon the law as a very good joke. He laughed at it. All that he feared was *vendetta*, the people's law. Why, he knew plenty of men, yes, and women too, who ought to be hanged, if the law was to be believed; and yet nobody was safer than they. They were more safe than honest people were.

So much for Bruno.

Vittorio, who knew enough about him, was sometimes minded to put him out of the garden. But the thought that he might then have to go himself restrained him. Not to be able to see the woman he loved, to reproach her, to watch her, to be tormented by her, that he could not endure. For him, all outside that garden-wall was a desert, though within all was misery. Still who knew, if he should stay, what sudden, unexpected happiness might start up some day! He was still so young that utter ruin seemed impossible. And who knew, if the happiness should fail him, what sudden vengeance, almost as sweet, might break through all this darkness and uncertainty, and drive them asunder, as the lightning breaks the cloud and lets the sunshine out? He could not believe that he was to have no one drop of sweetness in all his poisoned life. For if Adelaide did not love him now, then she never had loved him, and he had not even a memory.

"I wish she were dead!" he cried out more than once, in his anguish.

The Countess Belvedere had had an eccentric freak this summer, though it was a freak not unknown to ladies of fashion. She had chosen to bury herself in a solitary place to rest her complexion and her hair, and to get a little lustre back to her eyes. So she had said. And she had gone, with only Bruno and her maid, to Nettuno, had taken an apartment in the old Palazzo Doria, and was passing the months of July and August in taking baths, reading novels, and going to bed at Ave Maria.

Vittorio, who had seen no diminution of her beauty, did not believe the story she told, though it was half true. But there was no help for it. He must wait for her to come back. And it was like waiting in flames of fire. What was she doing, and whom did she see? There was a certain person whom he hated, and who was also out of town. Where was he?

He walked the garden studying this problem, and stared into the flowers, as if for an answer. He walked the street, and tossed on his sleepless bed, thinking it over. He paused in his meals, with the food or the glass half raised to his lips, studying over it. His cheeks were burnt away with the inward fire, and all his flesh consumed. People started when they met his large, glowing eyes.

" If she were dead, I could be at rest," he thought. " But never while she lives, never! never!"

The Countess Belvedere was very far from being dead. She was in high life and health. She was learning to swim from some people who came over almost every day from Porto d' Anzio. She lay in bed in the morning until, through tiny cracks in the shutters, the sunlighted ripples of the sea sent in reflections, as into a photographer's camera, and all the dusky painted ceiling seemed to swarm with dancing fireflies. Then she went out and plunged into the warm green water, and swam up to the high rocks, and took the spray they sent back over her. If she was alone, Bruno followed with a boat, and perhaps took her back. But she was seldom alone.

In the evening she leaned in her balcony over the sea, where Olympia Maldacchini had once leaned. For this was her palace; and the black foundations of her ruined baths were there beneath the *loggia*, rippled over by sunny rollers when the tide was high and the weather calm, but wreathed and hidden in angry foam when the scirocco or the ugly south-west wind blew. When the waves rolled in and struck, and tossed their foam up along the walls of this castle by the sea, and even into the *loggia*, then the Countess Belvedere shut herself into her room, and read novels, or she was entertained by visitors. She saw no beauty in a storm or an angry sea. When a tempest of thunder and lightning came, she wrung her hands and prayed. She knew that she deserved to be struck dead. When it cleared away she received her lover.

On white moonlighted nights she went out boating, and sometimes stayed till the east began to quicken with another day. On dark starlit nights she stayed in the house. She hated darkness, and she hated solitude.

Of course she was never alone. Carriages came up from Porto d' Anzio by day, and boats by day or by night A boat could come over that soundless, trackless highway, and land its passengers just under her *loggia*; then a dozen steps round under the dark archway, and they were at her door.

It was all very pleasant as long as the novelty lasted. When that was worn off, she went back to Palazzo Mitella. And then, seeing a white muslin curtain over the window of the *casuccia*, she demanded who was there, with the result which we have seen.

12

CHAPTER XIX.

REJECTED HELP.

THE Countess Belvedere was beginning to be alarmed, and her alarm increased as the weeks passed. Her husband had ceased to accuse her, but he was more than ever watchful. Her father scarcely addressed a word to her, except in the presence of others. Even before the servants he disregarded her. Some of her relatives had fallen into the habit of coming to see her unexpectedly, and of questioning the servants rather awkwardly as to her whereabouts when she was not at home. Apparently people were beginning to fear that they could no longer pretend ignorance of her character.

The winter months passed in a keen and silent battle, full of pleasure and excitement, but full of fear; and with the spring a crisis approached.

Cardinal Meronda, a Spanish prelate of distinguished reputation, was coming to Rome in Easter week, and everything depended on him. Many years before, when he was a young Monsignore, and the Prince, new in his purchased title, was living in Naples, the two had been close friends; and their friendship had never entirely ceased, though their meetings had been few and brief. Monsignor Meronda had passed several years in Naples, and was the godfather of the Donna Adelaïde. It behooved her to stand well with him.

Was it only pressing occupations which had made him delay so long in answering her cordial invitation to make Villa Mitella his home during his stay in Rome, and rendered the letter of reply so much more courteous than friendly? He would first pass a few days in a monastery, and he could not decide upon her invitation till he should be in Rome.

Her father and her husband both looked at her with lowering brows as she read out this ambiguous and chilling reply.

"If he does not come, it will be because he has heard tales of you," the Count exclaimed, and flung angrily out of the room.

"He is such a brute!" she muttered, looking after him, and not daring to glance in her father's face.

"The truth is brutal," he responded gloomily, "and you may yet find it become more so." He rose from the table where they had been lingering after dinner. "See to it that our invitation is accepted, or that we have some reason which will not be suspected. And if these scandals do not cease, remember Cecilia Bari!"

She shivered at the name, for Cecilia Bari had been suddenly snatched by her family out of a too free life, and had disappeared into a seclusion from which she never again emerged; and though she was at this time insane, it was well known that insanity had been the effect, not the cause of her confinement. That was at the South; but the same might happen at Rome.

"What can it mean?" she said to her maid that night. "I have been as careful as possible."

"Bruno says that it is the *Americana*," the girl whispered. "She is always at the window, and she must have told. Marta says that she sits there sometimes in the dark. To-day she saw Bruno talking with Marta, and she looked at him with *certi occhi* —" She laughed. "He told Marta that her signora had taken a fancy to Vittorio, and was jealous of me."

The Countess was too much disturbed to laugh. "It is a good idea to say that," she remarked, "but that is not enough."

It was now mid-Lent, and she set herself to work

without delay. She went to confession and Communion in a much-frequented church, and she committed these sacrileges with such devotion that every
one was edified. Then she began to go to Mass daily ;
and she called upon her most respectable friends, and
interested herself in selling tickets for a raffle for
some impoverished nuns. When Holy Week came,
she spent half of each of the last three days in church,
dressed and veiled in the deepest black. And she ate
fish all the week, and fasted on Good Friday.

On Easter Sunday she again sacrificed to Satan and
Society in a Communion in the morning ; and in the
afternoon she appeared at solemn vespers in a new
dress and bonnet, and a smile of joy for the Resur-
rection.

Her convent education had taught her what senti-
ments were proper to the occasion, and she imitated
them admirably.

The Countess had a suspicion of what was, in fact,
the truth, that she had less to fear from the lady
in the *casuccia* — from any one, indeed, who was not
necessarily connected with her affairs — than from
the zeal of her own assistants. Still, the American
must be got rid of.

She studied over the matter. Miss Pendleton,
whom she knew well, could easily be made to believe
that Valeria should leave the place, and to recommend
her to some other where all she should say would be
known ; and it would be easy to find some one to talk
to Miss Pendleton. For the Countess herself must
seem to know nothing of the matter. There was a
certain Miss Crankey, a gossiping American, who was
known to busy herself very much in other people's
affairs, and to talk a great deal, and with ill-concealed
ill-nature, of the Signora Valeria. This little woman,
excellent but ridiculous, and not a little jealous, had
an ambition to know as many Monsignori as pos-

sible, and to be considered a person of great influence in the church. She was one of the most active in preventing these reverend gentlemen visiting that black sheep, Miss Cromo. Of course, the fact that, had Miss Cromo been orthodox and honest, she would have reduced the Crankey to a nonentity in her own province, could have had no effect. Well, undoubtedly this little woman would not in the least object to have something to tell of the Signora Valeria, and she was sure to tell it to Miss Pendleton. It could easily be arranged. The Countess, through some of her gossips, knew all about these people. And there was a person who occasionally visited the Crankey on purpose to learn all the gossip that she knew, and tell her all that they wanted to have spread about.

Everything succeeded perfectly. The Countess thought that Providence plainly favored her in reward for the pious example she had given. For even though one should be guilty of some little private omissions of duty (she called them *mancanze*), it is always a virtue to set a good example in public.

Cardinal Meronda arrived, and having heard from a friend of the admirable behavior of his goddaughter, took up his abode after a few days in Villa Mitella. An apartment in the south wing was given up to him, a carriage placed at his disposal, and he could order luncheon at whatever hour he pleased for himself and any persons whom he might choose to invite. He was offered a private dinner; but he graciously preferred to dine with the family.

Moreover, after a few days, when all the Catholics of any distinction in Rome had paid their respects to the great man, a grand *papalina* reception was given for him in Villa Mitella. These *papalina* receptions had become a thing of the past, the great Catholic families having hung their harps on the willows on the fall of the temporal power; but they could not refuse to honor this distinguished visitor, whose name was equally illustrious for virtue, learning, and elegance.

Therefore, one evening late in April, Palazzo Mitella "flared like a beacon;" and the streets in front echoed to the carriages that set down their loads at its *portone*, through which a scene of enchantment was visible beyond the entering guests, and the servants in their gay liveries.

For the garden also was lighted, not too brightly, but with a fairy-like sprinkling and clustering of colored lamps, that left here and there a shady walk. One of the pine-trunks in the temple of Undine was wreathed about with tiny gold-colored lamps, and others shone above in the dark boughs; and light was so arranged from unseen lamps about the fountain that the nestling jet arose like molten gold, and fell and scattered like sparks of fire. Nearly all the water was lighted. Only one slender fountain showed white and ghost-like among the roses; and the roses were all in darkness.

"I have never seen anything more beautiful, dear child," the Cardinal said to his goddaughter, when all was ready.

He was exceedingly well pleased with her; for the Countess, intending to make assurance doubly sure, and to consecrate her *festa* as almost a religious ceremony, had again made a Communion in the villa chapel that morning, receiving from the hand of her godfather. The Prince had served the Mass, and all the household had assisted. Even the Count, a late sleeper, had crept in, yawning, when the service was nearly over, and made himself visible at the benediction. "Cursed hypocrite!" he muttered, on seeing his wife go up to the altar steps. But her father, having something of the Cardinal's own sweetness and piety, hoped for her.

She still remained on her knees when the family had retired; and even when the Cardinal had finished his thanksgiving, there she was kneeling with her slender hands folded, and a veil dropped over her face, like the most hidden of vestals. "God bless you!" he murmured, and laid his hand gently on her head in passing. It took a load off his mind, and disposed him to be pleased with everything.

It was rather a stately company that assembled that evening in his honor. Among the chief guests, a dignified grace and scrupulous ceremony learned in courts, or inherited from a courtly ancestry, had become a habit. If the man and the woman of the period were present, and doubtless they were, they were overawed by the chief personages, and laid aside their flippancies and their superciliousness to be used in another presence. In all, there was that repose and harmony which result from perfectly defined positions and differences; and the least was certain of being courteously treated by the greatest.

"After all," whispered an abashed, but admiring stranger to a friend, "such a ceremony is not only noble, but it looks to me more simple, and truly worthy of human beings. When I see how profoundly and gravely they salute each other on being introduced, it reminds me that for two persons to become acquainted may have consequences more serious than a waltz or flirtation."

A great number of clergymen were present, more than one cardinal among them; and there were archbishops and bishops a full score, and half a hundred Monsignori of lesser grades, both young and old. The ladies, especially the married ones, were brilliant. But the loveliest of all was the Marchesa di Mirandola, the bride of a year, whose romantic story was still a topic of conversation. In her robe of white Canton *crêpe*, heavy with embroideries, and white velvet with

pale blue linings, and turquoises and diamonds, she
looked a goddess.   And her husband was worthy of
her; for there was not a handsomer man in Rome than
Don Filippo di Mirandola.

These two were particularly distinguished guests,
for Don Filippo was a nephew of Cardinal Meronda,
and he and Madama Camilla, as the Marchesa was
usually called, were to accompany him on his return
to Spain.

The apartment was a noble one, comprising a long
vista of magnificent chambers, with several smaller
rooms running backward in the wings; and the little
modern furniture which had been introduced, chiefly
chairs, tables, and sofas, was modest in form and color,
however rich in material.   The great cabinets of
carved or inlaid work were hundreds of years old;
the vases and pictures, each a work of art meriting
attentive study, were separated by panels or draperies,
that they might not interfere with each other.   The
ceilings glowed with color, the old tapestries had the
mellowed tints of a misty summer's day, and the velvet curtains had ripened like fruit, such lights slid
along green folds that looked like sunny moss, or
folds of red that took the light like rubies.   Over
all was a soft illumination from hundreds of wax
candles.

There was but little of what is called entertain-
ment.   The Countess Belvedere did not stir from her
place for nearly two hours.   The supper was elegant;
but people went to it when they would.   Then an
improvisatrice who had lately arisen to notice gave a
few recitations.   Otherwise, the guests entertained
themselves.

The elder prelates went away rather early; and
Cardinal Meronda, having walked down the rooms
with one of them, came across a group of young
Monsignori on his return.   They were standing a

little apart, and talking with a mingled earnestness and merriment which attracted his attention.

They immediately became silent as he drew near, looked at him with smiling, expectant faces, and bowed lowly.

" If I had the power," he said pleasantly, " I would give you an obedience to continue your conversation just as though I were not present. I should be sorry to interrupt what seems to be a very interesting conversation."

" A conversation could only become more pleasant when your Eminence condescends to join it," one of the young clergymen replied, and was confirmed by an assenting murmur from his companions.

We were speaking of the new American Cardinal," he continued, " and wondering who will be chosen to carry the *berretta* to him. Half of us are longing to go, and the other half dreading to go."

" The longing I quite understand," the Cardinal replied. " It would be pleasant to visit the New World on an agreeable mission, and have all one's expenses paid. But what can the dread mean ?"

"Oh, the ocean !" exclaimed another. " Fancy all the uncertainties and perils of such a journey, the being out of sight of land for more than ten days, besides the misery of not being in Italy."

" The latter is a misery which the greater part of the world bear with remarkable equanimity," the prelate remarked dryly. " As for the perils, let us try to be men, since nature has denied us the privilege of being women. The ocean is a good monitor. If I had to recall a sceptical and hardened sinner who never crossed the ocean, I would send him on a sea voyage. I am sure it would give him a few solemn thoughts."

" Eminenza," said one of the young men, with soft insinuation, " there are some things in which I am a very hardened sinner; and I am sure that a journey to New York would do me great good."

The Cardinal looked at the speaker, a tall, handsome young man of thirty, with the boyish lightness of twenty; and his smile died away.

" I have no power to send you to New York," he said gently; " but I can procure another ocean voyage for you. How would you like to go to Japan as a missionary ? "

The young priest shrank back.

" It is settled, Don Cesare ! " cried one of the other Monsignori. " When his Eminence makes a promise, you may safely get the frying-pan ready." And they all laughed.

" Pray, what may the frying-pan mean ? " asked the Cardinal.

" His Eminence has but just come to Rome, or he would not ask," said Don Cesare. " Perhaps you may have heard of Mentana, whom we call the laureate ? "

" Certainly ! And I remember that he has written some cantos said to be worthy of Tasso," the Cardinal replied, with an air of serious respect for the person mentioned.

" Well," Don Cesare continued, " he writes little occasional poems on Vatican affairs, and when he reads them the Pope usually makes him some gift. Last month some one in Porto d' Anzio sent to the Vatican a present of a basket of the finest fishes ever seen. Mentana immediately set himself to write a poem on the subject, sitting up half the night to finish it. The next morning, as soon as he could possibly hope to be received, he dressed and set out for the Vatican. ' Get the frying-pan ready, Violante,' he called out to his wife, as he hurried out of the house. He found the Pope with some of the household about him, and read his poem, — a good one, too, they say, — then waited for the biggest fish in the basket to be given him. The Holy Father complimented him on his poem, and presented him with — his benediction. The fishes had already been divided, and sent to the different convents about."

The Cardinal smiled, but he looked thoughtfully at the men before him. He knew what was going on in the world. They, wrapped up in themselves and their environs, and utterly ignorant of the meaning of anything outside of Italy, seemed to fancy that Rome was still imperial, and the world a suburb. They saw people coming to them from all parts of the earth, and did not know that, for more than half of those who remained, Rome was but the dressing-gown and slippers of a weary or indolent life. These men laughed and trifled, and heard nothing of the nineteenth century roaring outside their gates. The one salt wave that had broken in could not convince them. They picked their way through the *débris* it made, and as long as it did not tarnish the buckles on their shoes, shrugged their shoulders, and believed that it was nothing.

But this elder, deeper-hearted man knew, and while they laughed, he trembled. Serious business had brought him to Rome, and such a load of serious thought lay upon his soul that it would have been too much, but that sometimes he felt the arm and shoulder of Christ slip under the burden, and lift its weight with him, and lift him with it, and bear him along in some miraculous hour of heavenly comfort.

"I am sorry for Mentana's disappointment," he said. "But though he missed a fish he found a parable which lasts longer and serves a greater number. Let us profit by it, Monsignori. Let us not count too much upon the loaves and fishes, and let us remember that though our faith is founded upon a rock, our fortunes are not."

He saluted them and passed on, but not to rejoin
the company. Stepping hastily aside, he went down
to a little curtained alcove on the lower floor, a tiny
room quite lined with purple curtains, in the midst of
which hung a small gilt lamp like a star in the twilight. There was no door, but only an arched opening.
Opposite that behind the curtain was a long, open
window looking out into a *loggia* a few steps above the
garden. From this *loggia* a broad stair led to an upper landing outside the windows of the state rooms.
Across the steps leading downward a gate was shut.

All the curtains in the alcove were down, but not a
breath of air stirred them. Cardinal Meronda took a
breviary from his pocket, seated himself under the
lamp, and began to read his office.

The Countess Belvedere, meantime, freed from her
duty of receiving compliments, was going about
among her guests, and allowing them to amuse her.
She was looking triumphant, and very beautiful,
though simply dressed. Her long black velvet dress,
swathing and disclosing her form as her custom was,
had no drapery except a lace scarf tied around just
below the hips. Rich yellow laces shaded her arms
and bosom. A wide necklace of rubies with a dia-
mond medallion and ear-rings were her only jewels,
and she wore only one spot of color. Just above
where the sombre folds of her train swept out on the
floor, was caught an immense bow of red satin, looking as though a butterfly of fire had alighted on her
train for a moment, and would fly away again.

In a side-room a group of young people stood
around a German lady who held a book, and seemed
to be telling each one something from it.

"What! telling fortunes, Baroness!" the hostess
said. "What if the Cardinal should catch you?"

"Such an interesting book, my dear!" cried the
German. "I must borrow it from you. Here one

finds all the influences under which one is born. Here are the pagan divinities, the angels, the demons, the animals, birds, and trees which govern each month of the year. Only tell me in what month of the year you were born, and I will tell you your fortune. October? *Ecco!* you have Pallas; your angel is Barbiel; your demon, Baal; animal, the wolf; bird, the owl; tree, the olive. How delightful! And, dear Lady Camilla, come and have your fortune told. Is it July? Listen. It is a lordly month, and has Cæsar for godfather. Your pagan is Jove; your angel, Berchiel; demon, Belzebub; animal, the stag; bird, the eagle; tree, the oak. It is the royal month."

The Countess escaped. Such things did not interest her. Italians have great moral subtlety, but little or no subtlety of the imagination. She could not understand this Northerner's delight in the mystic. For imagination is a Northern flower.

Lifting a curtain, she stepped out to the *loggia*, and looked into the garden. As she leaned there, a whisper came up to her, cutting the silence like a blade.

" Adelaïde ! "

She turned quickly to the side where the steps went down, and saw Vittorio leaning on the gate below. That part of the garden had no lamps, but a dim, rich light shone out through a purple curtain over his beautiful face.

She glanced about her, then ran hastily down to him. He stretched his hands, caught hers in a strong grasp, and held her.

" My poor Vittorio! " she whispered.

" Why did you invite that Monteforte? " he exclaimed. " I have been up there looking in, and I was tempted to rush in among them all, and tell who I am, and say that I am your lover, in the hope that some one would kill me. But here, Adelaïde, let me die here! " He bowed his head forward on her bosom. "Have you the courage to plunge the dagger in my neck? It does not require much strength. You have kissed me. Do me the only other grace possible: kill me!"

"Hush!" she whispered soothingly. "Some one will hear. You are cruel."

"Nothing hurts you women of the world," he said, raising his head. "You have ways of escaping. But for me there is only one escape. Let my blood flow where my life has died, at your feet. Kiss me once again and strike. I turn my head. You will not? Then, I—"

, "You are mad!" she whispered, arresting his arm. "Let me go now, and I will come out later. When they are gone, I will come."

As his hand relaxed its hold, she snatched her own away, and fled up the stair.

He opened the gate, and seemed about to follow, hesitated, then turned away. She was coming again later.

A burst of brighter light shone over him, a hand swept aside the purple curtain of the alcove window, and a quick step followed him.

Vittorio turned.

"Go on!" said the Cardinal commandingly. "I must see you! If you are not a coward, lead to the light."

Vittorio, without a word, led to the grove of Undine, leaned back against one of the large pine boles, and, folding his arms, waited to be addressed.

The prelate recoiled a little at sight of his face and dress. "Who are you?" he exclaimed.

Vittorio smiled. "I am two men. I am the only son of the late Duke of Monteforte, and I am Vittorio, the gardener."

The Cardinal was confounded. He stared a moment, then his eyes fell. He began to walk slowly to and fro on the dewy turf. The delicate golden lights glimmered on his pale face, on the rustling red silk of his robe, on the little red skull-cap set on his thin gray hair; and when he caught his robe about him away from the dew and his steps, the fairy radiance played with his shoe-buckles, found out the red of his stockings, and lighted another lamp in the diamond-rimmed emerald on his right hand.

At length he paused before Vittorio. " Are you not afraid of what they may do to you?" he asked gently.

" Not in the least!" was the brief reply.

The Cardinal paused an instant to look at him, then walked across the sward, and, coming back, paused again. " Are you not afraid of what may happen to her?" he asked.

" What can they do to her?" demanded Vittorio. " They can only beat her and shut her up. I wish they would!"

" Yet you were pleading like a lover ten minutes ago," the prelate said, looking at him steadily. " Do you not, then, love her?"

" Love her!" repeated Vittorio passionately. " She is too cruel, too false!"

" You hate her, then?" said the other, still regarding him fixedly.

Vittorio caught his breath, and held it a moment. " Hate her!" he said, with a slight faltering of the voice. " I have felt her little hand steal into mine. I have felt her brow with all its braided hair nestle into my neck. To-night, even, she kissed me, and I seem to feel a roseleaf yet on my forehead where her lips were."

" What, then, do you wish for?" pursued the Cardinal quietly.

Vittorio, in his turn, began to walk to and fro. " I ask back my youth and my trust! I ask a motive for living! I have nothing and I am nothing!"

The listener's eyes brightened. A solution of the difficulty had occurred to him the moment he knew who Vittorio was.

" You can be something if you will live for God ! " he said, with earnest haste, taking a step nearer. " Only one life can give harmony and peace to a man in your position. It is not yet too late. I will place you in a monastery where you can study. I am sure that you have talent. And you shall have a career. As you are now, you will always be discontented and violent. Your life will be one of strife and of peril. You will always be hoping for impossible things. But leave all this, give yourself to God, and he will give you peace. I will do all that I can for you."

Vittorio made a decided gesture of denial. " It is too late. If Jesus Christ and his Apostles would come by now, I would follow them to the seaside, the desert, the cross. But a monastery, no." He pointed at the silken robe and the ring. " I would not do it to wear those ! "

A faint blush colored the prelate's cheeks, and tears started to his eyes. " You are rash and unjust," he said. " When you change your mind, come to me, and I will be your friend. And, meantime, remember this, that a chaste and humble heart may beat under a silken robe, and a proud and sinful one under a blouse."

He turned as he spoke, and went back to the house with a swift, light step, entered by the alcove window, and went up to the great drawing-rooms.

The last visitors had just taken leave, and the Prince and his son-in-law were disappearing toward the smoking-room. Only the Countess stood in the farthest chamber, and looked down the long vista where the servants were already extinguishing the candles. One room after another was growing dim before her, when she saw far away the form of Cardinal Meronda coming up' toward the still brilliant chamber where she stood.

"I see that you are not yet sleepy," he said pleasantly, as she went to meet him. "And I am glad of it, for I want to say a few words to you. Will you do me the favor to come to the chapel a moment?"

She gave him a startled glance, and the blood redly bathed her face and neck as she stammered an assent.

He turned, called her to his side with a gesture, and walked past the servants with her, giving them a smiling glance as they bowed before him, and raising his hand to bless one who knelt.

"I have promised Prince Borghese to go out to see them at Frascati to-morrow," he said, loudly enough to be heard by all, "and I shall probably be off while you are still sleeping in the morning."

"Oh, I shall certainly see you before you go!" she exclaimed anxiously.

"I shall not expect to see you." They were now in the corridors, and his words fell with a chill precision. Reaching the chapel, he entered, and left her to follow as she might. It was ominous.

This chapel, built by a cardinal belonging to the family which had formerly owned the villa, was furnished in singularly pure taste. It was like the inside of a golden casket. The walls were lined with gold-colored satin damask, laid plain, without an ornament or a picture. Only over the altar was a St. Joseph. A sanctuary lamp hung high, and threw a soft light through the sacred stillness. Under the lamp was a *prie-dieu*, and beside it a chair.

Both bent their knees before the altar; then the Cardinal seated himself, and the Countess knelt on the *prie-dieu* beside, and a very little behind, him. Her heart was beating thickly.

"I was reading my office in the lower alcove chamber when you met that unfortunate young man in the *loggia*," he said abruptly. " I have been talking with him. What have you to say ? "

She had nothing to say. Terrified and over-whelmed, she dropped her face into her hands, and while he waited, she sobbed.

" I shall go away to-morrow morning," he resumed. "The question is, whether I shall go in silence, or talk first with your father. Have you nothing to say?"

She broke out into entreaties, protestations, and excuses. She hated her husband, she had pitied Vittorio — and — and — she was sorry. She would · never —

" You have promised to see him again to-night," he interrupted. " I forbid you ! "

" Oh, I will obey you in anything ! " she began ; but again he interrupted her, speaking with a sort of passion.

" What can I say to you, Adela ! Only this morning you invited the Lord to enter your heart. You forced him to come, and he could not refuse without performing a miracle. He has placed himself help-less in our hands in the Eucharist — as helpless as he was when an infant on earth — more helpless, since he has no longer a Mary and Joseph to protect him. The helplessness of the Infant Jesus was pitiful ; the helplessness of our Lord in the Divine Sacrament is terrible ! It is an abandonment of love so utter that only damnation is a fit punishment for one who despises and insults it. You believe that his passion ended long ago ? Not so. He is still bound to our stony hearts and scourged by our passions. Every day Judas kisses him anew, and Peter denies him, and the Apostles stand afar off while he is crucified. Every day men and women who call themselves Christians, while their hearts are full of worse than pagan malice, come to the altar and mock him, ' Hail,

King of the Jews!' He was in your heart this morning. Was he as mute there as he was long ago before his accusers, or did he speak ? If he was mute, how dare I speak ? If he spoke in vain, what can I say ?"

He ceased, and she only wept.

" Do you remember your first Communion, Adela ?" he went on more softly. "I went to the convent where you were prepared for it, and said the Mass for you. You were a child then. Oh, you must have been innocent! Can you not recollect that you were happy? And were you happy this morning? Are you so hardened that you could be indifferent ? The Magdalen came weeping before the crowd, and caring nothing for them. She washed his feet with her tears, while they reviled her. The dust on his feet were her jewels. But she was loving. And you — you are false and cruel. Nothing will recall you till you are crushed by some great misfortune. If the guilt of blood is not on you now, it will be. You played with fire when you cast your eyes on this Vittorio. A man of the world has some prudence; but this one has nothing to lose, and he knows no bounds. Only your perfect repentance will save you from him, and him from you."

Still those weak, hysterical sobs. He could not bear them ; for he knew that they only meant grief at having been found out. He rose abruptly.

" I leave you to God," he said. " Never let me see your face again till it is the face of a true penitent. And if ever you should come to me so, Adela, I will receive you with a love and joy that no words can express ; and the sorrowing woman will be dearer and nobler in my eyes than ever was the innocent child."

His voice trembled slightly. He turned hastily away, and left her before the altar.

"That Vittorio!" she muttered when the door had closed, and there was a shudder of passion in her voice. "I could tear his heart out!"

———◆———

CHAPTER XX.

THE BEGINNING OF THE END.

VALERIA'S winter was scarcely a pleasant one, though she rejoiced in having a house of her own. There are troubles against which we cannot bar our doors.

Monsignor Fenelon had been sent by the Pope on a mission which would detain him out of Rome several years, and she was sorry to lose him. Towards spring Monsignor Nestore died.

The occasional conversation of these two men had been a pleasure to her, and their advice and countenance invaluable. Besides, in a society which has, perhaps, a lower tone than any other in the world, it was a privilege to know two persons whose minds dwelt habitually in the *piano nobile* of existence.

She had still another cause of disturbance, and one that involved a mystery which for some time she was not able to fathom.

In one of those days of early spring Miss Pendleton came to see her, and was received with an affectionate welcome. She had seen this lady several times since their first meeting in Casa Passarina, and the slight unfavorable impression made on her at that time had worn off. It could not resist the invariable sweetness and kindly interest which the lady had displayed toward her. With the most of us a good person means one who is good to us.

The object of Miss Pendleton's visit was to persuade Valeria to give up her house, and go to live in
a convent which her visitor would recommend. But
this object was revealed only after a long preparatory
conversation.

To Valeria, as to others, Miss Pendleton was a nun
in all but name, and therefore a privileged person. A
Catholic never looks upon a religious as a stranger.
The first impulse is, not only to pay a particular respect to those who have been in an especial manner devoted to God, but to regard them with an
affectionate confidence. They may enter where others
may not; they may ask questions which are not permitted to an ordinary friend; and confidences are
spontaneously made to them on a short acquaintance
which would scarcely be made to the tried friend of
many years.

Nothing is more sweet and nothing should be more
sacred than such a confidence, both to those who give
and to those who receive it. One who has renounced
those family ties which we fancy will bring happiness, though they as often bring misery, and that
possible freedom of will which might never have had
its way, is consoled when he sees a broader and more
devoted family gather about him, and affection and
confidence spring up wherever he treads. The privileges of people in religion are, in fact, greater than
their renunciations; but that does not lessen the
merit of the sacrifice; for in thus devoting themselves, they renounce not only what they have and
might be sure of, but that which their highest hopes
and imaginations tell them the future might have
brought them. And on the other hand, in our esti-
mate of _religious_, we recognize not only their sacred
profession; we regard with a reverent enthusiasm
that element of Christian heroism which we do not
doubt of finding in their characters. We have ever

before our imagination that sublime hour in which, nailing their quivering souls to the cross in the sight of all, they swore to die to the world, and live thenceforth only in God.

The soul which returns to worldly goods and worldly ways after having been shut into the sepulchre of Christ by such a vow is a moral putrefaction and a minister of death.

Valeria had the most perfect confidence in those who have thus separated themselves from the world. She replied, therefore, simply and fully to the many questions which Miss Pendleton asked about her most private affairs, wondering a little sometimes, but never doubting that they were justified by the most sincere and noble friendship, and the intention of preserving the most inviolable secrecy. Viewed in any other light, the lady's inquisition would have been the height of impudence.

But when the proposal was made for her to leave her house, she protested.

"Why! I have only just taken it," she exclaimed in astonishment. "And I have always wanted and needed a house of my own. Why should I change?"

Miss Pendleton calmly persisted, ignoring arguments and opposition; and she gave no reason for her advice, except that a house must be expensive. But when Valeria showed her account of expenses, and proved that she could nowhere else have what she needed for less, her visitor betrayed clearly that this had been an excuse, and not a motive. Neither did her plea that she might not be able to pursue her writing in a convent have any effect. Her visitor, who was uneducated and unimaginative, believed that where one could knit a stocking one could write a book. She was one of the innumerable company described by Liszt, who "aspire to give laws in provinces to which nature has denied them entrance."

Moreover, it did not seem to matter whether Valeria could write or not.

"If you will do what we wish," Miss Pendleton said, "we will give you any necessary help, if you should ever have need."

The matter had evidently been arranged already; but with whom ? and for what reason ?

The proposal was at once cruel and tempting. That indefinite promise of friendly interest, oversight, and aid was particularly pleasant to one who found the world too rough to be willingly faced alone. But on the other hand, her life had already suffered too much from the misconceptions and impositions of others for her to consent to place herself now unreservedly in the hands of unknown persons that they might do what they would with her. If any reason worthy of a reasonable person had been offered, or any hint of danger given, she would have considered the question, and possibly have yielded; but the consent required of her was a blind one, and for that Miss Pendleton and her unknown company had most certainly come to the wrong person.

When, astonished, distressed, and confused, Valeria begged for time to think over the proposal, her visit or passed from an ever-disproved, yet ever-renewed argument to pleading. She had taken this matter before God, she said, and asked for light upon it; and she believed that her advice was such as should be followed.

Irritated by a persistence which seemed invincible, Valeria could not but think that she was able to pray about her own affairs, and that if Miss Pendleton had been made the medium of an illumination regarding them, she had failed to reflect any light to the person most interested.

Utterly exhausted at length with the combat, she proposed to write to Monsignor Fenelon on the sub-

ject, and abide by his decision, and with this her visitor was forced to be content.

The interview lasted more than two hours.

As soon as Miss Pendleton was gone, Valeria
wrote the promised letter, and sent her servant out
with it.

It was already past noon, and she sat down by the
garden window to quiet her disturbed mind; and, sitting there, she reviewed her mode of life, and tried to
discover if any fault could be found in it.

Every morning she went to Mass, and thus had a
short walk. Besides that, she seldom went out, except when obliged to do so. The morning was spent
in study or writing; in the afternoon she usually saw
one or two visitors. At *Ave Maria* her doors were
closed for the night. "Could any life be more harmless or more guarded?" she asked herself.

That part of the garden directly before her eyes was
completely hidden from the palace by groves of orange-
trees, oleanders, and camellias. Under a clump of
oleanders, at the farther side, stood two persons, the
sight of whom made Valeria start to her feet. Some
rose-bushes nearer by hid half their figures; but there
stood Vittorio and the Countess Belvedere, she leaning
with her clasped hands on his shoulder, talking rapidly
and coaxingly, and caressing him now and then; he,
with his arm around her, gazing searchingly into her
face. It was evidently no new thing. The gardener
showed no sign of surprise, and no flutter of pleasure
or elation. He merely gazed with those searching
eyes that were almost stern. He did not move; but
the lady kept glancing behind her toward the palace,
as if afraid that some one might discover her.

As Valeria gazed, fixed and breathless, the Countess
glanced at the *casuccia*, perceived that they were in
sight of its window, without seeing any one in it, and
hastily drew Vittorio behind the trees at their side.

A moment later she was visible gliding rapidly toward the palace, slipping from tree to tree, and avoiding the windows as she made her way to the rose-garden.

Valeria took breath, and sat down. She felt a little faint. She sat thinking, looking backward through the months she had passed in that house. She recollected the delightful evenings that she had spent in the dark at that window, when often she had seen a shadow slip from tree to tree, as the Countess Belvedere had done just now. She had thought nothing of it. She recollected all that Miss Cromo had told her of this woman, — stories that at the time had made not the least impression upon her, but which now had a new meaning.

It is a terrible moment when first we *know* that there is crime in the world. We have heard of it all our lives; but it was always afar off. Possibly some one was pointed out to us as the sinner; but we could not realize it. Surely no one near enough to touch us was guilty of crime. We carry our ignorance as a lamp that makes a circle of light all about us wherever we go. The shadows are ever beyond. Then suddenly we find hanging close by us the little string which, if pulled, will bring the thunderbolt down.

Valeria sat thinking. "How that woman must want me to go away from here!" she said at last; then started at a sudden thought. "Pshaw! what nonsense!" she added. "But, certainly, the Countess Belvedere cannot like to have me here."

She rang the bell, and sent Marta to ask Miss Cromo if she was too busy to receive her a little while.

The girl returned saying that Miss Cromo would be glad to see her; and Valeria went down.

"I have come to play Saul to your David," she said. "I am out of spirits. Are you in a tuneful mood?"

"I suppose Miss Pendleton has been talking religion to you," Miss Cromo said. "I happened to be

putting down the curtains this forenoon when she
went away, looking the very essence of a little sancti-
monious bore. What has she been catechising you
about ?"

"She has made me hate the interrogative mood,"
Valeria replied. "It would bore us both to repeat
her conversation ; though, after all, she is very good
and kind. She made me tired, that is all. Don't you
dislike to hear a person say the same thing twice ?
Only nightingales and lovers should repeat themselves.
Tautology is a demon. What were those old stories
about demons that were first a lion, then a tiger, then
a serpent, and so on, fighting somebody under all of
those forms ? How confusing it must have been!"

"She is very prying and meddlesome," Miss Cromo
replied with decision. "They say that she questions
people's servant-girls about their family affairs. Miss
Campbell — you know her, she is one of your *nerc* —
told me that Miss Pendleton wanted her to join some
pious association or other that they have over there,
and her confessor told her not to. He said that it was a
gossiping assembly, and that they wanted to know
and direct everybody's affairs. And that, my dear,
was an Italian priest. If you don't believe me, you
can ask Miss Campbell."

"I don't doubt it," Valeria said. Then after a while
she added, "I don't wonder that the Turks call us
'dogs of Christians.' I don't suppose there ever was a
more insincere set of people on earth than professed
Christians. We have n't a virtue in which the pagans
have not excelled us. Compromising, we lose all.
The motto of Christianity should be *in estremo ratio.*
There is no middle course."

"They are all alike," Miss Cromo declared. "It is
all a sham."

"Oh, no !" Valeria replied. "I know so many good
people. But I have always said that the worst enemies

of the church are within the church, and that much of
the hatred and distrust which outsiders feel is perfectly
excusable. There is no country nor sect which would
not honor a true Christian. We need the apostolical
virtues back again, and there is nothing else which
will save society. We need the glorious old courage,
and imprudence, and literal obedience to God. We
need adversity. Christianity is one of those plants
that is fragrant only when it is crushed. — By the
way," she added suddenly, "have you ever been acquainted with the Countess Belvedere ? "

Miss Cromo was in an uncommonly amiable and
truthful mood. " I was introduced to her once at a
friend's house, and talked with her for half an hour ;
and the next day, meeting her, I bowed. She stared
at me, and passed me by."

" I wonder you would bow to such a woman as you
say she is," Valeria remarked.

" My dear, she is the ' very best of bad company ! ' "

" Nevertheless, if I were introduced to her I would
not salute her," Valeria declared. " If she should come
to my door, I would n't allow her to come in."

" Oh, I know that you pretend to despise society ! "
Miss Cromo said. " But I am not so sublime."

" You mistake," was the quick reply. " Although
I agree with Voltaire, that ' Good society is a scattered republic, of which we encounter a member now
and then,' still I was never so silly as to pretend to
despise that which calls itself good society. It is the
guardian of the elegances of life if not of its loftier
verities, of its proprieties if not of its honesties.
Then it makes a fair setting to those human jewels
whose fortune it is to seem, as well as to be, great.
That it does not always recognize or respect rough
diamonds is nothing against it, any more than it is
its fault if it sometimes frames pudding-stone. Cut
you must be in one way or the other. Why, even

the Koh-i-noor was not *chic* till it was cut.   The chief
fault of some people in society is the believing that it
is everybody's Grand Mogul, just as it is their own.
And another fault is that it will pretend to be good,
instead of being content to be only pretty."

"It was never immorality which excluded a person
from society; it was bad style," said Miss Cromo, who
pretended to know all about the matter.

"But don't you think it would be better not to pretend to be so very moral?"

"It would be bad style not to pretend to be moral,"
was the reply.   "If you don't want to hear any lies,
you mustn't ask any questions. Society isn't a father
confessor. All it asks is, 'Are your boots blacked?'
Vulgarity can come in, and vice can come in, and the
devil is welcome; but they must black their boots.
It is *de rigueur.*"

They talked of other things, and presently Valeria
returned to her apartment.

Evening came, and she knew not what to do.   The
serpent had appeared in her paradise, and she could
take no pleasure in looking out there.   Yet she went
into her studio, and seated herself back from the
window.   It was possible to see the sky, at least.

Some one, Vittorio probably, was locking the gate
under her window, and she heard the voice of the
Countess Belvedere's maid talking with him.

"The Countess has gone to the opera," she said.

Ah! then the garden was clear.   Valeria waited
till they had gone away, then took her seat near the
window.   Disturbed and wakeful as she felt, that
quiet hour was more than ever necessary to her.

The window looked toward the north, with glimpses
of east and west, if one leaned out.   There was no
moon, and the stars almost danced with brightness.
There was the North Star with its ever-circling companions.   Dim, and far, yet steadfast, it burned like

a hope of heaven seen through the mists of earth.
How many a time she had seen those northern stars
shining over feathery snow-drifts or glittering snow-
crust, with the cold, pure blood of the Northern Lights
sweeping over them in delicate fleeting blushes!

Now there were roses and ripening oranges down
in the garden dusk under their slowly circling lamps.

She leaned out, and saw the gardener's window
alight and open, a wide arched window framed in
jasmine. In the midst of the light sat Vittorio, reading, his elbows on the table, and his hands buried in
his hair at either side. Behind him in the yellow
wall was a little blue niche with a white Madonna
in it. The lamp was a long brass one with movable
burner, and all three of the wicks were lighted.

"Three lights are an evil sign, Vittorio," said Valeria; "and you are in an evil way, poor boy!"

He looked like an old picture on a gold ground; the
yellow walls and light glowed about him.

She observed after a while that he did not stir, nor
turn a leaf of his book, and that his hands were
pressed behind his ears, not over them. He seemed
to be listening intensely.

There was a slight sound under her window, and
the gate was softly opened. Valeria drew noiselessly
back. There was a faint, rustling step; then a shadow
crept up the stair, and away toward the palace. The
gate was softly closed again.

Leaning out, she saw Vittorio stirring uneasily.
He turned the leaves of the book, pushed his hair
back, and at last rose, and, taking a lanthorn, came
out into the garden, and walked about. He came
and tried the gate. It was locked. All was silent.

Valeria drew back terrified. It was evident that
he was watching for or suspecting some one who
had come in by the gate.

He returned to his house and shut himself in.

Valeria went to her bedroom and locked the door, bidding Marta close the studio window. "And take a light with you," she said.

"If any one should look, they will see that I am not there," she thought.

In a few days Valeria received an answer to her letter to Monsignor Fenelon. He saw no reason why she should not remain where she was.

She gave his letter to Miss Pendleton.

"Very well," the lady said, and made no further opposition. "But if you had gone we should have been ready to do anything for you."

It was her only intimation of displeasure, and her only intimation of diminished friendliness.

It was April now, that heavenly season of Rome when the shade is yet cool, though the sun is hot; the season of wild-flowers, of drives to the Villas Borghese and Pamfili-Doria, and of loiterings in the sunny spaces, or sun-flecked dusky avenues of Villa Medici. Valeria began to feel seriously the restraint which is placed upon the movements of unattended ladies; for, having but few acquaintances, she was often obliged to go out alone. It struck her that it was becoming uncommonly disagreeable for her to do so.

She mentioned the subject to Miss Cromo.

"We cannot help ourselves," was the reply. "I have several times been grossly insulted in the streets here; but I always pretend to know nothing about it. Only last week the Countess Marini was followed the whole length of the Corso, in broad daylight, and treated in such a manner that the attention of everybody was called to her. And she had another lady with her."

"But," Valeria urged, "these are such men as do not notice ladies. They look like well-dressed workingmen. I should guess them to be low fellows who had just drawn a prize in the lottery."

"There is no help for it," Miss Cromo declared.

Valeria sat a moment in troubled silence. "Is there anything odd in my dress?" she asked then, rising to turn herself about before the mirror. "Is there anything that would be likely to attract attention?"

"What should there be, my dear?" Miss Cromo exclaimed. "Your dress and your behavior are both perfectly modest. You are merely suffering an annoyance which none but ugly old women can escape. It isn't worth crying about."

Valeria was not satisfied, but she said no more. It was impossible to put the subject out of her mind; for, without suspecting the meaning of it, she could not rid herself of the impression that there was a hidden meaning. These annoyances were all about her own house, and seemed to be designed as annoyances by persons who knew that they would displease her.

She set herself resolutely to solve the mystery; nor was it difficult to unravel when once the clue was found. For, when she ceased to go out, people came to her door. Scarcely a day passed but Marta came to her with some strange story.

"They ask for the queerest names," the girl said, "and say the strangest things. I am sure they are doing it to be impudent."

Two or three times Valeria sent the girl out to follow those who had been at her door, and she always traced them to the same point. She understood at last. The Countess Belvedere was trying to drive her out of the *casuccia*.

It was a relief to know the truth, though it plunged her into a new sort of perplexity. For while she saw that peace might be purchased by leaving the house, she found herself unable to leave it. She had a lease for several years, and the loss would be a serious one pecuniarily. Besides, she could not, in any case, go

out of town that summer. Miss Pendleton's proposal
crossed her mind, and tempted her a moment; but was
soon rejected. She must not commit herself to a mode
of life which might have still greater discomforts, and
render her work of writing more difficult, if not impossible.

For a moment she thought of complaining to the
Questore, or asking the protection of the American
Consul. But she was unwilling to try either remedy.
It would hardly be possible to make a complaint
without explaining the situation fully, and she was
resolved not to accuse any principal offender, however
she might point out the instruments. She would say
nothing but that which she had herself seen, and
scarcely all of that, indeed.

At length an incident occurred which made her
decide to take advice. Coming in one evening from
a drive, she was met by Marta outside the door.

"That same man, the Signor Conti," the girl whispered, pointing over her shoulder toward the anteroom. "He has been waiting half an hour."

Valeria passed the dim anteroom, where a man
rose at her approach, and, ordering the girl to bring a
lamp and then show her visitor in, entered the *sala*.
She knew what·" that same man" meant. This man
had already been at the house twice within a few
days, asking if she were in, and seeming very curious
to know in what room of the house she might be, and
going abruptly away when told that he might enter.
Both times she had sent Marta to follow him.

She considered rapidly while waiting. There was
a police-station near. Should she send Marta for the
guard, making some excuse for sending her out ? But
that would leave her alone in the house with this
man. Could she herself slip out on some pretext,
and call a policeman ? He would be sure to suspect
her purpose, and escape.

He was shown in. On the former occasion he had been gorgeously dressed, and full of a coarse jollity. Now he looked rather shabby, and had an air of exaggerated humility. He presented a subscription-paper which had not a name written on it. He was a poor man, he said, and wished to take his family back to Turin, from whence he had come to Rome, hoping to find employment. Would she kindly give him a little toward paying his journey?

She reflected while he was speaking that it would be better to pretend to believe him, and let him go. It was not impossible that this visit might be intended as a cover to the two others, which had been too flagrant for the prudence which these people usually showed.

"I can give but little," she said, rejecting the paper he offered.

"If it were only a *soldo!*" he whined. "I have five children, and we have not eaten bread for twenty-four hours."

"You have, then, been making yourself sick on roast turkey!" she thought, glancing over his full-fed form and face.

She gave him a few *soldi*, and he went away breathing benedictions upon her.

Valeria had already made a serious mistake in not putting these people into the hands of the *Questura*. She now committed a still greater mistake. She went down to ask Miss Cromo's advice.

"I am in great trouble about something," she said; "and I want to tell you what I can tell of it, so that you may advise me. I cannot tell all. But first promise me solemnly that you will never mention it to any one. I would not have it come out for the world."

Miss Cromo made the most profuse and solemn promises. She would keep the matter a perfect

14

secret. "It shall be to me as sacred as a confession!"
she declared.

It did not occur to Valeria at the moment that for
a secret to be as sacred as a confession to Miss Cromo
did not imply a very high degree of sacredness. She
took the meaning as she would herself have con-
ceived it.

Her story was told in a few words, all names and
places being suppressed. The only fact she communicated was that certain persons whose doings she had
it in her power to know were trying to drive her away
from the neighborhood.

"It was those people I have already mentioned to
you," she said. "I thought that it meant something.
I do not know what to do. I am tied hand and foot.
I cannot go to another house, and I cannot go into the
country. And of course I have no way of making
such people understand that I really do not wish to
meddle with them, and should have known nothing
if they had not forced me to examine."

"Pretend that you do not know," Miss Cromo said.
"Such people can torment your life out. But how in
the world have you learned this?"

"Please don't ask me to say any more," Valeria replied. "I would rather not. I don't like to speak of
it at all."

"Of course I don't wish to know any more than
you choose to tell me," Miss Cromo said, rather
sharply, and began to speak of other things. But
her visitor soon found that the discourse which followed was a clever hook and line for further revelations.

There is a way of catching a secret by telling a
secret; and it is a very good way, since one confidence naturally draws another. It opens the heart,
being an appeal to the generosity. Moreover, the person so speaking, having given an hostage, is supposed

to be safe.   Emulation is excited, too.   Who likes to
be outdone in story-telling ?

Miss Cromo tried this expedient.   She disclosed
the most piquant secrets regarding her friends, and
showed in the darkest colors several persons supposed
to be respectable.   But the effect was not what she
had hoped for.   It suggested to her listener's mind
that she had just foolishly added a new story to the
lady's repertory of scandal, without herself having
received any benefit ; and, moreover, that the details
which she had not given, and did not mean to give,
would, very likely, be added by her friend's imagination.

Finding her first step ineffectual, Miss Cromo went
still further.   She included some of her own nearest
relatives in the holocaust, and did not leave even her
own dead father's name unblackened.

" Oh, why have I told this story to a woman who
holds nothing sacred ?" Valeria said to herself in
terror.

She evaded the conversation, and rose to go.   "And
pray, don't forget your promise not to mention what I
have told you," she said.   " It would do no good to
either of us."

" Of course I shall never mention it," was the reply.
" But then," Miss Cromo added irritably, " you have
really not told me anything definite."

Another complication had already shown itself in
Valeria's position ; for, in searching out the meaning
of the persecution she suffered, she had learned that
others were employed in the same search.   She had,
in fact, come across one or two men posted by Count
Belvedere to watch the Villa.   This put her between
two fires ; for while Bruno and his company knew
that nothing could save them from exposure if Valeria should choose to communicate with the Count,
the Count himself might suspect that she was in com-

munication with his wife. That she would not have
taken either side in an affair which, on the one hand,
would have given her safety and friends, and, on the
other, would have punished the persons who had annoyed her, she could not hope would even be imagined
by persons whose lives, barren of every noble pleasure
or duty, were passed in an apparent lassitude and
monotony which barely covered the wildest games of
intrigue.

A woman like Miss Cromo would have known perfectly how to meet the difficulty. Unable to change
her residence, she would have complained loudly of
these annoyances, and, while as loudly proclaiming her
ignorance of the meaning of them, would have called
on the authorities for protection. Valeria, whose life
had never made her familiar with any such affairs,
committed the fatal mistake of confiding in women,
and of shrinking from the possible publicity of an
official interference. It did not occur to her that
there is no publicity so great as that to be feared from
the tongues of a few malicious and tattling women.

Looking out into the street the day after her interview with Miss Cromo, she was startled to perceive a
person whom she supposed to be young Mr. Burton,
the portrait-painter, who was unmistakably engaged
in watching the Villa. He walked about with pretended carelessness, smoking a cigar, and observing
everything. Bruno came out of the garden-gate,
passed him by without seeming to be aware of him,
and returned by way of the palace. Tito went out
through the palace, came back by Via Claudia, passed
the new sentinel with the same affectation of unconsciousness, and returned by the gate. But both
had taken the opportunity to fix his image on their
minds.

Valeria hurried down to Miss Cromo, and reproached her with her betrayal.

"I told him to walk about this neighborhood a little, and see what wonderful thing was going on," Miss Cromo said boldly. "But I do not see how he could have come so early. And you say that he was smoking. Burton never smokes in the street; so it cannot be he."

"How could you do such a thing when you promised secrecy!" Valeria exclaimed. "You will get both yourself and me into trouble. And I must tell you now that it is a lady of rank whom you have put a spy upon."

Miss Cromo looked startled. She rang the bell for her servant, and, seating herself, wrote a hasty note, and sent her out with it. "Take this to Burton immediately," she said. "But I am sure that it was not Burton," she repeated to Valeria.

"How could you do such a thing!" was all Valeria's answer.

"Pretend that you do not know!" Miss Cromo said impressively. "If you say a word of this, they will say that you are insane, and shut you up in an asylum."

It was not Burton, as it turned out; but a new agent of the Count Belvedere.

A few days afterward Valeria dismissed her servant Marta, having good reason to do so. She made no explanations, however, merely telling the girl that she no longer needed her services.

"You have done me a harm in sending me away," the girl said in going out the door, "and I will be revenged. I know how to."

It was not a pleasant threat; for however little, theoretically, a servant's word may be worth in Rome, where their dishonesty is proverbial, malice can always use them.

Valeria went to Miss Pendleton, and told her all her troubles, giving the Countess Belvedere's name.

Here, at least, she thought, her confidence was safe.

Miss Pendleton showed less surprise than she expected. A quick smile and a brightening of the eyes showed that some new light had broken into her mind on a subject not clearly understood before. Perhaps she understood better the influence which had induced her to beg Valeria to leave her house.

"The Countess Belvedere never had a good name, even as a girl," she said. "And last year a very excellent French maid who had been living with her a little while came to beg me to find her another place. She was not willing to live with a woman who conducted herself so."

Again Valeria was disappointed of any suggestion of help. It was nothing but gossip with them all.

But at home a pleasant letter awaited her. Her book, sent to America the autumn before, and ever since that time circulating round in a purgatory of critical publishers, till she had got to look upon this temporary state as its final Inferno, had at length been accepted, and would be published at once. It was a little ray of light in so much darkness.

"And now, if I could only escape all these people, and go out of town," she thought, "I should be happy."

CHAPTER XXI.

SOLE IN LEONE.

VITTORIO had watched all to no purpose. He had reproached and begged and threatened, and all to no purpose. There were times when he was tempted to kill himself; not that he wished to die, but from a nervous fury at being so thwarted and baffled. The amused look which he caught sometimes in Bruno's face put him in a passion which it required all his pride to conceal. The smooth evasions with which he was met maddened him.

Violence, he knew, would avail him nothing. He must oppose guile to guile.

He knew, moreover, that his time was short. It was incredible that the Countess would not find some means to have him sent away, without herself seeming to have anything to do with it. He had caught a spark of anger in her eyes more than once, and seen her straighten her neck with an arrogant scorn which did not promise a long patience.

If he were ever to know the truth, then, he must know it soon.

He asked leave to go to Palestrina. He had to see Marco on business, he said, and would stay but one night.

Permission was readily accorded.

" Cannot you come back in the evening of the same day ? " asked the Countess sweetly.

" How can I ? " he replied. " I should not have two hours to stay."

" Then if you stay two days, you can take a commission from me. They say that Maria Magistri has an antique white intaglio of Augustus that they found in one of their vineyards. Tell her that I would like to see it, and that if it should please me, I will buy it. She can give it to you to bring me."

Vittorio started at early dawn, and reached Villa Frattina just before noon. He had not meant to go to the villa; but there were four or five hours on his hands, and he knew not how else to employ them. He did not dare to spend them alone thinking. He knew what he meant to do. There was nothing to study out. He meant to return to Rome, conceal himself in the garden, and see who it was who came in by the gate. He would see his face, and then put him out into the street with a strong hand, and with whatever roughness the moment should dictate. To identify this man was a longing so engrossing that it hid all which should come after.

Marco was eating his dinner when Vittorio arrived at the villa, and the first notice he had of it was Rosa's glad cry. The girl, who came down frequently from the palace during the day to see her father, was serving the table for him when she saw her step-brother through the window.

"Vittorio!" she cried; and, running out, flew down between the green hedges and the gray statues, and flung her arms about his neck.

He kissed her on both cheeks, smiled at her, and went to the house with her hanging on his arm.

Marco had raised himself a moment from his chair to see over the window-ledge, then had resumed his dinner. He greeted his step-son with a serious "*Ben venuto!*" and a grasp of the hand, and, pulling a chair to the table for him, bade Rosa prepare him something to eat. He asked no questions. He and Vittorio understood each other too well to ask questions. Each sympathized too thoroughly with that moody discontent which makes a life of routine intolerable, and an occasional caprice a necessary relief. Routine is pleasing only to dull minds or to contented ones. These caprices in Marco had almost given way to age, and to the sweet influences of Rosa, who was like oil on the troubled waters of his soul; but he more than suspected that Vittorio had found in his new home a greater trouble than he had carried there.

Marco's first feeling of triumph on perceiving the impending relations between his step-son and the Countess Belvedere had arisen from a forgetfulness of the difference between Vittorio's character and his own. In Vittorio's place, he would have made a fortune from such a connection ; would have procured wealth and place by means of it, and would have made the woman's disgrace at last as plain as had been that of Felicità. He had learned his mistake, and he now feared that, instead of conqueror, Vittorio was to be a victim. The poor and obscure are always the victims, he thought. Though they have the axe in their own hands, and the great seem unarmed, the blade will turn in the hand even of him who wields it, and wound where it should have avenged. " We have no help in heaven or in earth," he thought, as he glanced into Vittorio's worn, yet burning face.

" I took a caprice to come here to-day for a change of air ; but I am going back to-night," Vittorio said.

Rosa began to expostulate. Could he not go up and stay at the palace that night ? Chiara had a spare bed. And she wanted him to walk up through the town with her.

" I 'll walk up with you if you go early enough," he said. " But I must go back in the evening train, and it will take me an hour to go over to Valmontone."

" I will go back to Rome with you," Marco said, without looking up ; and since he received no answer, lifted his eyes inquiringly, and saw that Vittorio was hesitating and embarrassed.

" Go and get a bottle of rosolio," he said to Rosa ; and when she was out of the room, added, " Will it put you out if I go ? "

" I did n't mean they should know that I was coming back," Vittorio said in a low voice, his eyes downcast. " I said that I should stay here all night."

Marco's suspicion was instantly confirmed, as was also his wish to go.

" I will keep quiet," he said, "and go wherever you

like. If I should be in the way in the house, I can go somewhere else."

"Come with me if you can be quiet," Vittorio replied.

It occurred to him that once he should know the truth, he might like to have Marco's advice. He had so far gone on in his own way; but this misery of love and jealousy had made him as weak as a woman. Marco was his only friend. On the whole, he would like to have him near. Marco had loved once in his life, and had been betrayed, — for Vittorio knew all his mother's story, — therefore he could understand. But Vittorio never placed Felicità in the same category with the Countess Belvedere. He reverenced the memory of his mother, and still more since he had inherited her fate. To him she was a flower rudely broken by cruel hands. He never remembered her without imagining what he would feel if Rosa were to be so sacrificed.

After dinner was over, Marco lighted his pipe, and, seating himself in the window, with his arms resting on the sill, smoked gloomily, looking out toward the terraces with their low green arabesques of hedges, their soaring oaks and cypresses above, and the laurels that stretched right and left. Gray and mossy stone figures looked down at him, fixed forever in one attitude. He, too, was forever fixed in one position, and could never escape from it except by death.

"And who knows if death may not be another sort of tyranny?" he thought.

Rosa came to him, put her arm around his neck, and kissed his dark face with her fresh lips.

"Good-by, papa! Vittorio is going up with me now. Be sure you come back to-morrow morning. I shall come down just the same."

Vittorio understood that the poor child was almost

as solitary as himself, and that it was a proud delight for her to be escorted by her brother; and he humored her. Hateful as it was to him, he walked up the long, tree-shadowed avenue where all the town came out later for a promenade, and through the piazza, where everybody congregated, and took the most frequented ways, to show that poor little Rosa had some one besides an old woman to think for and protect her.

If he had been less troubled, he might well have been proud to have that pretty creature at his side. Rosa had lengthened her skirts, and discarded her handkerchief for a veil, and in her sweet and simple dignity looked quite the lady. It was evident that she was proud of her companion. Her shining eyes seemed to ask of every one they met if they did not see this beautiful brother of hers. And yet her eyes searched his face wistfully now and then, and tears rose in them more than once, she scarcely knew why. Perhaps she had learned to feel that love is not always joyous. Perhaps she felt some unusual gloom about him, though he had never been gay.

The unspoken pain of others had never oppressed her in the days that were past. She had thought that people cried out when they were hurt, and that gloom and sadness were only a way that some had, even as they had fair or dark hair, and blue eyes or black. But now she was more touched by a sad look than by a spoken sorrow.

" Is your painter up at the palace this summer ? " her brother asked.

" No; but the Signora Maria says that he will come again this winter or next spring."

They walked on awhile in silence; then she said, with a slight effort, " I suppose Madama Valeria has gone somewhere for a *villeggiatura* this summer."

" I don't know," he replied; then, recollecting,

"You mean the American in the *casuccia?* No; I believe she is there now. I hardly ever see her. I have never spoken with her. When you come to Rome I will give you some flowers to carry her."

"I wish I could go to Rome with you to-day!" Rosa said, her voice becoming tremulous.

"You can't go to-day, *carina;* but you shall go soon, this autumn, surely. It is dull for you here. You can stay at Sor Bianca's house. Will that content you? I promise that you shall go."

"Yes," she replied, smiling through her tears." But someway it seems to me as if I could n't wait. Did you ever feel as if you would like to throw whole months behind you, like that?" flinging behind her with a gesture of sudden passion a bunch of half-wilted flowers that she had brought up from the villa.

"Yes!" said Vittorio, looking at her with awakened interest. "Has anybody been annoying you?" he asked after a moment.

"No; but sometimes I get nervous. I think it's the weather."

They had reached the wide-spreading steps that lead up to the palace door. Vittorio released Rosa's hand from his arm, and took it in his, leading her up the steps so. They looked as bright and beautiful and dainty as two birds might who had come up to build their nest in that gray old pile.

At the door they stopped. "I have n't time to go in," Vittorio said, holding still his sister's hand. "Remember, now, you are to come to Rome and stay a month just as soon as the summer and the fever-season are over. And now, *addio!*"

They stood smiling in each other's faces an instant, then leaned together with a mutual embrace and a double kiss.

"Is there anything else you want?" Vittorio asked, half turned to go.

· " Nothing," she replied faintly.

He went down the steps ; and when he had crossed the street, looked back, and saw her still there in the door, looking after him, her head drooping a little to one side.   In all that grayness of carved and piled-up stone, her small bright figure looked like .a flower growing in an old wall.

For a moment the image of her drove every other thought out of his mind.   She was not pale, nor pining, nor, apparently, unhappy ; but where had her . laughter gone ?

Marco and Vittorio started at five o'clock on foot to go to Valmontone.   Instead of taking the road, they plunged into a path that led down among the vines opposite the house.   This was the shorter way. Sometimes they were shut in closely by a green wall hanging thick with unripe bunches of white grapes ; sometimes they passed through a scattered grove of walnut-trees ; and then they plunged into an ocean of yellow wheat that leaned with all its red and blue poppies and bachelor's-buttons half over the narrow path ; and then the way grew rough and rocky, and flowering elder-trees, and dried branches wreathed with large white convolvuli and tangled ivy, half hid with their screen the yawning caverns at the roadside ; and then all that wildness gave place to a gayly blossoming field of lupines, planted for dressing.

" The wheat is good this year," Marco said.   " It gives us twenty for one. , It is a good year for everything."

" When wheat grows, everything grows, — both bitter and sweet," said Vittorio with a slight emphasis.

" Vittorio, what are you going to do ? " asked Marco suddenly, coming beside the young man and touching his arm.

"I only want to find out something," Vittorio replied lightly.

"Don't you know your man?"

"I think I do; but I am not sure."

"And then?" asked Marco in a half whisper.

"Then I shall think it over."

"You mean to take time to think it over?"

"Certainly. When a man catches too hastily at a knife, he may catch it by the blade instead of the handle."

Marco gave a low growl like an angry chained dog.

"We always take the knife by the blade," he said. "It has no handle for us."

They walked on in silence, and reached Valmontone just as the train from Naples was coming in sight. Vittorio did not take their tickets for Rome, but for the last station before arriving at Rome. There they found a carriage waiting that took them to the Porta Maggiore, where they descended.

It was now quite dark; but as they hurried through the lonely ways or the crowded streets, Vittorio did not go straight to his home, nor reach it without stopping many times and looking about him. But at length they were at the door.

"Do you want me to do anything? Speak the word if you do!" Marco whispered, when they had entered the house.

"There is nothing for you to do but go to bed and to sleep."

"Are you sure that there is no danger?"

"Sure."

They took their shoes off at the landing of the stairs. All the doors and windows of the house were open. Marco went softly to an inner room, and threw himself on to the bed, without undressing. He meant only to content Vittorio, not to go to sleep.

But the fatigue of a day's work and a journey, added to the heat, overcame him, and he slept.

Valeria was sitting in her study window when the two men arrived. She had avoided it of late; but it seemed probable that the Countess Belvedere was out of Rome at this season; and, moreover, she was thinking of something else at the time.

The night was magnificently dark, and sparkling with stars, and the flowers in the garden showed phosphorescent lights and flashes here and there. She had been sitting at her window a long time, watching first how a sunset that is golden in the west will look in the north; then seeing how the stars come out, first a doubt, then a hint, then a twinkle, and lastly a lamp. Then she had wondered why there came first a breath of rose, then a sigh of mignonette, then a rush of orange-flower, or a dream of a breath of pansies, then, all at once, a full sigh of them all mingled in inextricable sweetness, and almost too rich to breathe.

Finding the air oppressive, she rose and walked about the house. All the doors and windows were open; and as she reached a window looking out on Via Nera, a close carriage came slowly down Via Claudia, and stopped before reaching the corner.

There was the spurt of a match under the archway near her window, a momentary red light, then silence and darkness again.

"Pah!" she muttered, and went away from the window.

Still walking about, she heard the garden gate open, not so softly as usual; and then there was a moment of silence.

"When a woman of low station misbehaves," remarked Valeria to herself, "she is *demi-monde;* when a woman of rank does the same, she is *le monde et demi,* which makes a world of difference." And then she went back to her own interrupted thoughts: "First, I will write a book which shall be a fragmentary piece cut out of life, like a square of turf you cut, with perhaps no whole weed in it; and people who like a story will be disappointed, because nothing is concluded. And then I will write another, which shall be like a single root pulled up, and all the roots and weeds that naturally cling shall be pulled away; and then the story-readers will say, 'At last here is something complete.' And — " The words and her breath were checked on her lips, and the blood in her veins, by a sound that was neither a word nor a cry, but breaths strongly and sharply drawn and expelled, mingled with a crunching of gravel under struggling feet.

She waited a moment for this strange noise to cease, then ran into the study, half wrapped herself in the curtains, and looked out. In the shadows before her window two darker shadows were struggling, a third precipitated himself upon them, and a fourth rushed in from the gate. All passed in a minute. There did not seem to have been a word uttered.

' Then, as suddenly as it had commenced, the struggle ceased; there was a strange sound, not loud, but more terrible than thunder. It was a gurgling sound of one who is suffocated in his own blood. Then something fell.

There was an instant's pause; then three figures hurried to the gate. One, a man wrapped in a cloak, ran up Via Claudia, entered the carriage standing there, and was driven away; after a moment, the other two came out into the street, walked off in opposite directions, looked about, and came back. These were Bruno, and a man who had sometimes worked in the garden, one Tito, a large black-browed man, with a seamed and wicked face.

Seated in the garden window, with the curtains

almost drawn together before her, and shaking as with an ague in that heat, Valeria fixed her eyes on the shadows and waited. There was not a sound, except one of breathing that came from under the arch, and showed that the two men below were also waiting.

They waited in vain; for there was no stir amid the shadows under the camellias. But after a while a figure came rustling along the flower-beds from the direction of the palace, and Bruno went out to meet it. There was a whispered conversation; then the Countess Belvedere's maid went back to her mistress, and Bruno returned to his post.

The waning moon came up in the east, pale and languid like the ghost of an exhausted passion. It threw a melancholy white light over the tree-tops ; the beams moved downward and blanched the lower shrubs, and slid along the walks, and touched the edges of the heavy shadows. Inch by inch it crept over the grass, and two dark heads were stretched out from under the archway of the gate, and followed its course. There were three pairs of eyes strained to see what would come next. First appeared a daisy, and grasses that looked stiffened ; and then a hand, as white as though it belonged to a marble statue fallen there, lay out, the palm upward.

One of the three who saw it slipped down to her knees. The two men stole forward, lifted the motionless figure, and bore it toward the gardener's house, stepping carefully over the sward.

There was no lamp ; but the moon shone in, and laid a square of whiteness on the floor. They laid him in that ; then Bruno lighted a lamp, and the two men knelt, one at either side of Vittorio, and began to examine him. It was a mere form ; for one glance would have told the tale ; and Bruno knew but too well where he had struck, and how the warm blood had spouted out from the neck he had aimed at.

" Fool ! he would have it ! " he muttered in a trembling voice. " Why did n't he let go ? "

Hearing a slight noise, the two turned their heads, and saw Marco's face gazing out from the darkness of an inner door. His head was stretched out, his body invisible, and his eyes were fixed upon the mute form on the floor.

At the first glimpse of him Bruno started up, with a faint cry of terror, and fled out of the room and through the garden.

" You here, Marco ! I 'm glad of it ! " said Tito, looking steadily into his terrible face. " But it 's a pity you had n't been awake to prevent this. Poor Vittorio has had a fight with somebody."

Marco came slowly forward, and stooped down over the prostrate form.

" I 'm afraid it 's all over," said Tito.

The words were scarcely uttered before Marco was on the track of the fugitive. Their swift steps flew over the garden walks, out through the gate and into the silent street. Bruno, winged with terror, flew he knew not whither; Marco, nerved to the energy of youth by the wild spirit of vengeance, followed the echo of his footsteps in the close-shut walls, and his fleeting shade in the pallid lights.

At a cross street a carriage was just starting from an open door. Bruno threw himself under the step; for he could go no farther. The door closed as Marco came round the corner, and there was no one in sight. He believed that Bruno was lost to him for that time.

He waited a moment, then went back to the villa.

Tito asked no questions as he came in. " It 's a bad thing," he said; " but what 's done is done. I 'd have given a good deal to prevent it. I was outside, and heard the scuffle; and when I reached them, it was too late. But I don't know who it was struck him, on my life I don't ! It was too dark to see."

Marco said nothing.

" It would be best to hush it up," Tito went on. " You see, nothing could be done, and they might say something against Vittorio. He went away, and said he should n't come back till to-morrow; so no one could believe there was a plan to kill him. I thought he was in Palestrina till I saw him on the ground out there."

Still Marco said nothing. He was sitting where he had dropped into a chair on entering, and staring into Vittorio's face.

Tito waited a moment, then found a lanthorn, lighted it, and went out into the garden, saying that he would return presently. He got a spade, and a watering-pot full of water, and went toward the ca-mellias. He took up the stained gravel, and washed the stained grass; he went away and brought fresh gravel, and washed it down with water. He peered about in every direction. When all was done, and he had started to go away, he turned back, and flashed his light up at the window of the *casuccia*. It was open, but the curtains hung straight over it.

Valeria was there out of sight, on her knees. She could not rise. She seemed to have become stiffened into that position.

A few moments afterward a faint light showed across the garden, behind the oranges, where the pas-sion-flowers grew. There was a muffled sound of shovelling earth, which lasted till daylight, and there were steps that went stealthily, and a rustling of the shrubs, as if something were carried past them.

At daylight all was quiet.

Tito came out from the direction of the gardener's house shortly after, and paused beneath Valeria's window again, and stood there a moment looking up with his evil face. Then he went away. And at last the sun came up.

When its first beams touched the tree-tops, Marco's work was done.

"Go and tell the Countess Belvedere to come down here," he said to Tito. It was the first word that he had spoken since he came out.

They stood in the little opening between the orange-screen and the passion-flower draped wall. Two sides of this jutting square of wall were covered with the vines. On the third side Vittorio had prepared the earth to receive other roots. This bed had been newly disturbed.

"Now, Marco, what is the use?" Tito said coaxingly. "The Countess knows nothing about it, and it will upset her. What do you want to do? I've given up to you in everything, and helped you, for peace' sake. The Countess thought a great deal of Vittorio, and this will make her sick. Why can't you let go now? I'm sorry; but there's no help for it. Nothing will help. Nothing can be done. It will be said that Vittorio came back here last night, when he had said that he shouldn't, that he had a quarrel with Bruno, and that Bruno defended himself. If you go to law about it, what good will you get? And what good will you get by talking with the Countess?"

"Go and tell her to come out here!" said Marco.

It was evident that he would not yield.

"You can't imagine that she will come," Tito said. "She will be afraid of you."

Marco took his knife from his belt, and held the handle out to Tito. "It's all the arm I have," he said. "You may keep it till after I have seen her. Don't be afraid; I don't mean to touch her now. I only want to say a word to her. And if she doesn't come, I'll go into the palace and drag her out before them all."

Tito went toward the rose-garden, got behind a tree, where he could be seen only from the *loggia*, and when the maid came out there, beckoned her down.

Ten minutes later, the Countess Belvedere, wrapped in a dressing-gown that was scarcely so white as her face, came out with a hesitating step, and slowly approached the place where Marco awaited her. She was closely followed by her maid and Tito. She paused at some distance. Marco, standing beside the wall, beckoned her.

"Oh, Marco, I am so sorry!" she cried, bursting into tears. "I will have Bruno taken and hanged! I don't know how it happened!"

If Marco had not believed that Vittorio had rushed upon a death that was not premeditated for him, or, at least, not then, he would have torn her in pieces with his hands, in spite of his promise. He cared no more for a promise to those people than he cared for the sands under his feet.

"Come here!" he said.

She glanced behind at her attendants, then drew tremblingly nearer.

"There he lies!" said Marco, pointing to the flower-bed under the wall. "I have wrapped him up in my cloak, and fastened it around him with his own dagger. It was in his belt. He had not drawn it. See to it that he is not disturbed. If his body is n't there when I come, or send for it, I will cut you into a thousand pieces!"   .

"Oh, I will do anything you wish!" she cried in abject terror.

"Get down on your knees and swear it!"

She dropped on her knees in the gravel.

"Not there!" said Marco. "Kneel on the edge of his grave."

She rose, and, though shrinking with terror, did as he commanded her, and held up her hands and swore.

As she finished speaking, Marco bent forward, and spat in her face. "Now get out of my sight!" he said, and turned to Tito. "Give me my knife."

Tito gave up his knife; and the Countess and her maid fled to the palace.

Marco stood one moment looking down on the grave at his feet, then went back to the house. He prepared Vittorio's possessions to be removed, told Tito what to do with them, then went out of the door, and walked away.

CHAPTER XXII.

IN A WHEAT-FIELD.

WHEN Marco had turned backward, believing his chase to be a vain one, Bruno crept out from his place of concealment, and ran in an opposite direction. He could not convince himself that he was no longer followed. He stopped only when he had reached the Palace of St. John Lateran.

There was no person in sight; but he heard a tinkling of little bells from the road that came up from the Roman Forum, and presently there appeared a wine-cart. It came nearer, piled with empty hogsheads that had been exchanged for full ones, and he could see the driver quite alone, nodding in his seat.

Bruno spoke to him.

"Let me go out a piece with you. I want to get away, and I will pay you anything. I will get up behind. Only stop that dog, will you?"

The man said a word to the little white dog that, perched on the top of the hogsheads, was barking furiously, and waited while Bruno crawled in at the back of the cart, and lay down so as to watch the road behind them; then the cart rolled on, and out through the gate.

The cluster of little bells beside the driver's seat tinkled softly; the dog, after barking awhile longer to assert his importance, lay down, put his nose between his paws, and slept with his eyes shut and his ears open.

Bruno lay bathed in perspiration, yet shivering. He began to be sorry for having got into the cart; for the noise of it would prevent his hearing any sound of pursuit; and, if caught thus, he would not be able to extricate himself. He lay on his face, with his head lifted. Now and then he pushed back the hair that fell over his staring eyes. The hand was red to the wrist, and the fingers left red marks across his forehead.

The stones gave place presently to an unpaved road; the houses grew fewer, and disappeared; and the thin mists of the campagna, through which the stars looked like tear-dimmed eyes, wrapped them round.

He lay and watched the road with straining vision for a shape or a sound. His eyes searched the tree-shadows, and fancied that they moved. Sometimes he imagined that some one was beside the cart, and leaning round the corner of it, with an uplifted knife. If Marco found him, he would not merely be killed, he would be cut into a thousand pieces. He had always feared Marco, who was dark and strong and silent.

Moments of intense suffering or of rapt delight give one a faint idea of the mystery of eternity; for time drops out of sight like a bird that is shot on the wing, and there is no motion across the crystalline surface of impassive immensity. The sunshine of heaven is wrapped about us, or we are caught in the toils of everlasting torment, and there is no end."

The white light of early dawn came faintly up against the white light of the waning moon. It was the meeting of two ghosts. They passed through each other, gliding on their ways. A long road stretched itself out, blanching to a chalk-white through the green country, and there was not a person to be seen on it.

A faint hope of escape stole into Bruno's mind, hurting him as it released the tension of his fears, and with that tension the strength and wakefulness which it had upheld. Utter exhaustion fell upon him. He dropped his face down, clasped his hands up over the top of his head, with a last confused instinct of hiding himself, and sank into a trance that was half sleep and half a swoon.

He was awakened by a chorus of birds. He tried to move, and could not. Then, opening his eyes, and lifting his head a little, he looked out on a dewy, sun-swept landscape rejoicing in all the gladness of a summer morning in the country. The sickening sense of his condition returned upon him, and he was about thrusting his head out farther to find, if possible, where he was, when he heard voices talking. Quickly resuming his former position, he listened.

It was a fresh, girlish voice that spoke, with laughter between the words; and the rough voice of an old woman answered. They were quite near, and the driver of the cart exchanged a salutation with them. They must have almost passed by, when the girl spoke again.

"See, Chiara! there is a man asleep under the hogsheads. And, see! one of his hands is all red."

The bitterness of death swept over Bruno's soul. He seemed to be floating on a great tide that tossed him to and fro, and stifled him.

Gasping for breath, he lifted his face after a minute, and looked out.

Rosa and Chiara were at some distance, just entering the gates of Villa Frattina. He had believed that he was going toward Albano; and instead of that, he had gone into the very jaws of the lion !

All the frenzy of his first flight possessed him again. Extricating himself from his hiding-place, he dropped out into the road, tossed his purse to the driver, and plunged into the path which Marco and Vittorio had taken the day before. At first he ran, then he advanced more warily, avoiding the cabins of the guardians, and making for a wooded ravine not far distant. He had reached it, and was about letting himself down the rocks, when he came face to face with an old woman. She stared at him, uttered a faint scream, and dropped a bundle of green herbs she had in her apron.

Bruno turned from her without a sound, and fled in another direction. He knew presently that he was not far from the highway, but it was impossible to turn back. A great wheat-field was near, and he slipped into it.

This field was a sea of splendid, rolling gold, sprinkled through with scarlet poppies, and it soared far over him as he crawled carefully in till he could see nothing on all sides but the myriad slender stems of the ripe grain. Then he sank down and listened, panting, and yet trying to hush his heavy breaths.

He crouched on the ground till his limbs felt cramped; then he sat. The sun ran over the wheat-heads, rose higher, and a dazzling rain began to sift through the stems. Bruno's heart was thumping hard and high in his breast, and his thoughts started out like sparks from an anvil. Marco would come back to Palestrina; Rosa would know, and would tell of the man with the red hands hidden among the

wine-hogsheads; they would find the driver, would
learn the path he had taken, would question the old
woman he had met, and — there they were now!

There was a sound of men's voices, but they were
quiet and far away, and some one was singing a
vintage-song. Not yet!

He lay down, stretched at length, to feel the coolness of the earth, and be out of the sun for a little
while longer. Ah! why had he left Rome? There
was safety, a thousand hiding-places, and friends at
hand who were bound to protect him. He saw now
what a fatal error his fright had led him into, and he
knew not how to remedy it, even if he could have escaped into some other town. Why had he not run into
the palace itself and claimed protection? He had his
story all ready to tell. They were always prepared,
and no event could be unforeseen to them. He was
prepared, then, "in case any accident should happen
to Vittorio," or certain others. Of course, it meant
that Vittorio or one of those certain others might
attack him, and force him to defend himself.

How red the poppies were! How horribly they
sprinkled, drop by drop, all the ground about! And
his hands — he tried to wipe them; but Dives himself could not have found a drop of water here, and
the stains would cling. And presently there was a
sound, faint and thin, no sound of voice or step of
man or song of bird, but most like a faint intermittent whistling of wind in the rigging of a ship at sea,
when the spirits of the air go before a tempest. It was
sharp and thin, and it came from right and left and
from before him. They were reaping the grain toward
him from every side.

Bruno raised himself on his hands and knees, and
gazed about; but saw nothing. The field was large,
and they were yet far away. There were five sickles.
He could count them in the sultry silence, and they

were in a semicircle about him. At the other side was a path, and open spaces, with probably no nook to hide in.

The sun went up and hung in the meridian, and the reapers stopped; and still he had not seen them. Could they reap all the afternoon and not reach him? He stayed there on his hands and knees, like a beast, and waited. The sun slanted toward the west a little, blazing down with its long rays. The reapers began again, and he crawled inch by inch away from the sound of them. How he hated the daylight with all its blinding red and gold! His head was swimming with the heat, and with hunger and thirst too; but he did not think of that. He could hear the severed handfuls of wheat drop on the pile, and fancied that he could see dark blotches of human forms through the yellow wilderness.

"O God!" he muttered, and crawled away, carefully parting the wheat-stalks, that they might not see the tops move as they came steadily toward him with their five crooked blades. Who knew but that it was Marco's revenge that they should hem him in so, step by step, till they should reach and kill him with their sickles, that he could hear whispering and hissing nearer every moment?

The sun declined, and changed from gold to orange and from orange to red. He could hear distinctly now each cut of the blades, each drop of the handfuls of grain, and now and then a word or a cough; and the figures of the men were seen in glimpses. As he crawled on, the sweat of his torment fell upon the ground.

And by and by other dark shapes, showing through the wheat before him, terrified him anew, till he knew that they were tree-supported grape-vines that ran along beside the path.

The crimson of the sunlight deepened; soft shadows

rose from the ground, pushed the red off the wheat-
tops, and faded into the air.

And now Bruno could see the forms of his pursuers,
and the glistening of the steel, quick and curved.
He crawled to the tree directly before him, peeped
out, and saw that the land was nearly open at the
opposite side of the path, and that there was a cabin
not far away.

He was longing to look out, to see the path, to
look up to Palestrina, which he knew would be just
above him, and to see how far he was from the highway; but he dared not. The vines did not grow
thickly enough; the wheat was golden, the light was
rosy, and his head was so black, so black! And how
did he know but a knife was waiting for it to be
thrust out?

He crept close to the tree, and looked at the vine
full of unripe grapes. They cast a merciful shadow
over him. All day long he had fled before the reapers, — how horrible it was, like a nightmare, to fly,on
one's knees!—and this was the first touch of mercy
that he had felt. It had been all burning red and
yellow.

At the other side of the path were vine-laden trees
thinly set, and a small wheat-field that had all been
reaped. An old woman was going about, gathering
up the scattered stalks, and laying them on a yellow
wall of wheat that stretched along the field.

It was the woman he had met in the morning.

He watched her, wondering if she would betray
him. She must know that he was somewhere in
the neighborhood. He looked at the cabin door, and
fancied that he saw some one inside. Then he turned
his head backward, and listened. There was no sound.
The reapers had ceased their labors.

Then he laid his cheek to the earth, where the
weeds would cover his head, pushed it out toward

the path, and looked up to Palestrina. Nearly all
the city was in a clear pale light, only the higher
points being still red. There was a movement along
the road of men and women and animals going up
to the town after their day's work, as they used to do
when he was a boy. On the mountain-top the hamlet
of San Pietro blazed out like a beacon.

As he looked, voices came up the path. He drew
quickly back, and peeped out at a party that sauntered
by. There were the reapers, with their scythes on
their arms, and with them two girls who had been
washing clothes at a fountain farther down in the
plain. The girls carried large baskets of clean linen on
their heads, poised lightly, without touching a hand
to them; and they laughed and jested, and stepped
out of the path to break off the fresh vine-tendrils
and eat them. One pulled at the vine that a minute
before had been over his head. He felt as if she had
caught at his heart-strings and given them a pull.
They passed on, and went out into the highway by
San Rocco; and he was alone.

"*Maria Santissima!*" he whispered, and began to
cry with his face against the brown earth. He sobbed
bitterly, and felt deserted, and remembered what a
host of boon companions he had had but a few days before. His hands shrank away from the slippery poppy
flowers, with their warm petals, and the horrible feel
of the little urn in the centre. He wished that he
had let Vittorio alone. After all, he only wanted to
uncover the man's face, and see who he was; and
what harm if he had seen?

He heard a step, and again fear came uppermost;
and he raised his head, and looked stealthily out. It
was the old woman of the cabin, and she came down
between the two rows of vines from her door to the
path. She held something in one hand with her
apron thrown over it; she looked neither to right nor

left, but upward; and her lips were moving, and tears dropped down her face. She was but a common old woman in a faded skirt, and patched corsets, and a cotton neckerchief, with gold rings in her ears, and a silver dagger stuck through her gray hair, but she reminded him of a picture he had seen on the wall of some church, he had forgotten where. He had never thought of the picture since the moment when his careless eyes glanced over it; but now he seemed to see it again, not lacking the nimbus.

The cool dark vines and the yellow stubble were lifted behind her; and as she came nearer, he could hear the words that trembled over her lips. She was praying in the words of the *Salve Regina,* "To thee we cry, poor banished children of Eve. To thee we lift up our sighs, mourning and weeping in this valley of tears;" and her tears dropped down.

She reached the tree behind which he was hidden, and with her eyes still uplifted, and her lips still moving, hastily drew her apron from what she held, set something down under the tree, and pushed it into the screening vine-leaves. Then she rose quickly and went back toward the cabin.

A rude, dark man came to the door and called her. She answered, stopped an instant in the stubble, picked up a few wheat-stalks, furtively wiped her eyes, and went in.

When she had disappeared, Bruno looked among the weeds, and found there, folded in a large grape-leaf, two slices of gray wheaten bread spread with a *ricotta* of goat's milk, and in another leaf a little flask of white wine. Only then he knew that he was fainting with hunger and thirst.

He made the sign of the cross with his red right hand, and ate and drank. It was the saint of the fresco who had fed him, he thought. He could not know that all day long she had watched his progress by the moving wheat-heads, and that she had given him her own supper, and would go hungry that night. He ate and drank, and did not inquire how she had known, sure now that she would not tell. Then he sat without thinking, his mind as dim as the twilight air about him; till again his heart swelled suddenly, something rose in his throat, and he wept outright, with his face to the earth.

The sound of the Ave Maria bells came down from the town, all their voices at once, with a faint tinkle from the mountain-top, floating like a bubble over all. Mingling with these bells he heard a man's whistling. It seemed to be some one coming down from San Rocco, slowly sauntering, and whistling fitfully.

With his first start of renewed terror came a something of surprise and attention that did not dare to be hope, but was a piercing doubt. There was something peculiar in this whistling. It was like the call of a bird, followed by a little strain that spoke of safety, not fully played, but in fragments, with short silences. It told of safety, while enjoining caution.

Bruno crept forward, and peeped out.

A man stood farther up in the path, gazing at the vines and trees, as if he were a stranger, his hands in his pockets; and as Bruno looked out, he whistled again, and glanced about with seeming carelessness.

The fugitive's heart gave a bound. He half rose, and, still stooping, ran through the wheat till he came opposite the spot where his comrade stood, gazing in another direction, but with his head intent on the rustling of the grain behind him.

Bruno whistled softly. It was like the distressed chirping of a little bird, so well imitated that one might have believed that a nest had been disturbed, or that the mother-bird had had a dream of cats and serpents, and had wakened with that little cry.

The man in the path, without looking his way, drew nearer to the spot whence the sounds proceeded, and stood, still with his back to it, looking up into a tree.

"For God's sake, get me out of this!" whispered Bruno. "Is anybody watching?"

"Not that I know of. Follow me, but keep out of sight all you can. If I cough, stop."

So saying, he sauntered up the path to the gate, Bruno following in the wheat till it ceased, then gliding from tree to tree. At the gate his leader paused. There was no person in sight.

A little open city carriage that had been waiting farther along the road came slowly by. There was a woman in it. It did not stop; but the two men ran out and got into it while it was in motion.

For a while nothing was said. They passed San Rocco, and the wine-shop opposite, and took the road to Rome. Then the woman put her hand on Bruno's arm, and said, "What a fool you were to run away! Don't you know that you are always safe with us?"

"Marco was after me," he said, shaking. "Where is he now?"

"He started off to Albano. He did n't seem to know where he was going. Some people said that they thought he was crazy. I should n't wonder if he would kill himself. He was always a gloomy fellow."

"Is — is all out of sight?" Bruno asked.

"Everything is arranged," said the other. "We convinced Marco that it was better to let the matter drop. He could do nothing, and he knew it. He will study over it, and he may lose his head, and say something; but you are safe. Say that the fellow attacked you, and that you defended yourself. You were sorry; and while you were trying to revive Vittorio, Marco appeared, and you ran. That is all you know. But nobody will ever ask you."

Bruno breathed freer. He had certainly been a great fool to run out of the city. Slowly, like water filtering into an empty reservoir, courage came back to his heart. Life grew secure, then bright, and his crime excusable.

To-morrow he would smile, the day after he would laugh, and in a week his nerves would have regained their tone. Another time he would show more prudence, and would depend more on his friends.

Moreover, his friends could now depend more securely on him, for he was in their power.

———◆———

CHAPTER XXIII.

ON THE SEA.

MARCO had gone to Albano, as Bruno's friend informed him, and he had gone unconsciously, or nearly so. He was, in fact, so sunk in gloomy perplexity and silent, bitter grief, as to have no consciousness of any present save the terrible event of the past night. With a sort of instinct of returning home, he had gone to the station; but he could not be aware that the habit to which he resigned himself for guidance was not the habit of later years. As in old age, delirium, or death, the soul sometimes strips itself of later years, as of a garment, and goes wandering back amid the scenes of its childhood, so he, convulsed by a more ruinous blow than any which had yet fallen upon him, gave himself up to a habit of his early youth. He was a native of Nettuno, and had been gardener first in the Villa Borghese by the sea; and to Nettuno he bent his way when he thought to

16

go home. If he had been a younger man, or a less
clear-sighted one, he would have been frenzied by
what had happened. As it was, he was paralyzed.

His head hanging forward, his face haggard and
vacant, he had gone to the ticket-office because the
others went, without looking to see what train was
advertised; and when the man at the window asked
him if he wanted third-class, he answered yes. He
would have answered the same if he had been offered
first-class. He looked out the car-window as they
rolled over the campagna, but saw nothing; or rather
he saw only the scenes of the past night. To the
present scenes his eyes were sightless. If some faint
sense of familiarity was touched, it only helped him
to go on.

Leaving the station at Albano, he took the old
familiar western road to the sea. A cart came along
presently, and he accepted the driver's invitation to
ride. He rode almost to Porto d'Anzio. The driver
thought that he was sleepy, and after the first few
minutes did not urge him to talk. Marco shut his
eyes, dropped his head, and let his mind wander
about. It wandered calmly enough, for its passions
were benumbed. It reasoned clearly enough, too, and
told him that he could do nothing. Of course he
could kill Bruno, and meant to the first time they
met; or that he chose to seek the fellow. That was a
matter of course, and a trifle. But how could he
reach the power behind Bruno, and for whom that
insignificant fellow acted? He had an impulse in
the night, and again in the early morning, to rush
into the palace, and kill all that he met there, — not
the servants, but the family. But what would he
have gained? They would have killed him perhaps,
before he had succeeded in doing anything; and his
class and his cause would have been the worse for
his violence. If he could have died at the head of

a conquering army doing bâttle for the poor, then he would have gone to death with all the fire of youth; but he had learned how ruinous to the principle he would serve are all these ineffectual outbreaks. They were worse than useless. Either be strong enough to overset all, or do not move.

The cart stopped.

" Are you going to Porto d'Anzio ? " the driver asked.

Marco opened his eyes and knew where he was.

He answered in the affirmative as he got down from the cart. The man offered him some bread and wine. He accepted them, gave the driver some money, and went forward on foot. He was glad that he was not going to Villa Frattina, or to meet any one whom he knew. He wanted to be alone and silent while his mind was wandering in this laby- rinth.

It was now afternoon, and the slanting sun-rays were deepening in hue. He struck into a shady ave- nue, and, avoiding Anzio, went toward Nettuno, with- out knowing what he should do there. The avenue was long and still. He met a carriage or two, but no foot-passengers. All the town was in the piazza where the band was playing. He stopped a moment, and seemed to listen to the music, then went onward to the road that runs along the seaside, where the town ends, and Nature resumes her empire.

Marco went down to the wide flat beach outside the town. His manhood was up in arms, all engaged in a moral struggle; and his childhood, rising like a flower that the tempest has swept the dry leaves away from, lured him into the old, childish path; as when he went down there, long ago after a storm, to gather shells that the sea had left, or bits of precious marble, or tiny crabs.

The sea was of a bright blue, all sparkling with

ripples, and came in in long rollers of shifting hues and shadows, and broke softly in a narrow fringe of foam on the beach, or tossed and caught prismatic colors against the high rocks farther along, where the shore makes its long, fading curve toward the far-off promontory of the Siren.

There was a boat near by coming toward him, propelled by short strokes; and there were two men in it. They pushed up on the beach; and while one held the boat in its place with his oar, the other stepped out into the shallow water, and shouldered a fishing net. There were bright fishes glittering in the sunlight at the bottom of the net, which swung to and fro as they leaped. The sun showed only a spark on the horizon, but a faint blush lay on the sea.

Marco went down to the water as he saw the man in the boat putting off again, when his companion had gone away across the road, and asked for his boat for an hour.

The man stopped rowing, but looked at him doubtfully.

"I will pay you in advance," Marco said, "and leave a security in your hands. In an hour or two I will come back here with the boat. I only want a row."

The man looked at the money offered him, and came back. He took his net with the fishes in it on his shoulder, as the other had done, and went homeward on foot, telling Marco where his house was on the shore, half-way to Anzio, and asking him to leave the boat there when he was done with it.

Marco nodded and rowed himself away from the shore.

The fishing-boats were going out from Porto d'Anzio, each with its two pointed sails spread, looking like a flock of gray moths hovering over the water.

Sóft in the soft air, they skimmed lightly out to drag
their nets all night under the stars, and come back at
dawn with their glittering freight. The light-house
shone like a red-gold star in the west; and far out to
the eastward, at the other horn of the sea-crescent,
the promontory of the Siren floated in a violet mist.
It was like a woman cast down on her face, her limbs
outstretched, the whole outline tapering to the ankle
and foot. Her arms were folded under her face, her
dishevelled hair fell over them, her head was toward
the sea. The figure lay as the deserted Ariadne
might have fallen when she had seen her traitorous
lover's sail go down below the horizon.

Marco glanced over it all as unmoved as a mirror
which reflects indifferently whatever passes before it;
more unmoved, indeed, for he did not even brighten
outwardly. He darkened instead in the midst of this
scene, so full of peaceful splendor. The rough roads,
the rattling train, the dark, brigand-haunted, malaria-
poisoned forest he had passed through had been
fitted to his mood; but this clear light and serene joy,
on which his fate stood out black and distorted,
stirred the sleeping fury in him.

He began to row hard, straining at the oars, and
muttering. All his baffled hopes and hates and
loves, all his imprisoned and despairing aspirations,
all the rage which years of self-control had kept mute
within him, biding its time, began to gather and rock
to and fro in his soul as the water rocked under his
boat-keel.

It had never occurred to Marco to appeal to the
law. He despised it as much as Bruno did, though
from a different cause. He well knew that the law
would never punish the great for a crime against the
small. He had never looked for justice, save from
Garibaldi, or from his own strong hand. The law
meant to him nothing but a cunning labyrinth by

which the powerful escape the punishment of their
crimes, and in which the weak are hopelessly lost.
There was no help anywhere. " They destroy everything beautiful ; Felicità, Italia, Vittorio — "

He raised an oar and struck at the smiling, dim-
pling sea, as if it were a face that mocked him, —
struck with a fury that nearly overset his boat. A cry
like the roar of a lion broke from his lips, and rolled
across the water.

Why had he not killed that woman when she was
in his power, and so struck one blow, if but a futile
one ? Why had he let those people pass him, day
after day, in their insolent prosperity, and go un-
harmed ?

He leaned and clutched at the waters, and they
escaped his grasp ; he shouted his curses, and shook
his clenched hands backward to the shore; foam fell
from his lips.

He was killing himself, just as Felicità's father had
done long ago ; and he knew it, and did not care.

And meanwhile the long twilight had faded, and
it was deep night. The lighthouse burned steadily
in the dark west, the stars burned tremulously in
the dark sky, and faint firefly lights showed where the
fleet of fishers hung over the live treasures of the
deep.

And then a soft, ineffable splendor shone around
the eastern mountains, but so faintly that the Milky
Way lay unblenched before it. It was as though the
melancholy spirit of darkness had looked out from
under her dusky eyelids, now that all the world was
asleep. Scarcely parting the heavy shadows, she came,
holding aloft the pallid crescent of the dying moon for
a lamp. A flickering path of silver ran across the
peaceful waters, and crossed a flickering golden path
that stretched from a southern star. A whiter whiteness shone in the face of Marco Bandini, lying in-

sensible in the bottom of the boat that idly tossed upon the water. The hours wore on, and the light breeze that precedes the day began to give its delicate touches here and there. The east whitened, and then warmed with ruddy gold.

Marco opened his eyes, raised himself painfully, and looked about, and remembered all. He looked at the water, and wondered if he should throw himself into it, and so end all. He looked off to the dim sea-line beyond the Sirens, and wondered if he would row toward that, and take his chance of meeting a ship which would bear him to some other country. He could never go back to this accursed shore.

There was a small cloud over the east that was a bright pink with the sunrise. It hung there in a motionless ecstasy with the coming day. The water reflected it, and seemed to kiss it, dyeing its little ripples red with the touch. Its image passed unheeded over Marco's wandering eyes, then presently touched some chord that gave a faint dream of a sound. He did not heed it; but the sweet murmur continued till he looked up at the cloud, with just a cold idle thought that it was as red as a rose.

Rosa!

"Little Rosa!" The words came in a hoarse whisper, and all his strained soul melted as he uttered them. Where was she? What would she do without him!

He took up his oars, and rowed backward to the shore, and tears rose to his eyes, and dropped down, one by one. He sobbed now and then, a sob as pitiful as that of a lost child that is tired of weeping, yet cannot help but sob. Poor little Rosa! He would not leave her to weep. If he was good for nothing to himself, he was good for her. It was because she was hidden unseen in his heart that he had not died that night, he thought.

He looked at the palace on the shore, at the trees behind, the long beach, and the solitary sanctuary of the Madonna set close to the water; and scenes of his childhood came back to him. The water had not been so high when he was a boy, and a wide beach ran round outside the palace walls where now a barrier of stone-work had been built to preserve the foundations from the gnawing waves. In those days the procession that carried the image of the Madonna on her festa had walked quite round the beach where now the waves rolled perpetually. He was one of a choir of boys who sang as they walked, and he wore a little white *cotta* ironed into herring-bone stripes. The gray beach was gay with color; for the peasant-women wore their scarlet robes with gold-embroidered sashes fringed with little silver or gold bells, — a dress fit for a princess, and brighter even than Monsignor the Bishop's cope of gold cloth. He remembered the keen Arab faces of these women; he remembered how the little shells crunched under his feet as he walked singing before the Madonna, and how the sea came up the shore and sang with them, and was never out of time or tune, and how the men out in the boats took off their hats as the procession passed along to the sanctuary. He remembered how his eyes had roved about the smooth, firm sand in search of what the tide had left, fragments of many-colored Egyptian marble, bits of red porphyry, dark serpentine with its tiny blocks of lighter green, and the dimmed sunshine of antique yellow. Seeing a bit of lapis-lazuli that showed its splendid blue under the pearly lid of a shell, he had started out of the procession, caught it up, and returned to his place, without ceasing to sing.

The boat touched the beach, and its owner stood there wondering and displeased. Marco made some excuse, and paid him liberally. Then he went to the piazza, and got into the diligence that was about starting for Albano. He was quite alone. At this season people were coming to the sea, not going away.

They drove off through the wood by which he had come the night before. The driver, finding that his passenger did not wish to talk, dropped the curtain between them, and solaced himself with a cigar.

Marco was saying the rosary; and since he had no beads, he said them on his ten fingers. At the Our Father he clasped his hands. He was praying for Vittorio.

At Albano he took the railway to Valmontone, and from there he went home on foot across the vines and fields by which he and Vittorio had passed two days before.

When he reached the old road, Rosa stood at the villa gate watching for him. She uttered a cry, and came to meet him.

"Papa! why did n't you come home yesterday? I waited all day, and I would n't go back at night, but stayed here."

Then, seeing his face, she added, "What is the matter?"

"I 'm not very well. I think I may have a touch of fever," he said, and leaned on her shoulder.

Silently she supported him across the road, and in at the gate. When they reached the crumbling Janus, he staggered and fell against it.

"Don't cry!" he said faintly. "Go and get me some wine. It 's nothing." And he thought: "I can do nothing, because she must not know."

CHAPTER XXIV.

UNDER THE PASSION-FLOWERS.

TO those of her friends who wondered that she should remain in Rome so late, the Countess Belvedere explained that she was waiting to see some friends from the East who could not possibly stop to visit her out of town. Her dear Gabriella had been for a long time in India, where her husband, the Marquis de Massy, had a French government appointment. Now the Marquis was sent to London, as an attaché of the French embassy, and Gabriella was obliged to go across the world from east to west almost as rapidly as the sun did.

The Countess was very circumstantial in her account, and even told the whole story to persons who never asked her anything. There is nothing like the frankness and clearness of people who have a great deal of mischief to conceal. They are always prepared. It is only honest people who can afford to refuse to give reasons to everybody for their conduct.

To her father, who did not recollect to have ever heard of this suddenly beloved friend since the days when she was his daughter's schoolmate, and not her favorite one, another reason was given. Gabriella had a large collection of Indian shawls, and the Countess hoped to persuade her to sell one at a bargain; and she had heaps of Indian embroideries, and had been especially commissioned to bring to her friend a gold-colored crêpe shawl, heavy with embroidery, of which the Countess proposed to make a tunic which should be richer than cloth of gold. With all these toilet splendors in prospect, one could bear Rome in August.

These travellers from the Orient arrived the afternoon of the day on which Vittorio went to Palestrina.
They were too much fatigued to leave their hotel that
evening; but the next day Gabriella was to spend
with her friend, and the Marquis would come to
dinner. In the evening they were to pursue their
journey.

The Countess Belvedere had a bottle of chloral on
her toilet-table. She very seldom took it; for her
youth and health rendered it unnecessary as yet.
She took some after her interview with Marco, having first had a hot bath, or rather having had a hot
bath given her almost forcibly by her maid. For
Marco's treatment had thrown her into such a fury,
that she was near breaking all the mirrors and windows in the palace. That that beast, as she called
him, had received any provocation, or had any excuse, she did not for an instant own.

The hot bath and the chloral were not without
their effect; and, before Marco had reached Albano, she was sound asleep, soothed by her faithful
Lucia, who sat by her repeating that she was not in
the least to blame for what had happened, and that
she need not be in the least anxious about the future. Bruno would be found, there were scouts
out in search of him; and if, by ill luck, he and
Marco should meet, why, he would at least tell no
tales.

With all these soothing cares, the Countess Belvedere slept like an innocent babe, and woke refreshed.
While Marco was passing through the poisonous
macchia to Porto d'Anzio, and Bruno was crawling
away from the reapers in the Agro Palestrinese,
Madama Adelaïde was at her morning toilet. A
rose-colored muslin, a faint touch of rouge to her
cheeks, and a cup of strong coffee brought a look
of life into her pallid face; and when her friend

arrived just after midday, she was apparently quite herself.

The two ladies breakfasted alone, and, after half an hour's chat, retired to their rooms for a nap, both of them having drunk wine enough to make lying down quite as easy as sitting up. The Countess, who was still a little romantic, did not smoke, and her friend, who was past romance, enjoyed her cigarettes in private.

At five o'clock they went out for a drive, going up Monte Mario for the air, and at seven they came back. The Marquis had not yet come. He was to bring with him, to make a fourth at the table, a distinguished Monsignore from the Vatican, who was glad of this opportunity of seeing people just from the East who could give him the latest news, with all those particulars and corrections which one cannot hope to have from the journals, nor from less well-informed correspondents and travellers.

"And now let us go into the garden till they come," the visitor said. "I recollect that it used to be charming here."

The Countess had not invited her guest into the garden, and had tried to lead her thoughts elsewhere; but she assented readily to the proposal, and gayly led the way out through the broad glass doors that stood wide open, and across the black and white paved terrace where she had sat and known that Vittorio was watching her through the laurels.

They walked about among the flowers, talking gossip.

The garden was looking a little neglected that day. Two days' inattention at such a season tells. Nothing had been watered, and the opening flowers of to-day had pushed yesterday's flowers aside. The grass under the camellias was strewn with blossoms that were still fresh, though fallen. They had no stems, but the petals were bright. The colors were varied : some were white, others red, others mixed red and white. A pink carpet was spread under the oleanders, and the rose-trees stood in a rosy morning cloud of piled-up petals.

"What a profusion of flowers!" exclaimed the visitor. "You must have a good gardener."

"Excellent!" was the reply.

They walked on. Here and there, near the walls, a green lemon or a wild mandarin had dropped on the path.

"There is quite a little forest of oranges," said the visitor, pointing across the garden and turning her steps in that direction.

"The camellias are rather fine," said the Countess hastily. "Don't you want one to put in your hair?"

The lady returned.

"If you will give me a white one," she said. "That farther tree is white. But where is the gardener, dear? You will hurt your fingers."

"Not at all. I like to gather flowers." The Countess pulled a low branch toward her, and was about breaking one of the beautiful white flowers with which it was thickly set, when suddenly she cried out, and let the branch swing back.

"There was a bee in it, and I believe that it has stung me," she said, her face very red, as she pressed her finger in her handkerchief. And she hurried away, leaving the camellia ungathered. She had seen a dark red stain on one of its waxen petals.

She followed toward the oranges unconsciously, her face still red, her finger still held in her handkerchief, her friend pitying her volubly; till, finally, they found out that the bee had not stung her after all.

"But what is the matter, my dear?" the visitor said; for the Countess, finding herself beside the oranges, stopped abruptly, her color fading.

"Oh, nothing! But, really, I had such a start. I am afraid of bees."

The other, who thought her friend affected and uninteresting, tripped around the orange-trees with an exclamation of pleasure.

"Passion-flowers! There is nothing that I like so much." And she began to pull one after another toward her with her slender gem-laden fingers, and to look into their mournful faces to see which was the finest.

The Countess, after hesitating one instant, pressed her lips together tightly, and followed, standing at a little distance.

This retired spot, like a room with a roof taken off, and an orange-tree for a door, had a sombre and mysterious air. Poor Vittorio had called it the Chapel, and had banished from it every flower but the purple and white of oranges and passion-vine. In a rough niche in the wall he had set a small bust of some young unknown person that the Countess had said resembled him. This face looked out through the leaves. Two sides of the wall were draped with the vine; the third was bare, and had been meant to hold white jasmine. Under this bare wall the earth was newly turned. The setting sun shot across the top of the wall without entering, only a dull red glow falling into the shade; and the pointed leaves of the aloes set along the top of the wall seemed dripping in that light.

"The very largest one, by far the finest, is just an inch out of my reach, Adèle," her friend said. "I am quite longing for that. As you like to gather flowers, cannot you break it for me? You are taller than I. I am sure there is no bee here."

The Countess Belvedere smiled strangely. The other was looking up at the flower, and did not observe her face. She stepped forward, set her foot where her knee had touched the ground before Marco that morning, and stretched her arm for the flower. It grew at the end of a wandering vine that came out on the bare wall.

But her movement was too hasty. She snatched violently upward, and, feeling her foot sink in the soft earth, shrieked out, and in trying to extricate herself, fell at full length on Vittorio's grave.

The servants ran, her maid foremost among them. She was lifted, and helped, half fainting, into the house, where she sat shivering, and trying to drink the wine they brought her. Her eyes were staring as if she had seen a ghost.

"My dear, what is the matter?" her friend cried. "I cannot imagine why you look so terrified. Are you hurt in any way?"

"It is nothing. I am a fool." The Countess rose. "Is my dress all dust? The truth is, staying in Rome has made me nervous. Roman air always does make me nervous, especially in the summer. Do see if I am all covered with dust."

She went to a long mirror, and stood turning herself about before it,. and her maid shook out her dress, a lace-worked black grenadine made over red satin, and assured her that there was not a speck on it.

"But my shoe and stocking?" she said, and, seating herself, put her foot out, without looking at it, her face turned away.

The girl removed the small black satin slipper, and passed her hands over the black silk stockings wrought with red silks.

"There is nothing, Contessa, not a speck anywhere," she said.

"I have half a mind to go away with you to-night, Gabriella," the Countess said abruptly. "I have only waited for you to come, and I meant to leave immediately."

"It would be delightful, my dear, to have your company as far as Florence."

"I will go. There are yet almost three hours. In three hours one can prepare to go anywhere."

The gentlemen came shortly after, and there was a very bright little dinner, during which the politics of the East were thoroughly discussed by the two gentlemen, and the fashions of the East by the two ladies.

Three hours after the Countess Belvedere was on her way to Florence.

CHAPTER XXV.

ROBACCIA DI ROMA.

VALERIA took quite as much pains to conceal her experiences of the night as the Countess Belvedere did. As the stroke of six rang from a neighboring belfry, she slipped, shivering, into bed. When coffee was brought to her, she gave her orders for the day as usual.

"Lock the door well after you when you go out," she said; and was about to add that she would rest a little longer, when the woman asked her if she had slept well.

"I have n't waked once," she answered, taking alarm. "I am going to get up directly. Is the bath ready?"

When the house door shut, she rose and went to the window to make sure that her servant had really gone out, then to the door to see if it was securely locked. She had locked her study door before ringing the bell.

But sleep refused to come. There was that confusion of utter weariness and utter sleeplessness which is a torment. She had but two clear ideas : one, that she must conceal the events of the night from everybody with as much secrecy as if she had herself been an actor in them ; the other, that she must leave the house she was in as soon as possible.

It being Saturday, her servant, a woman sent to her by Miss Pendleton, had gone to the Campo di Fiori to buy fruit and vegetables for the week, and she would be away two hours ; but repose in her absence was out of the question. Every moment Valeria fancied that some one was at the street door, or climbing in at the study window. She was ready to imagine anything. She had a right to expect anything. But what she could never have imagined was how far more powerful than violence, how perfectly able to dispense with violence, are malice, subtlety, and cowardice combined. Such people as she had to deal with are the pet children of Satan, and he teaches them his finest diplomacy. They are smiling ; they are fond of the society of respectable people ; they are eminently prudent ; they can talk, at need, with such delicacy that their conscience might be a speckless lily, and their heart a thornless rose, both fresh with the dews of innocence. Above all, they are pious.

Valeria had felt herself growing cramped with terror, afraid to move or to resolve upon anything. She threw the fear away.

"It is best to be silent," she thought ; "but my silence shall not be a nightmare."

Opening her study door, she put back the curtains, and leaned for a moment into the garden, just as she might have done if nothing had ever met her glance there but flowers and fountains.

Then, seating herself, she wrote a full account of all that she had known in the past few months. The

17

initials only of the names were given; but the circumstances rendered them unmistakable.

This paper was securely sealed and enclosed with
directions to a friend in England. The person to
whom it was sent was to preserve it carefully sealed,
and in case Valeria should die without having recalled
it, was to open and print it. She knew that no scruples nor influence on the part of the person to whom
she confided her message would interfere with her
directions being followed out to the letter.

She promised to send later certain written testimonies to the truth of fragmentary parts of her recital. It would be easy to persuade the persons
concerned to write and sign these testimonies for
her, as they would seem to be trifles; and she could
make some laughing pretence of mystery which would
convince them that there was no mystery whatever.
And, insignificant as these documents would seem to
be, they would be as important as the little fragment
that finishes a broken statue, or the broken letter
which completes an inscription, neither letter nor
fragment having any sense, except so applied.

This done, she dressed herself and went out to mail
her letter, without waiting for her servant.

There was a head peeping out around the corner of
her house as she came down the street from the direction opposite the door; and when she turned to the
stair, she saw a man standing at the head of it, the
door being shut.

He was one of those men called brigands, to distinguish their dress; perhaps, also, to distinguish their
characters. He wore leather leggings, a peaked hat,
and a faded red vest. His face was thin and dark,
and might have been called beautiful but for its expression of sombre cruelty. His black hair fell on
his shoulders; the large black eyes, which devoured
his face, were wide open, and fixed upon Valeria

in an unwinking stare. Not a feature of his face moved.

"What do you want there?" she called out, standing in the street and looking up at him.

He neither stirred nor answered.

"Come down!" she said. "It is my house, and I wish to go in. Come down!"

He slowly descended the stairs without removing his eyes from her face, coming step by step, as though he counted in advancing. There was something chilling in his impassibility, and in those large black eyes, that seemed to be all black.

"What do you want?" she asked, looking steadily at him, as she would have looked at a wild beast, whom she could not fly from.

He growled out some inarticulate reply, and passed her by, turning his eyes sideways as he passed. He wore a handkerchief wrapped loosely around his left hand.

It was hard not to turn, not to run up the stairs, not to betray any sign of fear; but she succeeded in commanding her muscles till they touched the bell. Then she rang a peal that brought her woman instantly to the door.

"Come out here quickly and look at that man going up Via Claudia," she said. "He was standing at the door when I reached the house. Have you seen him? Had he rung?"

"No, Signora. No one has rung. And I would n't have opened the door to one like that."

"See that you do not! Never open the door to any person whom you do not know."

"What do you think he was here for?" the woman asked.

"*Chi lo sa!* Perhaps he wanted to sell goat's milk. I recollect to have seen two or three such men as that with a flock of goats in front of a large solitary house outside the gate of St. John Lateran."

It was scarcely possible to write that day; and Valeria went down to see Miss Cromo in the afternoon, and found her very gay and amusing.

"And by the way," she said at length, "how do your mysterious friends get along?"

"My mysterious friends? What can you mean?"

"Why, those very improper people you told me of some time ago," Miss Cromo replied. "Those people whose names you would n't tell."

"And whose names you tried so hard to find out," added Valeria.

Miss Cromo ceased to smile. "Well, how are they getting along?"

"You ought to know better than I," was the reply. "You proposed to put some one on their track. I really cannot tell you any news of them."

"You do very well not to occupy yourself with them," Miss Cromo said sharply. "It is n't nice for a lady to know about such things."

"I know nothing of such things except what is forced upon my notice," Valeria replied. "I believe that the most of my knowledge of such subjects has been communicated to me by you. No one ever hears me tell such stories. You know perfectly well why I mentioned this one to you, solely in order to have your advice on a subject which I saw you were familiarly acquainted with."

She rose as she spoke, and took a very cold leave before Miss Cromo had provided herself with a retort. Returning to her own apartment, she found a visitor waiting for her. She was somewhat surprised at seeing this lady, whom she had met several times at Casa Passarina, but had scarcely exchanged a dozen words with; and still more surprised at finding herself greeted with the cordiality of an old friend.

Any company was welcome, however; and she was, on the whole, rather pleased, knowing nothing against the lady, except that she was a little too cordial and friendly for such a very slight acquaintance.

Mrs. Morton was an Englishwoman of middle age, who was divorced from her husband, and lived as companion with a French lady, resident in Rome. She was agreeable-looking and pleasant-mannered, though a physiognomist would have called her bad-tempered. She was exceedingly useful in questioning servants as to the affairs of their employers, and in doing mysterious little errands for certain friends of hers; two of which errands she had to do this afternoon. One of them was to come to Valeria and find out what she knew, or would say, about the Countess Belvedere.

This woman was very pious. She had a rosary on her bed-post, a Madonna in a *chalet*, and a shell of holy water on the wall. She went to Novenas, asked people to pray for her, and went frequently to confession and Communion. One might accuse one's self of a feeling of curiosity to hear one of her confessions, after having known some of her doings.

When her errand to Valeria was done, she was to go to a certain lodging-house with the pretence of looking at rooms for some one else, and while examining the rooms, was to ask the mistress of the house a good many questions about a lady boarding there. Nothing was to be said against her; but the questions were such as could not fail to suggest suspicions of the person mentioned.

. That was all.

Satan caricatures God in all his works; and as in the Church there is a communion of saints, which is defined as a communion of all holy persons in all holy things, so in the church of Satan there is a communion of all evil persons in all evil things; and this communion is a sort of Freemasonry. The members understand and aid each other.

"Only tell me a person's name, and I will find out everything about her," this woman had said; and she said it with an air of pride. She had lost the instinct of honor.

When her second errand should be done, Mrs. Morton would be just in time to go to Sant' Andrea delle Fratte to the Novena which had begun for the Nativity of the Blessed Virgin, where, with every appearance of devotion, she would repeat her salutation to the Mother of the Love of God incarnate with the same lips that had a moment before insinuated a calumny, inspired by the father of lies.

Mrs. Morton began to compliment Valeria. She was full of smiles and friendly inquiries; she admired her apartment, and begged to be allowed to see the whole of it.

Valeria began to stiffen. "This woman is a little too sweet, and too much at her ease," she thought. And she ignored her request.

"You must have a view into the Mitella gardens," Mrs. Morton said presently, in no wise abashed at the tacit refusal. "Your house is partly inside the wall, is it not?"

"Yes; there is one window on the garden."

"How charming! I have always wanted a house with a garden adjoining. Even if it isn't one's own, that scarcely makes a difference. To be able to look at flowers and fountains, is about the same as to own them. I suppose you spend a great deal of time at that window. Do you ever see the Countess?"

"Very seldom. Naturally, when I see people in the garden, I draw back. And, indeed, though I sit near the window with my writing, I do not look out much, except when it is too dark to write, or when I want to rest my eyes for a moment. It rests one's eyes to look at green. The ancient stone-cutters looked at an emerald when their eyes were tired; I look at a tree."

" Does the Countess please you?" asked the visitor.

" I do not know her."

" I mean, do her looks please you? Do you think her handsome?"

" She would be called a handsome woman. I saw her once or twice in Casa Passarina."

" How I should like to look into the garden! Would you allow me?"

" Why do you not go to the Casino?" Valeria said. " They would probably let you go into the gardens. I presume that the family are away."

Anger flickered in the visitor's pale blue eyes, and distorted her smile; but she strove not to lose her sweetness.

" It did n't occur to me that the request was an improper one, I am so very open about everything," she said. " I never minded having ladies go to any part of my house when I had one. I never conceal anything."

" Then perhaps," Valeria said smilingly, " since you are so frank, you will tell me what it is you wish to find out about the Countess Belvedere and her garden. I own that I fail to see why either should interest you."

" Nothing in the world! What should I wish to find out? What should make you so suspicious?"

The visitor floundered in protestations, half angry, half apologetic, and, not being interrupted, rose to go.

" So happy to have seen you!" said Valeria, ringing the bell.

She rang it again when her visitor had gone out with a bitter-sweet smile upon her face, and gave orders that Mrs. Morton was never, on any account, to be admitted again.

" There 's another enemy for me!" she sighed, when she was alone. " I shall have all the *canaglia* of Rome upon my shoulders."

CHAPTER XXVI.

THE CLICK OF A LOCK.

IT was September, and Valeria was feeling very unwell, without once suspecting what was the matter with her. Fever comes so insidiously sometimes as not to be perceived. The weather was very hot, the summer had been an extraordinary strain of heat from the beginning of May, with scarcely a shower, or a merciful *tramontana* to temper the scorching rays of the sun. One can stay very well in Rome through July; but after that the system becomes prostrated.

She could eat nothing but fruit. Now and then her servant persuaded her to taste of something else; but she turned from it in disgust. She struggled to write, and the pen dropped from her hand. Her trembling fingers could scarcely form the letters.

And so September passed.

Bruno was back in the garden of Villa Mitella, swaggering and laughing as usual. He knew that Marco lay dangerously ill of fever, and he felt safe for the present.

Valeria always protested to herself that she did not know where Vittorio was, and that he must have found employment elsewhere. She refused to look at the thought that she had refused to utter. She scarcely ever went out now, and never alone. When she did go out, there was always some of that company near her; but their manner was changed. Their air was serious and threatening, but they never intruded too much.

The cool evenings came, and the sun, from being an

enemy, became a friend. It was pleasant, at early morning or toward evening, to stand in the yellow light of it at that season. But Valeria was no better. And now she could not sit up all day, and she tired of the few visitors who began to come.

Sometimes she thought of sending for Dr. Kraus. She felt nervous and irritable; the fever was slowly consuming her, and her strength slowly diminishing, and she did not know what was the matter.

One day, just before sunset, a visitor came in, — a very good person, who did not interest, and always vexed her a little. He was one of those persons who is always going, and never goes. When his visit was over, it still took him a great while to get out of his chair. He made little feints, half rising, smoothing his hat, and always settling again at a word. Then, once on his feet, he would stand, wait, turn half away, act as if he wished to say something and was trying to recollect what, till one longed to give him a push out of the room.

With all that, he was a good man in a negative way, and one liked him for the first fifteen or twenty minutes of his visit, and wished to be very civil.

There had been some rain early in the day, and it had cleared in the afternoon, and now, at sunset, a sharp *tramontana* was growing, and becoming, from cool intermittent puffs, a steady cold wind. The west window of the reception-room was open, and the wind came in and blew across Valeria's shoulders. But her visitor was now standing, and had turned and twisted to such an extent that it seemed impossible that he would not presently edge toward the door. If she should rise prematurely, it might be all to begin over again. If she should close the window and ring for a shawl, he might sit down. She meant to wait till he should get two or three steps toward the door, then rise briskly with an "Oh, you are going?"

give him her fingers, ring the bell, and whisk him away before he knew. Then turning to close the window, she could affect not to see him hanging about the door.

And meantime the cold wind was pressing like a block of ice on her shoulders, and a chill was creeping over her from head to foot, and penetrating to her heart.

At last the gradually attenuated leave-taking came to a point where she could sever it, and she was free, — free and deadly cold.

She wrapped a shawl about her and lay down on the sofa. She felt a little dull and confused, and took no other means to counteract the harm that she had received. Later, Dr. Kraus came. She hardly knew what she said to him or when he went.

After a while she seemed to dream. Her room was dim, and a black curtain hung round its walls, and behind this curtain she heard a step. Some one was running round between the curtain and the wall, as if seeking an exit into the chamber and finding none. The step betrayed agitation, and there was a breathless agitation in the voice that spoke to her.

It was the voice of her mother, dead for many years.

"Don't be afraid, Valeria! Your father will be near you," it said.

And still running, and seeking to pass the veil that separated them, and repeating over and over the same words, she heard the step and the voice.

"Don't be afraid, Valeria! Your father will be near you."

Then all went out in darkness.

She was delirious.

*   *   *   *   *

Like a candle that is lighted for a moment, her consciousness came back. She was lying helpless, and there seemed to be a mountain on her breast. She struggled to breathe, and could not. Dr. Kraus stood at a table preparing some medicine, half turned away from her.

"You have taken my breath away!" she gasped.

"No, I have n't!" he replied rudely, without looking round.

Then, like a candle, the light of her eyes went out.

Again it came back, but after what interval she could not guess.

Her room was dim, and she was alone. A light shone across the corridor from her study. Some one was there, and she heard the rattling of papers and whispered words, in which she presently recognized Miss Cromo's voice. She read out the title of a story that Valeria had begun, and made a comment on it.

They had, indeed, lost no time. Instead of locking her writing-table, and waiting to see how her sickness would turn, they had immediately begun to examine her papers.

And, again, she was aware for a moment, at another time, of Dr. Lacelles sitting at her bedside.

"And so they treated you very badly?" he said.

He had a calm, quiet way that was very soothing. One could not imagine that he would ever show the rudeness of Dr. Kraus to an unconscious patient, or one he believed to be unconscious.

"Yes, very ill!" Valeria replied mechanically; then wondered what she had been saying to him, and who had treated her ill; and, wondering, knew no more.

She was roused again by a sound at her chamber door. Miss Cromo, dressed for a visit, came in, and took a chair at a little distance from the bed, and facing her.

"She must not be made to talk," said the voice of some one out of sight, probably the servant.

"Very well! I will look about a little, then," said the visitor, and began to glance about the room, at the furniture, the walls, the floor.

"Oh, how pretty the toilet and curtains are!" she exclaimed. "How very pretty!"

Valeria was conscious; but she had waked only to the solemn struggle of life and death going on in her, and to a terrible sense of her own helplessness. Of the polite insincerities of life she knew nothing. All that she could bear of suffering was pressing upon her, and she felt this presence and triviality an insult.

"If you came here only to make comments on my furniture, you had better go home," she said with most uncompromising brevity, as dead to etiquette as a ghost.

Miss Cromo rose instantly and left the room without a word.

Little by little, came the faint, cold dawn of returning reason. It was no more a momentary glimmering, but a steady, though slow, increase of light. All was painful and cheerless. She was faint and emaciated; she needed simple medicines, which had not been given her; she needed nourishment, and some one to stand between her and all disturbances; and she had nothing. Never once had she opened her eyes and found any one sitting beside her, ministering to her, or saying a cheering word. If she waked in the night, she was in darkness, though her servant came when called. No vision of charity, nor even of humanity, had appeared to her.

She rose one morning and dressed herself. She staggered in walking, and her head reeled. She only reached the sofa in the next room, and sank down there exhausted. The servant came to her for orders, and she could hardly give them.

Later Miss Pendleton came to see her, and talked

till her head grew dizzy. She was kind, and very affectionate ; but she talked as no one should talk to a sick person, who was still sick enough to be in bed, and carefully tended.

"How long have I been ill?" Valeria asked her.

Miss Pendleton thought a moment, then replied, "Six weeks."

She had been ill three weeks. It was that day three weeks since the evening when the *tramontana* struck her.

Miss Pendleton had come for a special purpose. She wished Valeria to leave her house, and go to some hospital or institute where she could have proper care. It was impossible to have the care she needed from a servant, the visitor insisted, and she would never recover if something were not done for her.

"All I need now is quiet and nourishment," Valeria said faintly. "I cannot talk, I do not want to think. Only let me rest."

Miss Pendleton persisted. It was a repetition of the visit she had made in the spring, six months before, — the same wearing repetitions and urging, the same promises if she would yield, the same ignoring of all argument and reply.

Valeria took refuge in silence. Her mind, to which some momentary confusions still clung, like the rags of mist that linger for a little about the landscape when the tempest has passed, seemed about to darken anew and desert her under this torment. She would not answer, and Miss Pendleton left her, after having talked her almost into a swoon.

The next day several people came. She had told the servant that she would see no one, yet they were admitted. There were two doctors from some hospital, — an old man, who took her hand, led her to the strong, full light of the window, and questioned her, his eyes fixed immovably on her face ; and a young man, who, seated on the arm of a chair, swung one leg to and fro, and said nothing.

Valeria tried to give an account of herself, and could not. The light troubled her, the man's gaze distressed her, and she was annoyed at the manner of his companion, which was astonishing in the presence of a lady in her own house. She was expected to tell all the symptoms of an illness of which she knew almost nothing, and to describe her present state, which she only recognized as a misery of weakness and weariness.

The thought passed her mind that she would like to see an American doctor,—a man who would be gentle, soothing, and considerate, and on whose skill and honesty she could depend. These doctors seemed to her very strange people. Little Dr. Kraus was all the doctor she knew, except Dr. Lacelles. She would certainly never have employed Dr. Kraus in a critical case; and she quite as certainly had never dreamed of employing Dr. Lacelles professionally, however agreeable she might have found him as a gentleman.

This doctor who was questioning her had thin white hair and red eyes, and he looked sickly. By contrast, he recalled the figure of the doctor she had had at home, tall, strong, clean, and full of life and of gentleness. She could have dropped into his hands with strength enough for only one word, " Protect me ! " and been sure that her house would have been a fortress against all intrusion ; that whatever need she had would have been found out, every care provided, and her smallest flickering spark of life fed till it reached the full flame.

There were such men in Rome ; but she could not reach them. She had been taken possession of, and there was no help for her.

The doctors went, but other people came.

A gentleman and his wife came, seated themselves in two chairs, and looked at her. They were familiar acquaintances, but none the less unwelcome now. They did not talk, and she tried to talk to them, having nothing to say.

They went, and presently some man came about a repair needed in the house, and another with a little household bill, and she had to see them both. It would appear that the servant took no orders from her mistress; and whatever directions Miss Pendleton might have given her, to keep out visitors was not among them.

Later Burton the artist came, bringing her something that he thought might tempt her appetite. She was glad to see him, though she could neither eat nor talk. He was such a good fellow when left to himself. She thought that if she had him to see to her and keep everybody else away, she would soon get well.

The day passed, and the night. "Oh, if I could only be let alone to-day!" she said to her servant the next morning. "Don't let any one come near me! Don't open the door to any one. I want to lie still and not speak, except to you, all day. That will make me feel better."

They did not mean that she should be any better just then. They had plans which her health, if too quickly established, would have interfered with.

Miss Pendleton was shown in, and there was a repetition of their former interview. And again she went away, leaving Valeria exhausted.

The next day she came again, bringing with her an American friend of Valeria's, who had just come to Rome, and was going immediately away again.

Mrs. Marvin was one of the sweetest of women, and as gentle as a dove. She had but just entered the Church, and had all the enthusiasm of a convert, not only for the Church, but for Catholics. She invested her Catholic friends with all the beauty of the doctrines in which they professed belief, and the virtues which they professed to practise. Simply and transparently honorable, she had no conception of dishonor under the garb of religion. Theoretically it might be possible, but surely not of any one whom she had ever seen.

She had been talked to and prepared for this interview, and in adding her influence to further the object of it, she verily believed that she did service to God and to her neighbor.

Valeria was urged to leave her house, and go to a certain hospital where she would have every care. She was told that she could never recover where she was.

It was again a siege, with two voices instead of one.

-" You are nervous and you need a particular cure," Mrs. Marvin said, in her sweet, soothing way.

Valeria thought that she was not nervous. She felt no excitement whatever, but only weakness and lassitude; but she did not contradict them.

"I will go if I can be quiet," she said at last; " but I cannot see to my apartment, nor to anything. I don't want to think. Cannot you see that after such an illness one needs perfect quiet for a while?"

"Everything shall be done for you," Miss Pendleton said eagerly; "we will take all the responsibility. I know a nice family who will take your apartment till you want to come back. They would like to have a place for the rest of the winter."

"I think I may go to America in the spring," Valeria said. "I have had a letter from Sister Veronica, who is a nun in a Southern convent, and my dearest friend. I wrote them this summer that I was not well. They invite me to go to them and stay till my health shall be perfectly restored. I long to be with them so that I would like to fly there this moment. See! this is her letter."

Miss Pendleton took the letter, read the address written at the top, and gave it back.

"All shall be done for you," she said. "If you wish to go to them in the spring, we may know some one who is going, so that you shall have company. And now you will be well taken care of, and to-morrow I will take you to the place we have spoken of. Don't think of anything; leave all to me."

It was such a rest to think that she might leave all to some one.

Her visitors both kissed her affectionately.

"I am so grateful to you!" Valeria said to Mrs. Marvin.

"Oh, it is nothing! Christians must do for each other, must they not?" was the gentle reply.

As they were going out of the room Valeria thought to ask, "Where is the place to which you will take me?"

"In the Lungara," Miss Pendleton said, and they went.

In the Lungara! And she was to go there because she was nervous! In the Lungara was the great lunatic asylum of Rome, and they must have meant that. She had passed by its great iron gate more than once.

Valeria started up and began to walk the floor. She tried to think of some one to whom she could appeal. She remembered the American Consul, and put her hand on the bell-knob to call her servant to go for him. But no; the girl would go to Miss Pendleton instead. And even if he should come, could she talk to him in a way to convince him that she should not go there? This fear and distress, added to her weakness, would confuse her, would agitate her.

She seated herself, and wrote a letter to the Supe-

18

rior of the convent where Miss Pendleton lived. Her letter was blotted, her hand trembled so that she could hardly form the letters; but the meaning was plain.

She begged Madame de la Roche to let her come to them for a little while. "All I want is rest and quiet," she wrote. "I do want care, but not the care of a lunatic asylum." Her letter was imploring, and showed that she was terrified. When it was ended, and she had sent the servant with it, she sank fainting on the floor.

"They could easily drive me crazy or kill me in a short time," she thought, when she recovered.

The note was left, but no reply was sent then.

The next day Miss Pendleton and Mrs. Marvin came again.

They expressed warmly their regret for having disturbed her so much when they meant to do her good. She was soothed and reassured and coaxed. Madame de la Roche was very sorry not to be able to take her. Then Mrs. Marvin said that she had that day seen another place which she thought would suit Valeria. Did she know anything about Villa Barberini?

No, she had never heard of it. But the word villa was pleasant. It promised a garden.

Mrs. Marvin then described the place. It had large grounds and gardens, extending over a hill near St. Peter's. The house was fine, and Valeria's room would be the best in it. There were a few ladies there, who were not quite well, and wished to live quiet for a while. She need not have anything to do with them unless she wished to. Her meals would be served to her privately, and she would have the attendance of a servant who would be the same as a maid, and every care necessary from a doctor and nurse. The view from her window was lovely. Over a near hill quite in the garden looked the dome of

St. Peter's, not more than twenty rods distant; from the other window she would see a procession of great pines climbing the hill to a second villa.

It was an enchanting picture.

"I will go to-day if I may," Valeria said. "I am impatient to be quiet and silent."

It was arranged that she should go the next day. Miss Pendleton would come for her at two o'clock, would take the keys of her house, and dismiss her servant, and Valeria had nothing to do but to let herself be taken care of.

The rest of the day and the night seemed too long in passing. But at last the longed-for day came.

It was the 18th of November. Looking over her papers to put some of them into her trunk, Valeria saw by her diary that she must have been taken sick on the evening of the 27th of October, making thus twenty-two days from the first, without counting the weeks that she had suffered from fever without being aware of it.

After her trunk was prepared, she wrote a letter to those having the care of her affairs in America. Mentioning her illness, she said that Miss Pendleton would take charge of her affairs, and was to be trusted like herself.

The letter written, after resting awhile, she sat down by the window looking westward up Via Nera to wait.

It was a wild day, the sky full of sunshine and black clouds. Now a dash of angry rain came flying through the air and splashed itself, as sharp as hail, against the window-panes; then suddenly a rush of sunbeams broke through the clouds and turned the drops to gold.

It was the first time that Valeria had looked up to observe nature since the *tramontana* struck her three weeks before.

Miss Pendleton was long in coming. She had promised to come at two o'clock, and she did not come till four. When she came, the storm had subsided into a mournful calm. A watery sunshine shone through the windless sky, and now and then a few rain-drops fell.

"I was afraid that you would n't come," Valeria said, "and I could n't have stayed here another night, I am so impatient."

Miss Pendleton was serious and preoccupied, and had but little to say, except to excuse her delay. The few necessary preparations were made, the trunk was left to be sent for, and they went down to a cab that was waiting at the door, Valeria supporting herself partly on the banister, partly on Miss Pendleton's arm.

They drove through street after street in silence. Too weak to talk much in the house, Valeria was far too weak to make herself heard above the noises of the street; and her companion did not seem disposed to say anything. There were some familiar streets and others strange, and they seemed to go back and forth.

At length, when they had had time to go from end to end of the city, Valeria said, "It seems to me that we are going in a very round-about way."

"Yes," Miss Pendleton replied impatiently, "the driver is taking the longest road he can, so as to make it cost more. They always do that."

At length the houses ceased abruptly. They drove up a rise between high walls, made a turn or two, and stopped at a high iron gate that barred their way. The gate was shut, but the porter appeared inside.

And here a difficulty occurred. The porter would not admit them, not having received any orders to do so, and the *vetturino* refused to stay any longer without extra pay, which Miss Pendleton refused to give him.

There was a moment of perplexity; then the *vetturino* was dismissed, and Miss Pendleton begged Valeria to wait where she was while she should run to a house lower down for an order.

The cab disappeared, Miss Pendleton disappeared, and Valeria was left alone outside the gate with the porter looking out through the bars. The rain began to fall gently, the earth was wet, the air cold. It was past the middle of November, and she had been in bed only three or four days before with fever and congestion of the lungs; and she could scarcely stand. Apparently, her health had been, from first to last, but very little thought of.

At one side of the road there was a long chapel with closed blinds, and grass-grown stone steps leading up to it. Valeria seated herself on these steps, and waited. She began to grow afraid, not knowing where she was. She would surely be ill again if she stayed there much longer. And she could not sit up either. She had already exerted herself too much that day; and she could scarcely keep herself from lying down on the cold wet stones.

It was about fifteen minutes before Miss Pendleton appeared, accompanied by a young nun in a black dress, and wearing a black veil over a white one. She was a sister of San Carlo, an order founded by San Carlo Borromeo to take care of the sick.

The two were running. They made some hasty excuses, the gate opened, and they entered. It was a beautiful gate, and the road it opened into ran between a wall and a high slope, and was bordered with trees and shrubs, and there were flowers even now, and the banks were a bright emerald. Vines hung over the gate, and wreathed a little bridge that crossed over it.

They did not follow the road. The nun took them up a steep path leading to the bridge, where they entered the continuation of a branch of the avenue from the gate. The rain was falling, and the way seemed long; but the sister held Valeria by the arm, and helped her along.

At length they reached a house, and, passing under palm-branches that overshadowed the steps, entered a small garden enclosed in an angle of the *casino*. At the door another sister met them, took charge of Valeria, led her up-stairs, and helped her to bed.

Miss Pendleton took leave at once, promising to come again soon.

Supper was brought, and she ate a little, sitting up in bed, and served by the nun who had met her at the door. Then she leaned forward, and looked out through the window. Opposite was the Castle of St. Angelo, with the Tiber coming boldly forward a short distance, then turning aside out of sight. Beyond the castle were fields, and beyond the fields a long range of mountains, faintly rosy now opposite the rainy sunset.

They had not deceived her in saying that the place was beautiful.

"This is not your room," the sister said. "Yours is larger. It will be ready for you to-morrow."

Later, the sister came softly in again, and began setting the room in order for the night. She closed the shutters, placed a little flask of violet-water on a stand beside the bed, and smoothed the pillows and cover.

Valeria did not speak, nor open her eyes, but she smiled. This was something like care, like charity.

Those quiet motions were lulling, and when the sister went out, Valeria scarcely knew. It seemed to her that she heard the click of a lock when the door closed. But she forgot it immediately, and soon fell asleep.

CHAPTER XXVII.

LA CARITA ROMANA.

FOR nearly forty-eight hours Valeria lay and suffered herself to be taken care of without a thought. The sister and the doctor had discovered immediately the mistakes or the neglect in her treatment, and had remedied them. It was the ideal of care for a convalescent.

There were long hours of quiet loneliness, but never any neglect.

Now and then she raised herself in bed, and leaning forward looked out at the castle, the river, the stretching fields, and the far-off mountains. Once she rose and went to the window to see what was beneath. There was a narrow court, and beyond, nothing but a steep-dropping succession of roofs, looking like a shell-strewn beach with the multitudinous tiny curves of their mossy-lichened tiles.

A black old stone-wall was visible at the left, with weeds and flowers set in the interstices.

The house was, evidently, on the brink of a steep hillside. There were but two stories in front, and here there appeared to be four. At the left of the view was the Vatican.

The window was crossed by heavy bars of wood, so that she could not put her head out; but that did not surprise her; one sees bolts and barred windows everywhere in Italy, and though they are usually seen only on the ground-floor, it was not strange to a stranger to see them on the fourth, especially in a house inhabited by nuns.

The attendants were as pleasing as the place. A pretty young nurse came and went, ready to do any-

thing, and never doing too much, and Sister Agnes
came every few hours to visit her.

Sister Agnes had that charm which only a nun can
possess. Closed in a convent in her early youth, she
had preserved the simplicity of a child, while acquir-
ing the strength of character and experience in her
duties of a woman. She was rather small, and her
face had a severe and melancholy cast; but her smile
transfigured it with a sudden childlike sweetness, and
her manner, ordinarily calm and even taciturn, had
in conversation a charming vivacity. She had the
instinct of a nurse, the gentle authority, the soft
touch, the ready, supporting arms, the quick eyes, the
order and neatness. She divined what was wanting
without waiting to be asked.

On the second morning Sister Agnes came to conduct Valeria to her room, which had now been prepared for her. It was on the same floor, but looked
out over the villa instead of the city, and was at the
end of a long corridor, that had chambers at either
side. This was a new wing of the house, and Valeria
was the only person on the second floor.

Each door had a little slide in it, glass inside, a
movable iron screen outside; and the locks and han-
dles were on the outside. The doors could not be
fastened from within.

Beside these peculiarities, and the wooden bars at
all the windows, they were quite like any other comfortable bedrooms. There were carpets, the walls and
ceilings were delicately tinted, and they had the ordinary furniture of a bed-chamber.

Valeria's room was larger than the others, and had
a little dressing-room attached, with a large double
doorway without a door, and covered by a curtain.
From this dressing-room a window looked toward St.
Peter's.

The *casino* was built upon a hillside, not upon the

top, and the hill had been dug away a little more to build this new wing. Over the green summit, not three minutes' walk from the house, which was on the northern summit of the Janiculum, the dome of St. Peter's looked so large and near that it startled at first sight. The great cupola seemed to be set on the hill-top like a huge stone-ribbed bird-cage. All its form was visible; but nothing else was visible except the apostles of the façade, and two smaller cupolas, which might have been birds hopped out of that cage, so small did they look in comparison. In certain lights, the apostles appeared to be standing on the hill-top.

"Oh, there come the apostles to make me a visit! They are welcome!" said Valeria, without reflecting that this speech might seem strange to the simple, literal nun.

The bedroom window skimmed the backward edge of the Janiculum, gave a view of St. Onofrio, with its little *campanile* and one bell against the sky, and of the flat-topped cypresses of the mortuary chapel, on the steps of which Valeria had seated herself two days before. Higher up against the sky stood the *casino* of Villa Gabrielli, with a noble procession of umbrella pines leading down toward the hollow to the villa gate.

The grounds of these two adjoining villas were connected in a manner to puzzle one. The only way of passing from one to the other was over a narrow bridge. Under this bridge was the gate; and the avenue made the figure 8, both bridge and gate being at the intersection of the lines.

"Would n't you like to go out and take a walk?" the sister said, smiling at Valeria's contentment with her apartment. "It would do you good to take the air."

Certainly she would like to. Already, in but little

more than twenty-four hours, her life was beginning to come back. It needed so little help.

The sister went away, promising to come for her in the afternoon, and Valeria sank into an arm-chair by the window, and looked out at the pines. They were melancholy, but they were peaceful.

"Thank God for a garden that I am not afraid to look into," she thought, and then shudderingly put the thought far away. She must forget all that now.

There was an open gate beneath the window, and the avenue passed through, and was lost in a smooth curve on the hill, only a double line of tree-tops showing its farther course.

Close to the gate, and directly opposite the *casino*, was a building with *Tessenda* painted in large letters on the front. From the open windows and doors of. this building came the humming sound of many hand-looms, and now and then a woman, who might be a weaver, appeared for a moment, then disappeared to resume her work.

Valeria lay back languidly, and thought what a sweet gift is life, with all its burdens.

Her dinner was brought by the pretty nurse, Fidelia. This girl was a tall, black-haired Trasteverina, and, though serving with all necessary readiness and humility, had an air of natural stateliness.

Valeria found that she could eat something.

"I really believe that I have gained wonderfully already," she said.

"Certainly! And you will soon be well, signora," the girl replied brightly.

After an hour or two, the sister came.

They went down-stairs to an anteroom where two or three ladies were sitting with a nurse; and here Sister Agnes begged Valeria to wait for her in the *sala* adjoining, as something required her attention before she could go out.

The *sala* was a pretty room with frescoed walls and ceiling. Overhead, a few delicately tinted clouds sailed across a blue sky, and birds flew in and out. The walls represented a half-open veranda, with landscapes showing between the pillars, and vines and trees that pushed in here and there a branch, and a balustrade with vases and birds standing on it. Nothing could be more graceful than this decoration.

There was but one person in the room, a young woman of about thirty years of age. Valeria bent her head; but the lady, without responding, sat slightly turned toward her, and looked at her with a mild and sorrowful attention. She was very thin, but tall and elegantly formed, and her face was spirited and beautiful in outline. The nostrils were thin and sensitive, the upper lip short and curling, the eyes blue. The curly hair was drawn back into a cluster of thick puffs, and a blue bow of ribbon at one side brought out its rich chestnut shade. A black velvet dress contrasted with the exquisite fairness of her skin. Her face, from its shape, did not seem thin, and her cheeks were softly rose-tinted. One would have said that both head and face indicated an uncommon intelligence.

As Valeria was beginning to wonder at her continued gaze, the young woman suddenly clapped her hands together, started up, and began to pace the room from end to end. She carried a white handkerchief by the corner, and swung it about. She looked upward with her fine eyes, and gesticulated gracefully with hands and arms. Then she began to sing, or to declaim, in rapid words hard to follow. She seemed, with her mellow voice, to pour out supplications, accusations, and menaces, ever walking rapidly to and fro, and swinging her handkerchief.

Her excitement grew. Her short upper lip curled with angry scorn, her brows became corrugated and black, she bent her head forward, and her eyes flashed up from under the lowered lids, her voice rose to a cry.

What little of strength Valeria possessed seemed to condense itself into a crinkling flash of lightning which ran through her quivering heart. Who and what was this woman?

She could not bear it. She went out into the ante-room and dropped into a chair, rather than seated herself there.

There was a nurse with her knitting-work, and a little old lady walking to and fro, talking to herself in a whisper. Now and then she stopped to examine the floor, and picked up a thread or some small object.

"Who is that lady in the *sala?*" Valeria asked of the nurse.

"It is the Donna Claudia," the girl replied, still knitting, but looking attentively at the questioner.

"But that is not answering me," Valeria said, finding the girl's manner but slightly ceremonious. "Who is she?"

"She is a daughter of the Duke L——."

"And what is the matter with her?"

"Oh, she is only a little put out about something!" the girl said carelessly. "Donna Claudia," she called out, raising her voice, "please keep quiet!"

The Donna Claudia paid no attention. She was panting out breathless execrations in a strange, distinct whisper that was forced through her lips till it seemed to be close to the ear. Few tragic actresses have such grace or such a power of voice.

The nurse went to quiet her, and the little old lady came and seated herself beside Valeria, and began to speak to her in French in a low tone, and with a manner of delicate sweetness. After a moment she leaned and kissed her lightly on both cheeks. Then she displayed what she had been picking up from the floor, ends of thread, and colored lint, and a bit of pressed mud that had dropped from a shoe; and showed with an air of pride a piece of completed work, a bit of lace knotted out of odds and ends into the shape of a tiny bag. In this bag she had imprisoned a snail, perfectly closing the opening. Then she began a new piece of work, murmuring on her unintelligible talk in alternate English, French, Italian, and Spanish.

Sister Agnes returned with many excuses for being so late.

"I have spoken to this lady, and she does not answer me," Valeria said. She was feeling as if she should faint.

"Oh, the Donna Faustina is very deaf!" the sister replied. "But she is so good!" and she patted the old lady on the shoulder.

The Donna Faustina made a courtesy from under the hand, and walked away with a wonderful unresentful stateliness, her fingers busy with her tatting.

"Who is she?" Valeria asked.

"She is the daughter of the Prince of S——
C——."

They went out. The little garden, open to the south, but shielded from all cold winds, was bright with flowers. Two beds of pansies spread their rich carpets of purple and gold beside the path, the house was draped up to the height of one story with flowering vines and heliotrope, and a fountain tossed its slender jet of water into the air. There had been rain in the morning; but the sun was shining, and it was near sunset. They went down the steps under the palms, and walked up the avenue.

There was a Madonna in a niche of stones in the bank at the roadside, just outside the gate that Valeria had seen beneath her window, and beyond it an excavation with ancient walls and foundations, and beautiful fragments of sculpture, and alabaster and precious marbles over which the grass had been growing for centuries.

They had gone but a few steps when Valeria's strength deserted her, and she begged the sister to return to the house. A fascinated terror prompted her to learn more of this house without delay. She longed to find something to reassure her, yet did not dare to own to herself what it was that she feared.

"You had better rest a little while before going up-stairs," Sister Agnes said to her when they reached the anteroom. "I will bring you a glass of wine." And she left the room.

There was a lady whom Valeria had not seen before, and a nurse in the anteroom.

This lady was between fifty and sixty years of age. Her face was pleasing and intelligent. Her dark hair was very thin in front; but an enormous braid was looped at the back of her head. A plain gray wool dress was fitted somewhat too closely to her thin figure, and she wore black velvet boots on her exquisitely small feet. She carried her head very high with an air of mingled pride and affability.

The nurse asked two or three questions of Valeria. Was she English? Had she been long in Rome?

The lady turned and dropped her eyes for an instant on the girl.

"A lady can question a servant," she said; "but a servant can never interrogate a lady." Then, addressing Valeria, she said pleasantly, "You are going to stay here some time?"

"I suppose so," Valeria replied hesitatingly. "I have been ill."

"Oh!" The lady looked out for a moment into the garden. "I meant to have gone away to-day," she said after a moment; "but I have to wait for some dresses. I shall go to-morrow."

Valeria felt sorry; for the gracious manner, clear voice, and entirely natural and refined air of this stranger had pleased her. "I am sorry that you are going," she said.

The stranger replied with a slight bow and smile.

" Do you remain in Rome ? " Valeria asked.

" No ; I am going to Naples," the lady said, with an air of smiling pride and contentment. " A deputation from there visited me yesterday to offer me the crown."

Valeria remained silent.

" They gave me till this morning to think over their proposal," the lady went on in the same airy manner ; "and I have concluded to go."

She ceased, faintly smiling and proud, and sat looking out into the garden.

Valeria found voice to say, "You are then Neapolitan ? "

" No ; I am Roman. I am the Duchess of S——. I have visited Naples, however. I went there several years ago with the Duke. When we were near the city, the king came out to meet us with a troop of horse ; and when we entered, the people came about us with gifts of every sort, as they came to the Jubilee of the Holy Father. One had a basket of eggs, another a basket of oranges, another a pair of chickens. They all brought something."

She spoke with graceful, laughing ease, and all the indulgence of a sovereign pleased with her popularity, while amused by the simple demonstrations of her people.

The sister returned.

" I told the doctor what you wanted, Duchess," she said ; "and he will send it up."

The Duchess bent her head carelessly, without looking at the nun.

" I must go down to the community for a few

minutes," Sister Agnes said to Valeria. " If you want to go up-stairs before I come back, one of the girls will go with you." And she went.

The door of the *sala* opened abruptly, and a very large stern-faced woman came out, and crossed the anteroom to Valeria, whom she confronted angrily, " You are a rascal ! " she said violently in English.

"What have I done ? " Valeria asked, shrinking. For the woman seemed about to strike her.

" You have said that I am the Count de Morny ; and I am Louis Philippe, the king!" cried the woman.

" On the contrary, I always maintained that you were the king," Valeria replied.

" You are a rascal ! " cried the woman, unappeased.

" Will you say something to her ? " said Valeria to the nurse. " I cannot bear this ! "

" Go and sit down, Madama ! " commanded the nurse. " She won't hurt you," she added to Valeria.

Madama went and seated herself in a chair, and, losing after a moment her look of anger, began to smile and talk affably in English to an imaginary company, nodding and answering remarks unheard by all but herself, and totally unconscious of the people really present.

A young woman with yellow hair came out from the *sala*, and, walking to and fro, began to declaim violently against the Italian government, and to re-count the wrongs of the Pope. The Donna Faustina, who had been sitting quietly at her tatting, rose and began to make courtesies to Valeria, and insisted on kissing her hand. The Donna Claudia burst out of another room, followed by Fidelia, the nurse, who tried in vain to stop her. Her eyes were flashing with fury, her mouth was drawn down at the corners, and she growled fiercely, and ran about with her head down, like a wild bull, striking at everything in her way. All sign of beauty was obliterated from her face. She was a beast.

Without waiting for help, Valeria rose, and hastened, half fainting, to the stairway. One of the nurses followed, and helped her up to her chamber, and left her alone in the growing twilight.

This, then, was the quiet and peace which they had promised her! This was the house where ladies who were a little nervous went for quiet! They called the Donna Claudia a little nervous!

Valeria was too weak to feel indignant. She was simply terrified. She started at a slight sound, fancying that one of those terrible women had followed her up-stairs. She went to the door and tried to fasten it, but there was no lock nor latch on the inside. She longed to be locked in. Then things began to seem strange to her, and she doubted if she had not imagined that horrible scene below, and if it were not she who was mad. She was in precisely the state in which the persons who had planned, if not those who had carried out, her incarceration, had known that she would be, placed in her weak and sensitive condition in such a company. She was in danger of going mad.

Fortunately, her own feelings terrified her so much as presently to overcome the other fear. She went to the window, and watched the boughs wave in the wind, and the clouds sailing over the sky.

"The boughs always move that way," she said, "and the clouds sail before the wind. There is nothing strange in nature. But if I were shut up where I could see only the walls of my room, I should go mad. Oh, I must keep calm! I must not seem afraid. I must wait till I gain a little strength before I think of anything. My room is pretty, and I have good care. I must pretend to be content. If I show any excitement I shall be ruined."

19

They brought her supper, and the nurse helped her to bed. She scarcely said anything, except to ask what day of the month it was.

"I have had nothing to remind me of the day of the month or of the week for some time," she said.

"Oh, as you get stronger, your memory will come back!" the nurse said.

"I have not forgotten anything," she replied. "It is because the days in a sick-room are all alike."

The girl went, and this time the door was not locked. She was sorry for it; but quieted her fears with the reflection that women as violent as those she had seen were likely to be locked in and watched. Stretching out her hand for the crucifix that hung by her bed, she clasped it close, and wept in silent desolation.

"Oh, my Lord, this is what they call charity!" she said.

She would have been better off in a pagan land.

There were voices on the stairs from which one large chamber of the main body of the *casino* opened, and the Donna Faustina was heard snarling like a cat. The nurse tried to soothe her; the door shut, and there was silence.

An hour or two passed, and then Valeria with wide-open eyes saw a light shining in through her door, and heard a light step coming along the corridor. Her heart leaped, then grew quiet; for it was the black veiled head and white collar of Sister Agnes that appeared at the door.

Valeria closed her eyes, and lay still while the sister with a gentle hand smoothed the sheet and cover of the bed, and went softly about the room.

It reminded her of a time — how far back in her childish days! — when her mother used to come to her so at night before going to bed herself, and make sure that she was well. And the question, so often asked in those long-lost winters when the snow-drifts lay without thicker than the green boughs outside her window now, seemed to be spoken again: "Are you warm enough, Valeria?"

They were all dead that made her home, and she was in a foreign land and in a mad-house; yet even here something like mercy had found her!

As the sister came to her pillow again, Valeria put her arms up, drew the head down, and kissed her silently; and the kiss was not for Sister Agnes, but for her mother sleeping under the snows on a New England hillside across the sea.

"What! not sleeping yet!" said the sister, with a pretty chiding in her voice.

"No; but I think that your coming will bring me sleep. Are those women all locked up?"

"Oh, yes!" Sister Agnes said. "They are always locked in at night. And there is a nurse with the Donna Faustina, whom you could call if you should want anything."

She went away, and this time did not lock the door.

CHAPTER XXVIII.

THE WITNESSES.

"But these witnesses, were there any, or not?
"What! Do you think that they lacked witnesses? If it were a question of nailing our Lord to the cross again, do you believe that they would not find them? Of course there were witnesses, people who for the skin of a fig would swear to any falsity."

MARCO VISCONTI.

WHILE Valeria lay ill, telling in her delirium all the bitter story of the past months; and while, the flood of her malady passed by, she lay faint and exhausted on the shore of life, only beginning to live again ; and while, having detected and resisted their wish to take her to the Asylum, she had consented to go, and had been taken to Villa Barberini,— the people who, to use the Roman phrase, " interested themselves in her," had been very busy.

This illness, and especially the delirium, could not have suited them better if they had themselves procured it.

It is impossible to commit one crime alone, unless the criminal is willing to suffer the consequences. The wrong-doer who wishes to be held respectable is driven, almost in his own despite, to whatever means may best hide his fault, even though, as might happen, he should have to commit a greater crime to hide the first. This necessity is the scourge of the arch-enemy. They have, therefore, the poor excuse of self-defence.

There is another class of persons who presumably have not this excuse. They may be correct enough in their own conduct, but they are very useful to those who are not correct. Foremost among this class in Valeria's affairs was Miss Cromo. Her warning on hearing the story confided to her had shown how perfectly she knew what would be the wishes of those involved, and she made haste to anticipate them. These wishes could not have been carried out if she had opposed them ; with her assistance, they could easily be realized. She had, as she might have expressed it, the whip-hand in the affair. She had the doctor in her hands, and could decide who should be called in consultation. She had a great many acquaintances, and was one of the foreign centres of Roman gossip, and she could spread a report widely. From her came the first word which characterized Valeria's brief fever delirium as insanity.

Besides her willingness to do a harm to one who

had seriously offended her, she had two powerful motives: she could thus avoid the enmity of those who might suspect her as Valeria's confidante, and she could secure the friendship of the Countess Belvedere, who could scarcely be ungrateful for such a service.

She helped with a zeal which almost exceeded Bruno's; and she must have wearied even her own very active tongue in repeating to all her acquaintances the different inventions of Bruno's company of assistants.

The servant, Marta, whom Valeria had dismissed, was questioned by Miss Pendleton.

The girl had already been prepared. She was very quick-witted, and a hint was enough.

"Was n't the Signora Valeria a little strange?" Bruno had asked.

Of course she was. The girl poured out a hundred stories, — too many, indeed. It was necessary to select from them; and she was made to understand on which she was to insist.

When Miss Pendleton examined the witness, she was scrupulous in charging her to tell only the strict truth.

Marta at once related her inventions in the most pious manner, and swore to the truth of them.

Then it was necessary to have in readiness certain manias which could not easily be disproved; for Valeria could no longer be called insane. A person may have a dangerous mania, yet seem perfectly sane.

That some notable and flagrant examples of vice should have come to her knowledge could scarcely suffice. Unfortunately, the number of persons of the highest respectability who had said very nearly the same thing, and were still going about the world in the full enjoyment of their liberty, and clothed in their right mind, would more than fill all the lunatic asylums of the universe.

It was then found that Valeria was absolutely insane in money-spending, and that she was an opium-eater; two very useful manias. By means of the first, she could be deprived of the power to hold money; and without money, she was powerless; by means of the second, her friends at a distance might be made to wish that some restraint might be put upon her till she should have been enabled to break a habit which had already unsettled her mind and might destroy her life.

There was a little effort made to ascribe to an aberration of mind her known dislike of Miss Cromo; but it was found that people insane upon that subject were but too common, and the effort expired in a laugh.

Miss Pendleton went to consult with Miss Cromo; but, as the former was "devoted to God," while the latter was supposed to be in the other camp, it was necessary to begin with a disinfecting ceremony.

Miss Pendleton introduced the subject of religion.

Miss Cromo professed herself contrite, humble, and believing. The base metal to which she had confessed to Valeria had apparently been again plated over. She was under the deepest conviction. She, the clever mocker of sixty, almost went on her knees to a woman fifteen or twenty years younger than herself, whose mind and profession she had ridiculed and despised. She assured Miss Pendleton that she performed her religious duties regularly, went to Mass, and said her prayers morning and evening; and she listened with meekness to a somewhat lengthened advice and admonition against backsliding.

Prayers having thus been said before meat, they proceeded piously and lovingly to mangle Valeria's reputation, to plot against her freedom, perhaps against her reason and her life. They arrived at a perfect understanding.

It is doubtful if Miss Pendleton believed one word

of all the stories which she heard and repeated; but she persuaded herself that it was best, taking all into consideration, that Valeria should be discredited, so that whatever she might say of the Belvedere affairs might be called a mania, then sent away, if she should outlive the discrediting process, where her revelations would not annoy such precious sinners.

She certainly did not dislike Valeria; on the contrary, she liked her while she was submissive; but she considered it in some sort a duty to sacrifice her in order to prevent a scandal.

Having found herself strengthened by Miss Cromo, Miss Pendleton went to visit another lady.

Mrs. Harwood was a person of a very different character. She was a childless widow in good circumstances, but in bad health. She was a kind friend to Valeria, who had a sincere respect and affection for her. Of an upright and honorable nature, the qualities of her heart were even exceeded by those of her head ; and her intellect, if she had had the full use of it, would have been of an almost masculine character.

Like the most of the little circle of Valeria's acquaintances, she was a Catholic convert, and, being an invalid and advanced in age, her religion was her chief employment and consolation.

A peculiarity in her was the great respect which she professed and demanded for authority; and this sentiment was expressed less with a feminine reverence than with the masculine assertion of one who assumes to be authoritative in himself, and is defending the privileges of his own order. For while she denounced a popular independence of opinion and thought, she was herself notably independent with those whom she acknowledged to be authorities, and very hard to silence when not convinced that she was wrong. Once convinced, however, she submitted nobly. She had the partial justice of a good intellect ;

but justice is never perfect without imagination, and she was utterly unimaginative. She was incapable of fancying herself in any other position than that which she occupied.

This lady's malady, a nervous one, was peculiar. She was subject to short trances, into which she would fall while talking, or after any exertion of the mind. The face became vacant, the eyes fixed, the form motionless. If addressed at such a time, she did not seem to hear. She appeared to be insensible, sitting upright with her eyes open.

After a minute or so, during which her interlocutor would pause in embarrassment or fear, according to his degree of familiarity with this phenomenon, she would suddenly resume the conversation where she had left it, and go on talking, without seeming to be aware that she had interrupted herself. If the person had continued talking to her, she had either no knowledge, or a very distorted idea, of what had been said.

This nervous malady had other consequences. One was an impatience of being kept waiting or of being contradicted, which would sometimes throw her into a sudden fury, as startling to one not accustomed to her as a sudden squall across a glassy lake. Her face would crimson with an instantaneous rush of blood, her voice would rise almost to a scream, and, though infirm, she would for the moment be endowed with the agility of youth and health. Then, as suddenly, the squall was over, and she seemed as unconscious of it as she had been of the trance.

Her friends spoke of her with affectionate indulgence and pity. Among indifferent people she was unceremoniously spoken of as half crazy.

This lady, then, herself at liberty, was held to be an authority in deciding whether another should be put under restraint.

The subject pained and disturbed her; she was sorry for Valeria, and she did not feel herself well enough to take any responsibility in the affairs of others, though, on hearing the stories that were brought to her, she unhesitatingly decided that Valeria ought to be sent to an asylum. Shut up within the four walls of her house, and utterly lacking in that artistic curiosity and in the lively charity which might have made her, had she possessed them, wish to know what was going on in the world, she knew nothing and cared nothing beyond her own circle, and she held her exclusion to be a virtue. Those habits of observation which make the artist and the writer, she held to be a fault in Valeria.

It was not alone Miss Pendleton who talked to this lady; Miss Cromo, with whom she had no intimacy, and in whom she had no confidence, invited her to go out to drive, and came for her in a cab, that they might talk without interruption.

Miss Cromo began with praises of Valeria. She was so fond of her, so sorry for her; poor Valeria had so much talent; had Mrs. Harwood read her last story in the *Sunrise Monthly?* No? What a pity! She would herself lend it to her. She liked it better than anything she had previously read of Valeria's. .

Then came the object of their interview.

Mrs. Harwood knew Miss Cromo's character perfectly in a theoretical way. She had said to Valeria of a mutual acquaintance of theirs, "Clarissa knows her, root and branch." Yet practically she could be made by her to believe almost anything.

Miss Cromo, doing all that she could to prove that Valeria was fit only for a lunatic asylum, begged that she might not be sent to one, and Mrs. Harwood insisted that there was no other course possible. Though she knew absolutely nothing of the case except by hearsay, she considered it perfectly clear, and abundantly proved. Whether she would have considered such witnesses sufficient if it had been a question of shutting herself up, is doubtful.

Mrs. Harwood knew the American Consul and was known by him, and her word would have weight with him. It was for this chiefly that she was wanted.

The two doctors, though apparently the most important, were, in reality, secondary characters in the drama. An able and honest physician would have swept this network away like a spider's-web.

Good care was taken that no such person should be called. Dr. Kraus had been skilfully manipulated by Miss Cromo. He understood that he might make friends by pronouncing against Valeria, and enemies by resisting the influences brought to bear upon him.

He certainly did not expect that his dictum would ever be called into question, or he would never have dared to pronounce it. He had to choose between the weak and the strong, and he did not hesitate. Still he would never of himself have ventured to call such a physician as Dr. Lacelles in consultation. He would have preferred, maybe, to call a man of some reputation, and throw the responsibility off his own shoulders. He was not allowed to.

Dr. Lacelles was a familiar visitor of Miss Cromo's, and being, according to her, a solemn ass, was admirably calculated to sign the document which should put Valeria out of the way.

Dr. Lacelles was doubtless entirely honest, and certainly not malicious. But he was fond of the marvellous; and he naturally liked to be of some importance in his profession. This was probably the first time in his life that he had ever been called in consultation, and it is doubtful if his professional services had been required before in any way since his sojourn in the Holy City.

He talked with Valeria in her delirium, and listened to all the stories that were told him by others. Perhaps he consulted some medical volume. Finally, when, worn to a shadow by three weeks of severe physical suffering badly cured, or not cured at all, the patient was feebly creeping back to life in spite of doctors and visitors, Dr. Lacelles decided that she was hopelessly insane.

It had a fine sound, that "hopelessly insane." It was striking, and made people stare. And when the poor maniac was known to have a novel at the point of publication, the affair became dramatic, even tragical. If the book should receive attention, it might call the doctors into notice. It was not every doctor who could put a novelist into a lunatic asylum, however he might wish to do so. Then people would be sure to ask him questions about it, and he would have the pleasure of telling a striking story.

On the whole, such an opportunity of distinguishing himself might never again be offered to him, and he resolved to improve it. He did not get a patient so often as to willingly let one go who he knew was not likely ever to avail herself again of his services. He secured his prize by shutting her up. It was better to have had a crazy patient than not to have had any.

So much for the star performers, and the people who pulled the wires.

There was also a chorus. There were indifferent people, who, now they came to think of it, had always found Valeria odd. There must be something morbid in a person who does not appreciate the bliss of receptions, calls, dinners, and tattle. She had probably been queer for a long time.

It all helped. " *Quod non fecerunt barbari, fecerunt Barberini.*" What malice had not done, imbecility finished.

Many of them pitied Valeria, they even wiped their eyes in speaking of her when it was thought that she might die. They felt themselves to be very charitable toward her ; and, understanding the corporal works of mercy to be an unlimited use of their tongues, they performed that duty with an admirable zeal.

If she had died, it is probable that she would have had rather a grand funeral, and would have been found to be possessed of many virtues.

There are persons who are impracticable in this world, but they make such beautiful figures out of it that it seems very bad taste in them not to give their friends the melancholy pleasure of wreathing their cold brows with the *corona funebralis*.

As for the consul, his part was to sign the papers. He took for granted that all was right. He knew nothing of the lady except what had been told him ; and since they told him that she was insane, he took for granted that she was.

CHAPTER XXIX.

MAKING THE BEST OF IT.

VALERIA remained in her room the next day, and thought over her position. The one decision that she could arrive at was to make no protest. Everything was very comfortable as long as she did not see those women, and in her own room she was perfectly separated from them. She said nothing, therefore. To her languor and weakness, which made talking difficult, was added the conviction that she had better not talk.

Miss Pendleton came to see her the second day,

having learned from the sister that she made no complaint, and seemed unaware of the deception that had been practised upon her ; and even to Miss Pendleton she made no reproach. She was scarcely sure that the lady deserved any ; for she did not yet know that the lunatic asylum of the Lungara and Villa Barberini were different classes of the same establishment.

Miss Pendleton seemed very anxious that she should be comfortable, and was delighted with her apparent contentment. She reiterated her charges to Valeria not to give herself any trouble, and her promises that everything should be done for her. She promised to send her books to read, and to visit her often.

Valeria said but little. She was feeling a slight difficulty in breathing, and shivered a little now and then. Her exposure to the rain on coming to this place was bringing back both the fever and congestion of the lungs ; and she had added to her cold in going out into the villa that day. Sister Agnes, having had no idea given her of her patient's state of health, had taken no precautions.

Miss Pendleton went, and the Medical Director of the Asylum came to visit her, and stayed some time. He was a handsome, stately gentleman, and his title suited him. He was a cavalier.

What did she wish for ? She had but to command. Was she comfortable ? Did she like her room ? Let her say what was lacking, and it should be ordered for her at once.

Valeria felt more hopeful and secure after this visit. She had little confidence in women, not believing them capable of justice. They might have noble and generous impulses and tender hearts, but their principles were, in her opinion, very sketchy and pliable. She would never have given to woman the ballot, the law, nor the sole direction of any institution whatever where they would have unquestioned power over others. She did not believe in angelic women, though she knew that there were good women. She always suspected an angelic woman to be an illusion, a hypocrite, or a mere unproven piece of composition which would not stand fire. "No woman has a right to be an angel to anybody but her lover," she said; and, also, "I never saw a perfect woman who had not some serious imperfection hidden in her." Her only divisions of women were into those who listen and peep at keyholes, and those who do not; and the subdivision of those who do not, into women who are blockheads, and women who have brains. Her ideal woman was an intellectual one, who resolutely minded her own business.

As for those men whom she did not find either odious or indifferent, she regarded them with a somewhat ideal homage. In the shadow of a serious, strong, broad-shouldered man she sat down as contented as a lamb in the shade of a rock at noonday. She had the most tranquil confidence in their power to slay giants, lions, and dragons.

The entrance of a gentleman on the scene was, therefore, reassuring.

When he went, her feet were cold and her head hot. Later, she became so cold that she went to bed to warm herself; and when her supper was brought, she could not eat. She was shivering violently. Hot applications were made at once; but they came too late.

From that moment every care was taken of her; but she went downward. It was a return of the illness from which she had just begun to recover.

But the circumstances were different. Here were intelligent and authoritative medical attendance, and good nurses. Nothing that skill or charity could do was omitted; and thanks to such care, she was not delirious, though sometimes half unconscious, and incapable of all mental effort.

Miss Pendleton came to see her one day with Mrs. Harwood, but she could not talk with them; and they were not allowed to stay long.

The days dragged wearily, in that most frightful of all pain of suffocation. The doctors themselves became almost discouraged, and Valeria thought that she was going to die.

"Ask the Director if he thinks that I will ever get well," she said one day to Miss Pendleton, who had come to see her. "I ought to know the truth."

Miss Pendleton went, and returned with the answer, "He says that you may recover, but that it will take a long time, and a great deal of care."

A fortnight of misery passed; then one day life found a point for his lever to rest upon, and lifted, little by little, the weight of suffering. She could sit up in bed, and she wrote a few letters, with the reluctant consent of Sister Agnes.

On one of those days Miss Pendleton, who had undertaken all her affairs, and among them the care of her letters, gave her a letter and a magazine from America. The magazine contained a story of hers, and the letter the publisher's check. She indorsed the check, making it payable to Miss Pendleton, and gave it to her.

"Have you drawn for the other money I told you of?" she asked. "You know I cannot go to the bank. I have written them to pay your draft."

"Don't trouble yourself with any thoughts of business, my dear," Miss Pendleton said. "Everything will be done for you. We will see to everything."

"But it troubles me not to know anything," Valeria said. "Is there any one in my apartment yet? You said you knew a tenant who would like to have it."

"I have given up the apartment to the landlord," Miss Pendleton answered, not without a slight air of bracing herself for a possible battle.

"But the furniture," Valeria said, amazed.

"I have given that up, reserving some few things that I thought you might like to keep, your candelabra and the table things."

"But I had a lease, and I ought to have seen the man," Valeria persisted. "And, besides, there were two or three articles of rare furniture not easily found, and I don't want to lose them."

"The man does n't want to talk anything about the matter," Miss Pendleton said, telling a falsehood; for he had asked to see Valeria, and preferred to wait till he could see her. "I have given it all up. I thought it was best."

Valeria had meant to give up the house, but to do so in her own time and way, and she was stupefied at this high-handed proceeding.

"You know you said that you wanted to go back to America, and were invited to stay at the convent where Sister Veronica is."

"I thought of going, but was not decided to," Valeria replied. "I am bound to nothing. I hold myself free to stay or to go, or to live where I may like when I shall be well again."

"Well, don't think anything about it now," Miss Pendleton said, with soothing affection. "Think only of getting well, and all the rest can be settled afterward."

Valeria submitted. She had never dreamed of suspecting Miss Pendleton; she had never dreamed that she was not free, and that she could not leave the place where she was as soon as she should be out of bed. What motive could Miss Pendleton have but a charitable one? None, surely; and to such charity much might be pardoned. That the affairs of the

Countess Belvedere had any connection with her being brought to this place never occurred to her imagination. Of the wild stories going about her, she had no conception. She supposed that, having so few acquaintances, no one spoke of her affairs; and she believed that there was nothing uncommon in her circumstances.

A day or two after a letter came to her from a friend in Paris to whom she had written as soon as she became aware what sort of place she was in. Her complaint had been very gentle. "I was very sick, and needed care," she wrote; "but I think some other place might have been found than a lunatic asylum, or that I might have been left quiet in my own house."

The reply was an indignant one. "They had no right to put you in such an establishment," her friend wrote. "I have written a letter of expostulation to Mrs. Harwood. You ought to be taken away immediately."

Valeria wrote at once a soothing reply. "I am taken such good care of here, and every one is so kind, that I think it best to stay till I am quite well."

Every day her health improved. She could sit up, and she had the promise of going to church on Christmas Day. And a few days before Christmas Miss Pendleton came again to see her, accompanied by Madame de la Roche, the superior of the convent where she lived.

Valeria had known and admired this lady, and ran to kiss her hand with the greatest pleasure when she entered. "How good of you to come!" she exclaimed. "This makes my 'Merry Christmas.'"

The superior of the nuns in charge of the Asylum came to see Valeria the same evening, and said that she had talked with her visitors as they went out.

"And," she said, "Madame de la Roche said to me, 'Why, there is nothing the matter with that lady. Mademoiselle Valerie is perfectly reasonable.'"

Valeria made no reply. They had said that there was something the matter with her, then; and she had not been believed to have her reason perfectly!

From that day she began to take short walks in the grounds, accompanied by Sister Agnes or by Fidelia, and on Christmas morning she went to the chapel to communion, and to the *coretto* of the nuns for Mass.

This church-going showed her that the Villa Barberini was but a part of the Lunatic Asylum of the Lungara, to which she had absolutely refused to go. The chapel was in the Lungara, and the long way that led to it revealed everything.

Passing down the little terraced garden in an angle of the walls close to the *casino*, they entered a long passage which led over the arch of San Spirito, and connected the two parts of the establishment on the two sides of the street. Arrived at the Tiber side, they entered a labyrinth of dormitories, — long, sombre halls, with no furniture but a double row of white beds down the sides, and an alternate chair and table between them.

Nothing could be more mournful than these great deserted chambers, tenanted at night by a crowd of disordered brains, a strange, nightmare company of condemned and executed criminals against reason. What cries, what dreams, what mutterings, what wild terrors, must these dim walls have witnessed when the night-lamp threw its pallid ray along those lines of living graves wherein so many a soul lay dead to all but torment! What gesticulating hands, what eyes peeping wildly from under the pillows, what breaths more terrible than screams!

Valeria had heard a story of the men's department of this establishment. A large knife had been left with a plate, by some oversight, in the long dormitory, where a male nurse slept at either end. When all were asleep, one of the maniacs, softly rising, had fallen upon the nurse nearest to him so suddenly as to prevent any outcry, killed him, cut off his head, and set it in the plate. Going, then, to the other nurse, he wakened him, and showed him the ghastly head. " You see, he is still asleep," he said, pointing to the closed eyes.

" How dared they put me in such a place ! " thought Valeria, with a sudden blaze of horror and indignation. . " How dared they ! "

The boldness of her committal there stupefied her. She was almost incredulous of it. She looked back through all the time that had elapsed since, in her own house, she had emerged from the darkness of delirium, and she saw no excuse for such an act. Everything was remembered. She had forgotten nothing.

The dormitories passed, they came to an iron screen leading to a stairway and a long gallery looking into a court. Here there was a buzzing like the sound of a bee-hive. Poorly dressed women, those of the third class, sat along the sides of the gallery. Below, in the court, a crowd of women wandered about. One wore a crown of straws; another ran about searching for something which she never found; a third sat on a bench, and gazed before her with a face of despair; a fourth laughed like an idiot; — there was every form of madness.

The *coretto* was a small chapel, in one side of which a grated window looked down on the altar of a little church. A chair was placed for Valeria before this grating, and she tried to assist at the Mass in peace of mind. But it was impossible. All her self-control was necessary to keep the tears back. It revolted her to hear Mass through iron bars, she who had often longed to hear it in the open air, and scarcely liked the gilded roof of a basilica over her, or the tossing feathers of a lady's hat between her and the altar.

Then there was the wretched walk back through the dormitories. What a paradise the garden seemed when they came out into it from the arch of San Spirito !

The *casino*, which joined the wall of the villa on the Lungara side, was near the southern corner of the grounds, and the avenue beginning at the arch ran between narrow gardens at this side, laid in small terraced flats next the wall, but smoothly curved, and rising to the house at the other side. Every beautiful flowering tree and plant had been lavished here, and even now there were flowers. A gigantic pepper-tree hung full of red berries against the windows, and a beautiful palm stood like a fountain arrested in mid air, and turned to a tree, close to the lower veranda.

Following a foot-path through the shrubbery beside the *casino*, Valeria reached the garden in front, and seated herself on a bench against the balustrade there. All Rome, from the Castel Sant' Angelo southward, was stretched out before her, not flattened as in many views, but with all its various curves, and its hills and hollows. The Tiber ran past, and glimmered under the iron bridge, and the bridge of San Sisto, and away, away past the palaces and domes and towers that were laden with history as a toiling brain with thoughts, and weary with their memories, mumbled now through crumbling stones. Here rose the Quirinal with its palace, there the Pincio lifted its leafy coronet, far away the Esquiline showed its soaring *campanile*, and lower down the Cœlian and the Palatine with their gardens, and the melancholy Janiculum a confusion of piled and sculptured stone, and gardens, and pines and cypresses. It was glorious; but it was like all the glory of man, more than half mournful and cruel.

On the second side of the building enclosing the garden three long windows opened out on a veranda on the ground-floor. These three windows opened from three rooms belonging to the first class. The outer one was the Donna Claudia's, the inner belonged to the Duchess. In the central one the window was almost always closed, and had the blinds drawn together.

As Valeria sat there, this window was opened from within, and a tall lady, dressed in white, came out and seated herself on the bench at the veranda. She had an air at once of refinement and of suffering. This lady was called the *Signora bianca*, from her dress. She never spoke to any of the other patients, never went to walk, nor met the others at table. All her time was passed in her room, except that now and then, when the garden was almost deserted, she came out and sat in the sunlight for a moment. She was not insane, though she was nervous and excitable, and an air of mystery surrounded her. The beautiful toilets that she had brought with her showed that she had been in fashionable society. She never wore any of them. Summer and winter, she wore nothing but white. She was waiting for a gentleman to whom she was engaged to come and marry her, she said to her attendant; and she had waited there for years. Meantime her long, beautiful hair of loosely curling flax-color was turning white. She spoke Italian with elegance, but seemed to be German.

Sister Agnes came up from the Community, which, with the kitchens, officers' rooms, chapel, and third-class women patients, was at the other side of the Lungara. The *casino*, one might say, was the drawing-room of the establishment. All the ladies then came out into the garden for the air. As they ap-

peared, the *Signora bianca* rose hastily, and retired to
her room, closing the venetian blinds behind her.

Instantly the scene took a new character. It was
beautiful, but it became terrible. For all that beauty
of nature and art became at once implacable. It was
the vision of Paradise to Dives in hell. The streets
stretched away not far below, yet they could not set
foot in them. Within sight of them were women who
leaned from their windows, and went about as they
liked, and complained, maybe, of their lot, not realiz-
ing that they had the supreme good of liberty, and a
right to themselves. They would have looked on these
women shut up here as in some way radically different
from themselves, instead of being, many of them, but a
step in advance on the path of unreason. These women
walked in beautiful gardens, and their faces and their
hearts were sad. If they spoke, their words were
held as folly. They were not believed even when
they told the truth. If they should escape for a moment and run to the gate under the bridge, the porter
would not let them pass. The gate was high, and the
wall was high, and they could not fly over. If one
should steal away for a moment, slip through the long
passage over the bridge unseen, go down the stair, and
stand at the front gate, with only an iron screen between her and liberty, still she could not pass. She
would have to return. If she showed anger, even
such anger as a sane person might show, if not wise
enough to control herself, she would be locked into
her room, and perhaps put in a straight-jacket. When
they were conducted to their rooms at night and put
to bed, the light was taken away, and the door locked.
They were never lost sight of. It was the duty of the
attendants to keep them always in view, and to know
everything that they did. They had no privacy.
The same watchfulness which is necessary for the
most cunning and dangerous maniac is necessary

for her who shows little or no sign of mental disease. It is assumed that every person placed in such a house is placed there because she may do some harm to others or to herself, and although there may be no indications of any such danger, they are bound to look out for and expect them. One can never calculate surely upon the vagaries of an insane person.

Moreover, it is not solely the indications of real insanity which are commented upon and noted in such a place; but every little characteristic word or act, every mark of originality, every sign of anger or impatience which a free person may freely show unsuspected, — all are so many proofs of insanity. The nurse may be angry; the doctor may be angry; the patient, — no. You try to conceal some innocent affair of your own, from delicacy, or from a natural pride or reserve; and you are held to be cunning. The affair is searched out, as it may be something dangerous. By a strange sort of reasoning, the very desire to leave the asylum is held to be a proof of unsound mind, and contentment a sign of improvement. Precisely the acts and words natural to a sane person whom some plot has entrapped into an asylum of this kind would be held by one believing the person to be insane as proofs of insanity.

No crime is easier to commit against an unprotected person than to accuse him of insanity, prove him insane, put him into an asylum, and there drive him mad. The very accusation is strong to bring about its own justification; and the ignorance or dishonesty of physicians is seconded by the ignorance of the public.

People study books, but they do not study their neighbors nor themselves; and a thousand things in their own conduct or the conduct of those about them are passed over without the slightest notice, which

in a person whom they believed or suspected to be
insane would be to their minds the most palpable
eccentricities.

Let any one watch his dearest friend for one day,
trying to imagine that some one wishes to prove that
friend to be insane, and see how many times during the day he will tremble lest the proofs may be
found.

It cannot be expected that the persons having im-
mediate charge of the insane should be wiser than
their day and generation. The physicians are educated to their work; but the nurses, often ignorant
people, are not. And, unfortunately, it is in the
power of the nurse, by his very ignorance, to prejudice the physician against the patient.

We are all familiar with the story of the rustic
neighborhood which set down Wordsworth and his
friends as a company of lunatics. Who but lunatics
would wander about at night, gazing at the stars?
To the vulgar and the material, fancy and imagination are a sort of insanity. These people have a term
of their own; it is, " cracked." And the word is not
so badly chosen. The one they presume to criticise
has cracked the shell wherein they lie in complacent
darkness. One may fancy that the grub may call the
butterfly " cracked."

Valeria was thinking of these things as she sat and
looked at the patients: Sor Agnesina of the yellow
hair, forgetting the wrongs of the Pope in a new
pattern of crochet; the Duchess, happy over a journal
of fashion; Donna Claudia, walking to and fro, swinging her handkerchief by the corner; the Donna Faustina, making a bit of tatting into which she wove a
straw and some raisin-stems saved from her yesterday's dinner; and the Signora Eleanor, a young woman who had gone mad on the death of her husband,
scowling by herself in a corner, and refusing to speak

to any one. And she was among these! They were all crazy, and they were her companions!

Were beautiful flowers and trees and fountains, and a panorama of Rome rolled out from the walls that surrounded her, a compensation?

No; but they were a consolation and a preservative.

Valeria was settling in her own mind what she should do; and she was asking herself some questions that made her tremble. She felt now that she could not have been placed in this house as a person entirely in her right mind. She believed herself free to go away when she would, now that she was well and gaining strength; but she was sure that she must have been committed to the place with some sort of ceremony. Every restriction possible had been removed from her. Since the first night or two, her chamber door had not been locked; she was free to stay alone all day, and to go to walk in the villa when she would, though always attended. They said that she was outside the rules. The Director had told her that any time when she wished to go out into the city for a walk, or to visit her friends, accompanied by a maid, he would write a pass for her. She felt herself in a sort of liberty, — as much liberty, in fact, as could be given to any one in an establishment, where some regulations were imperative; and she had no anxiety for the future. But she shuddered at the past.

What, she asked herself, would they have done on the day she came there, if, when left alone outside the gate, she had had a misgiving, and gone away, and tried to return to her own house? She had positively refused to go to the Lungara asylum, and they had dared to deceive her by taking her to another door of the same establishment. They had been bold in everything. They had given up her lease, which

they must have searched her papers to find, and
arranged everything in their own way, because they
"thought it best." And this, when they could have
no smallest authority in her affairs except such as
she gave them. She was entirely her own mistress,
and accountable to no one in the world, except to the
laws of the land. No law could have placed her here
unless she had been complained of to the police as a
disturber of the community, and dangerous to herself
and her neighbors. They had taken the law into
their own hands.

And what would have been done to her if, on first
knowing what sort of people she was among, two
days after coming, she had insisted on leaving immediately? If they had refused to allow her to go, or if
she had been forced to enter on the first day, could
she have answered for herself? Could she be sure
that she would not have resisted with all her strength?
Resistance would have been madness, and they would
have used force. Nothing but her ignorance on the
first occasion, and her self-control and silence on the
second, had saved her. Remembering now how nervous Miss Pendleton had been, and how she had hurried away, — peculiarities which even in her miserable
weakness she had observed at the time, — she knew
that it was meant that she should enter and that she
should stay.

While she sat there, Sister Agnes came to her with
a letter.

"Miss Pendleton sent it to you this morning," she
said. "It was left at your apartment."

It was a foreign letter written by the editor of a
monthly magazine, who wanted her to write him a serial, and would be glad to have it as soon as possible.

Valeria smiled. "I wonder what he would say if
he knew where I am," she said to the sister, to whom
she communicated the news.

The Director and the Superior had waived their right of opening letters in her case, and she acknowledged their politeness by translating the contents of them to the sister.

The little incident was brightening, and started her thoughts on another train.

" My house is given up, and I do not care to go among strangers just yet," she said to herself. " The worst is over. I am here, and when in my room I am very comfortable. They say that I have been entered for three months. There are six weeks more. I will make the best of it, and stay the rest of the time. I can write this story here, and I can study the life of an asylum. It is n't every one who has the opportunity to examine a lunatic asylum from the inside. All is grist that comes to my mill. We 'll live and conquer, Valeria *mia*. And we will take good care not to trust any one too much again, so long as we have breath."

A carriage with a bay horse and a white one came down the avenue, and stopped at the steps. The back part was shaped like a great box, and there was a hood over the driver's seat. Two servant-girls came out of the *casino*, and went down to take out large tin boxes containing the dinner. It was cooked in the great kitchen below in the Lungara, and brought round in the carriage through the villa.

Valeria went up to her room, and sat looking out at the pine-trees, and at the tall eucalyptus that swung its slender branches against the bars of her window.

" Our Lord had his Merry Christmas in a stable," she thought, and was thankful that it was no worse.

CHAPTER XXX.

UNMASKING.

V ALERIA began at once upon her serial, — a
    slight thing, since, at best, it was impossible to
write well in such a place.   In her own apartment all
was tranquil, she was perfectly served and kindly
treated by all, from highest to lowest; but she could
not go out without encountering the insane, and the
shock always set her vibrating.   Th re was ever that
terrible bridge to pass in going from her own room to
the villa ; and though she might fly over it like Tam
O'Shanter from the witches, some taint of that wild
company always remained to spoil her first breath of
pure air, and first moments before that grand panorama, or her first hour in the tranquil privacy of her
own chamber.

The only employment in which she could really
forget herself was in studying the place and the people.   To look at them, thinking, This is my home and
there are my companions, was intolerable; but to
look at them as a new, strange book which she was
to read, was interesting, though still painful.

The site of the Manicomio of Rome is one of great
interest, even amid objects of such rich historical
value as are everywhere to be found in that incom-
parable city.

The arch of San Spirito, which, by means of a covered passage, connects the two parts of the establishment on the two sides of the Lungara, was built by
Pope Leo IV. when he built the walls around the
Vatican, enclosing the territory which was named,
after him, the Leonine City.   It was the principal
one of the six gates, and was then called the Porta di

Borgo. This was about the year 850. Early in the sixteenth century the Farnese Pope, Paul III., when he constructed the bastions of the Borgo, ordered a new gate to be made by Antonio da Sangallo. But some difficulties put in the way of the artist by Michael Angelo retarded the work, and he died before it was completed. When, early in the seventeenth century, Urban VIII. removed the wall between Porta san Pancrazio and Porta Cavalleggieri, in order to include the rest of the Janiculum in the Leonine City, the name of the gate was changed from Porta di Borgo to Porta San Spirito, from the near hospital. It remained useless, however, from this time, as did also the Porta Settimiana.

The covered passage over the gate of San Spirito was made by Pius IX. when he purchased the Villa Barberini and the Villa Gabrielli, farther back on the Janiculum, to add to the confined and gloomy Asylum in the Lungara.

The Villa Barberini was built by Urban VIII., a Barberini from Florence. This Pope, says an Italian writer, united Florentine elegance to Roman grandeur, and had a particular liking for sumptuous villas. As pope he began the magnificent Barberini place; while yet cardinal, he bought the Villa Visconti at Castel Gandolfo, and embellished it, and built the Villa Barberini, with both palace and *casino*, between the Porta San Spirito and the Porta Cavalleggieri; and after he became pope, he also built the papal palace at Castel Gandolfo.

This palace near St. Peter's was not only for his pleasure, but also for his convenience when there should be great functions at that basilica; and there exists to-day in that locality, close to the Colonnade, a defaced and squalid palace used for the manufacture of beer, which has over the principal entrance the arms of Urban VIII., the tiara, with the Barberini bees. The gardens extended back of this, up the hill, and contemporary writers give a glowing picture of its groves and fountains, of the riches in pictures and vases and majolica plates and basins of both palace and *casino,* and of the superb views caught through its flowering trees.

In building for Urban VIII. there were discovered the ruins of elegant baths, of pavements, and other remains of an ancient villa supposed, from an inscription found there, to have belonged to the poet Celio, of the time of Augustus. This house in which we find Valeria was the *casino* built by Urban VIII. ; and in the excavations under her window looking toward St. Peter's, were found some of the same ancient ruins discovered in his time.

The site of the palace near St. Peter's was the same as that of the palace of Nero (*palatiolum*), from which it is said that the emperor beheld the sufferings of the Christian martyrs in the Circo di Cayo, opposite his windows, in what is now the piazza of St. Peter's.

The *casino* of the villa, when Valeria first went there, had the arms of Urban VIII. painted on the ceilings of the anteroom and the long drawing-room ; but they were afterward painted over, in repairing the house. Outside, along the cornice under the roof, are the Barberini bees carved in stone.

The bastions of Paul III. were strengthened by Urban VIII. ; and one glance at those dark precipices of stone-work will show what a formidable fortress the Barberini family had when the death of the Pope left Rome in that lawless state which used to prevail during an interregnum, and when the jealousy which their prosperity of more than twenty years' duration had excited, if not resentment for any wrongs which they might have committed, had opportunity for revenge.

It is now about fifteen years since Pius IX. bought

the villas Barberini and Gabrielli, and built the passage over the gate of San Spirito, thus making, perhaps, the largest establishment of the kind in the world.

The *casino* of Villa Gabrielli, and two new buildings in the grounds, are assigned to the men, and Villa Barberini, with the buildings attached to it, to the women; and there are also separate quarters for men and women in the lower buildings. There are three classes in each, and the most excellent order is preserved.

Some amusement is provided for all the classes. A band has been organized among the men, who sometimes go down to play to the third class in the Lungara; a piano recital is given to the ladies of the *casino* twice a week, and the Deputy in charge gives them all occasionally a *festa*, especially in Carnival time. Besides this, walking in the villa grounds is encouraged; and these grounds are free to all classes, though no person can walk out without an attendant. Three times a week a carriage comes to take the ladies of the *casino* out for a drive in the city and environs. Formerly there was a livery; but they have had the good taste to lay it aside for the carriage. It is worn now only by the porters and male nurses.

Those of the third class who can be trusted to work are employed. The women wash, iron, weave in the *Tessenda*, and even do housework; the men work in the gardens, and perform various services about the place. The sum paid for their keeping is very small, only fifty *lire* (about ten dollars) a month, and no remuneration is therefore made them for their labor, except some little indulgence, perhaps an extra dish at table.

The Medical Staff is admirably arranged. It consists of a Medical Director, and four regular assistants, two for the men, and two for the women. These four make their visits every day, and oftener if necessary. Of these two couples, one of each is fixed, the other attends alternate three months on the men and the women.   This alternation lasts two years, when, if the physician has not a fixed appointment, he retires, leaving his name on the books for a vacancy.   No one receives an appointment who has not served two years in alternate attendance on both men and women. Besides the list of those who have thus received their diploma, there is another list of candidates for their vacant places.

The highest officer is a Deputy appointed by the government.   He is not a resident ; but the present Deputy (Tommasini) is a daily visitor, who may come in at any hour, and takes pains to drop in when least expected, keeping a strict watch over everything, severe if he detects the slightest neglect of duty, but kind and very much beloved by the patients.

But what interested Valeria more than the mere magnitude and direction of this great establishment was the patients themselves.   It seemed to her that this kindness in the treatment of the insane was but one step, though a great one, out of the barbarism of the past in Europe and America, and that the time might come when humanity and charity would find some means of curing those diseased minds in which the disease is not a temporary effect of physical illness. All that can be done for health and bodily comfort, and to keep the patient tranquil and cheerful, is done in this Manicomio ; but there is no time for psychological experiments, even if there were persons educated to make them.   Nature must first make such nurses, — for it is the nurse's work, not the doctor's, — and grace must confirm them.   The nurse is a far more important person in a lunatic asylum than the doctor, and should never be a vulgar and coarse person, and never an excitable one.

It is said that an insane person thinks every one about him insane; and it is no wonder; for the manner in which people usually treat an insane person would be insanity if addressed to a sane one. The patient, not believing himself insane, perceives this strangeness. The vague and careless answer, the evasions, the promises made in order to soothe and never meant to be fulfilled, the utter absence of any appeal to the reason, the disregard of reiterated prayers and requests, — all these are frequently unnecessary and injurious. Few or none of the insane are altogether insane, and they are capable of telling the truth. Their complaints may not be reasonable, but they may be a distorted image of a real grievance, and should sometimes receive attention. All of them think that they are the victims of a great wrong; but that is no proof that there may not be such a victim while the laws regarding their committal are so criminally negligent. No murderer is condemned unheard, no vilest criminal is executed privately without a warning. But the unfortunate who is insane, or supposed to be, is hidden away without defence. If he is seen, afterwards and talked with, there is ever between him and the spectator the wall of his supposed or real insanity. He talks reasonably ? What of that ? They all talk reasonably sometimes. He wants to go away ? They all want to go away. He says that there is a plot against him ? It is the old story. He begs you to have his case investigated, or to take a letter out for him ? They all want justice, and to send out letters. It is not permitted to send letters out. In short, there is nothing that the victim of a plot can do that an insane person has not already done.

There should be a jury for the insane as well as for the sane. It should be remembered that they are unfortunate, not wicked, and that their incarceration is more terrible in itself and in its effects than that of any criminal. They should be visited and asked to say why condemnation of worse than death should not be passed upon them. Nor is some agitation any proof against them. Their situation would naturally produce it. If undeserved, no horror could be greater, no insult more unpardonable.

Valeria found one exception to this rule of victims in an old man of the third class, who helped to bring up the supper through the bridge. For the carriage came only with the dinner.

She was seated in a great swing in one of the little flowery terraces as he came up. The gardener had given her a beautiful cane, cutting the dry leaves from the glistening yellow stalk, and leaving a faint ring of green above each knot, and she was dreamily pushing herself to and fro with it, and reading a news-paper, when she saw this old man looking through the fence at her.

" Well ? " she said.

He pulled off his cap.

" How do you do ? " she asked.

He shook his head. " I 'm crazy," he said.

"Oh, no !" she replied. " If you were crazy, you would n't know it."

" Yes; I am crazy," he persisted mournfully. " I can't remember anything but the Ave Maria. I can say that ; but I can't think. I don't know anything. I had a sickness, and I am crazy."

" He is saner than I am," she thought with a smile. " For if I am queer, I do not know it."

A month wore away, and Valeria began to think of finding an apartment for herself; and one day when she was out driving with the nurse, she glanced at the houses where there were notices of rooms to let.

" I am searching for an apartment," she remarked. " If I find a place that seems pleasant, I shall go in and see it."

Nothing more was said.

They returned to the Manicomio, supper was brought up, and at her usual hour she went to bed.

A few minutes after, just as she was dropping asleep, she seemed to hear some one lock the door on the outside.

The sound was rather in her heart than in her ears. But it was impossible to sleep with that doubt, and she rose to reassure herself.

The door was locked on the outside.

Can the reader imagine how terrible this might be? It was not the mere locking of the door, which could not well be more, in ordinary circumstances, than an inconvenience; as, except in case of sickness or fire, · she would not wish to leave her chamber in the night. The terror was in the reason for locking it. It meant that now, after having had full liberty for weeks, she was an object of suspicion, and that something had occurred to make them curtail that liberty. And this might be only a beginning. She had seen how utterly worthless are the judgments of most people when it is a question of one charged with a mania, or a slight aberration of mind; and for the first time since she recovered from the shock of finding herself in an asylum, she realized how unsafe it was for her to be there.

She thought over all the incidents of the day, and tried to discover what she might have done that could seem strange. It was her habit, while writing, to rise and walk to and fro, now and then, to relieve the fatigue of long sitting, and sometimes, while walking, she read or repeated a page that she had written.

The Donna Claudia and the Donna Faustina walked to and fro declaiming. Had they put her in the same category?

Then, in the garden that day, she had pointed out

the variety of clouds, — for a storm was passing off, and settled fine weather coming in, — and had told the names of the different classes of vapors.

The nurses might think that only an insane person would dream of naming the clouds.

At last she recollected what she had said to Fidelia about the apartment she was looking for. Nothing seemed so likely as that to be the cause of this strange precaution. She had not thought it necessary to speak to any one of her intention, meaning to seek an early opportunity to talk with the Medical Director about it.

No sleep visited her eyes that night. She had not slept when she heard the nurse who made her rounds at five o'clock in the morning, approaching her room. The girl unlocked the door and entered.

"What is the meaning of my door having been locked last night?" Valeria demanded, the moment she entered.

The girl professed to know nothing about it. She had come to the door in the evening, she said, and found it locked. Perhaps it was done by mistake.

"It is a very strange mistake," Valeria said, "and I hope it will not be made again. I am out of everybody's hearing, and I might have been sick in the night. I consider it a very strange proceeding."

The girl was as simply ignorant as only a well-trained Italian servant can be.

Later came Sister Agnes, with a glass of milk that she always brought in the morning. Valeria put the same question to her, and she made the same reply. She thought that the door was locked by mistake.

Valeria repeated what she had already said to the nurse.

"And do you think, Sister Agnes, that it is necessary to lock my door?" she asked.

"Certainly not! And you know that it has never been done before," the sister replied.

Later in the day Valeria had a visit from a monk, a man as honest and simple as he was learned, and whom she had known ever since she came to Rome.

"How did you find the signora to-day?" Sister Agnes asked him, when Valeria had left the two together a moment.

"Just as I have always found her ever since I first knew her," he said. "I see no difference in her."

"She was excited this morning," the sister remarked.

When Valeria was again with Don Giorgio, walking in the garden, he repeated to her what the sister had said, and she explained the reason of her excitement, or more literally, her disquiet; for the nun had said *inquietata*.

"Do you wonder at it?" she asked. "And I was no more disturbed than any other person would have been in the circumstances. You see, Don Giorgio, that, once a person is in a place like this, the simplest things they may do are suspected. I have seen both Sister Agnes and the doctor more angry than I was this morning, and for a less cause; and I don't mean to blame them in saying it. The only difference is that they can resent annoyances, and I cannot. You have been very good in telling me this, but do not you see that an unfriendly or even a stupid person might have made a great deal out of it to do me harm? Oh, I am not safe here! There could grow up about me a cloud of nothings just like this, which would be enough to ruin me in the end."

Later in the day Valeria asked to see the Director. He had always been very kind to her, and she had a great respect for him.

"In what can I serve you, Madamigella?" he asked pleasantly, drawing a chair near hers.

"The three months for which I was entered here will soon expire, Signor Cavaliere," she said; "and I would like to go away."

"You would like to go away?" he repeated.

"Can you wonder at that? Of course I have been taken excellent care of, and you have all been very kind. I am grateful for that, but—"

"I understand," he interrupted. "Of course it is not the place for you. Only, as it is now midwinter, and you have twice had congestion of the lungs, you must be very careful. Where do you propose to go?"

She told him her plans.

"I would not advise you to do so," the Director said. "You could never be sure that a private family would suit you. I would counsel you to go among foreigners whose customs and ways would be the same as your own. I know a pleasant French *pension* here, where you might be comfortable. I am acquainted with the family who keep the house, and with several of the inmates of the house. I will speak to Madame L. about it to-day. I am going there. Shall I do so?"

Valeria scarcely liked a boarding-house; but she liked still less to slight the advice of one whose judgment she had reason to rely on; and she consented.

"Miss Pendleton will have to come to see me," the Director proceeded. "As she consigned you here, it is necessary that she should receive you."

"Must I have any ceremony in order to go out?" exclaimed Valeria.

"There are rules," the Director said gently, "and no matter what the state of the person may be, the rules must be observed. Some one must receive the person going out, and be responsible for her support, and that she is placed in a proper home."

"But it is a mere form in my case. I support my-self, and I can take care of myself."

"It is, however, a form which we cannot omit," was the reply.

"And," he added, "I have another counsel to give you, if you permit me. It seems to me that you have had too many acquaintances. It would be better for you to know but few persons, and those, friends on whom you can rely."

"Why, Signor Cavaliere," she exclaimed, "I have lived the life of a hermit in Rome. I do not know twenty persons. If I had had a large circle of ac-qaintances, I should never have been brought here. Some one would have prevented it."

He regarded her with a look of surprise. "A great many persons interest themselves in you," he said.

"I do not interest myself in them," Valeria replied, beginning to feel uneasy.

"What could he have meant?" she thought when he had gone. "Why did n't I ask him? But he would n't have told me, probably. No matter; let it go. I can't stop to worry over every shadow." And she put the subject out of her mind.

The next morning he came again.

"Madame L. has some vacant rooms," he said, "and will show them to you when you go. Let me know when you wish to see them, and I will write the pass for you. Would you like to go to-morrow?"

"If you please; and a thousand thanks!"

The next morning, the pass was sent up to her. It was impossible to go out without one, no matter how well she might be. It was one of the forms which could not be dispensed with as long as a person had not been regularly discharged from the Manicomio; and it gave her but little trouble, as she seldom wished to go out.

Her first visit that day was to Mrs. Harwood, who

met her with the utmost cordiality. But when Valeria told her plans, she observed that her listener's face clouded over. But no comment or opposition was made, and though a little disappointed, she took her leave without any suspicion.

From Mrs. Harwood she went to the convent where Miss Pendleton boarded, and was received with open arms. Miss Pendleton was all "my dears," and smiles. But again, when she mentioned what she was about to do, the smiles died away.

"I don't know what we can do," Miss Pendleton said, with the air of a person who contemplates an immense difficulty. "I will see. Perhaps we can get you a place somewhere."

"But I am not going 'somewhere,'" Valeria said. "I am going to Madame L.'s. So you need not give yourself the slightest trouble about the matter. I will see to all that myself. But the Director says that, as you consigned me there, you will have to receive me; and he would like to see you. I am annoyed at being in a place where it requires so much ceremony for me to get out."

It was her first intimation of displeasure at having been taken to the Manicomio, and was uttered in a tone to show her displeasure. It seemed to her that, after more than two months of silence regarding an act which looked to her every day more high-handed and outrageous, they should make haste to liberate her the moment she asked for liberty.

"I thought that you would like to stay there till spring, and then go to America," Miss Pendleton said.

"I may or may not go to America; but I do not wish to remain in a lunatic asylum till next spring," Valeria replied. "It is an insult to me to propose it."

"But they don't call it a lunatic asylum here," said Miss Pendleton. "They call it a *casa di salute.*"

"They call it a *casa di salute* when they want to coax persons into it, and a *casa dei pazzi* when they have got them in. You're 'a little nervous' when you consent to go, and 'mad' when you are shut up. But the name makes no difference. It is a lunatic asylum, inhabited by mad people, and it is an insult to expect me to stay there. To think that I cannot step into the street without a written pass!"

"We are none of us free," Miss Pendleton said. "I cannot always go out when I like, and we have all of us some restraints. Try to be patient."

"There is no comparison!" said Valeria indignantly. "I am not quite free, even when I have my liberty, any more than you. It is absurd to compare the restraints of a lunatic asylum to the ordinary restraints of life."

Their conversation was interrupted by the entrance of Madame de la Roche.

Valeria rose to meet her, and asked permission to kiss her.

"*De tout mon cœur!*" said Madame, embracing her.

"Don't let's say anything to her of what we have been saying," Miss Pendleton murmured hastily.

Madame was very deaf, and heard nothing; and Valeria went away without having mentioned the subject to her, though she wished to do so.

"You have seen Miss Pendleton?" the Director asked when she entered.

"Yes; and I think that she will come to talk with you soon. We were interrupted. I was too late to go to Madame L. afterward, for it would have been the hour of their luncheon, and our dinner. But I would like to go to-morrow, if you please."

"Certainly!" he replied. "I have given orders that you are to be free to do whatever you please. You can go out when you like."

The next day was rainy in the morning, and
Valeria did not go out. The second day was Sunday,
and in the afternoon Miss Pendleton came to see
her.

Valeria received her cordially, believing that she
had come thus promptly to see the Director.

But Miss Pendleton did not mention it, and seemed
in a hurry to go away. Her usually sweet and smiling manner was quite changed. She sat at some
distance from Valeria, in a chair close to the door.

"Have you seen the Director?" Valeria asked
at length, after waiting in vain for her visitor to
mention the subject which alone could now interest
her.

"No," was the hesitating reply; "he had gone
away."

Valeria was silent.

"It will soon be time to pay for you again here,"
Miss Pendleton said. "You know it must be paid
three months in advance."

"But I am not going to be paid for again," Valeria
exclaimed in astonishment. "I have already told you
that I am going to leave this place on the eighteenth
of next month. I shall have stayed too long in staying three months."

"But what will you do for money?" Miss Pendleton said, rising, and showing a slight anger.

"The same money that pays for me here will pay
in another place," Valeria said. "I have drawn for
money, and never received it, though the draft was
given almost six months ago. I shall have money
now every month from my serial. And there is my
new book. I shall have enough after a while."

"You have n't any now," Miss Pendleton said, with
a shade of insolence, and that little vindictive tight-
ening of the lips which, through all her smiles, Valeria had always felt was possible to them. "And you

can do nothing without money." She opened the door. "I must go. It is late," she said, and went out into the corridor.

Valeria followed her, smitten with a sudden trembling and terror. "I am sorry that I left my house!" she exclaimed. "I am sorry that I ever trusted myself in your hands."

Miss Pendleton went down-stairs, and Valeria followed her, and stopped her in the anteroom, which was vacant.

"You must go to the Director and liberate me, as you put me into his hands," she said. "You are too bold to treat me so. I will not stay here after the three months are out."

"You cannot go out without money," Miss Pendleton said. "If you stay here, everything will be done for you; if you go out, nothing will be done for you." And her face showed that if Valeria went out everything would be done against her.

"I do not wish to have anything done for me!" Valeria exclaimed. "There has been too much done already. I have been betrayed. I should have got well in my own house. I was able to walk out the second day after I came here."

"You were sick a month here," Miss Pendleton retorted.

"I was sick three weeks; but I took the sickness here."

"No, you did n't!" exclaimed the other rudely.

"I did; and they all know it. Besides, that makes no difference. I am well now, and I want my liberty."

Miss Pendleton's mask of smiles and sweet speeches was quite off now, and the vulgar, cruel woman stood revealed.

"You are not well!" she cried out. "Your head is n't right."

Valeria recoiled. It was not possible to answer in words to such brutality. Helpless, terrified, insulted, she burst into tears.

"You can stay here till spring, and then go to America," Miss Pendleton added, seeming to think that she had conquered.

"Who are you, to tell me when I shall come and go?" Valeria replied, sobbing, yet fired with anger. "I will appeal to the American Consul for protection."

"You may appeal to him," was the cool reply.

"I certainly shall.

The other looked at her with a taunting smile. "Where will you go?"

"I will go into the street sooner than be shut up here!" Valeria cried with imprudent heat.

Miss Pendleton burst into laughter.

Sister Agnes appeared, and Miss Pendleton hurried away.

"Oh, why did I trust her? Why did I put myself into her power?" cried Valeria, while the sister was trying to soothe her. "I had an impression from the very first that there was something hard and strange hidden under her affected sweetness. It was n't natural. She has betrayed me. Oh, what shall I do?"

The confident insolence of her enemy showed a consciousness of strength. She would never have dared to be so brutal if she had not an assurance of support. Yet what that support was, Valeria had no conception. She could understand nothing. All was confusion.

CHAPTER XXXI.

DE PROFUNDIS.

THE morning found Valeria calmer; for all were so kind, and so much displeased at the insult that had been offered her, that she could not but be comforted. "She should not have addressed even an insane person so," Sister Agnes said, in commenting on Miss Pendleton's conduct.

The Director came up, and ordered that Valeria should not see her again.

"I do not wish ever to see her again," she replied. "I will not willingly ever glance at her, even. But suppose that she should come?"

"Excuse yourself," answered the Director. He was walking to and fro in the *sala*, talking with Valeria and Sister Agnes, and he was angry.

"You do not know her if you think that an excuse will answer, if she should wish to come in. She would walk into my room in spite of me. And you know there is no lock inside the door."

"Tell her, if she comes, that I forbid her seeing Madamigella," he said to Sister Agnes. "I will not allow it, mind!"

He then went, advising Valeria to go out for a walk into the city.

But she was in no mood to go out, and preferred to walk in the villa with Sister Agnes.

They went up the avenue to the excavations, and found the Deputy there, looking at some new baths that had just been uncovered. He explained the ruins to them, and gave Valeria permission to take away some records of the place. There were fragments of beautiful pillars in porta-santa and white marble, a

great deal of cipolline, and numerous fragments of
sculpture, earthen vessels, beautiful opaline glass and
serpentine, alabasters of different sorts, giallo-antico
and rosso-antico.

From there, they went round to a knoll called the
monticello, in the corner of the villa nearest St. Peter's.
Here a grove of shrubs shielded the back of a bench,
and an olive-tree strewed its black berries over the
ground. From this spot they looked down into the
piazza of St. Peter's, which was scarce more than a
stone's-throw from them, and off up the Tiber and
across the fields to Ponte Molle, and the country, and
the beautiful mountains beyond. A little to the right
lay the Castel Sant' Angelo, with all the city rolling
away southward. It is one of the few supreme views
of Rome.

They seated themselves on the bench, and looked
about awhile, then walked silently back to the *casino*,
and Valeria went up to her chamber and her writing,
and tried to forget her troubles in her heroine, and to
call up scenes of New England to blot these scenes of
old Rome from her mind. The next day would be
soon enough to go to look at Madame L.'s rooms. She
thought it probable that Miss Pendleton would come
to see the Director that day.

She did not come, however, and the next morning
Valeria prepared herself to go out into the city, and
sent one of the nurses down for her pass.

"Make haste," she said; "for I want to go early.
I don't know that a pass is necessary now, for the
Director said that I was to do as I please; but it is
better to have one, in case the porter should make a
difficulty."

She dressed and went down, waiting for the nurse
in one of the lower gardens. Presently the girl appeared.

"The Director says that you cannot go out," she said.

" Impossible ! " Valeria exclaimed.

" The Sister Agnes told me so," said the girl. " She asked the Director herself, and he said that you cannot go out."

" I will not believe it unless he tells me so himself. Go and find Sister Agnes, and tell her I want her to go to the Director with me."

" Sister Agnes is in the Community."

" Come with me yourself, then," Valeria said ; and the girl, though unwilling, accompanied her over the arch of San Spirito, down stairs and through passages, to where, near the Lungara door of the Manicomio, the Director's offices were.

" The Director is not in, but will return in fifteen minutes," the porter told her. " If you will wait inside there, I will call you when he comes."

Fifteen minutes passed by, and she was not called.

" I am afraid they have forgotten me. I had better go out into the passage," she said, going toward the great prison-like door that shut in the third-class patients.

" You cannot pass, signora," said the portress, laying her hand on the lock.

It was useless to contend. With what patience she could, she seated herself again.

Another fifteen minutes passed, and then the Lady Superior appeared. She was very grave and silent. " Come with me, Mademoiselle," she said ; and, taking Valeria by the hand, led her out to the Director's office. " Wait here till he comes," she added, and left her without another word.

Presently the Director appeared.

" How did you come here ? " he exclaimed.

" The Superior brought me ; and I want to know what all this change means," Valeria said. " Something strange has happened."

He went to his desk, and stood there a moment

frowning, and turning over his papers. " I have had a letter from the American Consul," he said, flinging out a letter from the others.

Valeria, who had risen and followed him, stood at the other side of the desk. " Well ? "

He was silent a moment. " He writes complaining that I let you go out about the city, and orders that you shall be kept confined inside the walls."

Valeria uttered a cry, and clung to the desk for support.

" You see that I could not let you go," the Director said kindly. " You know I never have refused you anything. But this is accusing me, as well as you. I am supposed either not to know, or not to do, my duty."

She had scarcely heard. She was almost fainting.

" Don't mind it so much ! " the Director continued, distressed at the effect of his communication, which he had not foreseen. He had been more occupied by the thought of the injury which might be done to himself by an official accusation of neglect in the fulfilment of his duties. He well understood that in a position so responsible, and one that was, moreover, desired by many, he must keep himself above reproach, and he was anxiously scrupulous that every smallest technicality of his office should be rigidly observed. He had found Valeria a lady, and had treated her as such. He now found himself required to treat her as a mad woman.

" I will see the Consul, and ask what it means," he said. " Of course, I cannot let you go out now for a little while, till this blows over; but you shall go again soon."

" You cannot believe that I have done anything strange ! " she said faintly.

" No, I do not believe it," he answered.

" I told Miss Pendleton on Sunday that I would

appeal to the Consul for protection against her, and
this is her answer! She has been to him, or sent
some one else, and they have made him believe something, I do not know what. I do not know what
they are doing. There is something hidden. She
was always before very respectful to me, as it was her
place to be; but on Sunday she spoke as if I were
under her feet."

"Try to be quiet now, and I will talk to him," the
Director said soothingly. "It will all come right.
There has been some mistake."

She went back to the *casino*.

Did the flowers console her, or the view? They
were all a darkness. The Donna Claudia was growl-
ing and biting her nurse. A new patient had been
brought in through the villa gate in a carriage, from
which they were vainly trying to persuade her to
descend. Half a dozen men and women stood about
waiting to help, if force should be necessary.

Up-stairs, the sister was preparing a chamber in
the same corridor as Valeria's.

"What! are you going to put an insane woman up
here?" she said in a trembling voice.

"There is no other room down-stairs," Sister Agnes
answered. "The house is full."

Valeria stood and held her hands clasped over
her heart, which seemed about to leap from her
breast.

In a few minutes the new patient appeared, two
nurses holding her feet, and two men at her head and
shoulders. Her face was deeply red, her eyes flashing, and her breathing loud; but she did not speak,
nor resist. She merely let them carry her, but would
not help them by walking.

Valeria shut herself into her room, and began to
write letters, some of which she sent out that
evening.

The next day Dr. Kraus, to whom she had written, came to see her, and was shown up to her room.

"I sent for you in order to ask you certain questions," she said. "They are not necessary to satisfy my own mind; but I wish to know what you will say. In the sickness through which you attended me before I came here, I had fever, congestion of the lungs, and delirium, and was ill about three weeks. The physical illness was enough to account for the delirium. Am I not right?"

He assented.

"Was I ever violent?" she pursued.

"I never saw you so. You used to speak of the room being full of people. But the servant said that you got up sometimes in the night, and that you asked for your keys, and she was rather afraid."

"I remember that part perfectly," Valeria said. "It was a lucid interval, when I did not know how long I had been sick, and wanted the key of my *scrivania*, as I always kept it by me, lest the servant should rob me. And now, another question: Was I in such a state that I could have been brought here if I had not consented to come?"

"No, you were not," he said. "But you needed a care that you could not have in your own house. Miss Pendleton said she thought you were insensible nearly all the way here."

"I was not. I can be silent without being insensible. She knows that I was not; for I remarked that the driver was taking a round-about road. I was a very sick person who ought to have been in bed, instead of dragged out into a cold November rain. My committal here was, then, illegal. If I could not be forced to come, I could not be deceived into coming, believing that I was going somewhere else. And if I could not have been forced to come, I cannot be forced to stay."

He began to shrug his shoulders. " It was thought best that you should stay here till you should be able to return to America," he said in a wheedling voice. "You are very comfortable, and you can drive or walk out when you like. You are very well off."

" I shall not remain here a day longer than I am forced to stay," she replied. " And when I go away, I shall order my life as seems to me best."

" I don't know how you will get away," the doctor said, changing his tone to one less complacent. "There is no one to take the responsibility, and you cannot leave without some one to answer for you."

It was quite true. She had no acquaintances in Rome, except this little band who had confined her, and kept her confined. It would be impossible to ask a stranger to be responsible for her, the more so that these people were on the alert to cut off every chance of escape, and to prejudice the minds of every one who might approach her. They had compromised themselves seriously; and if they had had no evil intention from the first, it was now for their interest to justify what they had done, since they did not mean to repair it.

" You knew, in placing me here, that I could not go away without some person being responsible for me ?" she asked, after a moment.

" Why, that is the rule of the place," he replied, hesitatingly.

" And you mean to say that the person who consigned me to this place — illegally, mind, by your own acknowledgment — cannot, be obliged to release me ?"

" But I do not know that you are well," he said, with an insolent smile.

Valeria restrained herself, and dropped her eyes, that he might not see the anger in them.

"I need not detain you any longer," she said, and rose to accompany him down-stairs, where she took a civil leave of him before the sister.

"But if I had the power, I would order fifty lashes to be given you," she thought, as he bowed his little pink-and-white impudent face before going out.

When he had gone, she went down to the garden beside the wall, and, seating herself in the swing there, pushed slowly to and fro with the long amber-colored cane. The air was soft, and the sky, brilliant with unclouded sunshine, was of a dazzling blue. Across this sky, at the right, ran the sculptured yellow cornice of the house, with vases full of aloes along the roof. At the other side, the same plants reared themselves against the blue on the near wall outside which dropped the great bastion of Paul III.

Into the hollow of one of these aloe-leaves, just where it folded to run into a sharp point, dropped a tiny bird, and, resting on the soft cushion of its own breast, poured out a sweet, though plaintive song.

Valeria looked up with a faint smile on her trembling lips.

> "'Che vuoi dirmi in tua favella,
> Pellegrina rondinella ?'"

The feathered singer stopped, seemed to listen a moment to the echoes of its own song, then raised its tiny wings and darted across to the house-top, and perched on a cross above the vane, her eyes following him.

How noble a mistress is Nature! With what a soft and potent touch she calms the troubled soul, and makes of every delight she offers a step upward! She opens the eyes of those who love her generously, and shows them the unlost antique paradise, while others grovel in the desert. All riches are theirs.

What tapestry does not look dull to one who has

been studying a flower-wreathed trellis, where bees and humming-birds contend for the honey of each scented blossom? What velvet is not coarse after a rose-petal, what lace not poor after the point of the frost-worker? What landscape satisfies him who turns from the mountains and rivers of the Master of the old masters, and what shape of marble or what painted face can equal the human face with an immortal soul in it? Is not the dome of St. Peter's insignificant to the gaze that withdraws itself dazzled from the dome of the sky?

The achievements of art are great only to him who is blind to nature, or who has studied the impotency of art to represent nature; and to appreciate those achievements, one must have served an apprenticeship to pettiness. The unlearned lover of nature looks at first with disappointment on the canvas of Raphael and the marble of Michelangelo; and to know how great these men are, he must first descend and study their difficulties and imagine their despair.

In this same sunset hour, a small company was gathered in Casa Passarina. To them entered a bright young couple, Mr. and Mrs. Clive Willis. The latter, on her independent cards, wrote herself "Mrs. Lilian Willis, *née* Marshall."

These two had first met in Rome, where they had flirted, and quarrelled, and gone their separate ways. But when the young lady returned to America, the gentleman found that he was not yet entirely satisfied with the corrections which he had given her, and that a great deal of unexpressed disapprobation still remained to trouble his soul. He followed her, therefore, and the result was a mutual agreement to quarrel amicably for the remainder of their lives.

This was their first appearance at Casa Passarina since their return, and they were joyfully welcomed by their old acquaintances.

"We have come to Europe for a few months to
escape congratulations," the gentleman explained.
"Americans in America have such odd notions.
They think that when people marry all is changed for
them in the twinkling of an eye, that they immediately become foolishly happy, and from that dwindle
off gradually into nothingness. Now, Americans in
Europe have no sentimental ideas about marriage.
No one here bothers us with any nonsense about the
matter. They know better."

"Men do not lie half so nicely as women do,"
thought Mrs. Lilian, as she calmly waited for her husband to finish his speech. "That poor fellow will
never be able to deceive me in the least."

"And now," she said, when an opportunity came,
"do tell me all the news about everybody. We are
going to Naples to-morrow evening, and may not see
you again. How is Miss Cromo? You know she
was my 'intimate enemy.' "

A little chorus of "Hush!" and enter Miss Cromo.
She seldom visited, because she was of no great consequence in any other house than her own; but now
and then she came to Casa Passarina.

"You want to know the news of everybody, my
dear?" she asked, after having made her compliments
to the bride. "To begin with, I suppose you know
that Mrs. Gordon has caught a count for her daughter.
You did not? Well, she has caught him; but she had
to pay fifty thousand dollars for him. But then he
was a very good article of the kind, having an old
name and some notable connections. Besides, last
year was rather a bad one; for there were some petro-
leum and bonanza girls here with no end of money.
However, they went in for princes and dukes."

"What a price to pay for a count!" exclaimed Mrs.
Lilian scornfully. "I have known of their going for
five thousand, and ten is a high price. With good

management you could get a real marchese for ten thousand."

"The man himself, yes. But connections cost. Besides, a nice young man will always cost more than a battered old reprobate of the same grade, unless the lady wishes to be a widow; and Mrs. Gordon's son-in-law is but twenty-five. Then, she is to live with them half the time."

"Oh!" says Mrs. Lilian, with a long circumflex. "He was not so very dear, after all. But do tell me about Miss Ellsworth."

Miss Cromo sighed. "Poor Valeria! I'm afraid there isn't much chance for her. Dr. Lacelles says that she is hopelessly insane. We are trying to manage some way to get her to America."

"How dreadful!" exclaimed the bride, really shocked. "I liked her so much. Do you think that we could see her? Would she know us?"

"It would only distress you, my dear," Miss Cromo replied tenderly. "She is violent against all her friends, even those who have done the most for her. I went to see her just before she was taken to the asylum, and she drove me out of the house. I thought best not to go again, lest it should excite her; but I have told them to let me know if I can do anything for her."

An elderly gentleman, who was waiting for a friend, had been sitting apart, looking over some newspapers. He was not acquainted with the company, and had taken no part in the conversation. But here he interposed.

"Pardon me!" he said quietly; "but I think that you must have been misinformed. I breakfasted to-day with the Baroness Hübner, and this lady you mention was spoken of. The Baroness has been at the Manicomio, and she talked more than a hour with Miss Ellsworth, and on a variety of subjects. She told me that she was stupefied at finding such a lady in such a place. There was not the slightest sign of mental disorder. The lady was perfectly calm and reasonable."

"It is not an insanity, as the word is usually understood," Miss Cromo said, without seeming aware that she was contradicting herself. "She has manias. She can appear sane at times, as many insane persons do. Besides, she would be on her guard with strangers."

"I also saw the Marchesa della Fontana," the gentleman pursued coolly. "She goes to the asylum occasionally to visit friends there ; and she had a long conversation with Miss Ellsworth. Her conclusion was the same. She found something very strange in the affair."

"There are plenty of other persons who give a very different testimony," Miss Cromo said, her eyes sparkling and her head stiffly erect. "The word of two noted physicians and of the American Consul must be of more weight than that of any chance visitor. She was, besides, so violent the last time that Miss Pendleton was there that they are afraid to allow them to meet again. And there is nothing which Miss Pendleton has not done for her."

"As what ?" asked the gentleman, who seemed to be rather a troublesome person.

"Why, Miss Pendleton took charge of all her affairs when she was sick, and has taken the greatest pains with them ; and she has written to her friends, and she made all the arrangements for her to go to the asylum, and has done a great deal for her since then."

"The question is, whether the lady or her affairs are in any better condition after having been so taken care of," the gentleman returned. "The most of us would think ourselves but little obliged to one who would take possession of us and our affairs when we were sick, and retain possession of both when we are well. I do not know all of this affair; but my idea is that the cause for gratitude is not so sure. I happened to be at Madame L.'s *pension* the day that the Medical Director of the asylum recommended Miss Ellsworth there. He spoke highly of her, said that there had never been anything like insanity in her case, but that she was brought there for care during the convalescence of a severe illness, and that she was now in excellent health. Such an authority is supreme."

"Every one knew that she needed a guardian," Miss Cromo said, losing temper. "She was killing herself with opium; and besides, she was insane in money-spending. Last year she spent three thousand dollars; and she ought not to have spent a thousand."

"You can't shut a person up for spending more than their income, nor for opium-eating," the gentleman replied. "And even if you could, the charges would have to be proved in every case."

Miss Cromo rose angrily, turned her back upon the speaker, and took leave of the others.

Her antagonist looked curiously after her.

"What interest has that lady in proving that Miss Ellsworth is insane?" he asked. "She professes to be a friend, and ready to do any service, yet I find her talk very inimical. Has she anything at stake?"

Miss Cromo had, in fact, won her stake. For the Countess Belvedere saluted her when they met — rather negligently, it is true, but it was a recognition — and one or two of her humbler friends had visited Miss Cromo's house. It was not to be expected that her services would be rewarded too quickly or openly; but she understood that in time quite a little circle attached to the mistress of Villa Mitella might honor her with their smiles.

CHAPTER XXXII.

FOUR-LEAVED CLOVERS.

THERE came a morning soon that was spring, though it was still called February. Nature had for some time been preparing one of her pleasant surprises; a multitude of leaves had stolen out in dusky dominoes, and held themselves ready to unfold and show a tender green at a moment's notice; there were countless flower-buds hidden under brown masks, where only the most searching eyes could detect their peeping faces; and it had taken a sharp little box-on-the-ear from a tramontana to keep the daisies from opening out a million million disks the day before, and turning all the world a premature pink and white. Moreover, slim rosebuds had been eagerly sipping a rosy ichor from the very heart's blood of the bountiful mother, and pushing their green sepals apart like the bars of a lattice with their swelling petals. All at once, at some signal, perhaps an air out of the sky, or a beam of the sun, or some rush of birds, or a pulse whispering under the earth, out they all burst at once. No one saw them appear, but there they were. It was done by the dews of the dark night, or in some magical hour of uncertain dawn. Ten kinds of flowers were open, myriads of birds flew, the trees were a mist of foliage, and the very thorns of the rose-bushes were so large and transparent and crimson that they seemed to be full of blood.

When Valeria went down-stairs in the morning, the doors and windows were wide open, and the ladies were all in the garden. The Duchess was seated on a bench, full of satisfaction over a plate of snails, which she picked out of the shells with a large pin, and ate, while talking airily of her near departure from the villa.

" We will take an apartment together," she said to Valeria. " I do not care for a large establishment. We can have a groom, a cook, and each of us a maid. Will not that be enough ? "

" Quite enough," Valeria replied listlessly, and went on.

The nun in charge of the *Tessenda* came to meet her. " When are you going away, signora ? " she asked.

" Oh, it is pleasant here ! " she replied.

" It is a pretty place, yes," the sister said; "but it is no place for you."

The Donna Faustina was busy with her lace-making, into which she was weaving a little white butterfly that she had found entangled in a spider's-web. The Donna Claudia walked to and fro, swinging her handkerchief, and declaiming in a voice that rose now and then like a tempest, then died away in a sighing cadence that was inexpressibly musical and touching. In the midst of them the English lady was affably entertaining an invisible company.

In one of the upper windows, clinging to the bars as she stood on the window-ledge, was the last patient, the Signora Agnese, talking with great volubility at the top of her voice. She had resisted all efforts to persuade her to eat, and was now celebrating her triumph over the doctors, who had just left her.

" *Dottori beneditti !* " she called jeeringly after them. " Do you think to make me afraid ? I am not afraid of you all, put together." And her scornful laugh ran down through the bars.

The young widow stood apart, as usual, wrapped in dark and bitter silence. The Sor Agnesina made tatting with swift, dexterous fingers, and wagged her yellow head, and seemed to talk inwardly.

"If I should stay here long," Valeria thought, "and watch these people, and be tormented by those others outside, I, too, might begin to do strange things. I wonder if they think of that in keeping me here ! I wonder if they never thought of it in placing me here !"

Turning away from the contemplation, she went up to her room again. But this was no longer a peaceful refuge. All night she had heard the ravings of the Signora Agnese, and it was now impossible to shut her voice out.

She tried to write ; but presently dropped the pen, and sat thinking. In spite of her, story after story came up before her of Italian vengeance, of people imprisoned without accusation or trial, of sane people shut into lunatic asylums, of sudden deaths that no one dared ask questions about — all these tales repeated, not by strangers and ignorant people alone, but by Italians and people of culture.

As she thought, her mind was like a smoke in which a thin flame flickers ; and the smoke was doubt, and the flame suspicion. This suspicion had been flickering in her mind ever since her interview with Miss Pendleton.

Now, as before, she put it away, and, rising, began to pace her room. The morning sunshine was reflected in at the window, and where it shone brightest on the wall, hung a picture of Tasso, the large luminous eyes looking out of his pallid face with the expression of a hunted creature which seeks for refuge, and finds it not.

"Oh, Tasso *mio !* " she said, looking into those troubled eyes, "you asked for love, and they gave you a prison ; you asked for bread, and they gave you a laurel crown. You were great, and I am small ; but we were both caught in the same net."

There was a tap at the door, and Sister Agnes came in with a letter and a package. " I hope it is something pleasant," she said, lingering a little.

Valeria opened the letter. It was from her publisher, and announced the issue of her book, of which he sent her a copy.

She opened the package, and saw a pretty green-covered volume with three four-leaved clovers on the cover. Here was what she had expected to receive with delight, and she received it — thus !

The sister was looking at her with kind solicitude. She had hoped to give pleasure, and feared that she had given pain instead. " It is pleasant, thank you, *suora mia*," Valeria said, trying to smile. " See ! it is my new book, and — and — oh ! I cannot bear it any longer ! "

CHAPTER XXXIII.

IN THE NET.

AS soon as Valeria had recovered from her second fever, and had begun to be displeased at the liberties taken in her affairs, she had written to several persons among those who were most interested in her ; and while, to spare them anxiety, she had made no complaint of any one, and had dwelt on the kindness of those about her in the Manicomio, she had stated decidedly her intention of going away at the end of three months.

It was now time to hear from her correspondents ; and one morning the sister came smiling into her room with both hands full of letters.

" I am sure there must be some good news among

all these," she said, and, laying them down, delicately
withdrew, and left Valeria to read them.

The first was from a publisher, and contained the
second monthly payment for her serial. The first had
come, and she had given it up to the Medical Director,
having been told that she would not be allowed to
hold money.

The second letter was from the American nun,
Sister Veronica, and had come to Miss Pendleton's
care, as many other letters had during her illness.

At the first glance Valeria saw that this letter had
been opened in Rome. It was so closed that the
lines of the Roman postmark, made over the fold, did
not form a regular circle, the edges of the fold were
worn, there were marks inside of the gum having
been put on twice, and a bit half torn off the envelope.

Sister Veronica had for many years been her most
faithful and devoted friend. Never had any one been
so solicitous for her good, so consoling in every trouble,
so helpful in every difficulty.

" Whoever has read it is sure to have been edified,"
Valeria thought, in unfolding the sheet; but as she
read, her pleasure changed to surprise, and her surprise to stupefaction.

Sister Veronica's whole letter was a prayer that she
would remain where she was till some other refuge
could be found for her. With sorrowful affection she
performed the duty imposed on her of withdrawing
the invitation given Valeria to make their convent
her home for a time. They could not, she said, give
her the care which she needed, and she was not herself in authority there, and could give no invitations
unsanctioned by her superiors. In conclusion, she
begged her to bear as patiently as was possible the
disadvantages of her position till they should have
decided what to do with her.

"If I were anything but a poor nun, I would come to Rome and take care of you, if I had to beg my way," she concluded, with a burst of love and grief.

Valeria read the letter through a second time to convince herself of its reality. She had already written to decline their invitation, and the letters had crossed on the way. That did not matter. But what did the rest mean ?

Her appearance was an odd commentary on this letter. Tall, full-formed, brimming with life and health from the tips of her fingers to the thick curly hair that was pushing out newly after her fever, one might have laughed at the idea of her needing care, if one could have laughed at anything suggested by that letter, which trembled all through with the pious and loving heart that had dictated it.

There were intimations which she did not understand ; but the next letter explained them. For this writer expressed herself more plainly ; and while, like Sister Veronica, she did not mention the source of her information, was more circumstantial as to what that information had been. She also began and ended her letter with advising Valeria to continue where she was till they should have made up their minds what was best for her to do.

After fifteen years of a life of entire self-dependence, uncontrolled and unaided, she suddenly found herself treated as a piece of unclaimed luggage which was to be moved from one place of storage to another by whoever might compassionately take the trouble of such removal. And at the same time she learned something of the grounds on which this guardianship was based. It was supposed that she was so addicted to the use of opium — a drug which, from some peculiarity of constitution, she could not take even as a medicine, and never had taken — that, if left free, she might be expected to appear in company stupefied or

wild from its influence; that she had so little idea of
the value of money — when, in fact, she was rather an
uncommonly skilful manager — that she was not to be
trusted to buy herself a pair of shoes; and that, while
in truth of a notably quiet and retiring disposition,
she was in danger of committing the most strange
extravagances. Everything that malice could invent,
everything that could be gathered from authorities
which they would have been ashamed to acknowl-
edge, had been gathered and written and told right
and left. Not only that: the story which Valeria
would not have made public even to obtain protection
for herself, but had confided — most unwisely, indeed,
but trustingly — to the honor of those whom she hoped
might suggest to her some remedy, now came back to
her in so distorted and changed a form as to be utterly
false, and contrary to every fact. And it came back
as a mania; which, indeed, it would have been, had
she ever dreamed of entertaining it. Her little confidences to Miss Pendleton in those days of weakness
when she had resigned herself into her hands, — confidences which she had never doubted would be held
sacred, the affairs of her house, her possessions, all
those petty details which would never have been
known except that she lay helpless, and could not
keep strangers out, — here they all were, blown to the
four winds.

And they had been believed, and believed on the
testimony of a stranger! It was but one example
more of what a few flattering words and pious pretences can accomplish.

Miss Pendleton — the informant could be no other
— knew how to tell her tale, with what seeming re-
luctance, with what excuses, with what expressions
of devoted attachment, with what doubts, and above
all, with what piety! And her correspondents had
lacked the penetration to see that, if really reluctant,

she need not have told; if doubtful and friendly, she would have sought to disprove such absurdities; and if really pious, she would have shown some mercy and nobility of soul. The proof of the dispositions of a story-teller is not in the professions which she makes, but in the effect which she produces.

"Are they imbeciles?" cried Valeria fiercely, crushing the letters in her hands, and flinging them away.

Two others remained. She tore them open, and found traces of the same work.

Both were from correspondents of Mrs. Harwood; and the writer of one of them, who, for some mysterious reason, assumed that that lady was a person of infallible judgment, and the most devoted friend that Valeria ever had, insisted that she would never have approved of what had been done without the best of reasons, and that she had acted on the surest information which she could obtain.

"What has Mrs. Harwood to do with the matter?" Valeria exclaimed, flinging this letter after the others, and taking up the last one.

And here, at length, was a beam of light through the chaos which surrounded her. A woman of extreme sensitiveness and delicacy, but of a clear and independent judgment, this writer had not been imposed upon by authorities nor by phrases; and she considered Valeria's confinement an outrage. The same reasons for it which had been written to the others had been given to her also, and she scornfully pronounced them worthless and null. Living at a distance, — she was in England, — she could do nothing personally; but she could procure the intervention of a high foreign official in Rome, who would demand an investigation of the affair.

It was useless. Unless he should know all the story, or should bring these people before her, it would avail nothing. As long as they could talk unanswered, they could always conquer. Their strength was in their secrecy. There needed a bold and resolute questioner, who would oblige each one to prove what she should assert, or give her authority, and who would tell Valeria everything. So pursued, they would have melted like shadows. They would have heard from some one, would have forgotten whom, would have shirked responsibility. They would have been a retiring fog, which could not be grasped, though they had been a thick fog to suffocate.

But she could not hope for such an investigation.

Neither could she hope for any active partisanship from the people of the Manicomio, kind as they were. Official reserve and Italian caution would prevent their taking any aggressive part. But that they would do anything against her she could not believe. The most that she could expect, and all that she could ask, was that they should make her detention as tolerable as it could be made.

But in this moment, even liberty was almost lost sight of in the misery of this inevitable *inferno* of wagging tongues.

"Oh! who will ever give me back the silence of my life?" she cried out.

Into the solitude where she had meant to hide herself with nature and art and religion for companions, had broken the full pack of yelping gossips.

There was a tap at the door, and Sister Agnes put her head in. "Well, signora," she began, "I hope" — then broke off. "Why, how red your cheeks are! What is the matter?"

"You hope that I have had pleasant news," Valeria said. "Come in, and hear them. Sit here. Excuse my standing, and walking about. And don't be alarmed if I should catch you and shake you. I feel as if I were a tempest shut into the puny form of a woman!"

" Why, signora —"

" Listen!"   And Valeria told her story.

The sister was shocked. She began to murmur consolations and exhortations, saying the best she knew. She begged Valeria to leave all in the hands of God, who would surely protect her, and raise up friends for her. She must try to forgive.

"Forgive!" Valeria burst forth.   "I would like to drive over them with wild horses!"

"Oh, don't speak so, signora! Try to wait; and God will right you."

"Oh, I must wait, for I am tied hand and foot!" she cried, wringing her hands. "But you may be sure that the time of God to right me will come the very first moment that I can right myself!"

"But, signora, a Christian must bear patiently —"

"Ah! ma sœur," Valeria interrupted, sweeping away the gentle voice, "'nous avons changé tout çela.'"

The sister was silent a moment. Then she said, "Miss Pendleton has been here."

"She has! Keep her out of my sight."

"She wished very much to see you," the nun went on. "She says that if you will receive her, she will never again interfere with your affairs in any way. And she wanted me to tell you that she loves you just as well as ever."

"I have no doubt that she does; just as well. Keep her out of my sight. Don't allow her to be in the garden when I want to walk there. And assure her that I do not love her as well as ever, nor at all!"

"I told her that the Director does not allow her to see you," the sister said.

"*I* do not allow her to see me!"

The sister had an inspiration. "Wouldn't you like to take a little walk?" she asked.

It was the best diversion possible. They went down-stairs, and out through the garden, Sister Agnes stopping to gather for her companion a bunch of purple pansies out of the crowd that stood all facing the sun, each with the image of an oriental bearded face painted on its rich petals. They went up the avenue under the delicate foliage, crossed the little bridge that would soon be draped with purple wisteria and snow-white multiflora roses, and came to a large green in Villa Gabrielli, where a few benches were set in the lee of a wide semicircle of laurels joined thickly into a hedge. And here the sister left Valeria in the company of a nurse they had met, and returned to her own duties.

The green was bright with daisies. In summer the grass would be over the head of the tallest man there. Everything in that place was luxuriant with a dancing growth.

Valeria seated herself by the laurels, and the nurse went about gathering daisies for her.

It was one of the days when the Manicomio was open to visitors, and two gentlemen were wandering about not far away. They went down the avenue toward the bridge, then turned back on to the green.

"Don't take any notice of them," Valeria said in a low voice to the nurse. "They show very little discretion in coming here."

She turned away in speaking, and began to examine the dark laurel leaves behind the bench.

The steps came nearer, and the voice of the nurse was heard talking with one of the strangers. In spite of the charge she had received, it was impossible for the girl to resist the compliments and inquiries addressed to her.

Hearing a step beside her, Valeria turned to go away, and found herself face to face with the Count Belvedere.

He looked at her with eager excitement, too much engrossed in the object for which he had sought her to even salute her.

"Signora," he said hastily, and in a low tone, "is it possible that I see the American of the *casuccia* in this place?"

"If you have any inquiries to make about the place, it would be better to go to one of the men-servants," she said coldly. "I do not play *cicerone*."

He regained his composure immediately.

"I do not mean to intrude," he said respectfully. "I only wish to say that I am sorry to see you here, and to ask if you have anything to say to me."

"Who sent you?" she asked.

"No one."

"And, pray, what could I have to say to you?"

He had dropped his eyes. He now raised them, and looked at her fixedly.

"I should be happy if I could be of any service to you. And I fancied that you might have something to tell me."

"I have nothing to tell you," she replied.

He continued to look at her with steady and penetrating eyes. "We were sorry to learn of your severe illness last autumn," he said, "and I am glad to see you looking so well. Your apartment is as you left it, and ready for you whenever you wish to return."

"Thanks! but I do not wish to return there," she said. "It has already been relinquished, — without my authority, it is true, — and I do not wish to renew the lease."

"Is that all?" he asked, as she made a motion to go. "You are resolved?"

"It is all, Signor Conte. Good-morning."

She called the nurse, and turned away. "It is the only reply I could make," she thought. "He wants to find out something, not to save me."

The Superior met her in the garden as she went in.

"Sister Agnes has been telling me of your letters, mademoiselle," she said, taking Valeria's hand. "Try not to think of them. Whatever those people outside may say, here every one loves and respects you. And those ladies certainly will do you no harm; they cannot keep you here."

"Those ladies, *madre mia !* Do you imagine that no one is concerned but a few mischievous women ? Do you think that they would have dared so much if there were not a stronger power behind them pushing them on ? "

"Who could it be?" the nun exclaimed.

Valeria was silent. To tell anything here would be to make a bad matter worse.

The Superior did not press the question. "I have brought up a pass for you," she said, "and I want you to go out and take a little walk or drive in the city. Don't sit still thinking of your troubles. It will do you no good."

How kind and thoughtful they were ! It was impossible to refuse the consolation and help, which was the best that they could offer.

Valeria dressed, and, accompanied by Fidelia, the nurse, went to visit Mrs. Harwood. She little dreamed what an influence this lady had had in her affairs, that her name had, indeed, had more weight than any other, and that to her she owed the Consul's letter which had for a time shut her within the walls.

Miss Pendleton, aware that she had by her violence committed herself irremediably, and alarmed at Valeria's defiance of her at their last meeting, had hastened to Mrs. Harwood.

Valeria was violent, would not listen to reason, and was so determined to leave the Manicomio that she would undoubtedly try to escape if she had the opportunity. It was true that she had no money; but she might claim the protection of the authorities, and make a great scandal. She ought to be strictly guarded, and not allowed to go into the street.

Well was it for Valeria in that day that neither Miss Pendleton nor her friends had power within the asylum. If they had had full authority there, nothing would have saved her.

They did what they could, however. Mrs. Harwood believed in Miss Pendleton as she did in the sun and moon. She was pious, and she paid great court to herself, and she had the gentlest manner in the world. Never had she seen her otherwise than complacent and "sweet." It would not have been difficult to make her believe that Miss Pendleton smiled habitually in her sleep. All that she said, therefore, was true and charitable.

Mrs. Harwood consulted with her, then went to the Consul, fortified with some such letters as Valeria had just received, — letters procured by the same means, and equally worthless as testimony or authority.

The Consul could not doubt her honesty, though he must have doubted her soundness of mind. He knew some of her relatives, and that they were very respectable people. And to this "distinguished consideration" Valeria had been sacrificed.

Of all this she was completely ignorant when she made her visit.

They talked awhile on indifferent topics; then Valeria gently complained of her detention. She had thought better not to speak of the letters received that morning.

"Your release depends on the doctors," Mrs. Harwood said, with an air of great reserve, dropping her eyes.

"The Director recommended me to go away long ago," was the quick reply.

"The Consul wishes to have the consent of the doctors who consigned you to him," Mrs. Harwood said after a moment's silence.

It was useless to argue with her. As there are none so deaf as those who will not hear, so there are none so dull as those who will not be convinced. Valeria knew that Mrs. Harwood would sit there in stolid silence, and listen as if to a whistling wind. The bitter thought came almost to her lips : " I wonder what doctors would advise your release if you were in my place !" but she did not utter it.

"I have learned from America this morning that the money I have been asking about so long was sent months ago, and is now in the bank here," she said. " I am sorry that some one had not the good sense or the good manners to tell me at once that I could not be allowed to hold money. It would have saved me the humiliation of asking for it several times in vain, and others the trouble of telling a good many falsehoods. Now, if it were offered to me, I would not take it. It can be used to pay any of my expenses, if the unknown powers which arrange my affairs choose to take it. But I will not touch it."

Mrs. Harwood, making no reply, glanced about the room, and her eyes fell on Fidelia, and on a gay purple shawl she wore.

"Where did she get that shawl ?" she exclaimed.

"I gave it to her."

Mrs. Harwood stared at the shawl.

"It was brought to me by Miss Pendleton and Madame de la Roche. I did not need it, but accepted it from courtesy. Now, of course, I will not keep any gift from that house. I had worn it once or twice about the gardens, so I could not send it back to them. Fidelia has done a good deal for me, and I gave it to her."

"But it was bought with your own money,"

Mrs. Harwood exclaimed. "It was to wear in the villa."

"And so they buy my clothes, even, for me, and make me pay for them! Come, Fidelia," she said, rising. "It is time to go."

She had not patience to talk any more. She preferred to go back to her prison. The great iron gate opened for her, and was locked behind her when she had entered. They went up the long stairway, through gloomy passages, passed over the arch of San Spirito, and up to the villa. Here sunshine broke into the dark archway, the great palm-tree by the veranda was softly waving its branches up and down, the ladies were out, and the gardener was clipping the trees.

Valeria went to ask him the names of some of his plants; but his flowers all spoke Latin, and he knew none of their familiar names.

"Botany is an exquisite science," she thought. "Why do not I study it? — if Madonna Nature would kindly pardon my curiosity."

The sister asked if she had had a pleasant visit.

"Oh! charming!"

The clean clothes had been brought up from the wash, and Sister Agnes and one of the nurses were folding them out of great baskets, and piling them on one of the marble benches set between the doors of the lower rooms, and trying to keep the Donna Faustina from sitting down upon them or walking over them. As they pulled the long sheets between them, leaning back to straighten them well out, the shadows of the palm-branches fell on the white linen, and brushed off the spots of reflected sunshine, that ever came dancing back again.

"You said that you should have something to send out to the post this evening," Sister Agnes said. "Pietro will soon come up, and you had better send out by him, if the letters are ready."

"They are not quite ready; and I am thinking about them. There is some manuscript, which will cost ten soldi. I want it registered. Then there are two letters, which will be five soldi each. And I have fifteen soldi left of the two lire that the Superior lent me last month. Do me a sum, *suora mia :* a certain poor maniac had fifteen soldi. From this she paid ten soldi for one thing, and five soldi each for two others. How much had the aforesaid poor maniac left ? I cannot find out the remainder. And do you not think that she will have to beg another lira before she can resume her foreign relations ? "

The sister smiled. " The Superior will lend you what you need. Or, stay ; I believe that I have four or five soldi." She searched her pocket, and brought out a few coppers. " But why do not you ask the Director — "

" I shall not ask the Director. Some one has been telling him absurd stories of my extravagance, and he believes them ; or he does n't disbelieve them. I will not beg for my own money."

She went up-stairs and finished her letters as well as she could for the noise about her, then left her chamber to carry them down.

The door of the Signora Agnese's room was open, and two nurses were putting the strait-jacket on her, while Sister Agnes stood looking on with an impassible face. The woman had so long refused to eat that it was found necessary to use force.

The strait-jacket, made of a strong double cloth of twilled linen, had very long sleeves ending in straps that were tied to iron bars at either side of the bedstead. An opening in the sleeves allowed the hands to be free ; but this also could be laced up so as to imprison the hands. The jacket was laced behind. Strong loops were set at the waist, the backs of the arms, and at the shoulders, through which wide bands were passed and tied to the iron railing of the bedstead.

Valeria remembered with a shudder that her own bedstead had these iron bars.

The woman did not resist, but she talked incessantly, her rather handsome face very red, her bright black eyes wandering about.

" Bind me tighter ! " she cried.   " Bind me tighter ! This is an easy martyrdom.   St. Peter, I suffer this for you.   I offer it up in your honor.   Do you know where St. Peter was crucified ?   *A Roma !* Do you know where St. Paul was murdered ?   *A Roma !* "

That *R-r-r-oma !* would have won applause for a tragic actress.

Her restless eyes fell on Valeria, who stood at the door.

" Who are you ? " she cried. " Are you the Superior ? "

" No.   I am a patient like you," Valeria said, going to the bedside.   " Only I 'm not so silly as to try to starve myself."

" I can't eat ! " the woman replied.

" Oh, yes, you can.   And you will grow worse every day if you don't try.   Here is some soup.   Try to eat it.   Don't be a baby ! "

" I 'll try it for your sake, but I don't want it," she said ; and she swallowed a little when the sister brought it to her, but pushed the rest away. " I cannot eat ! "

" This is the place where people who are nervous come to live tranquilly ! " Valeria said to herself as she went down-stairs with her letters, remembering the promises with which she had been enticed there.

When she went back, the Signora Agnese had been left alone.   The door was locked and the slide open. She looked in and saw the woman lying there bound. She was singing at the top of her voice, psalms and parts of the Catholic service, all in Latin, her tongue flying with inconceivable rapidity.   She sang prayers and responses, parts of the Mass, the Preface, the Pontifical benediction, and dwelt with particular unction on the high festa *Ite, missa est,* which she drew out in the long and rather cranky movement of a priest who has more music in his soul than in his voice.

Valeria heard some one laugh, and turned to see Sister Agnes. It was impossible not to laugh; for the woman lay shouting out this medley as if she were in the height of comfort and contentment.

The next morning, when the doctors made their daily visit, the Director came to the villa with them. He was always very welcome, for, though strict in discipline, he was kind and always courteous.

"You were at the bank yesterday," he said to Valeria, with a certain stateliness.

"No, signore," she replied, looking at him in surprise.

"You were at the bank and took out some money," he repeated in a measured voice.

"No."

"You have taken no money from the bank?"

"No; who has said that I have?"

"Mrs. Harwood."

Valeria smiled. "You see what kind of people are guarding me, Signor Cavaliere. I went to Mrs. Harwood yesterday almost on purpose to tell her that I would not accept the money if she offered it to me. I told her so plainly."

The Director uttered an exclamation of annoyance. "What kind of women are these? They go about making mischief for you in every way."

"If I had taken the money, I should have had a right to do so, should I not?" she asked.

"Yes, you would."

Mrs. Harwood had written her story to the Superior directly after Valeria left her. She had, in fact, fallen into one of her trances while listening, and the idea had entered her darkened mind inverted, like the images of outward objects into a *camerascura*. She had also complained that Valeria had been allowed to give the shawl to Fidelia.

"Signor Direttore," Valeria said later, "do you think it necessary to examine my letters?"

"Certainly not! and I never have."

"Did not I give you the check I received from my serial last month, when I might have concealed it from you?" she pursued.

"You did."

"Well, here is another letter from the same publisher. I have not opened it; I wish to open it in your presence, so that you may be sure that I do not steal nor hide anything out of it."

She opened the letter, shook the sheet wide, and gave him the check it contained.

"I have a right to receive and keep my own money," she said; "but when I tell you that I will not take any without your consent, I expect you to depend upon my word. When I choose to take my own money without your consent, I shall take it; but I will give you fair warning. Here — see! — is a letter which has been opened to make sure, I presume, that there was no money in it. Yet the money that I received before from this same person, as well as that from an American publisher, I put voluntarily into Miss Pendleton's hands. Honesty is thrown away on such people."

With an elegantly courteous bow, the Director tendered her the check that she had given him.

"Madamigella, keep the money, and whatever may come to you in future," he said.

He had such a fine, noble nature! One could not speak a generous word to him without meeting with a generous response.

"And, by the way," Valeria added, "Mrs. Harwood says that the Consul will not release me without the consent of the doctors who placed me here. Have they any jurisdiction?"

"Not in the least! Their work is done. It is for us to judge of the persons in our care," the Director replied.

"It would be rather amusing to have those two men come and talk with me to test my sanity. Hamlet had but one Polonius; I should have two. 'Very like a whale.' I can imagine them now with their eyes fixed on me, one at either side, our three chairs making a right-angled triangle. Dr. Kraus will look a little embarrassed. Dr. Lacelles will be full of a solemn feeling of responsibility. They will use the most elaborate diplomacy to introduce every possible subject, and will exchange glances at my replies. Do you know, Signor Cavaliere, I cannot promise you that I will not go in to see them with a crown of straws on my head, and walk about declaiming like the Donna Claudia. May I? Will you stand by me if I do it?"

"Imbeciles!" pronounced the Director, with an accent of superb scorn, as he slowly paced the room. "Imbeciles!"

That day Valeria was told that Mrs. Harwood had come and paid another three months for her.

"Don't let it trouble you," the Superior said, when Valeria uttered a faint cry. "That does not mean that you are to stay three months, or even three weeks. It is the custom to pay three months in advance, and the money is returned afterward, if the person goes away sooner. You are now on your fourth month, you know."

"Mrs. Harwood!" Valeria repeated.

"She wrote excusing herself for the mistake she made about the money," the Superior continued.

" And that very mistake, the reporting the precise contrary of that which was plainly said to her, does not make her doubt herself," Valeria said. " I have always spoken of her respectfully ; but now she has no longer any claim on my consideration which will prevent my defending myself to the utmost against her. I will never see her again. There is no knowing what wild reports she may make of me."

A few days later Mrs. Harwood came to see Valeria, who refused to receive her.

She went home and wrote her a pleasant note. " You will always know where to find me when you want me," she wrote.

" I shall never want you," Valeria thought, and made no reply. There was nothing that she could say or do that they would not turn into mischief. There was nothing to be hoped and everything to be feared from them. And where was there any hope ? Every one who was not knowingly malicious seemed to be imbecile.

It occurred to her to make a public appeal in some American journal. She could send away letters without examination. Could it be possible, if she wrote all her story to some journal at home, that her release would not be demanded ?

But even then she did not wish to write that story ; for, infamous as were the principals, they were less odious in her eyes than their tools. They were bad people, certainly, and they had been insolent and bold in their mode of protecting themselves ; but they had the excuse of self-protection. Could they have understood how little she cared to know of their affairs, and how averse she was to speaking of them, they might not have molested her. They had found her in their path, as she had found them in hers. She would wait yet a little longer.

Her thoughts turned to the Count Belvedere, and

instantly rejected his aid. He would have found some means of procuring her release, but always with the condition that she should tell her story to him, and to no one else.

No; it was better to have nothing to do with any of them.

But, oh, what could be done? It was maddening. Those people meant to keep her confined till she should consent to leave Rome, and to point out the length of her confinement as a proof of insanity, if ever she should speak of the real cause of it. Any intimation of hers that they had been dishonest, or even mistaken, was to be treated as a mania. And all this, that a Roman prostitute and her associates might go, — not unsuspected, for every one knew what they were, — but without fear of being caught.

Acteon must not look upon these trumpery gods and goddesses in the nudity of their crimes, or they change him to something monstrous in the eyes of the world, and set their dogs to tear him!

There was a good, kind chaplain at the Manicomio. He was not, perhaps, very penetrating, but he was very soothing, and entirely devoted to his duties.

"I will go and see if he can calm me a little," Valeria thought, "for all this is unbearable;" and she begged Sister Agnes to go down to the chapel with her.

They did not take the gloomy way through the dormitories, but went down the stairs leading to the *cancello* on the Lungara, turned aside into the section of the third class of women, passed a court, and entered the lower auditorium, which communicated with the chapel by a grating. It was a gloomy place, but the church was bright and pretty.

From this auditorium a door opened into a little closet. The priest's box opened into the church, and between the two was the tiny perforated screen of the confessional.

Did Valeria tell all her story to Don Domenico, does the curious reader ask? By no means. She went to tell her own sins, not the sins of others, and to listen to such comfort as the priest might be inspired to give. And it is wonderful how fresh and bright the lip-worn old truths will come out sometimes, when both speaker and listener turn their backs on life, and go down for a moment to look off over the incoming tide of eternity; as the dim, wave-rounded pebbles of the beach glow into gems when the foam rolls over them, and wakes the hidden glories of their coloring.

"Sister Agnes," said Valeria, as they went up-stairs again, "I weigh just three pounds."

CHAPTER XXXIV.

HOME AGAIN.

MARCH passed by, slow day by day, and April came to the twin villas in a shower of blossoms, like a laughing child that runs into a chamber where one is dying.

All the eucalyptus-trees — and there were many — hung out bright spikes and tufts of red and yellow at each point of their dark winter boughs; the sombre box-hedges and the laurels put forth fresh sprouts, and the cruelly nicknamed Judas-tree, waking to find itself leafless, blushed into a hasty blossom that veiled it to the tips of its uttermost twigs, as the Lady Godiva was veiled by her bright hair. Here a viburnum shrub held up its glossy spiked leaves, and bunches of delicate white flowers; there, from branches far overhead, hung long clusters of Imperial Purple.

24

There were shrubs that shonè with gold, and others
that glimmered with silver; there were the roses of
three months, for they had begun in. February; and,
climbing against the house, flames of red and yellow
nasturtiums, with the soft heliotrope between. It
was flowers everywhere, and all day. The Sor Agnesina snapped them off when she thought that no one
was looking, and flung them away by scores, and was
severely scolded when caught. For the Deputy interested himself very much in the garden, and constantly charged the gardener to have the flowers as
profuse as possible. The Signora Agnes broke them
off boldly and flung them into people's faces. This
woman was permitted to go about now, and was as
troublesome, and also as amusing, as a person could
well be; restless, swift, disdainful of authorities, with
a generous frankness which was pleasing to those
whose faces she did not slap, and a wonderful penetration. It was impossible to deceive, to flatter, or to
frighten her.

She had been placed at table with the ladies of
the second class in the dining-room, adjoining that
where the Duchess and the Donna Claudia ate, and
she amused herself in distributing sudden spoonfuls
of her soup into the wine-glasses of the others, and
in sending occasional telegrams of bones and macaroni
at the attendants. Her movements were so quick
and so unexpected that it was impossible to foresee
and prevent them, and she exhibited the utmost carelessness of the effects of her actions. One piece of
mischief done, she forgot it, and immediately addressed
herself to another.

Sometimes, when being taken into or out of her
room, she broke from the nurses, and ran into Valeria s chamber.

"Forgive me!" she would cry, flinging herself on
her knees; "I don't mean to be impolite to you, but

I don't like them. Will you forgive me? You are
my angel. I will do anything that you tell me to.
I am your devil to serve you."

"But I don't want to be served by a devil," Valeria
said, trying to calm her trembling at the shock of this
visit. "If you will be so violent, I shall not like
you, nor want you to like me."

"Well, now I will be quiet," said the woman, seating herself, her eyes scintillating with an excitement
which she could not control. "Here are some flowers
for you. I will change with you." And she pulled
out the flowers that fastened Valeria's collar, and
thrust into their place those she had brought. "This
is yours," tying around Valeria's arm a blue worsted
cord that she had snatched from some one down-stairs,
and tying it so roughly as to hurt the arm she was
decorating. "And these are yours. Everything I
have is yours," piling into Valeria's lap the different
objects that she had gathered about the house.

The nurse would have drawn her forcibly away,
but Valeria would not allow it. Terrible as this
intercourse was to her, she had too much compassion
for the sufferers to allow them to receive any reproof
on her account. Besides, there was something touching in the affection which these poor creatures testi-
fied for her; for even the Signora Ellen would come
out of her gloomy trance, and smile with a shy sweetness if addressed by her, would kiss over and over
the hand she offered, and run with jealous haste to
pick up anything she might have dropped.

There was a fascination in it, too. To enter the
labyrinthine windings of those ruined minds; to find,
where all seemed at first but dust and ashes, some
noble or exquisite monument still standing intact, or
some fragment which had added the pathos of a
tragical loss to its former grace; to study how, possibly, the original city of the soul might be built up

again in a fairer order than before, and to see even
now order and perfection where others found confusion, — it was an alluring study. But even so, she
went through these strange regions, as Dante went
through the shadowy worlds, shrinking within herself,
and, worse yet, with no "*caro Duca*" to guide and
reassure her.

Valeria was peculiarly fitted for such a study, for
she carried no positiveness to it. Absolutely passive
and unprejudiced when a new subject was presented
to her, she left it to make its own impressions on the
sensitive texture of her mind, and she formed her
judgments, such as they might be, in her own lab-
oratory, and from facts that she knew. To be unprejudiced, one must also be a little slow in credulity;
and she had as little respect as it is possible for a
human being to have for popular estimates of people,
when those estimates take the form of accusation.

But this very readiness to receive impressions made
her association with the insane at once perilous and
intolerably painful.

She went out into the garden one morning, feeling
that she must make some new effort to free herself.
The Signora Agnese had violently beset her as she
came down; the Donna Claudia had been wild all
night, and was now walking to and fro, muttering and
casting sidelong glances at the nurses, her whole
manner at once ferocious and cowed, like an inwardly
raging lion that fears his keeper. A very ladylike
and remarkably intelligent woman, whose sole weakness was the idea that some one was trying to poison
her, was watching with a trembling and fiery suspicion while her food was being prepared; even the
Signora Ellen, usually more modest and silent than
any other, was going about on tiptoe, with a strange,
mocking lightness, and seemed to be angrily mimick-
ing some one. The Donna Faustina had forgotten

her lace-making, and was pacing the veranda, and scolding *sotto voce*, in French and Italian. "Insults, and insults, and insults!" she muttered. "I have nothing but insults. I will have them imprisoned!"

The English lady was seated on a bench in the midst, shopping, apparently. A great variety of silks, velvets, and laces were being displayed before her, and she was selecting from them, and discussing their merits with the shopman and with her friends. "I must have a black velvet dress with white satin sleeves, for one. That lace is too wide. What! Do you think that it will do? Um! I'm afraid not. Now show me your pink satins and organdies. Yes, gauze looks well over satin." Then her thoughts went back to a little dance and supper that the Deputy had allowed them during Carnival, when, at the moment of breaking up, the dead Carnival had been brought in on a sheet. It was but a bedizened rag-doll; but to her it had been a corpse. "They drop dead frequently while dancing," she said; "but they should be carried out quietly, so as not to disturb the company. I could slip them out of sight. If I had to kill a person, I should do it quietly, and hide the body. People don't like to see those things. When I kill that woman, no one shall know it."

In the midst of this, the doctors had been listening to the sister's report, and were writing a few prescriptions.

The Duchess, dressed, as usual, in the morning to go away, had at length become incredulous and desperate. They had paid her compliments, written her passes, ordered her carriage, and evaded her every day for years, and every day her hope had revived. On this day a suspicion of the truth had come suddenly over her, and she was weeping bitterly. From the veranda where they stood in a splendor of summer and flowers, the city domes and towers were visible

over the walls; and beyond, against a sky blazing
with light, stood the Alban mountains, with Frascati
lying against their rich and misty purple, each storied
palace showing a silvery blotch, amid its groves and
gardens. Among them was her own family villa.
Down in the city was her own family palace, both
called by her maiden name, that had worn the coronet
of a marchioness before, as a bride, she had won the
ducal circlet.

Weeping wildly, she stretched out her arms to that
mocking vision of her vanished greatness set upon
the mountain-side before her eyes. "There is my
villa, and I cannot set my foot on its turf nor in its
halls," she sobbed. "Other people drive in my carriages and command my servants. I am mocked
every day with promises which they never mean to
keep. Oh! oh! to see it there, and not to be able
to go! Nobody shows me any respect, none to me,
the equal of queens! I have three coronets on my
head, I am a duchess; and I can call nothing my
own!"

No one noticed her. What could they do? They
could console her only by giving her freedom. She
must weep and rave till she was tired.

Do the carefully attended, the petted for the scratch
of a pin, the condoled with for an ordinary sorrow,
the readily helped in every trivial difficulty, understand what it might be·to stand wildly weeping for
the loss of more than life and friends, and have those
about merely raise their voices a little in speaking to
each other, so as to be heard, — the sobs that are
rending those hearts no more to these than the sound
of carriage-wheels in the street?

It was not their fault. Such scenes are the rule
in such houses.

Valeria stood a little while, then walked away into
the upper garden, followed by the chief doctor.

"Well, what are your friends doing about taking you away, signora?" he asked.

"I do not know. I hear nothing," she said. "I was told that the Consul wants the approval of those two doctors who consigned me here before he will allow me to come out. Have they anything to say about it?"

"Nothing at all!" he replied. "No one has any authority in the matter but the doctors here."

Valeria was silent.

"Signora," said the doctor, "what in the world did they put you in here for?"

"They said that I was insane," she replied.

He was silent in his turn.

"Doctor, you have had the care of me, have seen me every day, and had the sister's report of me. Now I want you to answer me frankly, on your honor, without fearing to give me offence. If you were asked what you thought of the propriety of my being put in such a place, what would you say?"

"In all that I have seen of you," he said immediately, "I have seen no reason whatever why you should have been shut up. But they said that you were a little wandering before you came here."

"I was worse than wandering, I was lost!" Valeria exclaimed. "I had an illness and delirium, just as any one might have. You may judge how sick I was, if you remember how I looked when I came here, when I tell you that before that illness I was as full in flesh as I am now. I was ill three weeks, and was beginning to get well. I had been quite insensible a part of the time. When I came here I was very weak."

"As your health improved your mind grew clear, did it not?" he asked.

"As you see. I had a week's delirium, maybe."

"I thought so," he replied.

There was a moment's silence.

"We must really do something to get you away," he said then. "It does harm to us, who only come up once a day, to see these people; how much more to you who are here all the time! I will speak to the Director about it. But you had better go in now. There is a shower coming up. See how black it is growing over there!"

It was one of those sudden tempests that sometimes come up on a bright day; and it had almost covered the western sky before they perceived it. As the doctor spoke, it struck the villa.

Holding on his hat, he ran toward the bridge.

Sister Agnes, with the double flaps of her bonnet, black silk over white linen, flying in the wind, ran about gathering the ladies, and getting them into the house.

Valeria went up to her chamber for a moment; then, seeking the sister, coaxed out of her an unwilling permission to go to the terrace on the roof, and see the storm come in over the city.

"Only don't stay out in the rain!" Sister Agnes begged, as she unlocked the terrace door.

When the first flight of large rain-drops came, flung against the house with a rattling like shot, she went down to her room again. There was a loud booming sound of the wind rushing through some fissure in the ceiling or roof over her window.

"Hear the Barberini bees!" she said, thinking of the great stone bees on the cornice outside, to the nurse, who was closing the windows.

The girl stared.

Before sunset the storm was over; and at evening the full moon rose superbly into a world all golden, and kissed on her silvery forehead by the last sunbeam. Even the sullen Tiber had been put into good-humor by this tempestuous *sfogo* of the skies. Could

that be the ugly, wicked Tiber, — that shining stream,
all delicate rose and silver, with every arch of every
bridge mirrored faithfully, and the first arrowy moon-
beam quivering in its tide?

Valeria had begged another favor of Sister Agnes;
and when the ladies were all shut into their rooms,
she came quietly out of her own. Passing along the
corridor, the light of her candle shining on the pretty
crimson borders of the doors, she saw a light at the
end, in the chamber opposite that of the Signora
Agnese, who was shouting her psalms as usual, and,
apparently, fancying that she was edifying a large
congregation as she lay bound to her bed. The door
of this second chamber was open, and a strange, pitiful sound issued from it, — a frightened whimpering,
and pleading words in a low trembling voice.

This was a new patient. She was a young woman,
with large, lustrous eyes, and rich hair that fell
about her; and she seemed to be almost paralyzed
with terror. The sister and the nurse were trying
to soothe her, and to find out what she feared, but
could understand nothing. When Valeria went into
the room, the woman caught her hand, and gazed up
into her face with those large, frightened eyes.

"O signora, what shall I do? O signora!" It was
all that she would say; but she clung so that her hold
had to be loosened, finger by finger.

"She is another one who will not eat," the sister
said.

Valeria, shivering, hurried away as soon as she was
free from that grasp, and went down-stairs. The
table for the nurses was prepared in the little dining-
room, and they were enjoying an hour of peace and
liberty after the long day of watchfulness, to be followed, in some cases, by a disturbed night.

Out-doors all the world was radiant with moonlight, and all was silent.

Valeria went down through the garden, touching the flowers as she went. The yellow roses showed in that light; but the red roses were known only by their sweetness. Wrapping a shawl around her, she seated herself in the swing, and sat there looking about and thinking, only moving the swing softly with a touch now and then.

Sister Agnes came out, and ran down through the trees toward the bridge. She was going to the Community to supper; and, the day's work done, the nuns also would have their little hour of recreation.

"If there is a letter for me, bring it up to-night, Suor Agnes," Valeria called out.

The nun assented, and hurried on.

She sat thinking in that scene of enchantment, which was also a scene of despair, till the sister came up. Then she went to her chamber and read the letter that was brought to her. Others came in the morning. Letters and papers were coming fast now; and they all told the same story, either of a success which might have been sweet to her, or of the poison which made that success worse than a failure. People liked her book, smiling faces were bending over it far away; and every word of praise was a feather to the arrow of a lie. People would look up with pleasure at sound of her name, and would listen to a story to make the smile die on their lips. Hands would be half outstretched, then coldly withdrawn.

It was not a great book, it was full of faults, much of it had been written in pain and sickness; yet it had touched kind hearts that might have been the hearts of friends, but for "these bonds," more cruel than the bonds of St. Paul, viler than the bonds of a murderer.

The praises that she had hardly dared to hope for came and beat upon the bars of her prison, and fell broken and worthless before her. Better far had she been the most obscure person on earth ; for then no one would have cared to know her story.

She read these notices that were sent her, and dropped them.

Yet there were times when they drove her almost wild. Was there no one in that far-off land of her birth who would have opened her prison doors, if he had known ? If she should send all her story to the journals, and call on the American public for protection, would they not demand her release ?

She resisted the temptation to call for help, and waited.

This struggle could not continue long without its effects on the sufferer. Perfectly sound in health, without any malady, and gifted with an appearance of robustness, Valeria had yet a sensitiveness of organization that left her body at the mercy of her mind. Sadness became a malady, and fear a disease. A fit of weeping made her physically ill ; a laugh cured her. She felt herself growing ill ; and as her courage died her strength died. Delight would have snatched her from the brink of the grave ; a lie could push her into it.

There was still left God and Nature ; but God and Nature are companions for other worlds, as well as this.

Little by little she dropped her writing. Her serial was finished, after a fashion ; and she could not begin anything else. She felt inclined to lie still and sleep. Her life was becoming a dream.

"Why do you not go out into the city ?" the sister asked. "You stay in the house too much."

"I have been thinking that I had better die," she replied. "I don't think that I know very well how to live in the world. I don't feel at home in it."

"Oh, you will not die !" the sister exclaimed. "There is nothing the matter with you. You must not lose courage. It is impossible that you can be kept here much longer. I think that you will go in a few days. Dress yourself now and come out into the garden. If you wish to go into the city, I will go down and get you a pass."

Valeria shook her head, but suffered herself to be helped to dress.

"Promise me one thing!" she said suddenly to the sister as they went down-stairs. "Don't let any of those people ever come near me under any circumstances whatever. Keep them all away from me."

"They shall not come near you. But they will not wish to."

"If I died, they might. They would come and look me over just as if they were friends. Listen to what one of them did. There was an American lady who died a few years ago in Rome. She was on unpleasant terms with that Miss Crankey whom you saw here with Mrs. Harwood, and who was never received by her. But as soon as the lady was dead, Miss Crankey went to her house, — there was no relative to keep her out, — and went into every room of it. The mistress of the house was in her coffin on the floor. That woman stood and looked at the coffin, as at any other piece of furniture, commented upon it; said that the occupant was older than she owned, and gossiped about everything. It was horrible. Don't let them come near me!"

"They shall not," the sister promised. "But cheer up! You are not going to die."

"Feel my hand : it is hot. And see my tongue : it was all white this morning. I have fever again ; and this is the third time."

The sister stopped. "You ought to go back to bed," she said. "I will call the doctor."

"No ; let me go out once again. You may call the doctor, though, if you like."

She went out into the garden, which was glittering with a splendid drench of dew that the sun had heated, but not yet dried, and, wandering down by the terraces, began to gather flowers. Every day she fastened her collar with flowers; and if she wore a veil, it was pinned on with a rose.

First came large yellow roses, pale and pure; then, against the wall, roses of a lovely pink; and, last of all, growing so high up in a corner that one had to pull the branches down with a cane, roses of so dark a velvet red as to be almost purple, and so fragrant that all the air about was heavy with the breath of them.

Large scented dew-drops rolled down as the stems were pulled; every green leaf was set round with a thick row of tiny drops; the rose-thorns, large and of a light transparent crimson, seemed to be full of blood; an intense, full life breathed in everything.

Valeria went back to the little garden, where the ladies of the house were. It was one of the visiting days, and there were two or three strangers staring about them, and making comments with as much freedom as if they were examining the wares in a shop.

One of the patients of the second class came to Valeria, and, pointing over her shoulder, said, —

"These people come here and look at us quite with an air of superiority. They seem to think that it is not necessary to treat us with good manners. I shall go to my room."

She went; and one of the visitors, thinking from Valeria's veil and shawl, and from her being unattended, that she also was a visitor, came to ask her some questions about the place.

Who was this lady? Who that? Were they violent, or dangerous? And what did they say?

Valeria replied with some reserve.

"Is either of those ladies insane?" pursued her

questioner, pointing to where the Duchess sat talking
with a friend.

A mischievous impulse seized Valeria, and she represented the visitor as the patient and the patient as
the visitor.

The lady watched the two eagerly. " Yes, one sees
that she is queer," she said, her eyes fixed on the un-
lucky visitor. " There is a certain wild light in the
eyes of an insane person which can never be mistaken. And how oddly she pulls at her dress ! Such
a dress, too ! Does she ever rave ? "

" I cannot say, but I have no doubt that she does,"
Valeria replied gravely. " But the other lady has a
very pleasant manner, don't you think so ? "

" She is exceedingly graceful and affable," the lady
said, gazing at the Duchess.

" You perceive the difference in their eyes at once."

" Oh, dear, yes ! "

The sister beckoned from the house-door, and Valeria went to the anteroom and found the doctor waiting
there.

" Why did you not remain in bed, and call me
earlier ? " he asked almost angrily, after having felt
her pulse, and looked at her tongue. " You must go
to bed at once."

She looked at him attentively. His face was very
much disturbed. " Give me five minutes, and then I
will go," she said ; and, without waiting for his permission, ran down a side door to the veranda, and out
into the garden.

. One more look upon the beautiful earth before the
bars of her windows should stamp their crosses on
earth and sky ! One more glance at a summer cloud
with nothing between them but the air ! One more
unfettered breeze straight out of heaven into her face !
Once more with her feet on the blessed green grass !

" Oh, merciful Christ, it is hard to give them up ! "

She caught the dew-wet rose-vines against her forehead.

" Sweetest Nature, can you not save me ? "

She bent and gathered a daisy from the grass under her feet ; then looked off over the city that had killed her and to the mountains. " I will look up to the hills whence help cometh."

If help should come now, she might live. With hope, her heart was strong enough to face twenty fevers.

There was no help in that hour.

" Come, signora ! " called the sister.

" You must not stay out here in the damp," the doctor said, passing by.

Valeria cast one more glance over the world, and in that glance her heart broke.

She turned and sank into the sister's arms. There was no more resistance. They might do with her as they pleased.

She asked to see a confessor when she had gone to bed, and taken the quinine that was ordered for her.

" I want him to-day," she said, naming the one she chose. " He knows me well. It won't be so necessary for me to talk much to him as to Don Domenico. If I am to take quinine, I must not put anything off ; for quinine confuses my mind. And, Sister Agnes, put the curtain down, and never raise it again."

At first she did not seem to be in danger. Her danger was in there being no resistance on her own part to the malady. She was like one who lies down and drowns in shallow water.

And that she was drowning they saw in a few days. All that skill and kindness could do was in vain. She only lay there and let herself die.

One day — it was May now — the sister came to say that a young girl wished to come in, and would take no denial.

Valeria assented faintly.

The door opened, and the girl entered, dressed in
black, and wearing a black veil on her head. She
hastened to the bed, dropped on her knees beside it,
and seizing Valeria's hand, kissed and wept over it.

At a sign, the sister drew aside the heavy curtain
before the dressing-room, and the red light from the
western window inside shone over the glossy black
hair strewn on the counterpane.

"Who is it?" asked Valeria; then, as the face was
raised into that light, she added after a moment:
"Rosa Prenestina!"

"Papa has heard!" the girl whispered. "He says
that he can take you out of here. He understands."
She looked eagerly into Valeria's face.

"No, dear, your father can do nothing. God is
taking me out of here."

"The Signor Eduardo is in Palestrina. He has just
gone there," Rosa said breathlessly. "I have been
with my aunt in Rome; but I will go to Palestrina
to-morrow. He will come here to see you."

"No; it is too late."

"What shall I tell him for you?" asked Rosa amid
her tears.

"Say *addio!*"

The sister interposed, and drew the weeping girl
away, and Valeria sank again into the dreamy half-
sleep from which the visit had roused her. Steps
entered the room, but she did not hear them; there
were low voices, and a sound of prayer. They did not
touch her.

She was wandering along a road in New England
where she had often walked in childhood through her
father's woods. They stretched eastward from the
town in hundreds of acres that no man's memory and
no history of man had ever seen other than now,
a stately growth of primeval forests. A thread of a
brook ran along beside the path. She watched it as

she walked, and stooped now and then for the little gold-colored violets that grew beside it. And there was pennyroyal too. She must gather some of that to take home to mother.

The prayers for the dying were being recited for her in Rome; but she knew nothing of them. She was in New England, and she was a child. Love, protection, utter safety, all that make the home of childhood, gathered themselves about her. They were close by, beyond the trees.

"I like to walk in this road," she said aloud.

A voice disturbed her, though it was low and gentle, — a voice used to speaking on the shore of life, where the waves of eternity come up and fill the ears of the dying as with the murmur of sea-shells.

"Are you willing to take this solemn journey?" asked the priest.

She roused herself a little.

"A journey? Does it cost much? I have n't money enough for a journey."

"It costs only love and penitence," the priest said, with impressive slowness.

She sighed with relief, and let the momentary care slip; and, turning her cheek to the pillow, her head drooped a little.

"I have love enough!" she said.

There was a pause. She sighed again; and more faintly — "I have penitence enough!" she whispered.

The priest bent suddenly forward, and called out in a clear, penetrating voice, "Jesu! Maria!"

The Heavenly Ones stood by her as their names were called out with all the passion of a consecrated soul that in that instant performed its most solemn function. Yet they did not come to her in Rome, but to the silent woods of New England. And as they found her, so they led her away, a child, with her hands full of violets and pennyroyal.

25

CHAPTER XXXV.

"SAID THE NORTH TO THE SOUTH."

IT was a sunny May morning in Palestrina, and Rosa Bandini, who had arrived the evening before from Rome, was at the old palace with her father.

Marco had been ill of fever all winter, with a relapse in the spring; but he was coming back to life again now, — the life of a broken old man.

"Never speak of Vittorio to any one," he had said to Rosa. "If people question you, do not answer a word. Look at them, and shut your lips. We shall never see him again."

She understood him. She never spoke; she only wept.

But when with the spring her father grew better, and she saw that he would be spared to her, a faint color began to come back to her face, and sometimes a faint smile flickered over her lips. You cannot beat a summer brook to death while it hangs only half-way down the mountain-side, so long as it has a rock to dance over, and sees the plain below; nor can you crush a young heart that is still on the morning heights of life, while it rests on a firm basis of household love and protection, and can still see through its tears the vision of a possible delight in the future.

Rosa was saddened then, but not broken.

The Signor Eduardo was in the Tempietto, painting. She had seen him come up early in the morning, and heard his step on the stair; and before his model should come, she was going up to speak to him. There was no difficulty in her going up alone; for beside the confidence which he inspired in all about him, Rosa had now much more liberty than Italian girls usually have. Her father would not allow her to be fettered, and was troubled only at seeing how little she cared for liberty.

What motive it was which had made the girl assume her *contadina* dress that morning, she would have found it hard to tell. She had not worn it for a year, not since she had seen the Dane the summer before. But now she arrayed herself in the dark blue corsets and petticoat, and white *camicia*, and draped a rose-colored kerchief over her shoulders. It was half pride and half fear which actuated her. He must not think that she was trying to play the lady, and so laugh at her perhaps; and she must not really play the lady, and make him forget, and then be annoyed afterward. In her corsets and neckerchief she was herself.

Yet her heart beat hard as she went up the stair, and stepped out into the crescent-shaped garden, with its wild luxuriance of dewy grass and weeds, and its broken statues, and her hand trembled as she pulled the latch-string of the gate that led into the enclosure outside the last story of the palace. A door stood open into this enclosure. She crossed a ruined chamber, and stood in the door of the Tempietto, with the painter at his easel before her, and a sunny world behind his figure for a background.

He was very intent upon the painting of a ragged boy who, on being caught by the gardener, must look up from the *finocchio* he was down on his knees to steal, with a certain mixture of bravado, deprecation, innocence, and confusion not easy to combine in one small face, and he did not look to see whose step it was in the door; taking for granted, moreover, that the boy-model had come.

Rosa stood and looked at him. The morning light seemed to shine through his pure, pale face; and it

steeped in a soft gold his fair hair and beard. Never
had he seemed to her so glorious. As he stood, a
dark blue wall of far-off mountain was behind his
head; and she thought that if some new great master
should want to paint an angel, he should paint the
Signor Eduardo.

"Come here, now!" the painter said, without looking away from his work.

Rosa understood his mistake; but she went toward
him without a word.

The figure struck him, probably, as too tall for his
boy-model, for he looked up quickly, and uttered an
exclamation.   Then, smiling, he laid down his palette
and brushes, and rose and went to meet her, and took
her hand, and, breathing quickly with a glad agitation, looked into her downcast face, and waited for
her to speak, or for her present image to take its
place in his mind before he could speak.   He had
only pronounced her name, and she had not uttered a
word.   She stood drooping, half with bashfulness,
half with sorrow, and moved, too, by a little flutter of
joy.

"I'm glad to see you, Rosa," the painter said.

She cast an eloquent glance upward to his face,
smiled in a swift flash of light across her trouble and
her tears, and then said, while her eyes drooped again,
"I have a message for you from Madama Valeria."

"Madama Valeria?" he repeated, with a momentary doubt.   Then, "Oh, the American who was here
last summer!   Where is she?"

Rosa went to lean on the parapet.   She felt a need
of support.   He followed her, and she told her story.
But while expressing his sorrow and his sympathy
with her, there was ever an undercurrent of delight
in watching that sweet, ingenuous face, now over-
flowed by a shower of tears, now lighted by a swift
smile, and the lustrous dark eyes, that were lifted for

a moment in self-forgetful earnestness, then dropped in self-conscious modesty under his steady gaze.

The boy-model came, and waited all unheeded; and, finding the couple so engrossed, seated himself on the pavement, and cast longing eyes on the brushes and colors, and on a certain pencil sketch of himself, and wondered how much he could sell any one of these articles for, if he should slip it under his rags while those two stood shut in by a golden wall of love. For little Beppo had heard of love, and already fancied that he saw it whenever his eyes fell on a man and woman talking together. To his mind, there were but two subjects which could occupy them: love and stealing. These two persons, being enormously rich in his estimation, could not be planning how to get somebody's money. They were, therefore, talking about love.

The story was told, the comments were made upon it, the mutual questions which friends who have not met for a year ask each other had been answered, and they stood leaning on the parapet in silence. The sun came round to them, and Rosa moved to the shadow of the pillar near, and half turned to go.

"Stay!" said the painter suddenly. "I want to see you a little longer. I will send this boy away, for I don't need him this morning."

Turning to address his model, the Signor Eduardo saw him slip a brush into one of the many loopholes in his vesture, and surprised also on his face the very expression he wanted for his *finocchio* stealer; but he not only seemed unaware of the disappearing brush, he did not stop to catch that precious medley of expressions.

"Come this afternoon," he said; and the boy slid swiftly away, as though he had been snapped off the finger-nail of the hand that only waved itself toward him.

"Rosa, are you willing to be my wife?" asked the Dane, facing his companion again, and sending the words out with the suddenness of a heart-throb.

She looked up with a startled glance and a swift momentary pallor; then dropped her eyes with as swift a blush.

"Oh, Signor Eduardo!" she said, and choked a little, then burst into tears.

"That means yes!" said the painter, and laid his hand softly on her hair, and smoothed it half timidly, as if he had never before touched a woman's hair, and knew not well what wonderful thing would happen to his hand in touching it.

"Of course it is yes, if you really mean it," said Rosa, laughing through her tears and blushes. "I shall be so happy! I don't know what to say. I do not understand how you can think me good enough. I will do all I can to please you."

Earnest little simpleton! who did not know that to be herself, and to stand there all tender blushes and sunlighted tears, was to please him more than words could tell.

The sun touched the meridian, and set all the town bells ringing for the vigil of Pentecost, and showed a curve of bright sea between the southern mountains, and gilded the rough stones, and filled the empty places with light, and set a glittering frame around the cool shadows, and glorified all this scene in which two, at least, of God's creatures were happy.

And the sunlight, like all things in nature, was but a sign repeating ever to our forgetful human souls how

> "God's greatness
> Flows around our incompleteness;
> Round our restlessness, His rest."

THREE NEW NOVELS

BY THREE OF THE MOST POPULAR "NO NAME" AUTHORS.

I.

THE HEAD OF MEDUSA. By GEORGE FLEMING, author of "Kismet" and "Mirage."

II.

BY THE TIBER. By the author of "Signor Monaldini's Niece."

III.

BLESSED SAINT CERTAINTY. By the author of "His Majesty, Myself."

ROBERTS BROTHERS, PUBLISHERS,

Boston.